OIL CITY LIBRARY
2 Central Avenue • Oil City, PA 16301

In Memory of

Lavina Cole

Presented by

Jean Marino & Norma Graham

NEVER FAR FROM HOME

MARY ELLIS

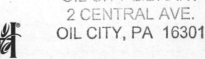

HARVEST HOUSE PUBLISHERS

EUGENE, OREGON

NEVER FAR FROM HOME
Copyright © 2010 by Mary Ellis
Published by Harvest House Publishers
Eugene, Oregon 97402

ISBN 978-1-61664-077-4

Printed in the United States of America

To the love of my life and best friend…
my husband.

~

I can't imagine how dull life would
have been had I not met you.

Acknowledgments

Thanks to Carol Lee and Owen Shevlin, who welcomed me into their home and opened doors for me in the Amish community.

Thanks to Dennis Miller and Carl Becker, who answered endless agricultural questions.

Thanks to my lovely proofreader, Mrs. Joycelyn Sullivan.

A special thank you to Joanna and Kathryn, and Mrs. Miller and her daughter Rosa, members of the Old Order Amish community.

Thanks to my wonderful agent, Mary Sue Seymour, who had faith in me from the beginning.

Finally, thanks to my editor, Kim Moore, and the wonderful staff at Harvest House Publishers.

And thanks be to God—all things in this world are by His hand.

ONE

April

Hannah Miller sipped her tea and gazed out the window over the sink, mesmerized by a winter world changing to spring before her eyes. Trees with only fat buds this morning now displayed tiny, tender green leaves. She had spotted a red-tailed hawk on her ride to Julia's, soaring effortlessly on wind currents warmed by the sun. Tomorrow it might turn rainy and cold again. Even an April snowstorm wasn't out of the question, but today God was giving them a small taste of good weather to come. Hannah's spirits lifted, despite having spent six hours on her feet helping with spring-cleaning at her sister's. With Leah only twelve, and Julia's hands unable to hold a sponge or wield a broom for very long, Emma had needed her aunt's help. But Hannah enjoyed the friendly camaraderie of women after a season too long cooped up indoors.

This had been a bad week for Julia's rheumatoid arthritis. Changeable weather, especially damp cold nights, increased the stiffness and pain in her swollen joints. Though steroid injections and prescription pain relievers had given Julia months of relief, her face revealed that a true cure was nowhere in sight.

Hannah listened to Phoebe humming a lullaby to her doll in the next room. The child was thriving during her first year of school.

Such a relief after Hannah's worry last year that she might never speak again. Now she rattled on in both *Deutsch* and English until Seth raised his hand and admonished, "Rest your tongue, daughter. It must last you a lifetime."

Refilling her cup from the teapot, Hannah leaned her hip against the counter and savored a few moments of quiet introspection. Supper was reheating in the oven—leftovers because she still cooked too much food for three people. Soon Seth would come home and tell her about his day in the low, husky voice she loved so well. Hannah enjoyed sharing a cup of coffee with him in the late afternoon or sometimes after supper if Phoebe had homework. But right now, Hannah was content to watch two blue jays tugging on the same twig…and then she saw a shiny green truck pulling up their lane.

What on earth? She knew before the driver's door opened who was paying them an afternoon call. The *Englischer,* a young sheep farmer who sold his wool to Audrey Dunn in Sugar Creek, stepped down from the pickup and headed toward the back door. Shaking her head, Hannah walked out onto the porch.

"Hello, Mrs. Brown. I hope you remember me, ma'am. James Davis from Charm. We met at A Stitch in Time." He swept a ball cap from his head.

"Of course, young man. You came here last fall looking for my niece." She glanced again at his vehicle, oddly clean compared to the mud-spattered trucks and buggies so common this time of year.

A corner of his mouth turned up in a lopsided grin. "Yes, ma'am. Your niece told me to stop by on my way home from Gram's to see your sheep operation."

Hannah vaguely recalled Emma suggested that the Davis family be invited to the wedding, which of course she had not done. They were complete strangers. But to the young man waiting patiently she said, "I'd be happy to point you in the direction of my sheep, and you're welcome to look around at anything you wish. But I'm sorry; my niece isn't here. Emma lives with her parents on Route 63, just around the corner. The second house you come to on your right. She should be home right now."

He looked disappointed for a moment until the subject of their conversation rounded the house from the back path. Emma was wearing a fresh pink dress and her skin glowed with youthful vitality. This wasn't at all how Hannah had seen her earlier, before leaving Julia's. Emma had cobwebs in her hair, a sweaty face, and a wrinkled and stained apron.

James must have caught Hannah's surprised expression, because he pivoted on a dime. "Hi, Emma," he called. "I'd hoped you would be working at your aunt's today." His greeting could only be described as enthusiastic.

Emma smiled demurely and offered a little wave as she approached. Hannah noticed she was walking rather daintily. Usually, Emma scurried wherever she went, only to be outpaced by Phoebe.

Not one to miss anything, Phoebe walked out of the house, letting the screen door bang behind her. She looked uneasily at the stranger before spotting her cousin. "Hi, Emma," she called and then ran to meet her.

"Hello, Phoebe," Emma greeted, enveloping the little girl with a hug. To the young man Emma said, "Hi, James. Welcome to Winesburg. I'm so glad you found us."

"No problem at all. Your directions were perfect." He stuffed his cap into the back pocket of his jeans.

Perfect directions? Hannah was thoroughly confused. Had Emma explained where they lived during their quick cup of cocoa in Sugar Creek last fall? That was a long time ago to remember an obscure township road on the other side of the county.

"Do you remember my aunt, Mrs. Miller?" Emma asked, glancing from James to Hannah.

"Oh, that's right," he said, his smile growing ever larger. "Miz Dunn mentioned coming to your wedding a while back," he said. "Congratulations. She said it was real nice. Great eats."

"Thank you, James," Hannah said, remembering to use only English. To her niece she murmured, "I didn't think we would see *you* again so soon."

Emma flushed. "I got a notion to walk over and check on my...I mean, your new lambs. There was still a bit of time before supper."

Hannah didn't comment on her quick bath and fresh change of clothing.

"Is it all right if James takes a look at our sheep, Aunt Hannah? I told him I'm going into business with you, and that I'm saving money for my own spinning wheel and loom." Sunlight reflected on her pretty face as she grinned with pride.

Hannah hadn't seen her quite so joyous in a while.

"Our Cheviots look pretty much like other Cheviots, same with our Dorsets and Suffolks. But if you'd like to show them off, I don't see any harm in it. I, myself, need to finish supper." She slanted her niece a curious look and then said to James, "Nice seeing you again. Please give my regards to Mrs. Dunn if you get to Sugar Creek before I do."

"Will do, ma'am. Nice seeing you again." He bobbed his head before putting his ball cap back on.

Neither teenager paid Hannah another smidgen of attention. They were watching each other with abject fascination.

Phoebe glanced curiously from one to the other until Hannah took her by the hand and they headed inside. An unsettled feeling was growing in the pit of her stomach.

I've come to see your sheep, indeed.

~

Emma waited until her aunt shut the kitchen door behind her before looking up at James. "Are you ready?" she asked.

"I've been ready for this all day," James answered. "I couldn't wait till I finished chores at my grandparents' house."

She tried to hide her pleasure with his comment. "My aunt brought mostly Cheviots and Dorset crossbreeds from Pennsylvania when she moved here, but my uncle added Suffolks to the flock. The sheep pasture is on the other side of the barn. Uncle Seth keeps the sheep separated from his cattle."

"That's smart, Emma," he said, "especially if you have a bull in with your cows. He could trample young lambs when he gets in a bad mood." James stuck his hands in his pockets and seemed to relax the farther they walked from the house.

"Our bull turns surly on a regular basis." She was anxious to keep the conversation going, although finding things to say hadn't been difficult in the past.

"Your aunt seems nice. So you're partnering up with her instead of your folks?" He pulled up some weeds and stuck the longest one in his mouth.

"*Jah*...I mean, yes," she said, feeling herself blush. "My father has just started liking sheep. Until recently, he used to call them smelly wool bags."

James laughed. "They do take time to grow on a person. I used to think something very similar to that myself. But if you concentrate on the fact that you never have to milk them and you can sell their wool on a regular basis, a person can overlook the fact they have the smallest brain in the animal kingdom."

"Smaller than that of a field mouse?" she asked as they reached the pasture.

"By half," he stated. James plucked a handful of dried Queen Anne Lace and handed it to Emma as though giving her a bouquet of expensive flowers.

Emma accepted the bunch and sniffed, knowing full well the weeds had no fragrance whatsoever. "Small brains or not, I like sheep. They have the world's sweetest babies. Look at those two young Suffolks with their velvety black heads and pink noses. They're much cuter than any dog or cat."

James focused on where Emma pointed. "You're right. Those are cuter than anybody's pet." He stepped up to the bottom fence rail and offered a hand. She glanced around quickly before joining him. "What's your dad's opinion now?" he asked.

"Oh, he likes them, at least he says he does. He's letting me start my own flock with Aunt Hannah's spring lambs once they're weaned. They will be payment for work I did." Emma didn't mention how little work she actually performed while Hannah and Seth were on their honeymoon. The compensation was overly generous.

"Is that right? Then let's hope for plenty of sets of twins," he said with a wink.

Something about his smile made her feel warm inside. It seemed as though she'd known James for a long time instead of as a casual acquaintance. *Are all English boys this friendly and relaxed around girls?* He wasn't bashful and tongue-tied like most Amish fellows. Not that she knew that many—her *daed* wouldn't allow her to attend Sunday singings yet, not until she turned sixteen.

"I suppose you're already done with school," he said with his gaze still on the lambs.

"Yes, almost two years ago." Emma felt her mouth go dry.

"You are one lucky lady. I've got a couple more months till graduation."

A lady? No one had ever called her that. She had been referred to as girl, child, female, *kinner*, but never a lady. The warm sensation in her belly spread from her head down to her toes. "I used to like school," she said, "but I'm glad it's done. I never wanted to be a teacher like my cousin Phoebe. That's all she talks about anymore."

"All I ever wanted to do is farm," James said, squinting from the sun dropping low on the horizon. "But now my dad's talking agricultural college. I don't need all that book learning to work my folks' three hundred acres." He pulled the weed from his teeth and tossed it down.

Emma nodded. "Me, neither. I want to raise sheep, sell the extra sandbag," Phoebe announced, pushing a tomato slice to the edge of her plate.

Seth and Hannah burst out laughing. "The ball is a baseball and the sandbag is called a base. Baseball," Seth concluded, adding ranch dressing to his greens.

"*Jah*, I forgot. At first the boys wouldn't let us girls play until the teacher made them. She said the other *opp-shin* was sittin' on the long benches twiddlin' their thumbs. So they decided to let us play."

"Boys can be troublesome at times," Hannah murmured, winking at her husband.

"I would say they made the smart choice." Seth took a roll from the basket.

"*Jah*, the girls hit the baseball with the wooden stick more times than the boys." Phoebe looked up with confusion. "How come that made some boys mad?" She pushed the other tomatoes to the edge of her plate and began to eat the lettuce.

Seth looked to Hannah, but Hannah shook her head, stifling laughter. "The wooden stick is called a bat," he said. "And the boys had because they were jealous. Apparently, they're not as smart as them credit for." He leaned over and brushed a kiss across her silky dark hair.

"Perfect explanation," Hannah added. "Now who wants stew?" Bowls were immediately thrust in her direction. She filled them and handed them back, and the two began to eat heartily.

Mealtime was Hannah's favorite part of the day, when her little family gathered to give thanks, eat something warm and sustaining, in the company of loved ones. What a blessing to have your family at hand. She had once read in a newspaper that English families had grown too busy to eat meals together. What a shame! Before they knew it, their *kinner* would be grown and gone while they dallied here and there.

"Honey is coming by tomorrow at first light," Seth said, ...ce.

wool, and maybe knit a warm sweater or two during the winter." She smoothed a damp palm down her skirt.

He nodded in sage agreement and then jumped down from the rail. "We'd better start back." He offered his hand to her.

Normally, Emma would have hopped down from the fence the way he did. But now that she was a lady, she accepted his hand and stepped down with dignity. "Would you like to see our barns and the shearing room?"

"Better not. I don't want any trouble with your aunt on my very first visit."

The two walked side by side back to the house without speaking. Each seemed lost in their private thoughts.

Emma didn't know what James was thinking about, perhaps what his mom might fix for dinner or maybe what time the baseball game would be on TV tonight, but she couldn't help pondering his choice of words: *I don't want any trouble with your aunt on my very first visit.*

That only meant one thing—James Davis planned to stop by again!

~

Hidden behind a swamp willow, Emma watched James' truck pull onto the highway and head south. When his taillights disappeared around the bend, she picked up the rubber muck boots she'd hidden behind Aunt Hannah's barn and tugged them on over her shoes. Although the boots were quite practical for walking the path between the two Miller brother farms, she had preferred not to be wearing something so unfeminine when she met James Davis again.

She had begun to think he'd forgotten his promise to stop and see Aunt Hannah's flock. How she yearned to visit his parents' three hundred acres! She was sure she and her aunt could learn a lot from him, despite the fact that he was English.

your chores. And don't develop an overfondness for money. That is how the devil gains an inroad."

"The devil will have no chance at my soul," she said without thinking.

Simon looked shocked as his brow furrowed with worry at the bold statement. Amish folk usually refrained from speaking with such assuredness. "Get inside, Emma, and help with dinner." His tone brooked no further discussion on the matter.

"I'll put away my things up here and go right in," she said, regretting her impetuousness. She didn't want to rile her father on this perfect spring day, further improved by the visit from James Davis.

Warmth curled in her belly remembering his gallant presentation of the bouquet of wildflowers. Others might call them weeds, but if a person found value, they were weeds no longer. Emma allowed herself a minute to mull over everything he had said and done during the tour. She knew few English boys since the school she'd attended in Winesburg had been all Amish. But James seemed much nicer than the loud, rowdy boys she'd observed in town with their baggy pants sagging to near indecency. He was polite, hardworking, gentle with animals, respectful of both his parents and his *mammi* and *dawdi* in Mount Eaton. James seemed like a person her parents might like—if not for one tiny little detail.

~

Hannah had watched the pair return from the sheep paddock from the side window. Emma had waved and headed down the path as the young man drove off in his truck. The unsettled feeling in Hannah's stomach had not gone away, but she sent her concerns up in a prayer and let the matter go. *I do have the habit of making mountains out of molehills, as has been pointed out to me more than once.*

"Umm. What smells so good, *fraa*?" Seth asked his bride from the doorway.

"You know full well what it is—the same thing we had yesterday,"

Hannah replied, unable to suppress a smile. With oven mitts she moved the pot from the stove to the table trivet.

Seth pulled off his boots in the hallway, hung his felt hat on a peg, and then wrapped his wife in a bear hug. "I missed you."

"You went as far as Mount Eaton and were only gone a few hours," she said, halfheartedly resisting his embrace.

"*Daed!*" shouted Phoebe. Her doll momentarily forgotten, she da[rted] across the kitchen like a hornet.

Seth swept her up into a three-way hug. "Can I help it if I [love] my two girls?"

"I missed you too, Pa," Phoebe said with her *kapp* ask[ew]

Seth kissed her forehead before setting her down.

Hannah pulled away from them. "Go wash your h[ands] Phoebe. I'll set the table so we can eat. I'll bet both of [you]

"How 'bout we scrub down together?" Seth ask[ed] got a bucket of road dust on me from all the plo[wing]

As the two marched off, Hannah sampled a[nother] store tomato she was slicing for their salad. [Hav]ing been harvested green so it wouldn't brui[se] had turned red but hadn't ripened since [being] picked. How she yearned for sweet gar[den] pickled-this and pickled-that all winte[r] with a heap of chow chow for color ju[st] back to the table.

"Something wrong with her leg[s]

"They're mighty tired from all [this] said, pulling over the basket o[f] when she reached for a biscu[it] silent prayer.

Ma. What music to H[annah] she'd married Seth Mill[er] ing the word still brou[ght]

"I hit the ball with t[he]

Hannah's head snapped up from her meal. Owen Beckley sheared sheep, Angora goats, and alpacas for a living. "Whatever for?" she asked.

"To shear the spring lambs, of course. Doesn't lambswool fetch a better price than regular wool?"

"*Jah*, it does, but it's too soon." Hannah set down her spoon on the side of her plate.

"It's not too soon. It's the middle of April." Seth scraped the last of the stew into his bowl.

"Nights still get chilly," Hannah reasoned. "I think we should wait." She sipped some water to soothe her dry throat.

Seth turned toward his daughter. "Stop playing with your food and eat." The child popped a spoonful into her mouth. To his wife he said, "There's no more frost at night, Hannah. I want to get this done before everybody gets involved with spring planting." His voice took on an intensity Hannah hadn't heard in a while—if ever.

"They're not even weaned yet, Seth. I don't see what the big hurry is." Hannah's own tone sounded a tad clipped.

"Phoebe, take your milk into the front room while your ma and me talk about this."

The child, who'd been glancing from one adult to the other, slid off her chair and scampered out, leaving her milk behind.

Seth leaned back in his chair and inhaled, filling out his broad chest. "The big hurry is Owen Beckley has time to shear them tomorrow before he starts setting his soybeans. Now is the best time for me too. Maybe I should've mentioned this earlier, but I just ran into Owen today in Mount Eaton." Seth rose from the table and threw down his napkin. "Don't make a big deal out of this, *fraa*, when it's really no matter a'tal."

Seth walked into the living room without another word. Hannah was left with a table full of dirty dishes and with her temper flaring in a most un-newlywed way.

Two

Emma thought Tuesday would never come. For the past week she'd been the perfect daughter—finishing the spring-cleaning, doing the mending and baking, and yesterday she'd washed clothes almost single-handedly while Leah had been at school. *Mamm* had stood nearby to offer suggestions. Emma's reddened and chapped hands offered proof of her hard work.

But finally *mamm* had given her a day to herself, and she was on her way to Sugar Creek.

She'd bathed and dressed carefully, rubbing in as much hand cream as her skin would absorb. Because the day turned out sunny and mild, her fourteen-year-old brother, Matthew, had hitched the team of smaller Belgians to the open wagon. She would be able to deliver the sixteen grapevine wreaths, all the finished packets of dye, and the last of her wool—spun, carded, free of debris, and ready to be woven into cloth.

After a quick tally in her head, she estimated she would earn enough for half the portable loom she'd admired in Mrs. Dunn's shop. It was perfect for her. It could do everything Aunt Hannah's could, and yet it weighed far less and could be easily moved when she had a home of her own someday.

After all, she wasn't a child anymore.

As Matthew tightly held the lead horse's bridle, Emma stepped into the wagon, smoothing out a lap blanket to sit on. *"Danki, bruder,"* she said when he handed her the reins.

"Wait up there, daughter," Simon hollered from the kitchen window.

Matthew snickered. "If you had been a bit quicker, you might have made a clean getaway." He grabbed hold of the bridle to steady the horses.

Emma frowned. As much as she adored her father, she had no time for a dozen questions. Sugar Creek was more than two hours away with this slow team, plus she still had to pick up her aunt.

Simon hurried down the back steps with his napkin, dotted with maple syrup, still tucked into his collar. "Your *mamm* says you're delivering the wreaths to Mrs. Dunn."

"Jah," she answered, "my wreaths, dyes, and wool. I should earn a tidy sum when she pays me for this." Her hand flourished over the wagon bed, where Matthew had covered the contents with a canvas tarp.

"I need your help today, son, to set soybeans. In fact, I could use both of you." Simon grabbed the other horse's leather lead.

"I'm not going anywhere, Pa," Matthew said, tightening the ropes on the tarp.

Simon looked at Emma with eyes rounding like an owl's. "You're not going all that way by yourself. Not driving a wagon team."

Emma smiled patiently at her father. "Of course not. Aunt Hannah is coming with me. She needs to deliver wool too. And I'll be happy to help you plant beans tomorrow. This nice weather is supposed to hold."

Simon's brows knitted together, but he released the horses. "All right, but get your business done and come home. No dillydallying."

Matthew walked the team in a half circle so that the wagon was pointed down the driveway. After Simon had returned to the porch, Matthew said with a grin, "Remember, absolutely no dillydallying." He slapped the horse's rump and the wagon lurched down the lane.

Excitement began to build in Emma's blood. They had a glorious spring day for the outing, and who knew whom they might run into in town?

Aunt Hannah stood waiting in the yard with her bags lined up next to the driveway. Within ten minutes they had loaded her wool and were trotting down Highway 62, each woman lost in her own thoughts.

"How's the weaning coming, Aunt?" Emma asked after a while, hoping not to sound too pushy. Although the lambs had been promised in return for farm-sitting, they weren't hers until the payment was made.

"Good," Hannah said. "Most are grazing a little, beside nursing from their mothers. Only a few have yet to acquire a taste for grass." Hannah held the reins since she had more experience keeping the wagon on the side of the road. Emma was allowed to control the lead horse only when the road widened with a designated buggy lane.

"*Wunderbaar.* I'm ever so grateful for them. I'm eager to increase my flock. Maybe next year I'll sell some of the male babies. I wonder what price they're fetching this year."

"I'm sure I wouldn't know, child." Her aunt slanted her an odd look and slapped the reins against the horses' backs.

Emma then remembered that Hannah never sold her spring lambs to the meat processor. Once Emma had overheard Uncle Seth say, "If my wife had her way, each lamb would be named, groomed with a pink or blue ribbon round its neck, and live to a ripe old age in our pasture."

Emma changed the subject to her recent attempts at dye extraction. She described boiling down various combinations of roots, bark, and berries to create some interesting shades of color. Before they knew it, their wagon had reached Sugar Creek and was rumbling down the alley behind the shop known as A Stitch in Time.

"Look, Mrs. Dunn is out on the loading dock. What perfect timing for us."

"I'd say it is," Hannah agreed, slowing the team. She squinted her eyes, trying to focus. "And isn't that the same green pickup that rolled up my driveway last week?" Hannah's tone sounded a touch frosty.

Emma craned her neck, even though she had spotted the truck long before her aunt. "I think it is. James did mention he might be delivering today. I thought we could spare Mrs. Dunn extra work if a large supply arrived on the same day."

"How very thoughtful of you," Hannah said, with a hint of a smile. "Please hold the reins and stay with the wagon. There's nowhere to park. We'll just wait here until it's our turn to unload." Hannah stepped down and tied the ribbons of her heavy black bonnet.

Emma noticed her aunt had started wearing the conservative head covering after her marriage instead of her usual white cotton *kapp*. Now she must turn her head fully left or right to see, since the bonnet blocked any side vision. Her aunt's pretty face was all but hidden, but she didn't seem to mind. *Perhaps wedding Uncle Seth has been worth the trade-off*, Emma mused, her face blushing from the thought.

Emma curiously watched Hannah start to approach Mrs. Dunn and then hang back shyly until the *Englischer* spotted her. Handshakes, embraces, even a buzz to the cheek followed in rapid succession amid laughter from both women. One woman Plain, the other fancy, yet it didn't seem to affect their friendship. Hannah waved from the loading dock and held up one index finger to signal a wait before disappearing into the back office. In a little while, the truck blocking the loading zone pulled away but no vehicle moved up to take its place.

Emma leaned from side to side, trying to get a better view.

"Good afternoon, Miss Miller." A voice spoke from behind her. Emma might have fallen out of the wagon if not for some quick action. James Davis grabbed her arm, pushing her back from the edge.

"Good grief, you scared the wits out of me!" Emma exclaimed as color flushed up her neck. "The last I saw you, you were standing in the doorway. Did you purposely sneak up on me?"

James put a foot up on the wagon rail and one hand on the back of the bench. "I did. I read in a magazine in the dentist's office that women like surprises."

Emma scooted back from his close proximity. She could smell his cinnamon chewing gum. "I believe startling and surprising are two completely different things." She tried unsuccessfully to sound cross as she smoothed down the folds in her skirt.

"Mrs. Dunn said I should pull your wagon up and start to unload. She and your aunt are going to have coffee and talk women-talk." He stepped onto the rail. "Scoot over, little missy."

"Little missy?" she asked. Now Emma did sound cross as she moved to the far end. "That's a silly thing to call a grown woman."

"Beggin' your pardon, ma'am." He tipped the brim of his ball cap. "I heard that in an old movie once, and I've been waiting to try it out."

"Neither your choice of magazines nor movies is serving you well today."

James swung up onto the seat, grabbed the reins, and clucked to the usually slow-to-react horses. They began stomping toward the delivery area immediately.

What is it with men and horses? Those two Belgians are usually stubborn mules for me.

As soon as he set the brake, she got down as ladylike as she could and began removing the tarp. Her grapevine wreaths, decorated with every type of nut, dried fruit, wildflower, and seedpod growing in the county, had weathered the trip nicely.

James leaned in for a look. "Wow," he enthused. "Did you make all these yourself?" He lifted out a particularly bright red one, loaded with holly berries, dried bittersweet, and interspersed with red oak leaves. "They are really nice. I might just buy one for my ma. Her birthday is coming up."

"I did." Emma grinned with pleasure, lining up four on her arm to carry in. "If you help me take them in, I'll give you a discount on your favorite."

"Looks like you're a smart business woman besides a pretty gal." James didn't wait for her reaction to the compliment but marched up the concrete steps with his arms full of wreaths.

It was a good thing, because Emma's cheeks had turned as bright as the red ribbons. She knew she shouldn't encourage such meaningless flattery, but so far she hadn't been able to put her foot down.

Once she had carried the boxes of dye packets inside, James wouldn't allow Emma to help unload the wool. He insisted she join the other ladies having coffee.

How nice to be treated like an adult for a change! Emma poured a cup from the carafe while Mrs. Dunn inspected her handiwork lined up on the counter. She proved to be as equally impressed as James. Mrs. Dunn took on consignment everything Emma had made during the last six months, plus she paid her outright for the packets of dye. Emma was pleased beyond measure once the wool was inspected and weighed. Her share of the profits far surpassed the estimate that had been bouncing around in her mind.

"That's wonderful, Mrs. Dunn," she said. "Thank you." Emma jotted the sum into her little notebook under the profits earned for the dyes. After a quick calculation, she said, "I'm halfway to the price of the portable loom right now. Once all the wreaths sell, I'll have more than enough, including the tax." Emma glanced between the shopkeeper and her aunt, arching up on tiptoes with excitement.

"I'm so proud of you, Emma. You're making real progress," Aunt Hannah said, patting her arm.

Mrs. Dunn clapped her hands enthusiastically. "Oh, Emma. Good for you. And I see no reason to wait until the wreaths sell since I'm certain they will. Why not pay for half the loom as a down payment? We can go six-months-same-as-cash for the balance, like that big furniture store in Canton. With the summer tourist season ahead of us, I'm sure the wreaths will be a hit. We'll just change some of the bows to blues and greens."

"Do you mean it, Mrs. Dunn? That would be ever so nice of you." Now it was Emma's turn to clap her hands.

"I'll ask James to load the loom into your wagon. I can use that space for a new knitting display I've been anxious to set up."

"Hold up here a minute." Hannah raised a hand as though stopping traffic. "I think we're getting a little ahead of ourselves. We shouldn't take anything home until it's fully paid for."

"But I promise to work very hard to pay every dime I owe as soon as possible," Emma said.

"I'm sure you will, dear, but I also know how your *daed* feels about buying on credit. We shouldn't make this transaction without checking with him first."

Emma wanted to argue—to point out it would save them an unnecessary trip back as well as free up valuable shop space, but after one look at her aunt's face, she bit the inside of her cheek instead. Besides, she didn't want to appear argumentative with James Davis lurking in the open doorway to the dock.

"Yes, ma'am," she murmured to Hannah. To Mrs. Dunn she said, "Please keep my profits for the wool on an account here—like layaway in the big furniture store. I'll send a note with my father's decision."

"Splendid!" Mrs. Dunn said. "Shall we have another cup of coffee and a slice of pecan streusel before you head for home? I'm longing for a piece but I never allow myself to indulge alone."

"Excuse me," James interrupted. He pulled a sheet of paper from his shirt pocket. "My mom gave me a list of stuff to buy at the bulk food store." He scratched his head while reciting the items, "Stone-ground buckwheat pancake batter, dried yellow currents, Havarti cheese, apricot chutney salsa...I don't even know what these things are, let alone where to find them. They're not like a gallon of milk and box of corn flakes."

The three women laughed while James slicked a hand through his hair.

"Emma, do you think you could help me find them?" he asked. "The store is just one block from here."

"No," said one voice.

"*Jah*, sure," answered another.

Hannah and Emma had spoken simultaneously, but Hannah continued, "I need to stop at that store too. We'll both help you with your mother's list." She turned to face the shopkeeper. "We appreciate the streusel offer, and it sounds delicious, but we had better be on our way before it starts getting dark. Goodbye for now and thank you, Audrey."

Hannah tugged Emma's sleeve all the way to the door, calling to James along the way. "We'll meet you inside Blanchey's Bulk Foods, Mr. Davis. I want to move our wagon out of the loading zone."

Emma stole a glance over her shoulder, but James had already gone out the side door. Drawing in a deep breath, she tried to calm her fluttery nerves. It would not do if anyone knew how excited she was about going shopping in a grocery store!

~

Hannah breathed a sigh of relief when their wagon pulled out of the hilly town of Sugar Creek and headed north. There hadn't been anything particularly bold or improper about Emma's behavior in Blanchey's; nothing she could admonish the girl for. It had been more of a feeling Hannah got each time she spotted her niece scanning the shelves with the young *Englischer*.

Did she have to giggle when they both grabbed the handles of the shopping basket and headed in different directions?

Must she appear so interested in the ingredients he was comparing between two brands of marinated vegetables?

Why had she tried to act so knowledgeable about baking apples when Julia could barely get her to pare off the skins when making a pie?

Although they did not stand too close or act inappropriately familiar, still Hannah didn't like the way they leisurely walked up and down the aisles…so like a couple!

Emma was not yet sixteen.

James Davis was not Amish.

And there was something else Hannah needed to get off her chest with her beloved niece. "Emma, have you been in contact with young Mr. Davis? Other than speaking to him the day he stopped at your uncle's farm?"

Silence—except for the clopping of horse hooves and the scrape of metal wagon wheels on the road. This wasn't like Emma, a girl who usually had plenty to say on every topic. Hannah waited a full minute while keeping her focus on the road ahead. Then, "I'm waiting for your answer."

Emma spoke in an almost childlike voice. "*Jah.* I left directions for him on how to find your farm. I gave them to Mrs. Dunn at your wedding."

"Why would you do such a thing?"

"He said he was interested in how our operation differed from his, especially how we manage without electricity. He invited us to stop at his folks' place, remember?" Emma turned toward Hannah on the seat, looking utterly earnest.

"I remember, *jah.* Why didn't you tell me you had left directions for him?"

She shrugged her thin shoulders. "Because I really didn't think he would stop, or that he would even remember meeting two Plain women."

Hannah inhaled a slow breath, trying to ponder the perspective of a fifteen-year-old. She had no wish to overreact to something not necessarily wrong, and so she opted to ask another question. "Was that your sole correspondence?"

"No. I sent Mrs. Dunn a note saying my wreaths were finished and that I would deliver them with our next wool order. That way she wouldn't take crafts on consignment from another supplier. And

I asked her to tell the Davis family about our delivery date in case she wanted her whole supply to arrive the same day. She had mentioned she fills big orders for a rug and carpet manufacturer."

"I see," Hannah said. On the surface nothing was wrong with Emma's logic. In fact, Hannah was impressed with her newfound business acumen. *So why do I still have a bad feeling in my bones?* "I get the idea, Emma, that you had an additional reason for sending the note to James. I believe you like the young man." Hannah exhaled her pent-up air with a *whoosh.*

"Well, I guess I do like him, Aunt Hannah. He seems nice, don't you think?"

"*Jah,* I suppose so."

"And isn't it important to have friends in your chosen line of work? Business contacts, like Mrs. Dunn and the friends Uncle Seth knows at the grain elevator...both Amish and English?"

Hannah felt she was about to be outmaneuvered, and she didn't like it. "True enough, but you're only fifteen years old." Nothing more reasonable than that came to mind.

"I'll be sixteen in two weeks, and I've been out of school for almost two years. Surely I'm not too young to have English friends."

"Let me ask you a question, young lady. Have you told your *mamm* and *daed* about James stopping by for a tour last week?"

Emma met Hannah's eye before gazing off at the countryside. Spring was exploding with each passing hour of glorious sunshine. "No, I didn't. Pa usually judges a book by its cover, and he wouldn't see anything beyond James' Englishness."

True enough, Hannah thought. What she said was, "But he is your father and knows what's best for you."

Emma crossed her arms over her apron, turning slightly away on the bench seat.

"I'll say nothing to Simon or Julia right now," Hannah said softly. "I don't want to interfere with a family matter between you and your parents."

Emma pivoted around on the bench, her face bright and eager. *"Danki*, Aunt Hannah—"

"Let me finish," Hannah interrupted. "But I also won't be part of any subterfuge in the future, niece. I won't assist you in deceiving your folks, no matter how much I love you." She reached out to cup the girl's chin with three fingers. "And I do love you, Emma."

The girl slid over until she was practically sitting on Hannah's lap. "I love you too. And soon I shall tell *mamm* and *daed* all about James since he's again invited us out to their farm in Charm. It would be rude to ignore the invitation, but I won't go without their permission."

At least they had reached an understanding. Hannah relaxed against the back of the seat for the remainder of the trip.

The day that the Lord had made was a blessed gift after weeks of clouds and rain. She could enjoy the companionship of her favorite niece without feeling disloyal to Julia.

She also felt mighty glad that her new daughter, Phoebe, was years away from such tribulations. *Danki, Lord God. Danki!*

～

Simon halted the team of Belgians to sop his brow with his hand-kerchief. The spring plowing was going well. The rains had been plentiful enough to leave the soil soft and tillable, but not overly abundant to turn his fields into a quagmire. With the sun just over the western hills, he decided this row was as good as any to stop for the day. He listened intently to the sound of an approaching wagon on the road. Was that his daughter returning from Sugar Creek with Hannah? When the wagon rumbled past his lane, Simon's anticipation changed to annoyance.

How a parent worried when a child was away from home. Every year the frequency of car-buggy accidents increased as more people moved into the fertile, rolling valleys of central Ohio. He would speak to Emma at supper. These trips needn't turn into all-day excursions, complete with picnics and those silly coffee drinks with whipped cream and chocolate sprinkles! Both women had chores waiting for them...not the least of which was supper. A growl from his stomach turned his thoughts along just those lines. What did Julia mention she would make tonight? Roast duck with sage stuffing. A rather fancy meal for a weeknight, but Simon wasn't complaining. Even his back pain lessened upon thinking about slices of moist, dark leg meat.

After putting the horses into the barn and sending in Matthew to rub them down, Simon decided to have a look in the unused washhouse. He'd spotted Emma scurrying in and out of the building from the kitchen window this morning. In this room his *mamm* had washed clothes in galvanized basins filled from a hand pump. And everyone had taken their Saturday night bath in an old copper tub. Water had been heated in kettles on the woodstove, steaming up the windows all winter long. Sometimes he yearned for how things were when he was young, but he was alone in such sentiments. Julia loved hot, running water to ease her stiff, arthritic joints. Now the outbuilding was cobwebby and vacant after they had added a bathroom onto the back of the house.

But unused it was not, as Simon pushed open the wooden slat door. Emma had commandeered the room, filling it from floor to ceiling with drying herbs, plants, weeds, and long stringy roots. Some hung from pegs, others dangled from lines stretched across the room at head level, while leaves and twigs lay across a makeshift table built from plywood and two sawhorses.

With his hands on his hips he surveyed the room. He'd never seen the porcelain mortar and pestle sitting in the middle of the table. The whole room took on an odd, macabre look that Simon didn't like one bit. He saw boxes of plastic storage bags of various sizes, and an array of cutting tools only a hospital surgeon would ever need.

First the barn loft workroom and now this? What is going on with my elder daughter? Simon hurried to the house, eager to rest his sore muscles, refresh himself with a cup of strong coffee, and talk to the voice of reason—his wife.

"Julia," he said as soon as he took his place at the table. "Have you seen what's going on in the old washhouse?"

"*Jah*, Emma uses the space for her dye-making." Julia placed a mug of coffee before him, refilled her cup from the pot, and then returned to the propane refrigerator for milk.

Simon noticed celery, carrots, and green peppers on the cutting board ready to be chopped. "Is the girl neglecting her house duties? I won't have you struggling with your bad hands while we have two healthy daughters." Simon gulped his coffee, scalding his tongue. "And where is Leah?" he asked when he was able to speak again. With her *kapp* off for the moment, Simon saw streaks of silver in his wife's dark hair.

Julia smiled patiently and stretched her gnarled hand out to him. "Rest easy, Simon. Don't upset your digestion before one of your favorite meals. I've sent Leah to the henhouse. I want to hard-boil some eggs while we eat supper. She'll be in soon to cut up those vegetables. This is her night to help with supper, not Emma's." Julia took a long sip of coffee.

Simon settled back in his chair. "First her own flock of sheep, then the dye-making, now all those wreaths she hauled to Sugar Creek. Don't you think she's getting a little too ambitious?"

"Young women today are all ambitious, *ehemann*, even Plain ones here in Winesburg."

Simon shook his head. "In 1 Timothy 6:10 we learn, 'For the love of money is the root of all kinds of evil. And some people, craving money, have wandered from the true faith and pierced themselves with many arrows.'"

"Sounds like money isn't evil, only an overfondness for it. We'll just be sure Emma knows the difference and makes her decisions accordingly," Julia said, squeezing his hand weakly.

At that moment, twelve-year-old Leah dashed in. She was bringing both a basket of eggs and tales of mischief by her brothers.

The topic of Emma would have to wait.

He had two sons who might need a wallop on their backsides if they really did lob eggs at each other in the henhouse. That would be wasting good food, besides leaving a mess on the floor and walls. Simon met his wife's gaze. She was trying to hold back a smile, but she offered him an affectionate wink instead.

Simon rose from his chair. "Set out that roast duck whenever you're ready, *fraa*. After I bring those two scoundrels back to the straight and narrow, I'm sure we will all be famished."

THREE

May

Hannah walked Phoebe halfway to school despite having plenty to do in her garden. But May mornings like today wouldn't last forever—sunny and warm without a hint of humidity, with a light breeze carrying the soft fragrance of honeysuckle and apple blossoms. Besides, it was the last day of the school year before summer vacation, and little Phoebe needed some extra attention. Laura Hershberger, the former Laura Stoddard, had announced to the class that she wouldn't be returning as their teacher in the fall. She was expecting a baby. Amish ways dictated she stay home and make her husband and growing family her priority.

Hannah could just imagine how filled with joy Laura must be. The young woman had been Hannah's first real friend in her new district other than Julia, her sister. Hannah laughed each time she remembered Simon's misguided attempt to fix the schoolteacher up with his brother, Seth. Both had been aghast since Laura had been secretly courting Joshua Hershberger and Seth had set his cap for Hannah. Laura and Joshua had announced their engagement soon after and married before Thanksgiving—one full month after Hannah and Seth's wedding. And now Laura was already in a family way, while Hannah wasn't.

As though Phoebe could read her private thoughts, she announced, "Mrs. Hershberger is going to have a baby. She said it should arrive in October with the autumn leaves."

"*Jah*, good. A bundle of joy to warm her heart this winter," Hannah said, clutching Phoebe's hand tighter as a car whizzed past on the road.

"We will get a new teacher, but she doesn't know who yet." Phoebe kicked at a stone with the toe of her tennis shoe. "Are you going to have a *boppli* too, Ma?"

The question that had haunted Hannah's slumber besides many waking daydreams just popped out of the child's mouth.

"That is in the Lord's hands, Phoebe. We have to wait and see." Hannah swallowed down the tightness in her throat.

"Pa says if it's meant to be, it will happen, and I will be the first person he tells, Miss Busybody. That's what he called me, Miss Busybody." She appeared pleased with the new nickname.

"Your pa is right. We must wait and see, but it wouldn't hurt to ask the Lord in your prayers."

Phoebe looked up with her dark eyes sparkling. "Is it okay to ask for a baby *schwestern* and not a *bruder*? Or do we just have to take what we get?"

Hannah hugged the girl to her side, grinning from ear to ear. "Both, sweet child. You can ask for a little sister, but be prepared to love the baby one way or the other."

"I promise I will. Look, we're almost there," Phoebe announced as they rounded a bend in the road. "I'll go the rest of the way by myself like a big girl."

Hannah stooped down to accept a kiss on the cheek, and then she watched Phoebe run toward the three-room clapboard schoolhouse. Her braids bounced down her back under her thin head covering.

"Bye, Ma. See you after school."

Ma. Hannah loved the sound of that word. How she yearned for a houseful of young voices saying it. She mulled over the possible reasons while she wasn't in a family way during the walk home. But by the time Turnip, the sheepdog Seth had given her while courting, greeted her at the end of the lane, she had sent her concerns up in a silent prayer.

If it be Your will, Lord. If it be Your will.

Turnip continued barking all the way up the drive. Once Hannah reached the barn, she saw the reason for the dog's agitation. A livestock hauler had backed up to the pasture gate. Hannah couldn't fathom why the truck, much smaller than the semitrailer that brought her flock from Lancaster County, was here.

Seth stood talking to the English driver near the pasture fence. Both held their hats in their hands, enjoying the warm spring sunshine on their skin. Her husband put his back on when Hannah approached and offered a welcoming smile. "Phoebe get off okay on the last day of school?" he asked. "Now she'll be underfoot all summer long." To the man he said, "This is my wife, Hannah." The driver touched his hat brim while Hannah bobbed her head.

"Good morning," she murmured. "Seth, why is this truck here? Have you bought more livestock?"

Seth scuffed his boot in the dirt, glanced at the driver, and then looked at his wife. "No, the truck is here to load up spring lambs. Now, that they're weaned, they are ready to go to market."

Hannah's facial expression required no words to convey her outrage.

Seth held up a hand. "Now, don't go getting upset. I haven't forgotten your promise of spring lambs to Emma. I picked out a half dozen healthy females and separated them out already. They're in a pen in the barn. Since tomorrow is Emma's birthday, I thought we could take them over when we went for cake and ice cream. I think she'll be more excited to get them than that book and the box of chocolates you wrapped up." He laughed with good humor.

Hannah could feel her ears pounding as her blood pressure rose. "You are selling off my lambs?" she squawked. "Without even discussing the matter with me?" Hannah couldn't help herself—she stomped her foot in the gravel, raising a cloud of dust. It was a childish, undignified gesture to be sure, but she couldn't remember ever being so angry.

"Excuse us a moment, Mr. Phelps," Seth said. He gently took Hannah's forearm and led her inside the barn. The driver busied himself by brushing mud off the truck tailgate. "Hannah, I don't like you losing your temper in front of English strangers." Seth kept his voice low and controlled, but Hannah knew she wasn't the only one who was angry.

"And I don't like you selling off my babies to a slaughterhouse!" Her words came out like a stray cat's hiss.

"*Ach*, Hannah," he said, twisting his head from side-to-side as though working out a crick in his neck. "They are not babies; they are livestock. And we can't keep that many young rams. We'll end up with a pasture of head-butting brawls the whole year long. No sheep farmer keeps all his newborns."

Hannah crossed her arms over her apron, shifting her weight from one hip to the other. "Well, I keep all of mine."

"That's another thing, *fraa*. They are not *your* lambs anymore. They're *ours*, and as your husband I get to make the decisions around this farm."

He might not have wanted his words to come out quite that way, but Mr. Phelps had appeared in the barn doorway, looking impatient.

"You folks want me to come back another day? I have another pick-up and delivery to do over in Mount Eaton later this afternoon."

"No, Mr. Phelps. You can start loading those lambs up. I'll be right with you."

Tears flooded Hannah's eyes. The last thing she wanted was to break down and cry like a child, but she realized then that nothing she could say would change the fate of her beloved critters. "Oh, Seth!" With her face awash in misery, she picked up her skirt and ran for the house. She heard him call her name, but she didn't slow her pace until she reached the quiet solitude of her kitchen.

Or was it his kitchen?

She broke down and sobbed on her sleeve at Seth's oak table in Seth's house on Seth's farm. Feeling sorry for herself and even sorrier for her lambs, she cried until every last tear was gone, and then she headed for her bucket and scrub brush. Now was as good a time as any to give Seth's kitchen floor a good scrubbing. Boot heel marks wouldn't stand a chance once Hannah focused her ire on them.

Later, with the linoleum gleaming, Hannah sipped a cup of coffee and contemplated washing the windows. She didn't hear Seth come in until he spoke quietly over her shoulder. "I'm sorry, Hannah, that I made you feel so bad this morning. I thought this might be a thorny issue, and I took the coward's way out. Next time I'll tell you of my decisions beforehand so you can speak your mind and stomp your foot in the privacy of your own house instead of in front of strangers."

Without another word, he walked back outside.

Your own house...it was as though he had read her thoughts. Or maybe he already knew her heart that well.

Just when she thought she'd cried herself out, one last tear slipped out and ran down her cheek.

~

A sixteenth birthday comes but once in a girl's life. So for that reason, Emma waited until after chores to take her bath. She had donned her oldest dress to feed and water the flock, clean the loft workroom, and move things around to make space. Then she helped Leah gather a dozen eggs and sweep out the henhouse. Leah and *mamm* would be cooking and baking without her help today. She had been given a day off from household chores since it wouldn't do for her to bake her own birthday cake, now would it?

While Leah mixed flour, eggs, and milk together in a bowl, and Julia simmered a pot of vegetable soup on the stove for lunch, Emma soaked in the tub until the water grew cold. Afterward she put on a pretty pale green dress. It wouldn't be many more years before she joined the church and wore dark hues like the other women members. Emma felt certain that when the day came she would be ready.

After brushing her hair forty extra strokes, she bound it up in a loose bun and noticed again that her forehead seemed too high and wide. She would love to cut a light fringe of bangs like the English girls wore, but her father wouldn't allow any hair cutting. When she'd asked him, he had declared, "No daughter of a deacon will cut her hair when the *Ordnung* specifically forbids it."

But today it hardly seemed to matter. Simon had agreed to allow the new loom to be delivered, despite the fact she'd only paid for half. "Your *mamm* seems to think it's a good idea, so I will permit it" had been his unexpected pronouncement. Emma mailed a note to Mrs. Dunn the next day, requesting the loom be delivered today, if at all possible.

She hadn't mentioned the significance of today, but nevertheless, Emma preferred not to be knee-deep in soybeans or rows of wheat sprouts when the deliveryman arrived. If her prayers were answered, James Davis would do the delivering. Emma knew her prayers had been shallow and self-centered, so she also prayed for rain for the hay crop, plenty of sunshine for *mamm*'s vegetable garden, and a good price for the corn harvest. Corn—that's all *daed*, Uncle Seth, and the other men ever talked about after preaching services anymore.

As she slipped a starched white apron over her dress, she thought how lucky she was in her chosen vocations. Grapevines grew wild and free for the taking in the woodlot, same as most of the roots, herbs, and berries she used for dyes. Wool grew back reliably after each shearing, never having to be planted, fertilized, or weeded.

All in all, Emma felt blessed on her special day, made even more so with the sound of tires on gravel and the toot of a horn.

Her prayers had been answered. James Davis climbed out of his truck, wearing pressed blue jeans, a white cotton shirt tucked in, shined-up boots, and a huge smile. Even though he couldn't possibly have known which room was hers, he looked up at her window and waved.

Emma felt her stomach somersault. She could only assume she should have eaten more pancakes at breakfast.

"Hi, Emma," he called when he spotted her in the window.

She offered a wave and then hurried downstairs before his yelling brought her brothers from the barn. Unfortunately, her mother was on her way out the door by the time Emma reached the kitchen.

Julia was standing on the steps as James approached the porch. "Mrs. Miller? I'm James Davis. Mrs. Dunn of Sugar Creek asked me to deliver a loom for Miss Emma Miller." With his ball cap in hand, he smiled charmingly at Julia.

"Oh, my. She'll be so pleased that it came today," Julia said, walking slowly down the steps.

Emma slipped onto the porch, not letting the screen door slam behind her.

James smiled at her, and then he turned his attention back to Julia. "Why is that, ma'am? What's so different about today?"

"It's my daughter's birthday. Oh, here she is now," she added, noticing Emma behind her. "This is James Davis. He's here to deliver the new loom."

"Yes, Mom," Emma said, choosing to use only English terms. "Aunt Hannah and I met him a couple times at A Stitch in Time. His family also raise sheep. I believe I mentioned that to you." She wanted to greet him properly, but suddenly she couldn't bring herself to meet his eye, let alone string words together to form a sentence.

"Does your mother spin and weave, James?" Julia asked.

"No, ma'am. She's a nurse in Canton and doesn't have much time. She wants to learn after she retires. My dad farms full-time. Not much chance for retirement there."

"*Jah*, true enough," Julia agreed. "I better get that birthday cake out of the oven before it burns. Emma will show you where to put the loom. She's been busy making room for it all morning. Nice meeting you, son." Julia struggled back up the steps, leaning on her daughter for support.

I'll show him if I can shake off this sudden bout of paralysis, Emma thought. Sensing his gaze on her, she felt every hair on the back of her neck stand straight up. "Our barn is this way, Mr. Davis," Emma said, marching down the path past him. Now that her legs were working again, they apparently yearned to run.

"Mr. Davis?" he asked, falling in step beside her. He pushed a wheeled dolly carrying the loom along the path. "Mr. Davis is my dad. It's me, James. Or you could call me Jim, or even Jamie like my gram docs, if you have a mind to. What happened, Em? Did you fall off a ladder and whack your head?" He laughed zealously at his joke.

"No, I did not, but Amish folk maintain more decorum than other folks."

"Okay, then," he said, "just as long as I know you're all right."

"I'm very well, *dank*—thank you!" Emma slowed her pace so she wouldn't be panting and sweating by the time they reached the loft.

"Being that it's your special day and all."

She huffed like a hen when someone stole her egg. "It's just a birthday. Everybody gets one once a year."

"But it's your sweet sixteen birthday. And from what I've heard from one of my friends—he's Amish like you and lives over in Farmerstown—sixteen is the age Amish girls start dating. Maybe you know my friend, Sam Yoder?"

She shook her head. "No, we don't all know each other. I've never been to Farmerstown." They entered the barn, but she paused at the bottom of the loft steps.

He looked bewildered. "I just thought maybe there was a chance you'd met. What are you so cranky about today? Did I say or do something to offend you, Miss Miller? *Already?*"

Emma clenched and unclenched her fists. *How can I explain he makes me feel nervous and giddy and bashful, all rolled into one?* "No, you haven't done anything. I guess I'm just a little overexcited, that's all. I'm sorry."

"So is it true then?" He lifted his eyebrows almost comically.

She glanced around the barn. The horses, the sow, even the tabby cat seemed to be waiting for her answer. "Is what true?" she asked and then held her breath.

"That now you're allowed to start dating?" James lowered the hand truck's wheels to the ground and leaned his elbow on the box.

"My parents must decide if I'm ready for courting, but yes, I imagine they will say I can." What she didn't add was that they wouldn't allow her to court an *Englischer* in a million years.

"That's good to hear. I mean, if I get a hankering to ask you out sometime in the future, and if you get a notion to say yes, we'd at least have this particular birthday behind you." He grinned with his clear blue eyes brimming with vim and vigor. She noticed that his eyelashes were dark, not the pale yellow many blond-haired people have.

"Look at you standing there...all full of yourself," Emma said, finally regaining some of her courage. "You look like your picture should be on a box of breakfast cereal."

"Thank you, I think." His laughter filled the barn, but unfortunately it also brought Matthew and Henry over to see what the fuss was about.

"Hey, Emma. What's in the box?" Matthew asked. He was eyeing the stranger with more interest than whatever he'd delivered.

"This is James Davis, a fellow sheep farmer and my friend. He brought the loom I've been saving up for. James, this is my brother, Matthew. And behind him is Henry." But her younger, shyer sibling was already wandering back to the horse stalls.

"How ya doing," James said, stretching out his hand.

Matthew shook it heartily. "Need some help getting that up the steps? Emma's not that strong."

Before she could protest James leaned the box on its side, and he and Matthew each grabbed an end. They carried it upstairs almost before she could walk up herself. "Please set it there," she said, pointing to the vacated area under the skylight window.

"Pa put that window in for our aunt before she decided to get married and move around the corner," Matthew said, dusting off his hands.

"Yes, I met your Aunt Hannah. Looks like your sister will reap the rewards of your dad's good idea." James was speaking to Matthew but kept glancing at Emma.

Both of them turned to stare at Emma...as if waiting for her to say or do something interesting. She was momentarily at a loss. Folding her arms, she asked, "Neither of you has anything better to do than gawk at me?"

"I've got plenty of better things to do," Matthew said, and then he headed downstairs.

James stood for a few moments as though pondering the question. "Nothing really *better* to do, but I did promise my dad I'd work on his diesel generator today." He started down the steps too.

Emma suddenly didn't want him to leave. Not yet, anyway. "Wait, James!" She hurried after him. He halted at the bottom and looked back.

"I want to give you something for your trouble," she said.

"No, Miss Miller, I won't take—"

"Don't call me Miss Miller. It's Emma. Plain folk aren't all that formal. Anyway, it's just birthday cake. Would you like to take a slice of cake home to have after supper?"

His grin grew so wide she could practically count each tooth in his mouth. "Sure, I'd like that a lot. I'll load the dolly in my truck and wait for you there."

Emma walked very slowly to the house—slowly because she would have to explain to *mamm* why she was cutting into a fresh-from-the-oven cake, not even frosted yet, before her family had a chance to sing "Happy Birthday."

∼

In the bathroom Julia swallowed two tablets of pain reliever with a full glass of water. "Work fast," she whispered. "I've still got plenty to do today."

She wrapped her gift to Emma and tied it with raffia from the dollar store. It was a hummingbird feeder made by a Mennonite glassblower from the next county. Two small bottles of red food coloring would tint the boiled sugar water that would refill it all summer long. It had taken two months of saving her egg money to afford it, but it was worth every penny. Emma so enjoyed the tiny, darting birds that zoomed in and out of the morning glories and foxglove by the kitchen window. Hanging a feeder there would keep the birds coming long after the blooms were gone.

Leah was frying chicken and baking sweet potatoes for supper— two of Emma's favorites. All that remained to be done was to wash some early spinach leaves for a salad and frost the chocolate cake. With a deep, steadying breath and silent prayer for relief from this flare-up of rheumatoid arthritis, Julia limped back into the kitchen.

Her morning accomplishment sat forlornly lopsided on the counter, tilting from a missing wedge. "Leah, did you eat a piece of your sister's cake?" As soon as the words were out, Julia realized the ridiculousness of her question. "*Ach,* I know you didn't. Was it your *bruders*? Did they sneak in and help themselves?"

Leah turned over another chicken leg in the frying pan before speaking. "No, *mamm*, it was Emma. She cut a big slice to give to that deliveryman."

"What deliveryman?" Julia asked, perplexed.

"That yellow-haired boy who brought her loom. He sure kept smiling at Emma, like she was telling him a funny story. But she wasn't talking a'tal." Leah glanced at Julia before she finished flipping the chicken pieces.

Julia mulled this over while reaching for the bowl of butternut frosting. "Well, it's her cake, isn't it? Nice of her to share," she said to Leah.

But passing out cake to *Englischers* who dropped by never had been Emma's habit. Had she taken a shine to the young sheep farmer? Emma, who never had given them an ounce of trouble while young, had become secretive and distant lately. She spent hours by herself in her herb shed, the loft, or walking woodland paths with a burlap bag over her shoulder.

Emma was growing up whether Julia and Simon wanted to acknowledge it or not. It was time for her parents to talk. As soon as the odd-shaped cake was decorated, Julia would find Simon and formulate a parental plan. Better to be prepared for this sixteenth birthday party than to be caught unaware.

Her husband wasn't hard to find in the least. He was headed up the path to the house from the barn. "Simon, come rock with me a while so we can talk," Julia said, shuffling toward the porch swing.

"Couldn't you talk at me while I wash up, *fraa*? I don't want to hold up my little girl's birthday dinner. Henry says we're having fried chicken." He tugged on his suspenders as though in anticipation.

"*Jah*, that's what I mean," Julia said, sitting down on the swing. "She's no *boppli* anymore. She's sixteen today. 'Spose it's time to give her a little more freedom."

With a weary sigh, Simon sat down next to his wife. "No need to rush things. Maybe Emma's not ready to start running around yet. She's so busy with her sheep and making those wreaths. And she'll have half a dozen new lambs to keep an eye on as soon as Seth and Hannah arrive. No time to think about young men." His scowl revealed much about the idea of his daughter starting to court.

"I see and hear things you don't. You've got your mind on your duties as deacon, plus getting the crops planted." She reached over to cover his hand with hers. "Emma is changing in small ways. She's growing more concerned about appearances—if her clothes are clean, if her face is sweaty, or if her nails are ragged. Did you know she asked me the other day if I thought her forehead looked too high? Imagine, how could a forehead be too high? It's right on her face where it's supposed to be."

Simon was staring at Julia as though she were speaking French.

Julia didn't wish to worry him unnecessarily, and for that reason decided not to mention the slice of cake given to James Davis unless Simon noticed the missing piece. Emma could have been just grateful for the timely delivery of the loom.

"Foreheads notwithstanding, I think we should tell our daughter she can start going to Sunday singings. Maybe after she opens her gifts, while we're having cake and ice cream. When she's ready, of course," Julia added quickly.

Simon gave his beard a long, thoughtful pull. "I don't know why you're rushing things, wife, when she hasn't started pestering us yet. The bishop said his daughter asked for months before they allowed her to attend singings."

Julia squeezed his hand, as much as the arthritis would allow.

"But you're the knowledgeable one on daughter-matters, Julia, so I'll trust your judgment." He struggled to his feet, his back having stiffened in the swing. "Just as long as she knows we're in no hurry for her to start courting. Twenty, even twenty-two, is still time enough for a gal to pick out a good husband."

Julia smiled as Simon went inside to wash up for dinner. He made it sound as though finding a life-mate were no more difficult than selecting a new standardbred buggy horse. But she wasn't in any hurry for changes within the family either. As far as she was concerned, everything could stay the same for many years to come.

And yet she also knew that God brought change to people's lives whether they were ready or not. One needed to trust Him and believe all things were by His hand, part of His divine plan.

Although Julia had tried to prepare Simon for what was to come, neither was ready for Emma's announcement later that night. Seth, Hannah, and Phoebe arrived on time for the fried chicken dinner.

Every last piece of chicken was eaten, a compliment to young Leah's skill in the kitchen. Emma opened the hummingbird feeder from her parents with wide-eyed wonder. "*Danki, mamm* and *daed*!" she exclaimed. "I love it." Leah's hand-embroidered pillow slips were praised and appreciated. Emma gushed over the box of pecan candies and the book on raising purple martins from Seth and Hannah. The birthday girl also thanked her aunt and uncle warmly for the six new lambs in the pasture.

But the surprise birthday present came from Emma's two brothers. The two boys marched a young Angora goat onto the porch to present to her through the screen door. They had hidden their purchase since the last auction day.

Matthew declared, "This is the perfect gift. It'll produce wool for you to shear and sell, plus we can tie it to a stake and he'll keep the grass short." The boys were clearly hoping to circumvent cutting the lawn around the house with the push mower all summer.

Everyone laughed, but no one more than Emma. "That's my *bruders*. Always looking for a way around chores."

Julia's energy level began waning as everyone was finishing their cake and ice cream. Thoughts of granting Emma new freedom had been forgotten in her fatigue. So Emma's announcement came as a surprise, if not an outright shock.

Emma looked from one parent to the other, cleared her voice, and said, "*Danki* for a wonderful birthday dinner, *mamm* and *daed*. Now that I am sixteen I want to take my full *Rumschpringe*."

No amount of porch swing chitchat could have prepared Simon and Julia for that.

FOUR

The next day Hannah was surprised to find Seth still at the kitchen table when she returned from the cellar. This time of year he usually ate fast to get an early start on spring planting. "Here, Phoebe, more strawberry preserves for your toast. Now finish breakfast. We've got plenty to do today."

The child spread a thick layer of jam on her bread and then used it to move oatmeal around in her bowl. "What are we doing, *mamm?*" she asked.

"We'll be very busy. You will wish you were still in school. We're planting peas, beans, and squash, setting tomato plants, and cutting spinach. Then we'll seed two more rows of lettuce to eat later in the summer. And that's just before lunch. Wait until you see how hard I work you this afternoon." Hannah reached over to tug one of Phoebe's braids.

"I'll be a big help," she said, pushing oatmeal over the rim of the bowl.

"Stop playing with your food," Seth ordered. "Put your bowl in the sink and take your toast outside. Your ma will meet you in the garden."

The child gazed at her father with wide-spaced, huge brown eyes. "Why can't I wait for her right here?"

Seth lifted a brow. "I don't need to give you a reason, daughter. But since the sun is shining and it's a Tuesday, I will. I want to talk to your *mamm*, and I don't want you to hear." He leaned very close to the small child. "Do you have any more questions?"

Phoebe didn't seem nearly as intimidated by her father as Hannah would have been at that age.

"Nope," Phoebe said and scampered out the door with her toast.

"I was wondering why you were still hanging around," Hannah said, refilling their coffee mugs.

"Does she always dawdle that much in the morning?"

"Pretty much. She's a slow starter and doesn't go strong till around dinnertime, when there's precious little day left." Hannah laughed, thinking how easily bugs, birds, and cloud formations distracted the child.

Seth shook his head. "I would amend your list of chores. With Phoebe along, you'll be lucky to get one row of beans planted by lunch."

Hannah studied Seth intently, trying to gauge his mood. "Maybe so, but it's just the first day of vacation. Is that why you waited to speak to me—to make sure your girl isn't sleeping on the job?" She sipped her coffee appreciatively.

Seth finished his in one gulp. "No, I wanted to tell you my reason for selling off your lambs yesterday." He met her gaze over the rim of the cup.

This was one topic Hannah would have preferred never to speak about again, but she waited for him to continue.

"Now that the pasture grass has come in thick, I'm not growing another crop of hay. Or soybeans. And if I can harvest my Turkey Red winter wheat by the first of July, I'm thinking about taking over that field too."

She stopped stacking the breakfast dishes to stare at him. "What are you planning to do? Dam up the creek and grow rice or maybe cranberries?"

One side of his mouth pulled into a grin. "Not this year. Maybe next if this doesn't turn out well." He laughed with a forced, hollow sound, while Hannah sat patiently waiting.

"I'm planting all corn this year, every acre other than my first hay crop."

"Nothing else?" she asked. "You've always made money on alfalfa and with your soybeans."

"Not that much once you subtract the costs and expenses. Not much profit to put toward taxes and equipment, let alone save for medical bills." He rubbed the backs of his hands absently.

"Corn prices have never been higher," he continued. "Other than my two pastures and woodlot, I'm putting every tillable acre into corn. We'll finally be able to put money aside for a rainy day." He scrambled awkwardly to his feet and then reached over to cup her chin with a calloused hand. "We don't know what the future holds, Hannah. Simon said Julia could be facing major surgery on her knees and feet. And those operations don't come cheap." He ran a caressing finger along her jawbone.

Normally, Hannah savored his gentle touch, but now the gesture seemed distracting. "*Jah*, the district will have to pitch in as much as possible."

"With the grain elevator buying up everything at great prices, we'll be in a position to help them. I stand to make a good profit if corn is all I plant."

Hannah got the distinct feeling he was trying to convince himself as much as her.

Unexpectedly, he leaned over and kissed her—in broad daylight, no less. "That's why I had to sell off your additional livestock, to raise cash to invest in seed corn." Seth left her to move to the stove to fill his insulated Thermos with the last of the coffee.

How far more benevolent "additional livestock" sounded instead of "newborn lambs" when describing taking animals to the market. Hannah's temper simmered, but she held her tongue. What was done was done; bringing up a sore subject wouldn't bring them back. Instead she asked, "What do you plan to feed your horses and cows come winter—buttered sweet corn? Cornbread with molasses? Popcorn with seasoned salt?"

Seth studied her expression before smiling tentatively, "Nah, I don't want to spoil them, *fraa*. I'll plant a late field of hay once the first crop of corn is in. I'll still have time. If necessary, we can grind the last of the corn and stalks into extra silage. Or we'll buy hay if we must—those prices are still pretty low."

"Seth, don't you think we should wait until—"

He didn't let her finish. "That's just it, Hannah. If I wait until everyone in the state is doing it, it'll be too late. It's about supply and demand. I want to get all I can harvested while the prices are high." With that he tucked his Thermos under his arm and settled his hat on his head. "I think this will turn out to be one of our best decisions ever. Opportunities like this don't come knocking every day." He buzzed another kiss across the top of her head.

Hannah couldn't kiss him back since she was too busy biting the inside of her cheek. *Opportunities like this? More like a chance to lose your shirt.* And why did he say "one of our best decisions ever" when she hadn't had a chance to utter a word on the subject?

Her exhale was very close to a snort.

She wanted to at least suggest he discuss the matter with Simon, but Seth had already made up his mind.

Maybe he was right. Maybe this was a good chance to build up the rainy-day fund. Right now they couldn't withstand more than a few days of drizzle, let alone a major calamity. Hannah had never questioned Seth's judgment before, but now she'd done so three times in two weeks. He knew his business—several generations of Miller men had tilled this sweet, fertile Ohio land respectfully and successfully. She had no reason to doubt him.

But something niggled at the back of her mind. Something didn't feel right.

Didn't their *Ordnung* have plenty to say about subsistence and not planting more than your family and community needed? But how could they possibly know what their needs might be six months from now?

One thing was certain—trusting in the Lord had always served them before. Didn't Hebrews 11:6 say, "It is impossible to please God without faith. Anyone who wants to come to him must believe that God exists and that he rewards those who sincerely seek him"?

But wasn't it also said that "God helps those who help themselves"? Hannah felt confused. Seth might be the head of the household, but allowing her some say-so only seemed fair in a marriage.

Right now, she yearned to put yesterday's foot-stomping bad temper and today's doubtfulness behind her. She loved her husband with her whole heart. Tonight she would pray for guidance and for understanding regarding his new plan. That way, just in case Seth decided to ask for her opinion, she would be ready.

～

Julia gazed out the window at the steady downpour. How the weather mimicked her spirits. Although the rain would be good for the new seedlings, she could use a little sunshine to lift the tension in her house.

All because Emma had announced her *Rumschpringe*! Some boys and most girls sailed through these years between childhood and baptism without choosing to "run around." But not her Emma.

Unfortunately, there wasn't much she or Simon could do. This period of trial and testing-the-water was her right prior to joining the church and agreeing to accept the district's *Ordnung* without question. After that, there would be no turning back. It would be different if she were a boy. A mother always worried that a girl would stray too far during this time and damage her reputation beyond repair.

Hadn't they raised her to love God and live by His Word? If so,

Julia needed to trust Him and trust that all things would be made right. But that wasn't easy to do when your little girl grew more secretive by the day.

When Julia asked her why she had cut into the cake before it was frosted, Emma had shrugged her shoulders and grown sullen. Julia knew that a girl didn't keep secrets about things that didn't matter, but she was also smart enough to know that asking too many questions would only drive the child away.

And Simon? Ever since Emma announced she wished a full *Rumschpringe*, he seemed to leave the matter entirely up to his wife. But Julia witnessed him shaking his head and mumbling under his breath even more than usual.

This had to be harder on Simon than on her. After all, he was a district deacon; people turned to him for guidance with household problems. Emma's decision to run around had put Simon in a quandary—and every other family member seemed to be scratching their heads as well. When she'd made her announcement, seven mouths dropped open wide enough to catch sparrows. Only Phoebe hadn't looked shocked but had simply asked, "What's a rump-spring?"

Matthew and Henry had then giggled, Leah looked worried, and Hannah had murmured to Phoebe, "I'll explain tonight before bed. Now hush." After that, everyone either went home or outside to his final evening chores. Julia had climbed the steps to her room and read several chapters from the book of Psalms. Psalm 34:19: "The righteous person faces many troubles, but the Lord comes to the rescue each time," remained with her still, offering comfort and hopefully patience in dealing with her elder daughter—the latter even more necessary when Emma arrived downstairs to help with breakfast.

Her blue cape dress and white apron were neat and tidy. The white prayer *kapp* was in place, while her long wheat-colored hair had been bound into a tight bun. But across her forehead was a fringe of bangs, longer on the sides, shorter between her eyes. Overall, they were spiky and uneven.

"Emma! You've cut your hair!" Julia said, unable to keep from stating the obvious.

"*Jah*, do you like my bangs? I think they keep my forehead from looking so high." Her blue eyes sparkled with delight. "Do they look straight? I found it hard to cut my own hair. I couldn't figure out how to properly hold the scissors."

Julia didn't know where to begin. "No, I don't much like them. And there's not a thing wrong with your forehead. It's no higher than anyone else's." Julia found herself gripping the chair back tightly as her knuckles turned white. "You know what the *Ordnung* says about a woman cutting her hair." Julia knew what the response to that would be as soon as she spoke the words.

Emma poured a glass of milk. "I only cut a few bangs, not all my hair, Mother." She set out the bowl of eggs and reached for the frying pan. "And after my baptism, when I join the church, I shall follow the *Ordnung*. This is my *Rumschpringe*, remember?" She glanced at Julia over the refrigerator door.

How could Julia forget? Now she would see a choppy reminder each time she looked at her daughter. "*Jah*, I remember, but I wish you would've discussed this with us first. We are still your parents, *Rumschpringe* or not."

Emma shrugged her shoulders. The bodice of her dress wasn't quite as loose as it had been when the dress had been made. "It's only hair. It'll grow out. Should I scramble the eggs? We've got mushrooms turning black; I could chop them and use them up."

"*Jah*, scrambled then. Melt the last piece of cheddar over the top." Julia walked to the stove to begin frying bacon. She caught the sweet scent of peaches on Emma. "What's that I smell?" she asked. "It reminds me of peaches, but we don't have any this early."

"Peach body lotion and spray mist," Emma answered without meeting her mother's eye. "I got them at the dollar store for two dollars each. Don't they smell nice?"

"Nothing wrong with the clean smell of Ivory soap," Julia muttered.

"I hope the hens appreciate all the trouble you've gone to this morning, because after breakfast I want you and Leah to scrub out the chicken cages and wash down the henhouse walls with bleach. Pour the bleach water over the floor when you're done. Shoo the hens outside and put up a gate so they can't go back in until you're done and everything has dried. Have Matthew haul over a couple fresh straw bales. That building is starting to smell bad."

"Yes, ma'am." Emma stirred the chopped mushrooms into her eggs and milk.

Yes, ma'am? Emma hated this particular chore and usually pleaded or bargained zealously to get out of it.

When Emma had poured the mixture into the pan, she washed her hands and sat down at the table. "*Mamm,* I'd like to ask you and *daed* for something." Her tone was as sweet as honey dripping down buttermilk biscuits.

Julia also sat down at the table.

"I'd like permission to accompany Aunt Hannah to the Davis sheep farm in Charm. We've been invited to tour their operation and we'd like to go. They are English, so we can't use many of their methods. It's more of a goodwill gesture. They supply Mrs. Dunn with wool for her customers same as us. They've already toured Aunt Hannah and Uncle Seth's farm and have invited us to theirs...twice."

Julia was at a loss for words. *The same Davis fellow who delivered the loom? The one who got the first piece of cake?* She swallowed down her petty thought and asked, "Hannah wishes to visit this farm in Charm, you say?"

"*Jah,* but she said I needed to check with you and *daed* first."

"This farm belongs to his parents? They will be home during your visit?" Julia asked.

"His mom has a job away from the house, but I'm sure his father and brothers will be there." Emma tilted her head to the side and seemed to be growing impatient.

"You will come and go in your aunt's buggy, not go riding in his pickup truck?" Julia tried to unclench her hands, but they'd almost locked into fists.

"Yes, Mother," said Emma in a tone Julia didn't care for.

Julia got up to turn the bacon and remove the egg pan from the burner. Though she took time to think, she had run out of questions to ask, and no good reason Emma *shouldn't* go came to mind.

She fell back on every mother's—Amish or English—last resort: "We'll see what your father says. It's okay with me if it's okay with him."

Emma locked eyes with Julia for a long moment, looking older than she had just ten minutes ago. "Okay. I'm going out to call everyone for breakfast so Leah and I can start on that henhouse."

Julia exhaled her breath, feeling that an argument had barely been averted. She knew she should trust her daughter; Emma had never given her any reason not to. But an Amish mother worried if her child ventured too close to the English world. There was much to tempt Plain young people.

During breakfast Simon proved to be angrier about the bangs than concerned about a visit to an English sheep farm with her aunt. "Why have you cut your hair, daughter?" he demanded. "And why do they run uphill from one side of your face to the other?"

Emma's eyes grew round and moist as she turned to Julia. "Are they that crooked? Oh, *mamm*, please say you'll help me make them even."

"I will, but first answer your father."

With tears in her eyes, Emma said, "I cut some bangs to see how they look. If everyone hates them, I'll let them grow back out."

Simon took a long drink of coffee. "They are too crooked to decide upon now. Have your *mamm* straighten them out. But then they'll look funny because they'll be too short."

Emma's face grew red as a male cardinal while tears cascaded down her cheeks. "Please wash the dishes by yourself, Leah, and I'll start scrubbing the henhouse. I'll do tonight's dinner dishes all by myself." She fled the kitchen with her face awash in misery.

"That's why Amish women don't go around cutting their hair," Simon yelled after her. He needed to have the last word on the subject.

Julia thought she'd better call the doctor to prescribe a larger dose of anti-inflammatory medicine and stronger pain relievers. She needed to be in better shape then this for the next few years of Emma's *Rumschpringe*.

~

Emma would have preferred waiting another month to visit Charm to give her hair a chance to somewhat grow back. Her *mamm* had tried to fix the bangs, but her arthritis wouldn't allow a steady grip on the scissors. So it had been up to Leah to even things out, and a hairdresser Leah was not. However, all things considered, she did make them straight. But as *daed* had predicted, now they were too short.

Time healed all woes, Julia declared, but Emma didn't have much time. She'd sent James a note the next day, informing him that she and her aunt would visit at his family's convenience. The day after that a reply was waiting in their mailbox. Oddly, it hadn't come through the U.S. mail. "Miss Emma Miller" had been written on the envelope. A tiny circle dotted the *i*. No postage stamp. James must have written back the day he received her note and then driven to Wineshurg to slip it into their mailbox.

Dear Emma,

My dad said any day is good with him. We're as caught up with chores as we ever will be. So I picked this Saturday, in three days. My sister promised to bake her special recipe of banana-walnut muffins and make us plenty of iced tea. I told the sheep to be on their best behavior in front of company. No head butting. No getting their horns tangled up in the fence. If you don't get word to us, I'll expect you and your aunt on Saturday.

James Davis

He'd written down his address and phone number and drawn a map with a black marker from their township road to his county road outside of Charm. Two big red *X*s indicated their houses. Emma studied the map so long she could probably find his farm in the middle of a moonless night.

Three days. Not enough time for her bangs to grow longer. Not enough time to sew a new dress. But why would she even consider making a new dress? James Davis was simply another *Englischer* probably more interested in her Amish ways than with her. He went to the large county high school that was attended by no Plain people.

Many *Englischers* considered them quaint—a nostalgic throwback to a bygone era. She was a curiosity to him, nothing more. And that was fine with her. Wasn't he a curiosity to her as well? Emma could count the English people she knew on one hand—Mr. and Mrs. Lee, Mr. and Mrs. Dunn, and Dr. Longo, besides passing acquaintances with the mailman, propane deliveryman, and the shopkeepers in Winesburg. She had babysat for a neighbor down the road, but she hadn't seen the children much lately. And none of those people were eighteen years old. There was nothing wrong with James being curious, but she wasn't about to make a fool of herself.

And Aunt Hannah was ready and able to also make sure that didn't happen.

～

Thanks to the map Hannah and Emma had no trouble finding the address as their buggy turned into a very long driveway. A private road would be a more accurate description, as it was paved and wide enough for two vehicles to pass. Acres upon acres of corn grew on the left, while wheat stretched off to the right as far as the eye could see. Even Hannah gawked at the number and size of the barns and outbuildings.

"My goodness," she said. "This must be one of the largest farms in the county."

Emma hadn't been expecting this either. "*Jah*, if there's one bigger, I don't think I'd care to see it."

Three members of the Davis family walked out to greet them as Hannah slowed the horse to a stop. A covered porch wrapped around two sides of the immense three-story farmhouse, while ornamental trees, lilac and rhododendron bushes, and flower beds surrounded the yard. Everything seemed to be blooming at once. Emma pulled her focus from the gorgeous blooms to lock gazes with her host.

James walked up. "Mrs. Miller, Miss Miller, this is my dad, James Davis Sr., and this is my sister."

Mr. Davis stepped forward. He was tall and wiry, with curly short hair, more silver than dark blond. "Ma'am," he said as he shook Hannah's hand. "How do, miss?" he asked Emma, nodding his head.

"Hi, Emma. My name is Lily. Jamie must've forgotten it. Welcome to Hollyhock Farm." His sister was tall, well rounded, and very freckled, wearing tight blue jeans and a red-checked flannel shirt.

"My wife had to work today," said Mr. Davis. "She'll be sorry she missed you." He held their horse's bridle tightly.

"Thank you. Please tell her we are sorry we missed her," Hannah said, stepping down from the buggy. Rows of irises and the namesake hollyhocks flanked the pebble walkway leading to the porch steps. "And give her our compliments on her lovely flower garden." Hannah glanced back over her shoulder. "Emma, are you coming or staying in the buggy?"

Emma sat motionless on the seat; the strange case of paralysis had returned.

"The cat seems to have gotten Jamie's tongue also," Mr. Davis said. He slapped his son on the back. "Help the young lady down while I unhitch the horse and turn it out in the corral."

"Nice meeting you, Mrs. Miller, Emma. If you'll excuse me, I'm cramming for my final exams. I'm a sophomore at Akron University in pre-veterinarian. But I'll see you later since I've fixed us refreshments that I hope you'll like."

Emma watched the girl stride away with her long, blond ponytail bouncing.

"Emma?" James asked. He stood at the buggy step offering his hand.

She realized she had been staring at Lily. "Thank you," she murmured. "Your sister seems very nice."

"She is, just a little overwhelming at first. I guess she had to become assertive growing up with three brothers."

Emma tugged her hand back from his after she stepped down. "Your family calls you Jamie. Should I?"

He laughed, a deep wonderful sound. "Everybody seems to call me something different. But if you don't mind, I'd like you to stay with James. I love the way it sounds with your accent."

"I don't have an accent," she said as they headed in the direction of Aunt Hannah and his dad.

"Sorry. I like how it sounds with your unique *lack* of an accent."

Emma shook off the compliment as they joined the two adults.

"Any particular place you want to start the tour?" Mr. Davis asked. "We breed and raise quarter horses and have one hundred head of dairy cattle and three hundred beef steers. We raise soybeans, wheat, and corn, besides animal feed and produce vegetables; and we have a small apple orchard."

The looks on Emma and Hannah's faces revealed their surprise.

Color flushed into Mr. Davis' already suntanned cheeks. "Begging your pardon," he said. "That sounded awfully boastful, and that wasn't my intention." He scuffed the toe of his boot into the gravel.

Hannah shook her head. "It's all right. You manage this by yourself with just help from your sons?"

"No, ma'am. Only James is serious about farming. I get some help from his younger brother, but my oldest boy is away at seminary to be a preacher. He comes home to pick apples and produce, but that's about it. And he eats as much as he harvests when we pick any kind of berries."

"Emma is interested in our sheep, Dad," James said.

"Oh, yes, you mentioned that. Let's head in that direction."

Hannah fell in step beside Mr. Davis, leaving Emma to walk with James. "How do you manage that many different operations?" Emma asked.

"My dad is pretty much the business manager. We have a full-time foreman and three other men who work for us. We also hire legal migrant workers provided by the Department of Agriculture. They stay with us from March through November."

"Good grief. They live with you in the house?" Emma had never heard of such a thing. "You have that many rooms in your home?"

"No, we have a men's dormitory plus four small apartments for those who bring their wives every year to work too."

She shook her head, trying to take it all in. "What exactly do *you* do?"

He laughed. "I graduate next week, and then I want to learn farm management from my dad. We're at a loggerhead—he wants me to go to college."

"What is a loggerhead?" She had never heard the expression.

He thought for a moment. "An ongoing disagreement."

Emma's blue eyes grew wide. "You're going to stand up to your pa? Disobey him?" Few Plain youths would admit to such a thing.

James studied her before replying. "I sure don't like arguing with him. I want us to reach a compromise."

Emma nodded as they followed the other two into the sheep barn. Once inside, all questions regarding seasonal workers, farm management, or loggerheads were forgotten. Her lower jaw dropped as her mouth gaped open. The huge sheep facility was brightly painted with clean pine stalls, fresh sawdust on the floor, and deep beds of straw in the pens. Light and airy, it smelled better than any sheep barn she'd ever been in.

"My word," she murmured.

"What lovely accommodations," Aunt Hannah said wryly.

"Yeah, much too nice for sheep," the elder Davis said. "But they are what this farm started with one hundred twenty years and many generations ago. So we maintain them in high style."

Hannah and Emma walked around in awe. The well-designed building had gathering pens, sorting pens, a forcing pen, and chutes. With plenty of ventilation and illumination, there were a dozen jugs for indoor winter lambing, so ewes and lambs could easily bond. The water tanks, salt blocks, and feeding troughs were clean and plentiful. They even had a room the visiting vet could use to treat sick animals, while the shearing room was a stainless steel wonder. Emma wouldn't have been able to even imagine such convenience. Aunt Hannah also was wide-eyed and silent as they wandered from area to area.

They took the remainder of the tour riding in an open jeep to save time. Without getting out of the vehicle, they drove past cattle barns, milking facilities, horse barns, corrals, and an indoor arena. They took a dirt lane through alfalfa fields, apple orchards, and around two ponds and one bass-stocked lake. They crossed a rushing river through a covered bridge to reach the higher pastures for cows and sheep.

By the time they settled into wicker rockers on the screened porch for their afternoon refreshments, Emma and Hannah were exhausted from looking, listening, and learning.

"I'll bet Dad and Jamie wore you two out," Lily stated, handing around glasses of iced tea and fresh-baked muffins.

"*Jah*," Emma said, blushing a deep rose color, "but we especially enjoyed seeing your sheep barn."

"I hope you'll forgive me, Mrs. Miller, Emma," Mr. Davis apologized. "I get a little carried away showing off the farm. I can't take much credit. My dad and grandfather built most of what you see. We just try to keep it up, adding something new whenever necessary."

Emma noticed that her aunt was eating her muffin quicker than usual, as though anxious to leave. She too suddenly felt like a fish flapping around on the pond bank. James kept watching her as though she might bolt down the walk to their buggy. The two guests finished their snack in record time.

"These are delicious muffins, Lily. Thank you for your hospitality, especially for taking time from your studies," Hannah said graciously.

"You're welcome," said Lily. "Please stop by any time you're in the area. We love company."

"It gives us an excuse to take a break from chores," added her father.

"Thank you again, Mr. Davis, for the tour, but now we must start for home." Hannah stood up abruptly, smiled, and walked down the steps.

"I'll bring your horse around and hitch her up," Mr. Davis said, following Hannah off the porch.

Emma met James' gaze for a moment, understanding how a deer might feel during hunting season. She turned toward Lily. "Nice meeting you...goodbye." Heading toward the buggy, she forced herself to walk while every instinct told her to run.

"Emma, wait up a minute." James grabbed at her sleeve halfway down the path.

She shot him an annoyed look and pulled back her arm. Once she knew the elders wouldn't overhear, she said rather crisply, "I can't imagine why you wanted us to see your farm, unless it was only to show off."

James' face sagged while he dropped his arms to his side. "No, it's not like that at all."

Emma perched one hand on her hip. "You couldn't have seen anything of interest in our small flock. And we can no more benefit from what we've seen today than we could from a visit to the moon."

He ran a hand through his hair. "I wasn't trying to show off, Emma. If the truth be told, I just wanted to see you again and couldn't think of any other way to accomplish that."

Emma's mouth dropped open while a blush rose up her neck. She felt herself turn pink up to her hairline. Nodding politely, she mumbled, "I see, James. That's a bit different. Well, now you've seen me."

With that, she ran to the buggy and climbed in, forgetting all about being ladylike. When Mr. Davis finished hitching up the horse, Aunt Hannah slapped the reins on its back and Emma waved goodbye. She didn't dare breathe until they were halfway down the lane to the county road. Only then did she glance back through the buggy window.

James Davis Jr. stood soldier stiff where Emma had left him in the yard. He was waving back and forth forlornly like a traveler stranded on a foreign shore.

FIVE

James watched the buggy turn onto the highway feeling oddly ashamed. Neither he nor his dad had meant to brag about the size or complexity of their farm, yet he knew that's how it must have seemed to Emma and her aunt.

Why hadn't he realized that such economic disparity, besides the cultural differences, might cause hard feelings? But how else could he get to know Emma Miller better? Since meeting her in Mrs. Dunn's store, that's all he thought about. Emma wasn't anything like the other girls he knew. And the fact she was Amish was only part of it.

The girls he knew through his church—Sunday school classes, vacation Bible school, and now youth meetings—he had grown up with. A person seldom develops romantic notions for someone they have known since playing in the sandbox. They were his friends, but he felt the same toward them as he did toward Lily.

And the girls from school only seemed interested in clothes, make-up, and guys with fast cars, in that order. They achieved good grades solely to get into prestigious colleges, considered shopping a competitive sport, and flaunted their designer purses or shoes to whomever would listen. He had no trouble getting dates in the past, especially not since he'd bought his flashy truck. With his paycheck from the farm, he could afford to take dates out to expensive Canton restaurants for dinner or to the movies. He'd never been shy about buying flowers or small gifts—being generous always made him happy.

But as soon as a girl heard he wasn't interested in playing college sports or even going to college, they looked at him as though he were addlebrained. *Why does everyone have to be the same?* He'd enjoyed playing wide receiver for his high school football team. Sports had taught him discipline, self-control, and teamwork—the whole was greater than the sum of its parts. But he had no delusions about college athletics. He didn't want to be just another farm boy, trying to compete in a world without possessing the necessary passion.

James loved working the farm. And unlike most rural young men, he wasn't ashamed to admit it. Maybe that's why he was so taken with Emma Miller. She was passionate about building her flock, increasing her wool production, and earning a living by raising livestock. She shared his interests and ambitions...besides having the bluest eyes and prettiest face in Ohio. She needed no beauty shop streaks with her natural highlights from the sun. And no blusher or lipstick could improve her peaches-and-cream complexion or soft rosebud lips.

Peaches—that's what he had smelled during the jeep ride. And the memory of her fragrance, the feel of her hand, and the sound of her laughter would stay with him for a long time. But standing in the middle of the road, staring after a buggy that was probably halfway home wouldn't get his chores done or, more important, figure out how to see her again.

He went searching for his dad and found him in the indoor arena with one of the horse trainers. This was as good a time as any for some advice. "What did you think about Emma...and her aunt?"

James Davis Sr. took his eyes off the new colt long enough to cast his son an odd glance. "I think they're very nice, but they may have been overwhelmed by our operation. I know you had no intention of embarrassing them, but nevertheless they were uncomfortable."

"That's not what I had planned," he said, loud enough to draw the trainer's attention. "I like Emma. She's really nice. Not that many gals I know are interested in livestock, let alone sheep."

His dad slanted him another glance, this one a bit sly. "She is awfully pretty too, but I suppose you already noticed that small detail." His eyes crinkled into a web of tiny lines as he lifted his boot to the lowest rail.

"Yeah, I noticed, but that's not why I like her." James Jr. labored to find the right words. "She's different from other girls."

"Andy, don't give him so much slack," his dad called to the trainer. "Tighten up that lead." The trainer had the colt on a long lunging rope. To his son, he said, "Emma's more than a little different. She lives in a separate world from ours."

James held his tongue. If he argued, he might betray his emotions. And since he really didn't know how he felt about Emma, that wouldn't be a good idea. The two men silently watched the spirited year-old colt fight against the rope for several minutes.

"Are you gonna stand here and chaw all day?" Dad asked. "Don't I give you enough work to do?" His laughter echoed off the arena's high metal roof.

"Yeah, I've got plenty to do. I'll check the feed order, update the inoculation records, and drive up to where those loggers are taking out some black walnut trees. I want to make sure they cut down only those I tagged and don't damage anything with their trucks or equipment."

"Good idea. I'll see you at supper," said James Sr.

"Not tonight. I'm driving over to Sam Yoder's after work to see what he's up to. I haven't talked to him for a while."

His dad leveled him a steady look and then grinned. "I just figured out why you made friends with that pretty Amish gal. I never took you for a matchmaker, son, but that's a right nice thing to do."

James nodded and then hurried off to his chores. Better to let that particular misconception alone for now, but fixing Emma Miller up with one of his Amish friends was the last thing on his mind.

~

Sam Yoder was washing mud off tractor tires when James arrived at his farm. The Yoders lived about ten miles away, closer as the crow flies. Because the family was New Order Amish, they used diesel tractors and other mechanized equipment for farming and had electricity in their barns.

"Hey, Jamie, long time no see," called Sam. He turned off the hose and dried his hands on his pant legs.

"It's been a while, way too long." They shook hands, never having adapted the habit of "man hugs" like some men their age. After preliminary updates on spring planting, news from mutual friends, and how the Indians looked in the new baseball season, James finally broached the subject he'd been mulling over. "Tell me again, Sam. How would you go about meeting Amish girls who weren't from your district...let's say, that were Old Order?"

Amish folk in Holmes County tended to socialize among themselves, especially the more conservative Old Order, the largest of the Amish sects. However, occasionally fund-raisers and other social events were held that welcomed all districts. Even *Englischers* were sometimes invited.

Sam began a slow smile. "When did you start taking an interest in my lack-of-love life?"

"It's not *your* love life I'm concerned with," James said, shoving his hands deep into his pockets.

Sam's grin now reached from ear to ear. "Is that right? And who is the lucky lady that James Jr. has set his eye on?"

"Things are still uncertain, but I promise when I figure this out, you'll be the first to know."

"Fair enough." Sam scratched the stubble on his chin as though deep in thought. "Well, come to think of it, my mom mentioned a big volleyball party over in Winesburg next Saturday. She's always pressuring me to socialize more."

James hoped his face didn't reveal his excitement over the name of the town hosting the event. "What will that be like?" he asked.

"Let me see. There will be probably close to a hundred people, mostly our age, some a little older. And all of them unmarried. Married folk don't attend these things. Several volleyball games will be going on, plus horseshoes, a big bonfire, plenty of eats, including some of the best pies and cakes you've ever tasted. The girls try to outdo each other with their baking." Sam rubbed his belly with a circular motion.

James wasn't quite as interested in the food. "You've been to a lot of these parties?"

"Nah, not that many, but maybe I should start going. Now that my classes are done at the vocational center, I won't be seeing many gals till county fair time. You run into few ladies down at the Feed-n-Seed." He swept off his hat and snaked a hand through his long hair.

"So you'll go?" asked James with anticipation building in his veins. *Is this what people mean by spring fever?* "And you'll invite me to come with you?"

Sam set his straw hat back on his head. "Yeah, I think I'll go. And you can tag along so long as you pick me up. The bishop won't let me drive my truck to a social event."

"You've got a deal," James said, a little too loudly.

"Did you eat supper yet?" When James shook his head, Sam continued, "Let's go see what my ma cooked up. I'm starving. And I'll fill you in on proper behavior and what to expect at this party. Mom will be happy to offer her two cents on that topic." He slapped an arm around James' shoulder and the two marched inside like comrades undertaking a daring mission.

And to James, that's exactly what it felt like.

~

Emma had been unusually quiet on the drive back from Charm,

and that had been fine with Hannah. The tour of the Davis' grand estate had left her feeling out of sorts. She wasn't jealous of such worldly wealth, and the Davis family seemed like genuinely good people, but the whole excursion had been a big waste of time.

Why had Emma yearned to see that vast, complex agribusiness? Plain people farmed to feed themselves and their families and earned a cash crop to pay taxes, medical expenses, and those things not easily grown or bartered. Their farms, although some were quite large, were far simpler and straightforward.

Hannah had a theory regarding Emma's fascination that had nothing to do with shearing facilities resembling hospital operating rooms. Perhaps the young woman's sullen melancholy on the way home indicated she might have lost enthusiasm for the fancy life. For Emma's sake, Hannah certainly hoped so. There was good reason why Plain people seldom mingled with *Englischers*, and it had nothing to do with covetousness.

After she dropped off her niece and watched the girl shuffle her booted feet up the driveway, Hannah released a sigh of relief. *That should be the last of the foolishness.*

Home beckoned. Her lettuce and green beans could use a few buckets of rainwater. She also needed to check her flock's feed supply since the pasture was somewhat sparse. But first she wanted to cut up a chicken and put it up to simmer. Chicken stew with baby carrots, new potatoes, peas, and celery sounded good with the rest of yesterday's buttermilk biscuits. Soups, stews, and pot roasts always worked when outdoor chores still remained. Even *she* couldn't ruin those dishes by overcooking if she kept the flame low.

As she unhitched the horse and turned it into the paddock, Leah appeared from the back path pulling Phoebe by the hand.

"*Guder nachmittag*, Aunt Hannah," Leah called.

"Good afternoon to you," Hannah said.

"*Mamm*," Phoebe yelled and ran to embrace Hannah as though she'd been gone for days.

Hannah lifted Phoebe to her hip. Soon she would be too big to pick up, so Hannah cherished the wonderful feel of a child in her arms. *Will I one day know the joy of nurturing an infant? Will I be blessed with a baby to rock to sleep in the handmade oak cradle used by four generations of Millers?* Hannah fervently hoped so, but so far her prayers had gone unanswered. Lately, she confined her prayer requests to other people's woes, lest the Lord think her unappreciative of the grace she'd been shown. She'd been welcomed into a new community, found a wonderful man to love, and given a precious child to help raise. She loved 2 Corinthians 9:11, which summed up being grateful: "Yes, you will be enriched in every way so that you can always be generous. And when we take your gifts to those who need them, they will thank God."

Hannah swung Phoebe around before setting her down and giving Leah a warm hug. "*Danki*, Leah. Did you two help your *mamm* pickle and can the first baby beets?"

For her answer, Leah held up her hands for inspection. The cuticles and fingertips were stained red from beet juice. Phoebe mimicked the gesture as they walked toward the house. "Come inside and have a glass of lemonade," Hannah said. "I have some cold in the fridge."

"No, *danki*," her niece said, stopping at the steps. "I need to get back and make supper. Emma ran straight to her flock when you brought her home. She didn't have one thought about helping me in the kitchen." She frowned with determination.

Hannah tried not to smile. Those two sisters were as different as strong coffee and cold milk—both refreshing but absolutely nothing alike.

"I appreciate you walking Phoebe home," Hannah called as Leah headed for the back path. After she disappeared from sight, Hannah entered the kitchen to find Seth sitting at the table.

"Afternoon, *fraa*," he said. A coffee mug sat before him.

"Seth, have you been waiting for me? Did you forget about my trip to Charm today?" Hannah hurried to take the seat opposite him.

Phoebe started to sit down too until Hannah stopped her. "Go wash up and play in the front room," Hannah said to the child.

Seth waited until his daughter left the room before speaking. "No, I remembered, but there's something I wanted to talk about before more time passed." He drained the last of his coffee.

Under the table Hannah smoothed her palms down her skirt with growing trepidation. "What is it?"

"I joined up with some men in the district to take advantage of the corn situation." He met her gaze with an expression of tenderness.

"*Ach*, the high corn prices. So you're not alone in wanting to plant extra fields with a moneymaker." She breathed easier. Her fears of illness or some other dreadful news had tensed the muscles in her back.

"*Jah*, a third of the district is doing the same, but there's more to it than that. Plenty of land in the county has been sitting fallow, mostly owned by *Englischers* who either aren't farming anymore or have reduced the number of acres under cultivation." He kept his focus on her steady.

It seemed as though he wanted her to guess what he was trying to say, but she hadn't a clue. Tension began to creep back into her shoulders. "Spell this out for me, Seth," she said, "so I can start fixing supper."

"We've formed an alliance to lease available tillable land. Together as a group, we'll put up equal amounts and share in the profits at the end of the year."

She stared wide eyed like a barn owl high in the rafters. "With what money would you invest in this scheme?"

Some of the tenderness faded from his eyes. "It's no scheme, Hannah. It's a solid business investment. I put up the money in our savings account."

"*All of it?*" she asked, annoyance replacing trepidation. The savings account included the remaining proceeds from the sale of her Pennsylvania farm to her brother, no small sum of money.

"No, not all of it, but a good chunk. We'll get it back and more after the final harvest."

"Seth, it's almost June. Isn't it late to be looking for land to plant more corn?"

"*Jah*, it would, but it's already done, *fraa*. We've leased the land and the crop is in. We're all praying nightly for rain, but not too much, you know." His laughter sounded hollow and brittle in the kitchen.

Hannah pulled off her *kapp* and slapped it down on the table. Her scalp had grown hot and prickly. "You've already done this, but you're just getting around to telling me now?" Anger replaced annoyance in her voice.

"Calm down. Don't work yourself up into a tizzy. We've both been so busy I haven't had a chance. That's why I wanted to tell you before I milk the cows tonight. Didn't want anymore time to slip by."

"Well, *danki* very much," she said, rising to her feet. She pulled the stockpot from the cabinet with a clatter. "I would've liked to discuss the matter with you before you went out and withdrew our savings, but since it's too late for that, I might as well start my chicken stew!" Hannah tried to keep her voice down so she wouldn't draw Phoebe to the kitchen, but there was no disguising her emotions. She took celery from the crisper drawer and began to chop stalks with zeal.

"Hannah, Hannah. You've got a bee in your *kapp*." Seth spoke softly as he walked up and placed his big hands on her shoulders. "Calm yourself, dear one. You're my wife now. You are no longer making independent decisions like you did following Adam's death. I'm in charge of these matters now." He patted her back, the same way she often stroked ewes before a shearing.

Hannah stopped attacking the celery stalk, fearful for her fingers. Her hands were shaking badly. Sucking air into her lungs, she gritted her words through clenched teeth. "I have no bee in my *kapp*; it's on the table."

But her pronouncement echoed in an empty kitchen. Seth had gone out to his evening chores before dinner. The screen door slammed resolutely behind him. Hannah was left alone to do women's work as she tamped down uncharitable thoughts toward the man she pledged to love, honor, and obey.

The first two were easy as pie.

The third was proving to be more of a challenge than she ever would have imagined.

~

They say a watched pot never boils. The same idea must be true about calendars. Emma thought Saturday would never arrive. The volleyball party would be her first social outing since turning sixteen and declaring her *Rumschpringe*. She had spent the week catching up with her barn chores and in the garden, besides helping *mamm* and Leah with the baking, sewing, and laundry.

Leah had it so easy. She didn't have farm chores, such as tending sheep or hauling feed buckets. Leah would also arrive late to weed or water the garden, and she usually found an excuse to leave early—either a roast needed to come out of the oven or the bread needed to go in.

But Emma wasn't complaining. Even drudgery tasks, such as coring apples or shelling peas, didn't bother Leah. While her sister loved helping *mamm* in the kitchen, Emma preferred the great outdoors. And whenever it rained, plenty of work waited in the loft or in her herb shed.

For the rest of today, however, play awaited. And Emma was ready.

Wearing new tennis shoes, she tapped her toe on the porch until Matthew finally brought the pony cart around. *Daed* had decided Matthew could attend the volleyball party since he didn't want Emma going alone. Even though her brother was only fourteen, this daytime party included those younger than courting age.

Courting age. She was finally old enough to attend Sunday night singings, summer corn roasts, fall hayrides, and winter skating parties with Plain people her age without her parents watching like a hawk. Now she could stay out late, as long as a young man asked to bring her home in his courting buggy. But the only young man occupying her thoughts lately drove a very big truck with four knobby tires across the back axle instead of the normal two.

Thinking about James made her feel a little sad as Matthew drove toward the center of town. Partly because she didn't want to miss activities Amish girls enjoyed, and partly because she knew how much seeing James would upset her parents. They would never allow her to court an *Englischer*, running-around years or not. That could easily lead to shunning and eventual banishment from the church, and no girl in her right mind wanted that.

"Woolgathering even when you're not with your sheep?" asked Matthew. Their *mamm* had trimmed his hair far neater than her bangs, and he'd shaven the first peach-fuzz whiskers from his chin, but he still looked like a little boy beside her in the pony cart.

"It's what I've gotten good at lately," she said. "Can't this horse go any faster? They will already have started the games by the time we get there."

He clucked his tongue to the horse, which seemed to have forgotten what that sound meant. "Nah, this old mare is just plain worn out. The pony cart is the only thing Pa lets her pull. She's pretty much only good for keeping the pasture grass trimmed."

Emma watched the passing scenery, occasionally waving to a neighbor. Why would she even think about upsetting her parents when James Davis probably had no intention of asking her out? She was sure she wasn't the only Holmes County female to notice him. People probably called him on the telephone all the time, or sent him those email messages—of which she had only a vague idea what they were.

In Winesburg the pony cart turned south. Within a quarter mile they heard shouting and general ruckus before the trees allowed them a view. But once the mare dutifully delivered them to the home hosting the event, both Emma and Matthew uttered simultaneously, "Good grief."

"Jump down, sister. I've got to park the cart and turn out Belle." Matthew had caught sight of nearly a hundred teenagers involved in three volleyball games, playing horseshoes, or already munching hot dogs under the food tent. He couldn't wait to join the fun.

Emma jumped down but then hung back under the shade of a willow tree, watching the goings-on from a distance. She'd been to barn raisings; her own family had held one last year after a fire destroyed their barn. She'd attended preaching services every other Sunday since she was a *boppli*. She'd been to weddings from time to time. But never had she been to a place where everyone was around her age.

"Hi, Emma," said two girls at once. Emma's time of shy observance came to an end when her friends Sarah and Martha approached. "We were hoping you would come. Isn't it wonderful? Everyone we know is here," Sarah said. Tall and very thin, Sarah Hostetler's brown eyes sparkled with delight.

"There are people from five different districts. And some folks from New Order have shown up too, plus some *Englischers*," her sister whispered almost conspiratorially.

"Do tell," Emma said, craning her neck around the pair to peruse the crowd. Her brother had already disappeared from sight.

"Do you know Samuel Yoder?" asked Sarah eagerly.

Emma thought for a moment and then shook her head. "I don't reckon so." The three girls looked toward the loudest of the volleyball games. Shouts of victory had drawn their attention.

"He's been asking about you—if you were coming, if anyone had seen you yet." Both sisters eyed Emma curiously. "Why would he be asking about you? Are you sure you're not acquainted?"

But Emma was as befuddled as her friends. She couldn't remember meeting any Sam Yoder. Of course, the surname was second only to hers in commonness. "I can't place him," Emma said. "What district is he from?"

"I'm pretty sure he's New Order and lives over by Charm."

Emma stopped dead in her tracks, causing the girls to leave her behind. *Charm? How does the mere mention of a town's name turn my stomach to gelatin?*

"What's wrong?" Sarah asked, turning back. "Do you remember him? Is he a pesky gnat you'd rather not run into?" She whispered so she wouldn't be overheard.

"No," answered Emma. "I've only been to Charm once and met no Sam Yoder." Oddly, beads of sweat formed above her lip though they stood in the shade.

Martha huddled close to Emma's side. "Well, don't look now, but he's coming this way—the boy who's been asking about you." Her hushed words drifted on the breeze.

Emma couldn't help but pivot around to see a tall, dark-haired fellow walking toward them. He wore a big smile and offered a friendly wave, but Emma was quite certain she'd never seen him before. Her two friends moved into protective flanking positions.

"Hullo, Emma Miller?" the stranger asked.

"*Jah,*" she said shyly.

"I'm Sam Yoder. I doubt you recall, but we met five years ago at a wedding of my second cousin to some kin of yours. The wedding was at my uncle's place, Abram Yoder."

Even close up she didn't recognize him, but five years was a long time. She nodded politely. "Sorry, but I don't remember you, Sam. Sometimes when a person goes to many weddings in a row, they start to blend together." She offered her hand hesitantly to shake. "This is Martha and Sarah Hostetler."

Sam nodded to the other girls as he shook Emma's hand. His focus remained on Sarah longer than necessary. "Shucks, that's okay, Emma. I might not have remembered you either, but I asked my ma what you looked liked. She's seen you somewhere else since the wedding."

Emma's forehead furrowed with confusion. "Why would you ask your *mamm* about me?"

Sam rocked on his heels, crossing his arms over his chest. "I've got a friend who was hoping to run into you again, and we both thought you might show up today."

Martha and Sarah watched her while suppressing grins.

The bottom of Emma's stomach seemed to give way. "And who might your friend be?" Her voice resembled the squeak of a mouse.

Sam turned and waved at the road. No one was standing in the vicinity he was looking, but then James Davis popped from behind an ancient oak tree, and he began walking toward them.

"Yet another stranger," whispered Sarah.

"And this one's English," added Martha.

"Oh, my goodness." Emma could manage nothing else.

Sam Yoder leaned forward. "Martha, Sarah, why don't we join that game over there?" He pointed in the general direction of the volleyball field. "They sure can use more people, considering the number of times the ball hits the ground. You don't have to worry about Emma. My friend is as harmless as a mayfly."

Both girls looked at Emma warily. "Is that what you want us to do?"

"*Jah,* go on ahead. I'll be there shortly. I know this *Englischer* from my wool business."

Martha cast her a worried backward glance as they walked off, but Sarah had already struck up a conversation with Sam.

"Good morning, Miss Miller," James said upon reaching her. "Are you surprised to see me?" He had on clean blue jeans and a navy shirt with short sleeves. For a moment, his arm muscles drew her attention. Plain men never bared their upper arms.

Pulling her attention away from his biceps, she said, "Shocked is more like it." She took a step backward from his close proximity.

James hooked a thumb in his pocket. "Good kind of shocked? Or the kind when you discover a snake in your boot?"

She couldn't help but smile. "That remains to be seen. I didn't know English people came to these parties."

"Sam Yoder invited me along. I think mainly because he wanted a ride."

"Yes, I imagine so. Well, are we going to play volleyball or not?" She felt nervous and fluttery again with him so close. She started walking toward the nets.

"That's why I came. I love the game! I strongly suggest you join the same side that I do." He easily caught up and fell into step beside her.

She smelled the spicy, cinnamon scent of his gum again. "Why should I do that?" she asked.

"Because then you'll end up on the winning team." He laughed and pulled one of her *kapp* strings, something her *bruders* did too many times to count. But this felt quite different.

A new volleyball game was getting ready to start as James and Emma walked up. Because people arrived at the same time from the opposite direction, they did end up on the same side of the net. Emma took a spot in the front row, while James squeezed into the middle of the pack. After some successful volleys back and forth, a few assists, and even one blocked spike, Emma relaxed into the game.

The day was sunny but not too hot. A light breeze refreshed overheated skin. The other players were loud, but friendly and noncompetitive. Emma played well and shouted encouragement to her fellow teammates. When other girls kicked off their shoes to play barefooted, she did the same. The thick grass felt cool and soft between her toes.

Even though their team lost two games in a row, they were just beginning to hit their stride. That is, until a particularly high ball proved difficult to judge. Emma continued to back up, positioning herself for the shot until a voice exclaimed over her shoulder.

"Right behind you, Emma. I've got it!"

The familiar male voice, soft and husky, startled her worse than any snake in a boot. She quickly pivoted around to meet almost nose-to-nose with her fellow sheep farmer.

James was smiling like a cat in the cream.

The volleyball landed next to them, just missing her head.

"Better call your shots, you two," someone shouted, "before someone gets knocked unconscious." Everyone at the game laughed.

Everyone but Emma. "Whew, I need a break," she called to Sarah. "The sun is flaming hot." They walked off the playing field together.

But what truly is flaming is my face. James made her nervous. She knew what that meant. And she knew only too well that letting members of her district know that was surely a bad idea.

"Wait up," James called, hurrying after them. "Let's get something to drink. I'm parched and can also use something to eat."

"All right. I'm a little hungry too," Sam called.

They all drank lemonade and ate a hot dog each. But during the meal James was entirely too silly and flirtatious. Emma wasn't accustomed to flattery and felt uncomfortable with the attention they seemed to be attracting.

As soon as she could, she found Matthew, pleaded a headache, and insisted they leave the party.

James walked her to their pony cart and helped Matthew hitch up the elderly horse. With only the briefest of goodbyes, Emma lightly slapped the reins on poor Belle's rump, something she wouldn't normally do. She was grumpy and confused and hadn't been able to locate her new tennis shoes when it was time to go. The last pair left by the net was dirty and worn-out, but she had no choice but to put them on. She couldn't leave barefooted.

And for some reason, she couldn't stop thinking about the cause of her irritation all the way home.

SIX

June

Emma had thought things would get easier once she reached *Rumschpringe,* but she felt more confused than ever. She wasn't used to making a spectacle of herself in public. When the volleyball hit the grass between them, she and James had locked eyes like two hawks vying for the same rabbit. Everyone had noticed…and laughed.

You're facing the wrong direction, Emma.

Don't use your head; this isn't soccer.

Did you two come to play or to make goo-goo eyes?

Goo-goo eyes, indeed. She'd never before felt so humiliated. Yet all morning long she couldn't keep from thinking about the man who had caused her mortification. First, she'd scorched the oatmeal at breakfast. Then, she'd forgotten to close the gate behind her, so several ewes retreated to the barn instead of marching to the pasture where their food and water were. Finally, she'd cut spinach and not lettuce in the garden and pulled onions instead of carrots to earn a scolding from *mamm.* Her mother kept looking sideways at her during lunch, expecting her to do something else senseless, but she managed to serve tomato soup with toasted cheese sandwiches to her father and brothers without mishap.

She didn't like the effect James had on her mental state, but that was only one thing she didn't like about him. When she'd headed to the lunch tent with Sarah and Martha, he and Sam Yoder had tagged right behind them. Both had asked her friends endless questions about the food choices as though hamburgers, hotdogs, baked beans, and coleslaw were unusual decisions.

Several Amish young men had noticed how much attention the *Englischer* was paying her. Emma didn't need gossip starting behind her back. The final straw came when he followed her to the pony cart, and then acted as though he'd run into a long lost friend with Matthew. They'd only met once before, for all of two minutes, when James delivered the loom.

What if Matthew started questioning her in front of their folks? Worrying them unnecessarily was a bad idea, especially since she didn't know how she felt. James was much too flirtatious to be friends with a Plain girl.

"Emma, mind what you're doing. You're slopping dishwater on my clean floor." Her mother put an end to her daydreaming as Emma scrubbed the morning's baking pans.

"May I go to Aunt Hannah's this afternoon?" she asked.

Julia, who'd been trying to let down Henry's trouser legs, slanted her an odd look. "Now that you've got your own spinning wheel and loom, I would think you'd have enough to keep busy here." Her poor bent fingers dropped the needle yet again. In exasperation, she pushed the garment away.

"*Jah*, I do," Emma agreed. "But it's questions I need to ask. I want to pick Aunt Hannah's brain."

Julia looked aghast. "I don't care for that expression, daughter. Where did you hear it? At that volleyball party?"

"Yes'm." Emma set the last pan in the rack to dry.

"Don't use it again," Julia said. Then in a softer tone she added, "You may go to Hannah's when your chores are done. Take that extra apple crumb pie on the windowsill. It's Seth's favorite. Be home in enough time to give Leah a hand with supper."

Emma nodded and flew out the door to get the laundry off the line. If she hurried through her ironing, she'd have plenty of time with her aunt. Hannah would know what she should do. She had straightened out a hornet's nest of problems with Uncle Seth before they were hitched last fall. If anyone could explain these strange feelings she had for an inappropriate match, it would be Aunt Hannah.

After all, she and Uncle Seth were still like two sweet lovebirds, roosting in the eaves, after almost a year.

~

Hannah lifted bedsheets off the line to fold, careful not to let them touch the ground. She was surprised a sudden storm hadn't undone her hard work, considering how the rest of her day had gone. First, there was her monthly onset, reminding her once more she was not in a family way. Would she ever know the thrill and joy of a baby growing inside her? Would she one day be able to present Seth with another precious daughter like Phoebe, or his first son? An Amish farmer needed sons to help when backs grew stiff and eyesight faltered. Who would take over Seth's farm and tend it with the same loving care?

Hannah sometimes felt selfish praying for a baby that might never come. Perhaps she should accept God's will and devote herself to the family she'd been given. Then she remembered Elizabeth in the Bible, barren for years and finally becoming pregnant when very old. *If it be Your will, Lord, please don't make me wait that long.*

Second, the unexpected visit from her niece hadn't set well with her. Emma had come asking questions about the new lambs, but Hannah quickly suspected another matter had motivated the girl to hike the mile between the farms. Emma had just attended her first social event. At first her amusing tales had reminded Hannah of her youth when everything seemed to conspire against a young woman. Emma had lost her new tennis shoes and had to come home in a worn, ill-fitting pair. She had dribbled mustard down her dress in front of her girlfriends. And she had to leave the party early since Simon feared the old horse might become confused after dark. But when Emma mentioned that the sheep farmer from Charm had been there with his Amish friend, Hannah had grown uneasy.

Emma was obviously looking for some sort of guidance or advice without asking specific questions. Emma needed to talk to her mother about these things. Yet Hannah knew Julia could sometimes be close-minded.

"Talk to your *mamm* about running around barefoot," Hannah had directed. "Ask your *daed* if Old Order members are allowed to court New Order during *Rumschpringe*," she had advised. But when Emma asked if God loved *Englischers* as much as Amish folk, Hannah's reply had needed no deliberation. "Of course He does, but God is happiest when we listen to His Word and are obedient."

That seemed to satisfy the girl, but it had left Hannah feeling guilty. She felt disloyal to Julia and fearful that her counseling might lead the girl astray.

History had shown she was no expert on the district's *Ordnung*.

But how could she turn away her niece? She would not close off her relationship with Emma, because young people needed all the help they could get during this difficult period. Hannah would walk a careful line between the girl and Julia.

With the laundry down and folded, Hannah carried the basket toward the house. She spotted Seth and Phoebe strolling through tall grass on their way home for supper. He'd taken his daughter wading in the river because today had been very warm for the first week of June. Even though they were still beyond earshot, Hannah could tell Phoebe was talking up a storm. Her small hands gestured wildly to punctuate her sentences.

The sight warmed Hannah's heart. As recently as last year the child had been mute, responding to questions with only shakes and nods of her head. If her animated speech was any indication, the little girl was fully healed.

The three Millers met at the porch steps. "We took off our shoes and went in the creek up to our knees," Phoebe exclaimed. "*Daed* rolled up his pants and I held up my skirt. The water was cold, Ma."

She apparently hadn't held up her skirt very well since the fabric below her knees was sodden. "I'll bet the water still felt good, didn't it?" Hannah asked, smiling. "Go in and change, Phoebe, and put that dress in the laundry basket." Hannah turned her attention to Seth. His face was already tanned despite the fact he seldom went outdoors without his hat.

"How soon before we eat?" he asked, toeing off his muddy boots on the porch. He would leave them outside by the door.

"*Eat?* You just ate yesterday! Are you hungry again already?" Hannah loved to tease him about his hearty appetite.

He winked and held the door open for her. "I can't get enough of your good vittles, *fraa*. It's all I think about out in the fields."

"Ha-ha," she said. "My cooking is only an improvement over yours." Hannah set down the laundry basket in the hallway. "For tonight I have pot roast with carrots and potatoes on low simmer. It should be done in ten minutes."

Seth headed straight to the refrigerator. "Turn up the heat," he said, pouring them each a glass of iced tea. "I've got a meeting tonight. Let's eat as soon as we can."

Hannah turned up the propane burner and began to slice up vegetables for a salad. "A meeting, you say? What about?" she asked. Weekday meetings were rare. Men usually talked enough after preaching services, as did women, not to need time away from chores or family.

"The corn alliance. The county extension agent is coming out to discuss market conditions and tell us if any more land is available to lease in the area. The bishop should be there and probably both deacons." Seth sat down at the table with his glass of tea.

Hannah noticed he looked more tired than usual. Perhaps the warmer nights were interfering with his sleep and would take some getting use to. "In that case," she said, scraping the vegetables into a bowl from the cutting board, "I'll set the table and we'll eat soon. We can drop Phoebe at Julia's for Emma to watch and then be on our way. I wonder what my sister thinks about—"

The expression on Seth's face curtailed the remainder of her question. "There's no reason for Phoebe to go to Julia's. This meeting is for men." He spoke stiffly as he arched his spine against the chair back.

She pulled the roaster off the heat and cautiously lifted the lid. "I know better than to speak at one of these meetings, *ehemann*, but I see no harm in women sitting in the back, listening. I'll be quiet as a mouse."

"I know you would be, but you cannot come, Hannah. The bishop said men only, so men only it will be." Seth popped a baby carrot from the salad bowl into his mouth.

Hannah pulled off her apron and tossed it down on the counter. "The decisions made at these secret meetings affect the women too. We need to know if families will be eating boiled potatoes with fried eggs all winter long. We could start putting away dried beef now to have later on." To save time, she hacked the pot roast into smaller chunks while still in the pan.

Seth scooped salad onto their plates for all of them. "No need to assume the worst. Have faith. And these meetings aren't secret since I just told you about it." He gazed at her with dark eyes both earnest and sympathetic.

She speared a hunk of meat and transferred it to Seth's plate. "I have plenty of faith. I'd just like to have some say-so for a change." Her words slipped out unintended, making her sound petty and willful.

Seth scooped carrots and celery from the pot and began to devour his dinner. He finished faster than usual, even though the roast was still rather tough. Hannah supposed his speed wasn't solely due to the meeting.

"I promise, Hannah, that I won't go to bed until I tell you of any decisions made tonight. Then you can have your say-so to me for as long as you like." He drained his tea in one long gulp.

Hannah decided to let the matter drop. She called Phoebe, and the child started her dinner about the time Seth finished his. Hannah took her time picking at supper long after Seth was on his way to the gathering.

Your will be done, Lord, not mine. She repeated the words silently over and over. Lately, it had become her most familiar prayer.

~

"Jamie! Come in here. Your mom and I want a word with you, son."

James frowned. He had finally updated the computer program for the harvest forecasts and finished the daily ledgers, besides supervising the hookup of the new irrigation pump at the main pond. He'd hoped to take his horse, an Appaloosa gelding, for a trail ride into the hills. Nothing felt as satisfying as galloping across an open field on a beautiful June day. Or they would follow the shady woodland trail along the ridgeline where he could look out on the entire Tuscarawas River Valley.

Graduation was over. He'd enjoyed prom night more than expected with a non-romantic date from his church youth group, he'd endured commencement exercises in a stifling hot gymnasium, and he was officially a high school graduate.

His grandparents were proud of him.

His parents had thrown him a party for "just a few close friends and relatives" that had ended up with more than a hundred people. But his one *special* guest hadn't been there. He couldn't chance sending her an invitation, not until he knew how her father would react. James was finally a free man with the entire summer before him, and all he could think about was Emma.

"Jamie!" his dad called again from the house.

James dutifully dismounted, tied his horse's reins to a low-hanging branch, and went inside. His father was leaning against the kitchen sink while his mom sat at the glass-topped table with her Bible and papers spread out in front of her. "Preparing for your Sunday school class?" he asked.

Barbara Davis taught a women's class that was working their way through the Old Testament. She smiled at him over her half-moon reading glasses. "Among other things I've got started. I can't seem to tackle one project at a time on my day off. I begin several at once and hope for the best."

"Oh, you'll probably finish them all and paint the kitchen and sew up some new drapes," he said, only half kidding. His mother loved to immerse herself in domestic projects whenever away from her stressful job as an emergency room nurse.

She laughed, but his dad cleared his throat and put on a serious face. Barbara fished through her papers and pulled out a college catalog. "There's something we gotta talk about, Jamie. Time is growing short."

James felt his enthusiasm for the afternoon slip away. *Not this old argument again.* "Ah, Ma," he moaned, slumping into a chair.

She smiled patiently, but James Sr. wasn't so indulgent. "Hear you mother out, and don't be rude, son."

"Yes, sir. Sorry."

"I know you didn't want to think about more schooling during your senior year. And we let you alone about it…more or less," she said, adding a wink. "But times are changing for farm managers same as for everybody else. And you're too young to let new methods and technologies pass you by. It'll hurt this farm's productivity down the road."

James picked up the catalog she had pushed across the table. "Ohio State? I've been to Columbus and have no desire to live there. That is one big city."

Why couldn't he make his parents understand college wasn't for everybody? His older brother had received a bachelor's in Theology and was now in seminary to become a pastor. His sister was an undergrad, currently applying to veterinary schools. He was certain his younger brother would go to college—his nose was always in a book. Couldn't his parents be happy with three out of four of their children getting advanced degrees?

"You wouldn't have to move to Columbus," James Sr. said. "The OSU Agricultural Extension is in Wooster, not that far away—less than an hour. You could probably schedule your classes into four days, and come home to the farm for long weekends."

"Take a look at the catalog, Jamie. There are many courses that sound fascinating," Barbara added, double-teaming him with her husband.

James leafed through the catalog and paused on one page of course listings. He grinned as he found what he'd been looking for. "Entomology of Indigenous Flora Subspecies, Engineering Technology, and Applied Sciences of Agricultural Natural Resources. Do those sound interesting to you?" James asked, rolling his eyes. "They sound like a remedy for insomnia to me."

His dad's dimple deepened slightly in his cheek, but his stoic demeanor soon returned. "Well, don't sign up for those, but there are plenty of other classes that'll help you become a better farmer. You've got a lot to learn, son, and I'm not the one to teach you. I'm old school. If you want to survive as a farmer with the challenges out there in the twenty-first century, you'll need help. And if you're serious about taking this place off my hands so I can retire someday, then prove it to me."

James knew he couldn't argue with anything his father was saying. And the silver in his dad's hair, the slight limp to his walk, only underscored the fact that James Sr. wouldn't be able to run Hollyhock Farms forever.

James Jr. exhaled a pent-up breath. "I'll look over the catalog, but don't plan on me going away for four years…maybe two. And that's if I can stay awake that long."

The joy on his parents' faces was undeniable.

Honor thy father and mother. God commanded it, and James wished to comply more than anything. His folks had always been more than fair while he was growing up. And they had never asked for anything in return. How could he deny them this? Even if it meant going to school for two or more years, he knew he would do it to please them.

And what about sweet Emma Miller of Winesburg? He was young and she was even younger. Would she be willing to wait for him to finish agricultural college?

He knew that Amish girls married young—or at least began courting seriously by eighteen. They had only just met, and now he would be stuck up in Wooster most of the time. The only encouraging thought was that Winesburg was on his way to and from the college.

"I'll read this through tonight," he said, realizing his parents were watching him intently.

"There's a website where you can complete a preliminary application online. Then they'll send the rest out in the mail," his mom said. "Do it tonight, Jamie. It's already June. Time's a'wasting. They'll close enrollment, or some of the good classes might fill up. Then you will be stuck with Entomology of Indigenous Flora Subspecies."

Both his parents laughed while James felt like a bull fenced up in a tiny pasture. They had gone from "at least give it some thought" to "fill out the application tonight and email it in" within the space of fifteen minutes.

His dad put his cap back on and headed outside to chores. James dug around in the refrigerator looking for a soda and the bag of carrots for his horse.

"I thought you were going for a trail ride," Barbara said without looking up. She had already returned to her Sunday school preparations.

"I am, but there's something I wanted to ask you after Dad left."

She peered at him over her reading glasses.

"Amish people," he continued. "They're Christians same as us, right?" He popped open the soda can, trying to look casual.

Barbara thought for a moment before answering. "Yes, son. They have a slightly different approach to obtaining salvation that emphasizes earthly good works and self-sacrifice, but they use the same Bible and believe the same fundamentals."

"Okay. Thanks." He started for the screen door feeling immensely relieved.

She lifted an eyebrow. "Why do you ask, Jamie?"

He glanced back at her. "I was just curious. You know I have a good friend, Sam Yoder, who's Amish. And I ran into an Amish girl at the volleyball party. I just wanted to know what they believed." He hurried out to where he had tied his gelding before she could ask him more questions.

Or before he revealed something he couldn't even admit to himself.

～

Emma knew it was wrong to use the term "miracle" to refer to something most people would dismiss as insignificant. Miracles should be reserved for witnessing the hand of God in a manner that defied the logical outcome. But to Emma, that was exactly what seemed to have happened in her life.

She'd heard from Sarah after preaching service that many young people were going on a canoe trip on the Mohican River in Loudonville. The all-day social event would involve mostly older courting couples and their English friends. Since the town of numerous canoe liveries was too far to go by horse and buggy, and considering the length of the canoe ride, they depended on *Englischers* to take them in cars and vans. Her parents never would allow her to go on such a trip...or so she had thought, and that's why it seemed like a miracle.

After services Mrs. Hostetler had mentioned to *mamm* that she was permitting Sarah to go. Also the bishop's daughter would attend with her young beau. His daughter was two years older than Emma, and everyone expected them to wed in the autumn. Even so, *mamm* had originally said no when Emma had asked.

"But if the bishop thinks it's suitable for his girl, then I see no harm in it," *daed* had declared. And the matter was settled.

Emma found herself counting the days and holding her breath for fear she'd say or do something to change her parents' minds. She had pitched in with even the most onerous of chores and helped Leah with dinner when not her turn. She'd weeded the garden without being reminded and darned her *bruders'* socks to spare her mother's arthritic fingers. And she'd stayed out of her father's path as much as possible, since the sight of her bangs still rankled him.

Now that the day had arrived, Emma was so excited her shoes barely touched the ground when she walked. She'd heard from Sarah that James would be canoeing with Sam Yoder. Sam was the reason Sarah was willing to climb into a wobbly boat, perch on a hard wooden seat, and paddle downriver on a hot June day, swatting at mosquitoes all the while. The girl feared water most other days.

Funny how a heart plays strange tricks on a girl's mind.

Canoeing had always sounded like a silly pastime to Emma, but today she couldn't wait to see what fascinating sights waited along the riverbank. She'd begged her mom to let her walk to Sarah's so the English driver wouldn't have to make so many stops. The Hostetlers lived about a mile away, across the road from Aunt Hannah. Emma could easily hike the back path.

"*Jah*, sure," Julia said, "but you make sure the driver brings you all the way home. I don't want you walking through the bog after dark, even with your flashlight."

Emma readily agreed. With any luck, a tall blond-haired man would bring her home in his shiny green truck. That thought instantly made her feel guilty and deceptive, even though she hadn't done anything wrong…yet. Emma tried to tamp down her enthusiasm. Sarah might be wrong about James, since his responsibilities at the Hollyhock Farm might keep him from an afternoon of fun, but for some reason she didn't think so. At the volleyball party, he'd looked at her differently than the other girls—as though his face were glowing.

Her Plain upbringing wouldn't allow her to look at him that way, but she felt the same on the inside. "Bye, *mamm*," she called, feeling another pang of guilt.

"Don't upset the canoe and fall in the river," Julia hollered. "Sitting around all day in wet clothes won't be very comfortable."

Emma nodded, waved, and hurried toward the path. That was certainly true. Taking extra clothes was out of the question since changing facilities wouldn't be available. Ducking into the shrubbery wasn't proper for a modest Amish girl. Her *mamm* said she could take off her shoes and socks in the canoe but made no other allowances for hot weather. Her dress reached to her shins and her *kapp* was to stay in place at all times. But Emma didn't care; she wasn't ashamed to be Amish. She enjoyed feeling part of a larger community that loved God and worshipped Him with their whole lives.

The gorgeous June day wrapped around her during the walk to Aunt Hannah's. The warm air hung over the tranquil beaver pond as eagles and turkey vultures soared effortlessly on wind currents. Bumblebees buzzed from one tall flower to the next, while insects emitted a hum that amounted to near cacophony. Maybe it was her imagination due to her good mood, but Emma thought she glimpsed the elusive beaver lifting his head above the surface of the water.

Reaching her uncle's farm, she waved to him in the cornfield and then craned her neck to see if Aunt Hannah was working in the vegetable garden. But she had no time to go looking for her as she crossed the road and started up her friend's driveway.

And the best day of her life thus far just got better. James Davis stood in the Hostetler yard with Sam Yoder.

"Hi, Emma!" he shouted upon seeing her.

"Hello, James. Hi, Sam," she called, too excited to be nervous.

"Are you all set? We're planning to paddle all the way to the Ohio River." James grinned as she approached.

"I'm as ready as I ever will be." Emma headed toward the house where Sarah was standing on the steps.

Mrs. Hostetler walked onto the porch, letting the screen door slam behind her. "Sarah, take this along," she said, handing her daughter a soft-sided cooler. "It's full of Cokes and snacks for later. Hello, Emma." She offered Emma a pleasant smile. "You girls make sure the driver is careful and don't distract him. And no speeding."

"*Jah,* we'll be careful." Sarah took the cooler and walked toward Emma with smile. "I'm so glad you were allowed to come."

Emma waited until Mrs. Hostetler went inside before she spoke. "Me too," she said, "but where's Martha? Still getting ready?"

"She's not coming," murmured Sarah. "Only courting couples are going today." Sarah slanted her an odd look while Emma began to feel panicky.

Only courting couples? So that's what this is—my first date?

She grabbed Sarah's sleeve to talk before joining the others. "I didn't know that. I thought we would stay in a big group."

Sarah patted her arm. "Don't worry. We'll be together, but a canoe only holds two people. That's why it'll be mostly courting couples. Sam asked me the night of the volleyball party." Sarah's face flushed with pleasure with the admission. "You had already gone home or I would've told you."

"But James didn't ask me to come, you did," said Emma. Her uneasiness grew by the minute.

Sarah whispered conspiratorially. "He was afraid to. He thought it better if I asked and he just showed up, hoping for the best."

"Are you girls ready?" Sam called. "The river is waiting."

Sarah squeezed her hand. "It'll be fine. You'll see."

As much as Emma wanted to spend the afternoon with James,

she didn't like deceiving her parents. But then again…it was her *Rumschpringe.*

James approached wearing a look of concern. "Is everything all right, Emma?"

"Everything is okay, I guess." She said nothing about her misgivings. After all, this date could be nothing but a fix-up by Sarah.

"Let's get going," Sam said, opening the truck doors. "We still have to get two more people along the way."

Once the shiny green truck picked up the other couple, Emma sat back for the drive to Loudonville. Because they would be jammed together, the three females sat in the backseat while the men were up front. This separation didn't surprise the Amish fellows, but James looked a bit disappointed.

Emma caught him stealing glances in the rearview mirror more than once. Figuring out what she should do was hard enough, but with James being English it became nearly impossible.

Once they arrived at the livery, they met others from their district in line to buy tickets. She somewhat relaxed seeing how many others were taking the trip. But once they were handed paddles and life preservers and walked to the water, some of her confidence fled. A very swift current carried the canoes away from the dock the moment people got in. When their turn came, James jumped down into the canoe and reached for her hand.

Inhaling a deep breath, Emma stepped in gingerly and settled herself in front, careful to not rock the boat. "Don't make it tip over," she cautioned. "I'll get mad as a hornet." She was too nervous to look back at him.

"You have my word. I'll keep you safe and dry." His words drifted up on the breeze.

She chanced a smile over her shoulder as he paddled the canoe toward the middle of the river. James deftly dipped his paddle on one side and then the other. Although Emma had her own paddle, she seldom used it. After a while James needed only to steer, since the strong current from recent rains easily carried them downstream. Other couples bobbed in and out of sight. Sometimes it seemed they were alone on the river. Other times they rounded a bend and joined a log jam of boats. Emma leaned back and lazily watched the riverbank lined with willow and sycamore trees. Odd how ordinary scenes looked different when viewed from a passing boat.

After a quiet interval James cleared his throat, drawing her attention from the peaceful valley. "What are you thinking about, Miss Miller?"

"That I didn't know this would be a...date," she said, choosing the English word for courting. "And please call me Emma. I'm not used to such formality." She glanced back at him.

"I was afraid to ask. I thought you might say no because I'm not Amish. But if you got to know me better, you might give me a chance."

"I had noticed you were English. In the future, if you want to see me again, you should ask me directly." They quickly ducked their heads as the canoe passed under a low-hanging branch.

"And if I get up courage to ask you out, what do you suppose you might say?"

She swiveled around to cast a withering look. "I have no intention of answering that question right now. It will depend on whether or not I remain dry for the entire trip, for one thing."

They glided past two overturned canoes whose occupants were busy splashing each other in the shallow water. Emma shook her head but couldn't stop grinning at their antics. Styrofoam coolers and life preservers floated downstream as the splashing battle raged on. James steered to give them a wide berth.

Once well beyond them, James said, "On my honor, Emma. I'll do everything possible to make sure not a drop of water lands on you."

Emma discovered that she thoroughly enjoyed canoeing. Birds sang from cattails, dragonflies flitted just above the water, while small fish darted beneath the surface, their silvery bodies reflecting

the bright sunshine. Plenty of shade and a light breeze kept them cool. She couldn't remember feeling so relaxed, certainly not with a young man she barely knew.

James entertained her with delightful stories from his childhood. He was attentive and gentlemanly, and he kept them both dry for the entire trip. For one fleeting moment, Emma wished the day would never end. But all too soon they arrived at the line of canoes heading for the boat dock. When Emma spotted Sarah and Sam waiting to unload, she knew the eight-mile trip was over.

"What happened to paddling down to the Ohio River?" she asked, more to herself than to James.

He leaned forward. "And what provisions do we have left? That's quite a distance."

She peered inside the cooler. "Two apples, a bag of chips, and two bottles of water."

"Sounds like enough to me, but I'd better steer this ship into port." James paddled the canoe toward the dock. "I don't want to jeopardize my taking you out again."

Emma blushed, feeling warmth deep in her belly. He liked h And so far, she liked him. What did it matter if he was English? T had sheep-farming in common. Their ages were a good match. were both Christians and loved the Lord.

That's all that should matter.

~

But much more than that mattered to Simon Miller. waiting on the porch for his daughter to come hom When he finally heard a vehicle pull into the yard, h the steps to see who was bringing her home. A long-
around in front of the porch and out jumped E looked a little suntanned and her *kapp* was spot

He raised his hand to shake a finger at his

told your *mamm* you were going canoeing with Sarah Hostetler and a group of courting couples." He heard the fury in his voice but couldn't seem to control it. This words startled birds from their roost in the lilac bushes. "You said nothing about your young man being *English*!"

SEVEN

M r. Miller, sir?" the young man said, stepping toward Simon. Julia bit her lip. She'd had a bad feeling something like this would happen ever since this *Englischer* delivered the loom.

"I'm James Davis. I drove five people today to Loudonville. I just dropped Miss Hostetler off a few minutes ago, and she only lives around the corner. Emma wasn't alone with me."

An Amish young man whom Julia didn't recognize got out of the passenger side of the truck. *His being in the vehicle probably won't help Emma's case,* Julia thought.

"I know very well where the Hostetlers live, young man," Simon said as his face turned florid with anger. "But this is a family matter, and it's none of your concern. Emma is my daughter, and she's only sixteen."

"Daed," Emma said in a soft, pleading voice.

"No, young lady. We will not discuss this in front of outsiders." Simon pointed at the young men. "I'd like you two to be on your way," he said, and then he turned his finger toward Emma. "And you go inside the house right now." His hand shook with fury.

Emma's face reddened as she opened her mouth to argue, but not a sound came out. Instead, tears began to stream from her eyes. She looked at the English sheep farmer for a long moment before fleeing toward the house. She stomped up the porch steps noisier than Matthew or Henry.

Simon waited until the screen door slammed shut before he turned back to the young men.

James Davis glanced from Simon to Julia and back to Simon. "I'm sorry, sir. I meant no disrespect to Emma, and I don't want to cause trouble in your family."

Simon stood motionless, like a hawk perched on a power line. Julia wanted to thank James for driving Emma home from Sarah's, but she didn't dare. Blessedly, the two boys climbed back into the pickup and left without another word.

Simon stared down the driveway until the truck's taillights disappeared from sight.

"You lost your temper," Julia said. "You know what Scripture says about losing one's temper."

He turned to face her. "*Jah*, thank you, *fraa*. 'Stop being angry! Turn from your rage! Do not lose your temper—it only leads to harm.' Psalm 37:8 is much easier to quote than live by."

"We should have expected some rough patches when our daughter decided on a full *Rumschpringe*." Julia spoke as gently as she could.

"Emma going canoeing with an *Englischer*...you call that just a rough patch? I would call that a disgrace."

"No, Simon. I saw her climb out of the backseat. She wasn't sitting next to him. Do not falsely accuse her of doing something disgraceful."

He walked up onto the porch and lowered himself into the swing, looking like a man in his sixties instead of his forties. "I shouldn't have shouted. You're right, but when I heard Emma was going in a group of courting couples, I assumed everyone would be Amish."

She patted his knee. "I know, *ehemann*, but what we do and say now is very important. These are her running-around years. We want her to decide to become baptized and join the church by her own choice. If we distrust her, if we show no confidence in her ability to pick right from wrong, we will only drive her away."

He gazed at her with sad, weary eyes. "I am a district deacon besides her *daed*. I cannot turn a blind eye to disobedience."

"No one is saying you should, but she did nothing today that was disobedient. She told me an *Englischer* was driving them to Loudonville and that she would ride with Sarah. That is exactly what took place. I, myself, am glad that young Davis drove her home. I don't want her walking the back trail alone at night. There've been sightings of bobcats in the county. Although I believe all God's creatures have a place on this earth, I would prefer my *kinner* not cross paths with a bobcat at night."

Simon stood and offered Julia his arm to lean on. "You're right. I shouldn't have lost my temper. That was a mistake, but let's get you inside." Slowly, because the damp night air had stiffened her joints, the pair walked back into the house.

Emma was sitting at the kitchen table with her *kapp* off. A glass of water was in front of her. Her face in the kerosene lamplight looked painfully young and vulnerable.

"I didn't do anything wrong, *mamm* and *daed*," she said with her lower lip trembling. "I asked you if I could go to Loudonville and you said *jah*. How did you think we would get there? It's too far to go by buggy. If we were to canoe eight miles, we'd never make it back home the same day." The trembling of her lip stopped as Emma lifted her chin. She stared into Julia's eyes instead of Simon's. "What did you tell *daed*?"

Her tone was almost defiant. Emma seemed to be blaming her for Simon's overreaction, and while Julia didn't appreciate it, she had no wish to fan the flames.

"*Jah*, I told him everything you said, daughter, but he didn't understand *Englischers* were going along too."

Emma glanced at Simon and then stared at the wall. "We don't live in a world unto ourselves. The Bible instructs us to love one another, not only other Plain people. It's the second greatest commandment."

Simon snorted, not appreciating in his turn someone quoting Scripture to him, especially not a sixteen-year-old who hadn't taken the kneeling vow yet. "I'm well aware of what the Good Book says, including Matthew 22:39. Let me ask you a question: Who is this Englishman to you?"

Julia held her breath. Amish parents usually didn't ask *kinner* who they were courting—it was a secret until an engagement was announced. They gave young people a certain measure of privacy, trusting that they would make the right decisions.

After what seemed like a long time yet was probably only several seconds, Emma said in a not quite respectful tone of voice, "He is my friend, *daed*, and a fellow sheep farmer." The girl looked at Simon and then focused on her *mamm*.

Julia saw the challenge in those cornflower blue eyes.

"All right then, go up to bed. I'm sure you're tired," Simon said.

Emma immediately did as she was told. They heard her take the steps two at a time.

"We must learn patience, Simon, both you and I."

"*Ach*, my hair will either turn snow white or all fall out before this *Rumschpringe* is done." He exhaled a heavy sigh and also headed up the stairs to bed.

But not Julia...she sat at the kitchen table, knowing sleep wouldn't come with her current feelings of unease. She worried that Emma would venture too far off the accepted path and end up being gossiped about, if not shunned outright, by the district. Or Emma would become attracted to the English lifestyle to the extent that she'd leave her Amish world behind.

And Julia feared that she wouldn't have the necessary patience to guide the young woman because of her own personal physical pain. For more than an hour, she thought and worried, plagued by anxiety and self-doubts.

Finally, she prayed to God, who had sacrificed His own Son so that she and all believers might find salvation. Her own dilemma with a willful teenager testing her wings paled to nothing by comparison.

~

"Don't go getting any ideas, Curly," Simon warned the Angora goat. In the past few months since his sons had bought the ornery creature for Emma's birthday, it had done nothing but eat. It had increased in size by half while not improving its disposition an ounce. Even now she appeared to be watching, biding her time until he turned around to untie the rope from the stake. Then she would charge and butt his backside just for fun.

"You are supposed to be Emma's," he muttered. "And the boys should be moving you around the yard so you don't overgraze an area down to bare dirt. Come along, Curly." Simon led the goat around to the back of the house where the grass was rather long. He studied the length of rope and tied her to a tree just beyond reach of Julia's kitchen garden and the flower beds. "Eat grass!" he ordered.

Curly cocked her head to assess him, her jaws slowly grinding lunch into a watery green stew. Backing away slowly, he heard the sound of buggy wheels in the driveway. Simon didn't pause to shield his eyes until he was well past Curly's reach.

"Seth," he called. "You're a sight for sore eyes!" He hadn't seen his brother since the last preaching service and hadn't been able to share a word because all the men had been in a dither. Seth had been part of that fracas, but at least he hadn't been the leader.

Seth jumped down from his open buggy and tied his mare to the hitching post. "*Gut nachmittag*, Simon."

"Care to put her in the pasture?" Simon asked. "Why not stay for lunch? Julia and Leah are trying a new tuna fish casserole recipe. How dangerous can that be?" He laughed at his joke as Seth joined him near the flower beds.

"No, *danki* just the same. I get my fair share of cooking experiments in my own kitchen." He grinned like a man still happily discovering the mysteries of being a newlywed.

Seth looked over Simon's hayfield, where the tall grass was rippling in the warm breeze like a green river. "Ready to be cut, *jah*?"

"It is. I'm sharpening my blades today and will start cutting tomorrow if the dry weather holds. How 'bout yours?"

Seth crossed his muscular arms over his chest. "I won't be cutting a second crop of hay. I've still got plenty of bales under plastic from my first crop back in April."

Simon stared with confusion. "No second crop? What happens if we get a drought and your pasture grass dies back? What will you feed your livestock then...some of Hannah's cooking experiments?" His jest didn't sound that funny, so he resumed his sober expression. "What *did* you plant your hayfield in?"

"All corn—everything but Hannah's garden and the sheep and cow pastures."

Simon pulled off his hat and slapped it against his leg. "Just like that band of hotheads? I thought you were smarter than to fall in with that lot."

"I guess you overestimated my intellect, *bruder*, because I think it's a good idea, same as others in the district." He sounded very sure of himself.

"You're taking a big chance, a *gamble*." Simon imbued the word with onerous emphasis. "Something the Bible and our *Ordnung* caution us against."

Seth met his eye and then gazed off toward the horizon. A small bird seemed to be following and intimidating a red-tailed hawk in flight. "Scripture says nothing against planting corn."

Simon's back stiffened. *First my daughter now my brother telling me my business?* "You know exactly what I mean. You're engaging in speculation, hoping to make a great deal of profit."

Seth shifted his weight, planting both feet as though preparing for some kind of standoff. "Have you noticed what they're paying for corn at the grain elevator in Mount Eaton? Even higher prices if you're willing to take the crop to New Philadelphia to sell."

"Speculation, I tell you." Simon planted his boot heels in the grass. "There's no guarantee those prices will hold until fall."

"They're buying up all the available corn to manufacture ethanol," Seth said.

"According to what I read in the *Daily Journal*, it's still experimental. They don't know if these ethanol plants they're building can turn corn into fuel any cheaper than refineries can process fossil oil."

Seth pulled on his beard and appeared to be considering this. At least his brother would listen to reason, not like some of the hotheads.

"What you're saying is true. I read the same article myself, but I think we have no choice but to take the chance. And I would like you to join us. As deacon, you are respected—your opinion holds high authority. The county agent says there's more land available for lease in the southern part of the county. It's not too late to get in another crop of hybrid to harvest in October."

"Have you lost your mind?"

Seth straightened to his full impressive height. "Do you know how little is in our district's community fund?" he shot back. "I talked to the bishop about the balance. Several buggy accidents, some farming mishaps, the road usage fees, a couple of house fires—the coffers are nearly depleted." He shook his head sadly.

Simon found his back growing more painful by the minute. "The bishop shouldn't have discussed this with you. You're not a deacon or an elder." His tone sounded harsh and petulant.

"I asked him straight out and he gave me a truthful answer. That's all. I don't want to overstep my bounds, Simon, but Julia will need surgery sooner or later. There's no denying it. Do you know how much *that* will cost?"

The fight went out of Simon at the mention of his beloved wife's name. "Let's go sit in the shade." He shook his head and walked toward the barn with Seth on his heels. A rickety table and pair of chairs were under the barn's eaves—a good spot to sit and enjoy lunch in the fresh air. Simon sat down heavily and leaned his back against the wall. Seth sat too, resting his large hands on his knees.

"*Ach*," Simon said. "I've been afraid to ask the doctor what it'll cost. I suppose I've been no better than a foolish goose burying its head and thinking the coyote can no longer see it."

Seth put a hand on his brother's shoulder. "You're no goose. Just a man facing a difficult situation...one that has no easy answer. How is Julia?"

Simon dropped his chin to his chest. "The pain is getting worse. The medications and the therapies that once worked well no longer bring relief. She is suffering, Seth, and I am helpless to stop the pain. It's time we travel again to Canton to see that specialist."

Seth tightened his grip. "The money from selling this corn in the fall can rebuild our medical fund. It will go a long way toward paying her hospital bills. Join in with us. Give us your support."

Simon felt suddenly like a very old man. "I cannot. I am sorry. The Bible tells us, 'Plant your seeds in the morning and keep busy all afternoon, for you don't know if profit will come from one activity or another—or maybe both.' Let's leave it up to God. I appreciate what you're trying to do for Julia, but I can't in good conscience join in this." He struggled to his feet as his brother's hand dropped away. "Come in to lunch and sample Leah's tuna casserole. It might be a welcome surprise after all."

"No, *danki*. I shall go home and await my fate at Hannah's hands." Seth stood then and walked toward his buggy with far less confidence and pep than he possessed upon arrival.

This would be a summer of changes...a time of trials and tests by the Lord. Simon would pray nightly that he would be up to the challenge.

～

July

It had been a full month since the canoe trip. Emma had replayed every detail in her mind over and over. She'd heard not a word from James, even though she and Aunt Hannah had stopped at A Stitch in Time in Sugar Creek, but at least her father had dropped the subject of the English sheep farmer.

Since that night Simon had been patient and gentle as though he regretted losing his temper. *Mamm* still watched her like an eagle, vigilant that her fledging didn't fall from the nest. Julia hovered around the kitchen, even though Emma and Leah did the cooking and baking these days. Julia's hands had become painfully crippled with rheumatoid arthritis. To be truthful, Leah did most of the kitchen chores without complaint, allowing Emma time in her loft. Plenty of wool still remained from the last shearing to spin, while progress on the new loom was slow but steady. She had plenty to keep busy with. Mrs. Dunn had sold all the consignment wreaths, and the money Emma had received from them allowed her to pay off the balance on her new loom.

Whenever Emma got a chance, she would wander through the woods between their farm and Uncle Seth's with clippers and a burlap sack over her shoulder. Wild grapevines for new wreaths grew unceasingly in the plentiful July sunshine. On these solitary walks on misty mornings or in fading daylight after supper, her thoughts turned to a suntanned boy with sparkling eyes and a soft voice. Remembering his smile lifted her heart into the clouds. His laughter, his polite manners, his respect for all God's creation helped her to forget he wasn't Amish.

How she wanted to see him again. Wasn't this her *Rumschpringe?* This was her time to discover what she wanted and who she was, but four weeks had passed without a single word from him. Her fear of disappointing her parents apparently had been premature.

"Emma, Emma!"

She heard her brother's voice but saw nothing but an empty

path through the dense trees. Suddenly, Matthew galloped toward her on their newest colt. He rode bareback with only a bit, bridle, and reins, gripping the horse with his long legs. "I've been looking for you!"

"You've lost your hat," she said, stepping away from the horse's prancing hooves.

"*Jah,* it flew off a while back. I was pretending a pack of wild boars was chasing me and I needed to get away." He slipped smoothly from the back of the colt to the ground. He was becoming an adept horseman.

She glanced down the path. "Not a single wild boar in sight. I think you've outrun them."

"Good, I'll look for my hat on the way back. I was anxious to find you." He dug into his boot and pulled out a letter. It had been folded over several times.

Emma's heart skipped several beats upon spotting the envelope's distinctive handwriting.

Matthew grinned his funny, lopsided smile. "I saw your English beau down by the road when I was getting the mail. He was about to put this in our mailbox."

"He is my friend, not my beau," she corrected, stretching a hand out to take it.

But Matthew held the letter high, beyond her reach. "Why the personal delivery? Can't the guy afford a stamp?"

"He was probably driving by, that's all. Now hand it over, you imp." She lunged for the letter again, but Matthew was far quicker.

"Our farm isn't on the way to anywhere," he laughed, waving the envelope above her head.

Emma stomped her booted foot. "Matthew Miller, you give that to me or I'm telling *daed*."

"Oh, I doubt you'll tell Pa. But someday I might need help from a big sister, so here you go." He lowered it down to nose height, and she snatched it without hesitation.

"*Danki.*" She turned her back to him before tearing it open with trembling fingers.

Matthew leaned over her shoulder. "Care to read it aloud?"

Emma clutched it to her chest. "On your way! Go find your hat. A woman needs some privacy."

"You're hardly a woman, Emma. You're still just a plain ol' girl, but I'll leave you alone. He probably wants to talk about his dumb sheep anyway." Without benefit of a saddle horn, he boosted himself up onto the colt's back and swung over his leg with amazing agility. "See you at supper," he called. With a tiny kick, boy and beast took off down the trail.

Her hands shook as she removed the single sheet of paper and began to read:

> *Dear Emma,*
>
> *It is my fondest hope that absence has made your heart fonder for me. I have missed you, and I think about you each time I see the sweet face of one of my new merinos.*

A sheep? He thinks I look like a sheep? Emma didn't know what to make of this letter so far! From high overhead, the caw of a crow added insult to her injury. Dismissing the odd compliment, she continued to read:

> *A group of people are going horseback riding this Saturday at the stable in Berlin. They'll provide a picnic lunch to eat along the way. Sam Yoder and Sarah Hostetler are going, but tell your dad it's not just for courting couples. Plenty of other folk will be there. Please understand, I am officially asking you to be my date.*
>
> *Eagerly (and hopefully) waiting for Saturday,*
>
> *James*

Emma clutched the paper to the spot she believed her heart to be and made a frightening decision. She would go on the trail ride with her friends, even if it meant telling her parents a little white lie.

～

On Saturday, her mother was so distracted by pain and discomfort she didn't much question Emma about the outing. She commented only "you surely show little interest in the colts and fillies Matthew is raising," and instructed her to wear the one pair of trouser jeans she owned—*under* her dress.

"*Mamm*, this is July and close to ninety degrees."

Julia shook her head. "I know perfectly well what month it is, but you can't ride astride a horse in a long dress. You also can't wear jeans and a shirt like *Englischers*. So it's the two together or stay home and help Henry paint the fence." She lowered her head to lock gazes with her daughter.

So Emma wore the jeans and dress together, happy to be going despite the hot day.

Sam Yoder drove his buggy up her lane promptly at nine o'clock. With his new standardbred, a former racehorse, he'd made good time coming from Charm. Emma climbed into the buggy and offered a quick wave to her *daed*. Seeing a buggy and not a pickup, Simon stayed with his plow and didn't come charging across the field. Matthew studied her from his position in the hayloft window, no doubt curious about her response to the secret letter.

"Bye, Emma," Leah called from the porch swing. The girl was already shelling peas for lunch into a large pot. "Have a nice time."

Emma felt a twinge of guilt at how little fun her sister had, but her time would come soon enough. She was only thirteen. However, as soon as Sam's buggy headed up the Hostetler road, Emma felt nothing but excitement. She dug around in her tote bag, packed with bug repellent, hand wipes, and water, and pulled out a tube of pink lip gloss and a compact of rose blusher. These had come from the dollar store. Emma applied the cosmetics the way she'd seen English girls do in the ladies' room in town.

"You putting makeup on for Jamie?" Sam asked.

Emma glanced his way briefly. "No, I'm doing this for myself, to feel pretty." Why she'd said that she didn't know.

"Shucks, Emma, you don't need that stuff. Jamie and I were just saying that you and Sarah are the two prettiest girls in Holmes County. And we're the two luckiest men."

"Is that right, Sam Yoder?" Emma shoved her makeup back into the tote.

If Sam answered her question, she didn't hear because James had spotted the buggy and was walking their way.

"Emma," he said. "I'm so happy you came I think I could hug you!"

"Thinking is one thing, but don't try it," she said, sounding more confident than she felt.

"Ready to go?" he asked. "As soon as Sam puts his horse in the pasture, we'll be off in my ride. I gave her a bath for the occasion."

Emma was confused until they walked over to his pickup. The vehicle gleamed brightly in the sunlight. "Is this truck female?" Emma asked.

"Sure, doesn't she look it?" James opened the doors and windows to cool off the interior.

"The color could certainly be female," Sarah teased, joining them with her tote bag and a cooler hanging on her arm. "Green is for girls; blue is for boys."

Emma was happy to see that Sarah wore jeans under her dress too. This was all new to her, but then again, she'd never ridden a horse for pleasure before. Amish folk loved their animals, but horses represented a farming implement or a way to get from one place to another.

"I'm so glad you made it, Em. This should be even more fun than canoeing," Sarah said. She craned her neck to see where Sam had gone.

Emma grinned. Not only had Sarah climbed into a wobbly conveyance over water, today she planned to mount a huge, four-legged beast with flies buzzing around its head. The way Sarah looked at Sam when he returned from the paddock must have something to do with her change of heart.

Are my emotions also that obvious? Emma certainly hoped not as she squeezed into the backseat.

"You look real nice, Emma," James said, watching her in his rearview mirror.

"Keep your eyes on the road," she warned. "And no speeding."

"Yes, ma'am." James flashed a grin and then concentrated on the road during the drive to Trails End Stable.

When they arrived, an earlier group was preparing to go out. The English teenagers milled around while the trail guide matched the size and ability of each rider to a particular horse. Emma couldn't help but notice the girls in line. They all wore snug-fitting tops with even tighter blue jeans. Some wore Western boots while most had on tennis shoes. *Why must they wear their clothes as if they bought the wrong size?* There was no mystery to any curve of their bodies. Emma smoothed a hand down her solid blue dress, glad her clothing fit properly. She would be very uncomfortable wearing such constricting outfits.

One young lady spotted her watching them. She offered a wave and smile before turning back to her friends. If the girl thought wearing pants under a dress odd she didn't show it. And for that Emma felt grateful, because today she was with James, not someone Amish.

She touched her fingertips to her lips. The lip gloss was sweet like peppermint candy and a little sticky. She hoped it wouldn't attract gnats. Remembering 1 Peter 3:4, a Bible verse her father loved to quote about vanity stopped her from comparing herself to others: "You should clothe yourself instead with the beauty that comes from within, the unfading beauty of a gentle and quiet spirit, which is so precious to God."

"We're next, Emma," James whispered near her ear as the others left for the trail.

"I'm as ready as I ever will be," she answered. "My brother would be proud of me. He rides bareback, even at a gallop, and doesn't fall off. With a saddle, I hope I can stay on the horse the whole time."

James placed his hand at the small of her back. "You'll be fine. These horses aren't like the spirited stock Matthew bought. They're accustomed to people sitting on them who don't know what they are doing."

"Thanks a lot." She wrinkled her nose at him as she stepped up to the mounting block.

But her worries about horses were premature. Emma mounted gracefully and was soon trotting across an open field with a dozen other riders. At the edge of the pasture, a trail entered a dim, cool wood where wild violets still bloomed even this late in the season. She listened to the forest sounds around her and an occasional snort from her gentle mare, but otherwise the place was utterly peaceful.

She loved the woods, feeling God's presence in the soft light filtering down between the leaves and tree branches. And she liked James. He followed behind her, dutifully watching to make sure everything stayed cordial between her and the horse.

Their trail followed a winding river to a clearing where several picnic tables waited beneath a huge oak tree. "Chow time, folks," hollered the trail guide. He and his assistant quickly spread out an assortment of sandwiches, chips, grapes, apples, and a cooler of drinks.

"Where did all this food come from?" Emma asked James, while nibbling a sandwich.

"A pack mule trails behind the last rider, bringing food and a first aid kit, just in case."

"Oh, that's interesting," she murmured, averting her eyes.

But actually it was more unsettling than anything else. How did James know about the pack mule? Had he brought other girls here before? A pang of jealousy crept up her spine and soured her stomach. She couldn't finish the delicious lunch. And she could barely think about much else on the ride back to the stable.

Growing up and courting weren't easy...whether you were English or Plain!

EIGHT

M amm?" Phoebe asked. "Where do *bopplin* come from?"

Hannah dropped the pancake she was flipping down on the stove. Breakfast was off to a bad start. "They come from God. Why do you ask?" She scraped up the crumbles to add to the bucket headed for the sow and piglets.

"*Jah*, but how does He get them to us?" The big-eyed child looked utterly earnest. "One girl at school said God leaves them in the garden and the sunflowers bend over the *boppli* until the mom finds it the next morning."

With her back to the child, Hannah smiled at such innocence.

"Then another girl said that's not right. God puts the baby in the *mamm's* belly and there it grows until it's time to come out. Just like the cow babies and the little lambs."

Hannah turned to face her daughter. "The second explanation is pretty much how it goes." *Seven is too young for any more details,* she thought.

Phoebe paused and then asked, "When is God going to put a baby in your belly? I'm ready for a *schwestern* or even a *bruder* already."

"I am too, but we must be patient. And He doesn't give babies to all couples. We must pray and then accept His will for our family."

"Okay, but I hope He says yes." With that, Phoebe ate her pancake with gusto and drank her glass of milk.

I do too, dear one. I do too.

But babies weren't the only thing on Hannah's mind during the ride to Julia's later that morning. She planned to speak to Simon. He wasn't just her brother-in-law; he was her deacon, and she needed his advice.

She and Seth had been butting heads for weeks and that troubled her sorely.

Despite finding a man to spend her life with, Hannah struggled with losing her say-so in matters. She had managed her own farm following Adam's death, paid her bills on time, and sold her crops and garden produce. Plus, she had built a business selling wool and lambs to other farms to support herself. Now she had melded her life and livelihood with Seth, and he wasn't seeking her opinion. He made all decisions by himself and told her his conclusions after the fact.

Simon might not have been her first choice to turn to before, but stubbornness in the past had only multiplied her woes.

"*Guder mariye,*" she called upon entering his barn. Phoebe ran off to tell Julia they had arrived, and then the child would tag after Leah like a shadow on a sunny day.

Simon glanced up from the cutting implement he was sharpening. "Good morning to you, sister. How go things around the corner?" He refocused on his work.

"Not well, I'm afraid," Hannah answered without preamble. "That's why I'm here."

Simon's file slipped off the blade with a clatter.

He probably asked the question to pass time, not expecting a frank answer, she thought.

"*Jah?*" he asked. "You're not well? What's wrong, Hannah? Is it my *bruder?*"

"We are all fine in body, *danki*. It's my spirit that needs your help," she said, sitting down on a hay bale.

He set down the tools and wiped his hands on his leather apron. "Tell me what's wrong." He spoke so softly, she somewhat relaxed.

"It's me. I am willful and opinionated and rash." When she glanced up, he was pulling sagely on his beard, but he didn't deny her assessment.

"How can I help?" he asked.

"Tell me how a wife comes to accept that her husband gets to make all decisions in the household." She blurted out the words without regard to tone or volume. "Seth doesn't even ask my opinion in matters I'm knowledgeable about."

There it was—expressed succinctly in words—the matter that had her tossing and turning each night.

Simon gazed on her with compassion. "Stay there. I'll be right back."

Hannah sat, listening to the barn swallows cleaning out their nests. Bits of mud and straw drifted down to the oaken floorboards from their industry.

In a few minutes Simon returned with his well-worn Bible in hand. "Do you trust the Word of the Lord?" he asked.

Hannah nodded. "With my whole heart."

"Then let's see what Scripture has to say." Simon read her Ephesians 5:22-23: "For wives, this means submit to your husband as to the Lord. For the husband is the head of his wife as Christ is the head of the church."

"I will write down those verses for you to take home. Read them nightly along with your prayers. In fact, study the whole book of Ephesians."

She nodded while her eyes filled with tears.

He patted her hand. "It won't be easy, Hannah. We all struggle with obedience at some point or another, but I can say it will lead to greater contentment in your life and a surer path to salvation. Let your husband lead you. Even when he stumbles or falls, do not criticize him. Your joys will be multiplied and your prayers will be answered."

Silence spun out in the barn. Even the swallows stopped their cleaning. Hannah sat with fresh tears streaking her cheeks. She knew he was right, and she also knew it was the only way. "*Danki*, Simon. I will do it." Dabbing at her nose with a hanky, she rose shakily to her feet. "Right now, I'll go see what Julia is doing." She felt as though she'd just accomplished an exhausting task as she walked from the barn.

Thy will be done, she said to herself over and over. *And for better or for worse.*

~

She didn't make it to the house before her niece waylaid her. "Aunt Hannah, could I speak with you a moment?"

Hannah did a double take. Emma looked different—older, but then Hannah noticed the confectionary pink tint to the girl's lips. "Do you have makeup on?" Hannah asked, quite shocked.

"*Jah*, do you like it?" Emma stood in the doorway to her herb shed, glowing unnaturally.

Hannah shook her head negatively. "Where did you get it, and what did your *mamm* say?"

"I bought the makeup in Sugar Creek; the lip gloss and blusher were very inexpensive. *Mamm* just stared and frowned, with her nose wrinkling up, but she didn't *say* anything." Emma drew back her shoulders. "After all, it is my *Rumschpringe*."

Hannah cocked an eyebrow. "You are very pretty, Emma, if that is what concerns you. You were blessed with lovely features that often cause more problems than they're worth, but your prettiness needs no enhancement from cosmetics."

"*Danki*, but could we talk about something different? I need your advice on what to do when your heart tells you one thing and your head tells you something different. I like James Davis very much, and I think I want to court him."

Emma blurted out this private admission with no more restraint than Hannah had used with Simon last year. This was the admission Hannah had feared. "Have you told this to your parents?"

Emma dropped her shoulders. "No, I saw no reason to upset them until I figured out how I felt."

Hannah inhaled a deep breath. "I take it James Davis wishes to court you?"

"*Jah*," she answered without hesitation.

"You have much more to lose than James does. If you court him and marry him, you will be shunned. You will no longer be part of the Miller family and the Amish community."

"I know, but I can worship God in James' church. His *mamm* is some sort of Bible teacher and his pa leads men in the church, sort of like my *daed* does."

Hannah tried to absorb this. "You really wish to join the English world?"

"No, but I wish to date James. What should I do?" she asked, turning her blue eyes up to Hannah.

How simple to be young—but so complicated at the same time.

"Before bed," Hannah advised, "read your Bible every night. Pray that the Lord leads you to the answers you seek. And open your heart and mind. Make sure you are listening to Him and watching for signs and not simply following your own will. When and *if* you're sure you want to court an *Englischer*, tell your folks. Don't live a life of deception. The shame of doing so will harm you far more than anything you can imagine."

Emma hugged her tightly, smearing off some of the cheek blusher. "*Danki*, Aunt. I will read my Bible and pray. I'm so grateful to have you in my life. You're a wonderful aunt."

"And I am thankful to have you in mine," Hannah said, embracing the young woman. Emma headed back into her shed to work while Hannah walked toward the house. She was anxious to find her sister to gauge how she was faring during the teenager's crisis. If she knew Julia, there would be a few more streaks of silver in her dark chestnut hair.

～

Simon sat for a long time on his bale before returning to his tasks. He had plenty to do before cutting hay. All of the blades needed sharpening, one wagon wheel was out-of-round, and he needed to check the shoes on his Belgians.

But his heart was heavy after his sister-in-law's visit. He hoped the counsel he offered was sound, but lately he was having doubts.

Emma's decision to run around before her baptism and joining the church had unnerved him. Why did his daughter want a *Rumschpringe*? He was a deacon. Although she was entitled to this period of youthful experimentation, he would have preferred a smoother transition. First, she'd cut her hair into a scarecrow imitation and had started wearing English athletic shoes instead of her sensible boots. But the last straw had been that pink paint on her face. In his opinion, it only underscored the scarecrow image. He'd put his foot down and hadn't allowed her to come to the table with makeup on.

Unfortunately, he doubted this would be the last straw.

Next, Seth had come to him for support he couldn't give. A variety of crops protected them when one or more of the harvests fell short of expectations. The entire district planting almost every acre in corn could lead to disaster.

Or it could lead to huge profits and shore up the depleted medical fund, while allowing families to make repairs and replace worn out equipment. Even a Plain farmer could not live without hard cash.

Seth was a practical man, not one to fly off recklessly, and not one to follow the crowd unless he'd considered the matter carefully. He was correct that if money were to be made in corn, now was the time. The ethanol craze wouldn't last forever. Either it would die out as an impractical alternative to fossil fuel, or so many American farmers would increase corn production that the high prices would fall.

Seth believed corn was an answer to their problems. And their district had its share of problems—Julia's deteriorating health the most pressing on Simon's mind. What if her physician decided surgery with rehabilitation was the only option? They would be paying on those medical bills for the rest of their lives. Being in debt was not compatible with the Amish way of life either.

Simon rose from his hay bale and walked to the doorway. From where he stood, he could see his fields and pastures. In the distance, dense forest supplied the firewood for the stove for the coming winter. The stocked pond provided fish for his table besides an occasional break from chores with his rowboat and fishing pole. Balanced, sustainable farms met their needs, except when illness or accident forced them into the English world of doctors, lab tests, and expensive anesthesiologists. Then, without medical insurance, the Amish were at a disadvantage.

Simon turned his gaze toward heaven. His trust in the Lord was steadfast. Only in His Word could the answers be found, so that was where he would turn. By faith he would live his life and lead his district.

He had to believe he offered Hannah sound advice. Scripture was clear about a man's responsibilities and authority in the household. Now he must find patience to guide Emma and the strength to remain resolute while many in the community ran astray of the traditional ways.

But even though the path was clear, the journey wouldn't be easy.

～

The hot, humid days of July were Emma's least favorite time of the year. Upstairs in her bedroom, sleep proved impossible. Not a breath of breeze came through the open window. Her bed sheets felt damp along with her nightgown. She seldom yearned for English conveniences, but right now she would love a fan blowing across her overheated skin.

It was hard to imagine air-conditioning throughout the whole house. The blast of cold air when she stepped into the grocery store always shocked her system. *Do* Englischers *feel that jolt each time they go from hot to cold all day?*

Stretching like a cat, she swung her legs out of bed and sat up. Though dawn was still an hour away, she would get no more sleep. Her musings on fans and air-conditioning turned her thoughts to James. When she pictured him curled on his side with his silky blond hair across one eye, she ran to the bureau to splash water on her face.

Passionate daydreams had no place in her head. Her *daed* would never allow him to officially court her, so this summer infatuation must end by the time autumn leaves change color.

But for today Emma would permit herself this romantic indulgence, because she would see him tonight. The Hostetlers were hosting a gathering for Amish youths, and Sarah had invited Sam Yoder's English friend. Maybe the Hostetlers wouldn't notice his truck, and certainly her parents didn't know he would be there. And for that dishonesty Emma felt ashamed. Yet the deception also added a measure of excitement to an otherwise ordinary bonfire.

The party started around seven thirty. People would huddle around the fire pit to cook hot dogs and roast marshmallows. The hosts provided coleslaw and potato salad, while the girls would bring desserts. Emma dressed and hurried downstairs to start breakfast and begin her own contribution—Apple Betty bars. Similar to apple crumb pie in a square pan, the addition of molasses to the brown sugar stiffened the mixture enough to be cut into squares. Chopped walnuts added richness to the crumb topping. One of these treats was plenty. More than that and you risked your waistline…and a bellyache.

Leah was already frying bacon when Emma reached the kitchen. *"Guder mariye,"* she said.

"Good morning to you, sister," Emma answered. "Is *mamm* still sleeping?" She set the butter on the table to soften.

"*Jah*, Pa told her to stay abed longer and take more pills. Her knees are aching unbearably. She said we should scramble the eggs and add diced tomatoes and peppers for an omelet. I'm going to add leftover ham and melt cheese on top too."

Emma smiled as she reached for the chopping board. Her sister did love to cook and bake, changing basic family recipes this way or that, sometimes with disastrous results, but often they were delicious.

"Just tell me what you want me to do," Emma said. "You are head cook today and I'll be your assistant."

Leah handed her the tomato, pepper, and ham to chop. "You could help me convince *mamm* that I should be allowed to go to the bonfire tonight." She sounded like a pouty child despite her adult culinary abilities.

Emma thought before replying. As much as she loved her little sister, she preferred not to have her spying on James and her. "You're still too young."

"It's a bunch of kids roasting hot dogs and then building up the fire to a big bonfire. They'll be sitting around in a circle and singing. There's no reason why I can't join in that kind of fun. Elizabeth Hostetler will be there, and she's only fourteen."

"You are only thirteen, dear one, and Elizabeth lives there. Mostly it will be courting couples. Your turn will come soon enough."

Leah sighed. "I've had no fun all summer. I'm always working. I wish I could eat some marshmallows."

Emma hugged Leah's thin shoulders; the girl felt all bones and sinew. "I'll bring you some in my cake pan, along with a sample of every single dessert. How does that sound?"

Leah nodded with a sniffle. "*Danki*, Emma. I s'pose it's better than nothing. But tomorrow after chores, can we swim in the pond like we used to? It's been horribly hot."

"*Jah*, we can, I promise." Emma hugged her tightly for a long moment. The idea that she might be starting down a road that would take her away from Leah filled her with sorrow. Summer days were always busy, and she missed sitting on the swing with her sister and telling girl stories.

Leah returned to her bacon while Emma tried to tamp down her growing anticipation of seeing James. Grinning foolishly at a pile of vegetables would look mighty suspicious.

The day passed quickly, and promptly at seven fifteen Emma left for the Hostetlers with her dessert tucked inside a covered hamper. Because it was still daylight, she took the back path, knowing a safe ride home would be provided. Walking around Sarah's house, she spotted a knot of people milling down by the creek. The fire was already burning, tables and chairs had been set up, and sawed-off logs served as cook stools. Her heart began to pound and her palms perspired as she walked toward the flames leaping toward the sky.

"Can I carry that basket for you, Miss Miller?" James Davis asked over her shoulder.

She jumped but quickly regained her composure. "Carry, yes. Peek inside, no," she said, relinquishing the hamper to him.

James transferred the hamper to his other side so he could take hold of her hand. "Will you share a log with me?" he asked, swinging arms like little children. "I'm going to cook two hot dogs at once. How 'bout you?"

Emma thrilled to the touch of his strong, calloused hand. Hers seemed so small by comparison. "One will suffice to start. I'm saving room for marshmallows. And you had better save room for my Apple Betty bars or my feelings will be hurt."

He lifted her hand to his mouth and kissed the back of her fingers. "I'll eat every last one if you'd like."

The bold gesture startled her. She pulled back her hand just as they joined the group. "Start with one and see if you like them first."

"Hi, Emma." Sarah greeted with a smile. "What goodie did you bring? Set it here." As Emma walked to the table, Sarah created a front spot for her dessert. "I see James found you," she whispered. "He arrived early and has been glancing at his watch ever since."

"What can I help you with?" Emma asked, eager to change the subject.

"Carry these buns, ketchup, and mustard down to the fire. We'll leave the side dishes up here. The hot dogs are already there." Sarah handed her a tray and then walked to where Sam Yoder was busily sharpening points on long sticks.

Emma returned to the fire and set the tray on an upended log. She found James sitting on a log big enough for two with sticks already fixed with hot dogs. "Should I cook yours too?" he asked. Firelight sparkled and danced in his eyes.

She sat down beside him and glanced around. No one seemed to be paying them any attention. A dozen people were already cooking, eating, and talking. One *Englischer* and his Plain date hadn't stopped the world among people her own age.

"Yes, please," she answered. "I like mine sort of burned."

"Me too. Burning food is my specialty." James handled both hot dog sticks expertly, turning them often. Once sufficiently charred, they smothered the hot dogs with mustard and relish and then snuggled close on the log. Emma dabbed mustard from his chin with her napkin. James fed her the last bite of his second dog. Both smiled as though this was their best meal ever.

While they ate the evening star, Venus, appeared low in the sky as the sun dropped beneath the horizon. The heat and humidity of August lifted as a light breeze blew from the south. Emma roasted three marshmallows until light brown and then three more to take home to her sister. She ate hers straight from the stick, sparing her fingers the messiness.

Some people began to sing songs, while others just cuddled side-by-side to watch the blaze. Men added more wood to build the bonfire into an inferno. It crackled and sparked and shot flames toward the night sky.

Sitting beside James, Emma had never felt so content as he munched not one but two squares of Apple Betty bars. He *ooh'ed* and *ahh'ed* and praised her baking skills, giving Emma a tingle of womanly satisfaction.

"Can we take a walk together?" he asked quietly upon finishing dessert. "Not far, but there's something I need to tell you."

She glanced around and nodded, rising to her feet. Anticipation swelled deep in her belly.

James took her hand when they had wandered away from the noisy crowd. Despite almost total darkness, Emma felt no fear. They walked only as far as the pasture fence where he turned to her. "Emma, I decided to go to college after all. It's something that's very important to my folks. My dad never went, so he wants all his kids to go. I won't be far away—Wooster—but I'll be staying on campus in a dorm."

Emma felt the air leave her lungs, while the hot dog and marsh-mallows she'd eaten turned leaden in her belly. This wasn't the dec-laration of affection she had hoped for. "College?" she asked weakly. "Why would a farmer need college?" Yet she knew the Davis farming operation was far different from the Miller family's.

"Yeah, that's what I said too, but my dad made a good argument. The agricultural world is changing, and an English farmer needs to change with it. Advanced courses will help with that."

She nodded in agreement, but she didn't really understand. "This is what you want?" she asked.

"No, this is what my parents want, and I want to respect their wishes."

She tried to think, to sort the details in her mind. "When does school start? In late September?"

He squeezed her hand tighter. "No, I leave in two weeks for fresh-man orientation. That's why I wanted to tell you tonight. I'll be busy with the early harvest, so I might not see you before I go."

Emma tugged her hand back while her mind reeled with things she didn't like. He would be gone for four years, surrounded by pretty English girls in their tight jeans and snug tops. One Plain girl from Winesburg would soon be nothing but a vague memory. She had been foolish to think this was a serious courtship leading to marriage. "Good luck then, James. I wish you success with your studies." Her voice sounded distant and unfamiliar.

"Emma," James said. "Please don't be upset. I like you very much, and my going away to college doesn't change that. Since you don't have a phone, I hoped you would let me write to you—if your parents will allow it. I'll be driving right by your place to and from school, and I can stick letters in your mailbox."

She lifted a questioning eyebrow.

He laughed before adding, "Going by your place won't be much out of my way." Then he bent his head to meet her gaze. "What do you say? Do you like me well enough to write? And we could see each other as often as possible."

Emma didn't take long to make up her mind. "Yes, I'll write to you. I guess I like you plenty enough for that." She smiled as the breeze blew a loose strand of hair across her face.

James reached out to tuck it behind her ear, and then without warning he leaned in and kissed her. Not on her cheek or on her forehead as her family did, but squarely on her pink-glossed lips. She didn't pull back until after the two-second kiss was over.

"Umm," he said. "You taste like peppermint candy." He smacked his lips together. Apparently, some of the sticky gloss had rubbed off.

"It's lip gloss," she said. "What do you think?"

"Sweet, but you don't have to trouble yourself on my account, especially if it upsets your parents." He tipped up her chin. "I like you exactly how you are." His face grew serious while his blue eyes turned as dark as deep water. "I think you are absolutely beautiful, Emma Miller!"

NINE

With his cutting blades sharpened, his plow horses shod, and with his sons to help, Simon had planned to start harvesting hay. By the almanac's predictions and his own study of cloud patterns the past few days, plenty of good weather stretched before him. But lest he grow too confident or complacent, his best leather harness snapped into two pieces when he tried to use it. The older pair of harnesses looked dry-rotted and not worth the effort to even test on his Belgians. So with a final glance at the perfect, cloudless sky, Simon decided to visit the leather crafter in Berlin. His field of hay, bright green and shimmering in the sunlight, would have to wait.

As Simon led his gelding out of the barn, Matthew strolled onto the back porch. The boy was eating a peach despite the fact they had just finished breakfast twenty minutes ago. "What ya doin', Pa?" he asked. "Why are you hitching up the buggy? I thought we were cutting today." His straw hat was perched on the back of his head while his cheeks looked tanned and ruddy.

"I broke another harness," Simon called. "That makes two this month. I'm going over to the harness maker in Berlin. Hopefully, he'll have one ready to fit and I won't have to order and then wait. Tell your *mamm* I should be back in time for lunch." Simon finished hitching his standardbred and then inspected its harness too, as he was already making the trip.

Matthew ran down the path toward him. Simon noticed his work trousers were already a tad short, while his shirt pulled tightly across his chest. The boy needed new clothes again. Julia or Leah had already let out or let down every seam. He was growing faster than the pokeweed along the fence line.

When Matthew reached halfway, he yelled, "Can I come with you? The milking is done, and I've filled all the water troughs and moved hay bales to the cow and sheep pastures."

Simon could think of a dozen things the boy could do while he was gone, but his plaintive, freckled face looked desperate for a change of scenery. "*Jah*, all right, but go tell Henry to stay close in case your *mamm* needs something. There's no saying where Emma might be off to. She always has several chores started at once."

"Okay," Matthew called, "but don't worry about *mamm*. Leah's in the house." The boy disappeared back inside while Simon tightened the halter. Thank goodness God had made all his *kinner* different. At least Leah would see that Julia didn't overdo and that lunch would be ready when they returned. Emma would forget to eat if someone didn't set it in front of her...like one of her sheep.

"Can I take the reins?" Matthew asked, climbing into the buggy a few minutes later.

"*Jah*, sure," Simon answered, "but keep him over as far as possible. This is the busiest month for English tourists, gawking left and right instead of watching the road. I saw a station wagon pull to the side of the road the other day. A group of people got out and stood by our fence for a long while staring at the cows." Simon clucked his tongue with disapproval.

"What were the cows doing?" Matthew asked, slapping the reins lightly on the gelding's back. The horse picked up the pace to a full trot.

"Same thing cows do all day long—they were eating grass and

chewing their cud. Nothing else." Father and son enjoyed a hearty chuckle over the oddities of *Englischers*.

But once they approached Berlin, Simon found little to amuse him. Traffic had backed up to the outskirts of town. Buses belching diesel exhaust were filled with tourists eager to spend money on handmade items, quilts, and baskets. Pickup trucks and delivery vans were loaded with new oak furniture on their way to the dealers.

Matthew pulled hard on the reins to stop behind a car packed with white-haired ladies. "Not a good day to come to Berlin," Matthew declared. "They must be having a craft fair or some kind of festival."

Simon blew out his breath through his nostrils. He hated queues of traffic with all the fumes. "We should've gone the back roads, but I thought this way would be quicker. We'll never get home to cut hay at this rate."

Matthew, however, seemed far less annoyed, content to do his own share of gawking. At long last, they snaked through the quaint town of gift shops, restaurants, and small inns to arrive at the shop on the western outskirts. The harness maker had divided his farmland between his two sons and taken up leatherwork. If the warm smile on his face was any indication, the career change had been a good choice.

"Simon Miller," the man exclaimed when they entered the shop.

"*Guder mariye*, Amos," Simon greeted. The pungent smell of recently tanned leather assailed his senses. "This is my elder boy, Matthew." Amos lived in a different district, so it had been a while since they had seen each other.

"*Jah*? How do?" Amos asked. "Been a long time."

Matthew mumbled a shy hello while Simon nodded in agreement and then asked, "How are you fixed for harnesses? I need a new set for my Belgians to accommodate working teams of two, four, and six."

Amos pulled on his suspenders. "Belgians, you say? How many hands?"

Simon took out a piece of paper on which he'd jotted the specifics and handed it over.

Amos read the notes and pondered a moment. "I've got enough in stock, but I'll have to make adjustments. Sit down while I get what we need."

He returned carrying leather straps over his shoulder, a box of assorted buckles and hardware, and his pouch of tools. Pulling up a stool to his bench, he went to work with his glasses perched on the end of his nose. "My boy Joseph saw your daughter last weekend," Amos said without lifting his focus from the harness.

"*Jah*, at the Hostetler bonfire, I imagine." Simon wondered how the man could do such meticulous work in the dim light.

"Joseph said Emma's dessert was the best one there. He put two pieces in a napkin to eat the next day."

Simon's surprise bloomed across his face. "Is that right? Emma's not one to spend much time in the kitchen with fancy baking. I'll be sure to tell her what Joseph said. She'll be pleased."

Amos set down his awl and met Simon's gaze. "She's on *Rumschpringe* then, your Emma." It sounded more like a comment than a question.

Simon immediately grew uneasy. "Why do you say that? Was something wrong with her dress or clothes in some way?" He thought about the cotton candy-colored lip gloss and felt the back of his neck start to sweat.

"No, Joseph didn't say anything about her appearance, other than she turned out real pretty…and that she was courting an *Englischer.*" Amos watched Simon intently as though waiting for his reaction.

Simon ground down on his back teeth hard enough to crack molars but didn't reveal his inner turmoil. "Courting? No, that *Englischer* is just a friend of hers. He's another sheep farmer, and my Emma has grown plum attached to her sheep." He forced out a small laugh.

Matthew dropped a tool he'd been fiddling with by the window, drawing the attention of his elders. Simon had forgotten the boy was in the room. "Go outside and get some fresh air, son, but don't wander too far. We'll be leaving as soon as the harness is done."

Matthew glanced from Simon to Amos, opened his mouth to speak, but shut it again and headed for the door.

"He's just a friend of Emma's," Simon repeated.

"*Jah*, all right," Amos said. "My Joseph will be happy to hear that since he might have it in his mind to court your girl. But you tell Emma she ought not to hold hands with friends, lest she give folks the wrong idea." Amos slipped several brass fittings into place and began tightening everything up. He adjusted and measured and adjusted again while Simon stewed over the news.

Simon didn't like another man telling him his business or how to raise *kinner*, but because he couldn't cut hay without new leather, he bit back any retort he might have had. "I'll tell her, Amos. Now, what do I owe for the harness?"

Amos scratched his chin and named his price after inspecting the finished set one last time.

Simon refused his offer of coffee and muffins, paid the harness maker, and then he left with his son. He allowed Matthew to run the horse faster than normal on the less-traveled northern route around town. He was anxious to get home and have a word with his daughter.

Emma was feeding chickens when they arrived shortly after one o'clock. She waved and poured the remaining ground corn into a pile inside the pen. "Finally home?" she called, closing the gate behind her. "Lunch has been ready for over an hour." She carried her bucket toward the house.

"Hold up there, daughter," Simon demanded. "Matthew, put the buggy away, rub down the horse since he's lathered, and turn him out. Then come in to lunch."

"Now, Pa, why don't we—"

Simon didn't let him finish. "Go do what I asked. This does not concern you."

Matthew cast his sister a sympathetic glance before driving the buggy toward the barn.

Simon walked to where Emma stood by the fence. The holly-hocks had grown taller than her in the past few weeks of sunshine. "I heard some disturbing things today at the harness maker's," he said and waited.

But Emma only shrugged in confusion. "What did he tell you?" she asked.

"He said you were courting an *Englischer*. And that you two were seen holding hands at that cookout the other day. Is it true, daughter?"

Emma's complexion blanched to the color of new-fallen snow as she gripped the bottom of her apron with both hands. She appeared to consider her reply carefully. "*Jah*, James took my hand when we walked down the hill toward the bonfire. It was rocky, uneven ground, and he didn't want me to fall. But no, we are not courting."

The two locked gazes for a long moment until Simon looked away. "Good, that's what I told Amos. I'm glad you have not made me into a liar. Let's go have our lunch. I am hungry, never expecting to be gone that long. You can't believe the traffic headed to Berlin today... as if stores were giving things away for free."

Simon marched past Emma and climbed the porch steps, so he didn't see her expression change from surprise to utter mortification to sorrow.

She might have followed him to the kitchen table and gone through the motions of eating in front of her family, but Miss Emma Miller swallowed very little food that afternoon.

~

How could one lunch of toasted cheese sandwiches and tomato soup take so long? Emma thought her *bruders* and *daed* would never go out to the fields. But, finally, they slapped their hats on and left, enthusiastic about what they would accomplish by dusk. Supper would wait until dark—no sense taking a dinner break since they were starting so late. Julia headed into the front room to lie down because the upstairs was stifling hot. Emma and Leah cleaned up the kitchen.

"Don't forget," Leah said, "you promised to go swimming with me this afternoon." She carefully swept breadcrumbs into the palm of her hand.

"*Jah*, okay," Emma said, forcing a smile. "But later, after our work is done." Actually, she'd forgotten her plans with her little sister, but she would honor them despite the fact she'd rather hide from her family right now—preferably under a slug-covered rock where all deceivers and manipulators belonged.

Emma was ashamed of herself. As much as she loved James—and that notion had only occurred to her this afternoon—she regretted her sneaky behavior. Not until her *daed* backed her into a corner did she realize she loved James Davis. Why else would she lie to her dear father—the man who'd taught her to swim, how to eat ice-cream cones, and how to love the Lord with her whole heart?

Now she'd broken the ninth commandment.

But what else could she do? She was in love with a man whom her parents found unacceptable. It didn't matter that he was kind, gentle, and attentive. It didn't matter that he was respectful, honorable, and strong in his Christian faith. He was an *Englischer,* and that's all they saw when they looked at him.

Emma couldn't choose James over her family, especially not when he planned to leave for college in a few weeks. How could she break her parents' hearts for someone who might quickly forget her on a campus full of pretty girls?

When Leah headed off to the ironing, Emma filled water buckets for her sheep. In hot weather she needed to be extra diligent to prevent dehydration. After counting heads and checking for signs of illness of injury, Emma walked back to the barn. Sweat dripped down her neck and turned her scalp itchy. Gnats swarmed around her head, deepening her miserable mood. She hadn't bothered with cheek blusher or lip gloss today. Why make the effort for a bunch of chickens, sheep, and cows?

Hot and out of sorts, Emma couldn't bear the stuffy barn loft, so she headed for the herb shed, a quiet place to work and read. But first she stopped at the house and tucked the family Bible under her arm. She'd never read Scripture much on her own, content to listen to *daed* read in the evenings or during the preaching services. But today Emma realized she was no longer a little girl, sitting by her father's feet. She was an adult with grown-up problems to solve. Pushing open the door to her sweet-smelling retreat, she yearned for guidance.

Perched on a stool, she closed her eyes and turned her face upward. "Dear Lord, I am Emma Miller of Winesburg, Ohio. Please help me and show me the way."

Then she opened the well-worn Good Book on her lap to where a bookmark had been placed. It was the book of Proverbs and someone had underlined chapter 28, verse 7: "Young people who obey the law are wise; those with wild friends bring shame to their parents."

Wild friends? Did *daed* think of James as wild? James did not drink alcohol, smoke cigarettes, or use foul language. Would a *wild* person loosen the bits on several horses that had been too tight during the trail ride?

But even though James wasn't wild, she was bringing shame to her parents nevertheless. How upsetting for her father to hear about the hand-holding from the harness maker. Did she really believe her behavior on a farm not a mile away wouldn't get back to her parents? *Young people who obey the law*...for the Amish, their *Ordnung* was the law. But this was her *Rumschpringe*. She hadn't broken any law...yet.

Emma scooted her chair closer to the window, turned back a few pages, and read another underlined passage, Proverbs 17:25: "Foolish children bring grief to their father and bitterness to the one who gave them birth."

Is that what I am doing? Adding bitterness to the burdens mamm *already has with her arthritis?*

Emma flipped to another bookmark in the book of Psalms and read chapter 32:9-10: "Do not be like a senseless horse or mule that needs a bit and bridle to keep it under control. Many sorrows come to the wicked, but unfailing love surrounds those who trust the Lord."

Was she a senseless mule? She thought about their tired old pony, Belle. Belle would charge back into a burning barn just to get to her stall with fresh straw and a bucket of oats. Emma longed for unfailing love, yet knew her sneaky behavior was a form of wickedness. Would sorrow be *her* future?

Shutting the Bible, she clutched it to her chest and fled from her safe haven. She ran to the house and to her *mamm*. It was time to talk to the woman who had given her birth and had sheltered her from harm.

"*Mamm*, are you awake?" Emma asked, creeping softly to her side.

Julia had woken from her nap but hadn't moved from the couch. "Yes, child. What's wrong? You look troubled." Julia struggled to sit up and then patted the spot beside her.

Emma laid the Bible down on the table. "I am troubled. I've been reading some places *daed* had marked." She faltered, waiting for some response, but Julia only breathed heavily as though she'd been running hard.

"I haven't completely told the truth about James. I told *daed* we weren't courting, but I want to court him. I like him very much, and he likes me." Emma waited for Julia to absorb this.

"You wish to turn English?" Julia reached up to straighten her *kapp*.

"No, I don't. At least, I don't think I do. Not right now anyway." Her words trailed off to a whisper as her conviction vaporized.

Julia nodded. "You are sixteen and confused. That's understandable."

"That's probably why *daed* marked those Scriptures for me," Emma said.

Julia reached for Emma's hand. "Your father didn't mark those passages for you to find. I did."

"You did? But Pa is the deacon."

"Exactly, and as deacon he would prefer that you not read and study indiscriminately. But you are much like your aunt, needing to find answers on your own. I just thought I'd give you a place to start."

Emma nodded, yet she didn't completely understand. Her mother wanted her to read the Bible but her father didn't?

"James isn't wild or foolish," Emma said, remembering certain words.

"He can be a very fine young man and still not be the right one for you."

"How can I know for sure? How can you?"

"You must be patient and do nothing to seal your fate until you are sure."

Emma hung her head. "Fate seems to have already decided for me. He's going away to college in a few weeks. He doesn't want to go, but he will to please his parents."

Julia looked relieved, but maybe it was only Emma's imagination. "Then both of you will get a chance to grow and learn and see how you feel later."

Emma wanted to say her feelings would never change, that she would wait for James no matter what, but she didn't dare. Instead she said meekly, "He asked if he could write me when he goes away. Is that all right?" She glanced up to find Julia's face pinched and creased with fatigue.

Pangs of guilt and shame squeezed her heart once more. In spite of her honesty, she was still bringing anguish to her *mamm*.

"*Jah*, he may write to you. And you may write back, but make no promises, no commitments until you're older and sure of what you want."

Emma hugged her until Julia squawked. "Enough, daughter, before you crack a rib. Go find Leah and give her a hand. And don't neglect your promise to swim with her later. It's a good day for that, I will say." Julia tucked a stray lock of Emma's hair under her *kapp*. Despite the misshapen fingers, her touch was soothing.

Emma pressed her face against the gentle hand, wishing she could have stayed a little girl forever. How safe she was as a child! And how simple her life had been.

Should she have told *mamm* about the kiss? Her first kiss during the bonfire party had been bittersweet—a pledge of love coupled with the news of his leaving. But a girl's first kiss was an important milestone—one that Emma needed to keep secret for a while longer.

She would take baby steps along her new path. A person must know how to walk before learning to run.

~

James must have changed clothes three times that Sunday morning. He wanted to make sure he wouldn't offend anyone with his appearance or stick out like a sore thumb. He settled on black shoes, black slacks, a plain white dress shirt, and he borrowed his dad's black suit coat. He'd shaved his mustache off and the beard he'd been letting grow for ten days, ever since he asked Sam Yoder if he might tag along to his Sunday morning preaching service. His parents had exchanged puzzled glances but said little when he announced he wouldn't be going to church with them.

Because he couldn't keep Emma Miller off his mind for longer than ten minutes, he wanted to peek into her world. Would she be willing to turn English for him? What would she have to give up? Although he knew much about Amish dress, customs, and farming techniques thanks to his friendship with Sam, he understood little about the Amish Christian faith. If their relationship had any chance of survival, that was where he needed to start.

He arrived at the Yoder farm and parked his truck in the shade of an ancient beech tree. Sam came outside carrying two mugs of coffee when he heard the crunch of gravel in the driveway. "You're here bright and early," he called from the porch.

"I had no idea how long it takes to get to the service," James said, accepting one of the mugs. Accepting a ride to services in a pickup was out of the question. New Order Amish used horse and buggy for basic transportation, same as Old Order.

"Let's bring my buggy around. We'll go separately from my folks," Sam said, finishing his coffee in two long swallows. "That way you can ask me all the questions you want without my sisters and brothers laughing behind your back."

"That's good to hear, thanks. How do I look?" James hooked his thumbs into the lapels of his dad's dressy coat.

A slow smile deepened the dimples in Sam's cheeks. "Like an *Englischer* playing at being Amish for the day. But that's okay. I'll get you one of my extra felt hats and you'll blend in just fine."

Sam had his own buggy and spirited standardbred, plus he was diligently saving his money to build a house on the family property. Like James, all Sam ever wanted to do was farm. But until he married, he would live in the big house with his parents and siblings

With black hats in place, the two young men set off at an easy pace to the house hosting the preaching service. Unlike Mennonite, New Order Amish held church in a district member's home, not in a separate meetinghouse.

James was soon glad the other Yoders weren't there to hear his questions. "Okay," he began, "Emma is Old Order. How exactly is that different from you?"

Sam tipped up his hat brim. "So, this is all about that blue-eyed neighbor of the Hostetlers, is it?"

"Maybe, or maybe I've just become curious now that I'm about to expand my mind with higher education."

"Yeah, right," Sam laughed. "Well, depending on the bishop, we use electricity and phones in our barns and in our homes too. That makes a big difference for dairy certification. We can sell our milk as grade-A direct to milk bottlers. Most Old Order sell their milk to cheese producers. We farm with tractors and diesel cultivators; the motors don't have to remain stationary. But we can't own cars, can we, pretty girl?" He shook the reins lightly over the horse's back. He directed the question to his mare, who twitched her ears with interest.

"All of that I'd pretty much figured out," James said. "What I'm curious about is how your Christian church is different from Emma's... and different from mine, for that matter. Fill me in on what to expect before we get there."

"You probably should've asked my ma, but I'll try my best. We still use German for the singing and preaching, but you will hear some English thrown in. And the young people participate more in our service than in Emma's."

"So I'll be able to understand the sermon?" James asked.

"Probably not. Maybe some of it. The big difference is that we *talk* about our faith a lot more than Old Order. We read the Bible at home and discuss what we've read. We can go to hospitals or prisons or on missionary trips to spread the Word of Christ. Old Order has a less personal, quieter form of worship. They want to be known by their deeds and their lifestyle instead of what they say."

James nodded, trying to take it all in. "Sounds somewhat like the evangelical church we attend," he said, relaxing upon hearing similarities.

Sam cocked his head to the side. "Yeah, I guess so, in some ways. We have assurance of salvation. Emma's sect has the *hope* of salvation. But before you get too excited, Jamie, even New Order Amish would be no easy change for you: no alcohol, no tobacco, no card-playing, and no dancing."

James shrugged his shoulders. "No big loss. I don't drink, never smoked, don't understand the first thing about poker, and nearly broke my date's foot when I tried to dance with her at the senior prom."

Sam laughed and shook his head. "Okay, but no more big green shiny pickup truck, my friend. And it takes ninety minutes to go ten miles in a buggy, doesn't it, girl?"

The horse lifted her hooves higher into a fast trot as though she knew the conversation involved her.

James crossed his arms over his pressed white shirt. "Oh, yeah. I keep forgetting that part."

"Why don't you just start with our church service and not get too far ahead of yourself," Sam said, his buggy joining a line of others headed to the same farmhouse.

"Okay," James agreed, blushing slightly.

He knew he was getting way ahead of himself. Sweet, shy Emma Miller might simply be curious about him. Especially since this was her running-around time before getting baptized and settling down. Just because she allowed him to kiss her once didn't mean she was ready to seriously court an outsider. More pressure would be placed on her by her family than he could imagine.

Her father was a deacon.

She was only sixteen years old.

And he had at least two, if not four, years of college ahead of him. The prospect of their friendship growing into something more permanent looked bleak. But as Sam's buggy turned into the driveway of the family holding the service, James could only think about two things:

All he had ever wanted to be was a farmer.

And the only girl he could imagine spending his life with was Emma Miller.

TEN

Seth gazed over the acres of new corn, standing tall and green in tidy rows. The plentiful rain and abundant sunshine had brought the crop further along than expected. Some men in the district had counseled against planting more corn after his first hay had been harvested, but his decision had been sound. Ears were forming on the tender green stalks, and he felt confident this crop of hybrid would reach maturity.

But a stroll in the opposite direction presented a different dilemma. Turkey Red winter wheat, their plump brown heads nodding in the breeze, stretched for as far as the eye could see. These acres of grain grew on the highest and best land in the area. The fields were well drained, well fertilized, and free from rock debris. Usually, he sowed alfalfa after the wheat was harvested. But the price paid for dairy cow feed was nothing to crow about.

Dare he plant this field too with corn? Planting more this late was unheard of, but these acres received more hours of daylight than anywhere on the farm. While his bottom acres became shaded by late afternoon by the western hills, these fields received plenty of light until dusk. But would it be sufficient to ripen another crop before the first frost? He didn't know. Sometimes the growing season stretched far into November. Other years, an early October blizzard reduced plants to flaccid stalks, suitable for chopping into silage and not much else.

Seth pulled on his beard, ran a hand through his hair, and chewed on a long weed, yet still no great insight occurred. Seeing little alternative, he headed toward the house to the counsel of his wife. Although a man made the final decision in a Plain household, especially in financial matters, only a fool failed to consult with a spouse when uncertain.

And this was one of those times.

Hannah possessed good intuition about these things, and right about now he could use a second opinion. "Hannah," he called, stomping up the steps. "Hannah?" He entered the back hall, catching the screen door with his boot heel.

"I'm in here, Seth. Why all the shouting?" Her voice floated from around the corner.

Seth hooked his hat on a peg and walked into the kitchen, but the room bore little resemblance to the orderly, austere heart of the Amish home. It had taken on the appearance of some sort of vegetable disaster zone, what one might expect if an explosion occurred at a Del Monte plant. Tomatoes, peppers, onions, celery, carrots, and unrecognizable vegetables in various stages of being cleaned, sliced, chopped, pureed, or blanched covered every surface of counter and table. Pots the size of cauldrons simmered and spattered, throwing off a mixed bouquet of scents. Peels, stems, and seeds overflowed the trash can and littered the floor.

"Good grief, woman, has there been an accident or explosion of some sort?" Seth chewed the inside of his cheek.

"Ha-ha, very funny. No, no mishaps," Hannah said. "Things are coming along fine, I'd say. I'm canning a nine-vegetable juice—adding one more than the competition, while I'm also stewing and canning tomatoes." A grin filled her speckled face. "And I intend to try my hand at making homemade salsa with the hot peppers I grew this year."

Her *kapp* was askew and spattered red, her face flushed from the steamy heat, and her apron would probably never be white again, but Hannah looked positively joyous.

"Good work then, *fraa*. A tidy kitchen is highly overrated!" He picked his way gingerly over to the refrigerator. "Could you take a short break? I need your point of view. Let's sit and have some tea." Seth poured two glasses and pulled a pair of chairs to the table. He pushed a mound of beets with their lacy tops still attached to one side to clear a spot.

Hannah peered at him curiously before running her hands under the faucet and wiping them on her apron. She turned down the heat under her pots so their contents wouldn't scorch. "You are seeking my opinion, dear husband? Have you suffered heatstroke?" She sat down and took a dainty sip of tea.

"Maybe so. You can judge that after hearing me out." Seth also drank some tea and then explained his idea for the wheatfield. He tried to sound logical and pragmatic without unduly influencing her.

Hannah watched him with eyes as round as an owl's, but she didn't interrupt. Once he concluded she asked softly, "Are we talking about the wheatfield still standing?" She aimed her forefinger in the general direction.

He nodded.

"You plan to cut those acres with a grain binder pulled by draft horses, then feed those tied bundles through the threshing machine to get them out of your way, then re-plow the field and set young corn plants? *That* wheatfield, Seth Miller?" The smudges of tomato sauce on her chin enhanced the amused, comic effect of her teasing.

"*Jah*, that's the one—the only wheatfield I have." He shook his head. Hearing his idea put in Hannah's terms made it sound as impractical as it was.

"Hmm, let me think about this before jumping to a conclusion." She placed a finger on the side of her jawbone and gazed toward the ceiling.

Seth grabbed her hand and mimicked taking a bite. "I suppose there isn't enough time unless winter bypasses Holmes County altogether this year," he said, kissing her fingers instead of chomping down. "And I don't think that's going to happen."

"Dear *ehemann*, content yourself with the corn already planted. It should be sufficient to generate the income you desire. Don't put all your eggs into one basket."

Seth held her hand for another minute. It felt small and soft against his calloused palm. He would think on this long and hard. She was probably right—it was too late to set more corn. But what profits could be made with those additional acres. He dared not even add them up in his head, lest the Lord learn just how money oriented and greedy he had become.

～

Was she doing it again—bossing her husband around and telling him his business on a farm she only married into last year? Her brother-in-law had counseled her on a wife's role in a Christian marriage. It hadn't taken her long to veer from the path. The house was her domain—she could make decisions there freely, short of painting the walls pumpkin orange. But financial concerns, especially those regarding day-to-day management of the farm, were a man's responsibility.

Let your husband lead you. Even when he stumbles or falls, do not criticize. Your joys will be multiplied and your prayers will be answered. Simon's words echoed in her ears as though he were whispering to her from the porch.

Hannah snapped back from her reverie to find Seth still cradling her hand within his. He wore a sad, resigned look on his face. "Have I overstepped my bounds?" she asked. "Have I annoyed you with my pushiness?"

Seth squeezed her fingers as a smile crinkled the skin around his eyes into deep folds. "No, dear one, you haven't. I asked for your opinion, and you gave it."

Hannah exhaled the breath she'd been holding. "I stand behind you, Seth, whatever your decision."

"*Danki.* I'll ponder the matter, but you're probably right. It's too late in the season to plant any more corn. We'll hope for a good harvest with what we already planted. Now I had better start cutting wheat since it won't cut itself while I daydream about vast riches." He offered one last crooked grin, released her hand, and strode from the room.

Being a good wife was no easy job. A wife walked a thin line if she wanted to be helpful without being domineering. A man needed respect, while a woman needed love most of all. Did Seth know how much she respected him? His transition from widower to husband must have been difficult. One look at the kitchen confirmed she was no Constance.

Hannah glanced around the messy room and giggled. It *did* look like a giant tomato explosion. Shaking her head, she turned the gas burners back up to high. The sooner she finished canning vegetable juice and putting up tomatoes, the sooner she could put her kitchen in order.

God would put their life in order too, according to His plan. She would not concern herself with what grew in their fields. With a house to tend, garden vegetables to can, and a child to nurture, she had her hands full. God had answered her prayers for an end to loneliness when He brought Seth and her together. Maybe if she showed some faith, an answer would come for her other prayer too.

～

"What are you doin', Emma?" Matthew climbed up to the top rail of the forcing pen. His hat was tipped back while he chewed a long piece of hay.

When Emma glanced up, he appeared to be laughing at her. "What does it look like, *bruder*? I'm trying to wash mud off some of my sheep." Emma had managed to separate the untidiest sheep from the flock and herded them into the narrow chute. However, trying to get them to stand still long enough to use the long-handled brush was a different story.

"Why are you doing that?" Matthew asked, scratching absently at a mosquito bite.

Emma looked away from her task, just long enough for an irritable ewe to knock the hand holding the garden hose. A stream of water hit her squarely in the face, besides drenching the front of her dress and apron.

"Oh, my goodness," she exclaimed, stunned by the cool spray of water.

Matthew hopped down and took hold of her sleeve. "Come out of there before you get hurt." He pulled her from the pen and latched the gate behind them. "Now tell me again who's supposed to be getting the bath?" He handed her his clean handkerchief.

"Apparently me. These sheep refuse to be cleaned up." She cast them a frosty glare before walking outside to the bright sunshine.

Matthew leaned over and whispered in her ear, "No one ever gives a sheep a bath."

Emma flapped her apron and shook her skirt to hasten drying. "I don't know why not. If they were clean before they were sheared, I'd have less trouble on my hands with their wool. My shearer is coming in two days." Emma pulled off her *kapp* irritably and shook it out. "Not much else has gone right today, either. A bee stung me while I was taking down the laundry. Then that ornery Curly head-butted me when I was moving her rope."

Matthew appeared to be holding back hysterics.

The frosty glare focused on him. "I don't know if I should be grateful for my last birthday gift or tell you to try to get your money back." She put her soggy head covering back on. In general, Emma felt hot, sweaty, and miserable. Her foot throbbed where she'd walked barefoot over a bee. And the impromptu shower in the barn hadn't helped matters.

"I might be able to make it up to you, sister," Matthew said, sounding mysterious as he hopped up on the gate. He never could remain stationary for long.

Emma arched an eyebrow. "How's that? What are you up to, young man?" In truth, she was only two years his senior, but since her *Rumschpringe* she felt much older.

His crooked smile lit up his face. "I asked *daed* if I could go to Mount Hope on Friday to watch the horse pull competition. They're having one before the draft horse sale in the field behind the auction barn. He said I couldn't go alone and not with Henry, either. He said I would let him wander off, which of course I wouldn't." Matthew sounded indignant, because he spent a good amount of time watching out for his little brother.

Emma smoothed the wet creases out in her skirt. "And...?" she prompted. "I must finish chores and help Leah..."

"And I said to Pa, 'How 'bout if I go with Emma? She's sixteen.'" He spit out a wad of chewed up hay. "What do you think?"

Emma pondered while she glanced toward her sheep pasture. The mud-caked animals had backed their way out of the confining pen until they were able to turn around, and now they were merrily headed back to the flock. Her aunt had never explained how willful these creatures could be. The idea of a Friday evening in town sounded like a welcome diversion, even though horses dragging around a weighted sleigh had never appealed to her before.

"What did *daed* say?" She tried not to sound too excited. After all, she was a mature woman.

"He said, *jah*, okay, as long as we have fresh batteries for the buggy lights. He doesn't like us driving after dark." Matthew started to swing his long legs. "What do you say? Could ya stand being seen with your lit'l *bruder* for one evening?"

"I sure could, *danki*. I can't wait to see real live people and not just critters covered up to their bellies with mud."

"You've never been to a horse weekend. Some of those sellers and trainers get mighty dirty too." He hopped down from the gate and loped off toward the milking parlor to his afternoon chores.

But Emma didn't care how muddy the other people were because an idea had occurred. James was a horse breeder and trainer. He often sold young colts and fillies that he didn't need. The Mount Hope horse auction came only once a month. Maybe, just maybe, a bit of luck—and not another bee sting—might come her way.

Emma tried to keep a mouse-sized profile until Friday. She did all her chores and helped Leah in the kitchen even when it wasn't her night to cook. But *mamm*'s arthritis wasn't cooperating with her Friday night outing. That morning at breakfast Julia announced they were going to Canton to see the specialist. The medicine and pain relievers had become ineffective in bringing relief.

For a moment Emma was disappointed, but there would be other horse pulls in Mount Hope. *Mamm*'s suffering had become a seven-day-a-week agony. "All right. Matthew and I will stay home with Leah and Henry," she said, mustering a pleasant smile. "Shall we plan a late supper for you and *daed*?"

"No, we'll eat in Canton. And Henry and Leah are coming with us. Mr. Lee said there's room in the van, and they both want to go." Julia reached over to tilt up Emma's chin. "There's no reason to stay home once your chores are done. You and Matthew can go as long as you're both careful." Pain reduced her smile to a grimace.

"Are you sure? Maybe I should go to Canton with you," Emma said.

"*Ach*, no. The van would be too crowded. Don't worry so, daughter. This is just an ordinary doctor's appointment."

"*Danki, mamm*." Emma kissed Julia's cheek and then flew out to her chores. Anticipation began to build in her veins. By three o'clock, the hour Matthew had decided upon, steam would be ready to whistle from her ears.

With the rest of the family gone, she saw no reason to make a big lunch. She carried a sandwich, an apple, and a cold drink to the horse paddock where Matthew was trying to train a rebellious colt.

"What are we having for supper?" he asked in between bites of his sandwich.

Emma perched her hands on her hips. "You haven't even finished lunch and you're already worried about dinner?"

"Sure, I'm worried. Leah and *mamm* are gone." He winked and took a huge bite.

She ignored his taunt. "We'll have a bowl of soup and some hard-boiled eggs before we leave, but I don't want to fuss with a big meal. I'll treat you to a hot dog and ice cream in Mount Hope. Let's be ready to go promptly so we'll have plenty of time. Hurry with your chores." She turned and headed toward the henhouse.

"Don't get yourself too worked up, Emma. He probably won't be there tonight."

She stopped in her tracks. "Who do you mean?"

"You know exactly who I'm talking about. Horse pulls aren't a big deal for *Englischers* since they don't own draft horses. They like tractor pulls or drag races better."

"I don't know what you're talking about. I'm going to look at horses. Poor old Belle shouldn't be hitched to the pony cart anymore. She's too old."

Matthew shook his head. "Whatever you say. I'll be ready on time."

And the boy was true to his word. Ten minutes past three o'clock they were trotting down the county road to Mount Hope. Emma felt like singing, but she didn't dare. Then her *bruder* would know just how happy she felt with even a chance of seeing James.

Instead, she counted fence posts, then silos, and finally filed her nails down with an emery board. She didn't fool anyone with her distractions.

"You really like this James, don't you?" Matthew asked.

Emma considered denying it, but that would be lying. *"Jah,* I do."

"'Spose you've got lots of folks telling you what a bad idea that is." He glanced over as she nodded yes. "Then I'll just keep quiet and save my energy."

"Danki very much," she said wryly, wondering how anyone kept things secret.

But soon Emma had no time to ponder. Mount Hope was bustling with people—Amish, English, tourists, and farmers out for some harmless fun. Vendors had set up booths to sell food and beverages. So many buggies had arrived, the Miller siblings had to park quite a distance from the activities. But neither minded the long walk as they searched the crowd for familiar faces.

When Matthew sauntered over to talk to a group of school chums, Emma stood in line to buy their hot dogs. He chose to eat his supper with his friends close to the arena, but she preferred dining under a shady tree, away from the fly-populated horse pens.

"Why, Miss Miller," a voice said over her shoulder. "You came to a demonstration on the power of four-legged beasts? I'm rather surprised."

Emma nearly jumped out of her black boots. She still hadn't replaced the lost tennis shoes. "Hello, James. Still sneaking up on people, I see." She managed to swallow down the dry hot dog bun.

"I wouldn't have thought the competition would interest a delicate female such as yourself."

Emma pivoted to face him squarely, shocked by how close he was standing. The second jolt was due to how handsome he looked. His tanned arms bulged from beneath the short sleeves of his cotton shirt. The collar was open, as well as the first two buttons. She saw that even his chest was deeply suntanned, leading her to imagine him working his fields without any shirt at all.

Emma pulled her gaze from his chest and stared at the ground. Her face flushed a deep rose. "I like horses just fine. Most girls...women do." So he wouldn't get the notion she'd come tonight to moon after him, she added, "I'm here to price horses to pull my pony cart."

Graciously, James said nothing about her staring at him, but he seemed to stand straighter than before. "Ah, you might want to see the Appaloosas they'll be auctioning tomorrow—beautiful animals, gentle and intelligent. Would you like to take a look at them, Emma?"

He offered his arm like an old-fashioned gentleman.

She almost took hold but then remembered the gossip her *daed* had heard at the harness maker's. Her hand slipped down to her side. "Thank you, but I don't suspect there are any slippery patches along the way." She took a step toward the barns.

"In that case, I can't wait till winter. Then you'll walk a little closer, and I can pretend you're really my girl."

He spoke the last words softy, but Emma heard him clearly. She felt warmth in her belly and halted in the thoroughfare. Folks behind them were forced to detour around. "Why would you do that?" she asked. "You're off to college soon."

"Because nothing in this world would make be happier, and going to college doesn't change that."

Emma felt a little faint—too many jostling people and too much late-summer humidity. The hot dog sat like a lead weight in her belly. "Could we go back to talking horses, please?" she pleaded.

"If you prefer," James said. "Let's tell your brother we're going in the horse barn so he doesn't worry."

She nodded, sorry she hadn't thought of that. They easily found him; he was half a head taller than his pals.

Matthew took one look at James and started to smirk. "Hi," he crowed. "What a surprise! I didn't think you'd be interested in draft horses."

"I love all horses." James extended his hand. "Good to see ya again, Matt."

They shook hands, while Matthew's Amish friends kept glancing from one to the other.

"We're going inside just for a minute," Emma said. "I need to look at ponies if I'm going to retire Belle."

"Sure, we'll be over at the pull. It's getting ready to start." Matthew tipped his hat and walked off, his friends following after him. One of them looked over his shoulder at Emma curiously.

Emma exhaled through her nostrils. "I hope he doesn't make a big thing out of this."

"Of what, Em?" James sounded confused.

"Of you...and me...oh, never mind. I'm worried about nothing." She smiled politely, remembering it wasn't James' fault that an Amish girl's behavior was limited compared to that of English girls.

They found the smaller horses indoors. Although she had no intention of parting with any hard-earned money for a new pony yet, it was fun to compare and discuss different breeds. Emma easily picked out a favorite.

James agreed with her choice of an Appaloosa filly. "You've got a good eye. You have talents you've kept hidden from me." He gently tucked a stray lock inside her *kapp*.

Emma felt her heartbeat quicken and her palms grow damp. "You mustn't touch my face in public," she whispered. "It's not proper." She found herself on the verge of tears.

Not because he'd caressed her face, but because she had enjoyed it so much...and because she had wanted him to continue.

This cannot be.

Emma shook herself as though waking from a dream.

"Yes, it shall be an Appaloosa when I'm ready to buy. Thank you for sharing your expertise with me." She bobbed her head formally. "Now let's return to my brother so I can watch the horse-pulling competition."

"Of course," he said, looking abashed.

Emma forced herself to put one foot in front of the other to walk out the door. So much of her wanted to remain alone with James in the horse barn—surrounded by buyers and sellers, yet somehow alone just the same.

ELEVEN

August

Hullo, *fraa*. Is lunch almost ready?" Seth called, breaking Hannah's daydreaming.

Hannah straightened up very slowly, allowing each vertebra in her spine to ease back into place. Spasms in her arms and shoulders reminded her she had been picking vegetables for a long while. Shielding her eyes from the sun's glare with her hand, she spotted Seth by the garden gate. "Lunch?" she called. "How could you be hungry already? Didn't we just eat breakfast?"

"Hours ago, my dear wife. It's well past noon." Seth sauntered through the green beans, looking annoyingly fresh. How could the man spend the morning tilling between rows of sweet corn and not look as limp as a dishrag? Her shoes were scuffed, her apron was dirty, her dress was pasted to her back, and her scalp prickled beneath her *kapp*. She could just imagine what she looked like.

"How goes your day?" he asked when he reached her, midway down a row. He took the basket of beans from her grasp.

"I've been going round in circles. I suffered plenty of scratches to pick enough blackberries to make jam, and then Turnip ate half the bucket while my back was turned."

Her husband grinned from ear to ear. "Maybe he thought you picked them for him." Seth rocked back on his heels.

"That dog is supposed to be guarding sheep, not thieving in the berry patch. Then I only got half the peaches picked before spotting a hornet's nest at arm's length. I had to leave the rest behind. Suddenly, everything in the garden has ripened at once, needing to be picked and canned before it starts to rot." She wiped her sleeve across her forehead, leaving behind a smear of dirt.

"Is that all?" he asked with a mischievous grin.

"No, that's not all. My feet are so swollen it feels like I put on somebody else's shoes, and my back hurts from bending over."

Seth dropped his arm from around her shoulder to the base of her spine and rubbed in a circular motion. "Where is that imp, Phoebe? She's supposed to be helping you out here."

Hannah shook her head. "She said she was getting a drink of water half an hour ago. I haven't seen her since."

"Let's get you out of this hot sun for a while." Tugging her hand, Seth gently led her from the garden.

Inside the house, they found Phoebe sitting at the kitchen table. A glass of water sat in front of her, while her doll occupied the opposite chair. A toy cup had been provided for the doll's refreshment.

"Hi, *mamm* and *daed*," the child sang out when they entered the room.

"Are you having a tea party while your *mamm* works outside alone?" Seth asked, sounding sterner than Hannah had ever heard him.

"I'm sorry," she said, and ran to hug Hannah around the waist. Her dimpled face looked truly repentant.

"It's all right, Phoebe," Hannah said. She washed her arms and face at the sink while the child clutched her skirt.

"You help her make my big, gourmet lunch while I clean up next," Seth instructed.

"Seth Miller," Hannah said, tossing the hand towel to him. "We are having cold ham sandwiches and maybe a few spoonfuls of chow chow. That's it. There's no time to cook a big…"

He cut off her words with a finger pressed to her sun-chapped lips. "Easy now. I was joking. What happened to that great sense of humor you had when we got hitched?" Seth buzzed a kiss across her damp forehead and then took his turn washing up.

What did happen to my sense of humor? Hannah had been edgy, irritable, and emotional. Never one to cry over spilled milk or scorched oatmeal, lately she found herself crying…or fuming…over inconsequential things. The August heat and humidity weren't helping. Tonight, maybe they could try sleeping in the screened porch since the upstairs bedrooms were nearly unbearable.

Hannah fixed three sandwiches, adding a tomato slice to each, and poured cool drinks. She tried to smile pleasantly for the duration of the meal. Just because the weather and female hormones were making her cross, she had no right to take it out on—

Suddenly an idea, a possibility struck her like a thunderclap. The jar of pickled chow chow slipped from her fingers to land with a thud on the oak table.

Seth looked alarmed. "Are you all right, Hannah?"

"*Jah*, just fine. Butterfingers, is all." She wiped up the spilled vinegar with the dishrag and tried to eat her sandwich, while counting days and weeks in her mind. *Two, three…was her monthly really three weeks late?*

Hannah went over days and events as best as she could recollect, yet kept arriving at the same conclusion. Or was it merely wishful thinking? Phoebe and Seth seemed to be watching her, so Hannah ate her sandwich and drank her iced tea as normally as possible. *Could I possibly be pregnant?*

She felt different, both physically and emotionally. She felt bloated, clumsy, and painfully tender. Isn't that what happened when a woman was in a family way? Hannah speared a piece of pickled celery and marveled at the crunchy texture while she chewed. Either this was the best batch of chow chow her sister ever canned or something was different.

When Seth grabbed his hat and returned to the fields, and Phoebe carried their plates to the sink, Hannah mulled a dozen ideas in her head. What month would the baby arrive? What names would Seth like to use? Would her delivery be smooth or, because this was her first pregnancy, would she end up in bed for the final months like one of her cousins had endured?

How she wanted to run the back path to her sister's house. Having given birth to four healthy *kinner,* Julia could answer a bushel basket of questions. But she didn't dare. It was too soon, and she couldn't be sure. She would get no one's hopes up but her own. But, oh, how she hoped that she was expecting.

So she prayed.

She prayed while finishing the rest of the bean rows, and while picking zucchini and squash. And when she milked cows and fed the chickens, she prayed a little more, ignoring that her dress stuck to her back and her forehead dripped with perspiration. Finally, the sun dropped behind the western hills, bringing relief from the oppressive heat. While a chicken roasted in the oven and potatoes boiled for dinner, she enjoyed a cool sponge bath and put on a fresh dress. Phoebe busied herself with the blackberries Turnip had left, washing them and picking off the stems and leaves.

Seth returned earlier than expected from the fields and also took a quick bath. "There's a meeting tonight, Hannah," he announced while towel drying his hair. "Let's eat as soon as possible. All the men in the district are congregating at the Steiner farm."

Hannah only nodded and smiled. The fact that he was off to discuss family business without her didn't trouble her as much as it had in the past. She would heed Simon's advice to the best of her ability. After all, God rewarded those who were obedient—who listened and followed His Word.

This might be the sweet reward she had been waiting seven years for…a baby!

～

Seth hitched his fastest horse to the buggy and left right after dinner. The chicken and parsley potatoes had been quite tasty, even though Hannah had spent most of the day in the garden. She had a sunburned nose to show for her hard labor.

Iced tea and apple pie would have to wait until he returned home. Seth was eager to get to the meeting to gauge the district's sentiments. A lot of money had been raised to lease nearby available land. More money had been invested in seed corn and additional equipment. Many men like him had worked long hours planting a late corn crop after their regular chores were finished to maximize profits for the community fund.

The profits would only be there, though, if a killing frost didn't come early. Or if a late summer drought didn't shrivel the new plants to dust. Or if a plague of locusts didn't swoop down and devour every last kernel. Many things could go wrong, some that hadn't occurred to Seth while he was convincing his wife and brother that this was the answer to their prayers. Now he wasn't so sure. And that uncertainty soured his stomach, despite Hannah's delicious roast chicken.

Buggies lined both sides of the Steiner driveway. The turnout for the district meeting surpassed Seth's expectations. One of Jacob's sons unhitched his mare and led her to a round stanchion of hay, already crowded with visiting horses.

"That way," the boy said, pointing to a large barn with doors open wide to catch evening breezes. Seth heard the sound of voices raised in heated discussion long before he entered the hundred-year-old structure.

"Everyone calm down," someone commanded. Seth recognized the authoritative voice of the bishop. "We'll hear both viewpoints of the issue one at a time. We will not have a shouting match. Each side, pick a spokesman."

Seth glanced around. About thirty men were milling in two fairly equal groups. One group contained the district's younger men, while the other was a mostly white-bearded crowd. Seth recognized several friends, including those who had originally formed the corn alliance and convinced him of its merits. He also spotted his *bruder*, along with the other deacon and bishop on the other side.

Simon spotted him and tipped his hat in greeting. Seth nodded, smiled, and then joined the younger men as they were selecting a spokesman. Thank goodness they didn't ask him to plead their case. He'd said enough on the subject to last a lifetime and wished the controversy would cool down. Let those who had invested wait for the harvest without all the ongoing fuss.

His wishful thinking for a quiet compromise was not to be. Especially since the man chosen as spokesman was a well-known hothead. The young man stepped forward and talked about anticipated profits as though they were a foregone conclusion. Although he talked in a low, controlled voice, Seth saw that many of the elders disapproved of his assurance of outcome and cocky attitude.

One glance at Simon confirmed their spokesman wasn't winning any new converts. Simon looked like Curly when the goat's rope was too short to reach the tastiest grass. Some elders mumbled under their breath, while others shook their heads or pulled on beards. The younger men either defiantly crossed their arms or nervously shifted their weight from foot to foot. Most didn't like dissension in the community or alienating themselves from fathers, fathers-in-law, or other kin. Seth found himself in the latter group, despite his conviction the plan would work.

Soon the bishop called for silence, and Simon stepped forward to present the other side. It was simple, really. The Amish way of life, which had served them for years and was protected by the *Ordnung*, demanded subsistence farming. That meant growing only what the family and community needed—to store up riches in heaven without undo concern for earthly wealth. Scripture spoke directly on the matter in 1 Timothy 6:6-8: "Yet true godliness with contentment is itself great wealth. After all, we brought nothing with us when we came into the world, and we can't take anything with us when we leave it. So if we have enough food and clothing, let us be content."

The white-bearded men nodded in agreement.

As Seth saw it, the two groups differed only in defining the needs of the community. A depleted medical fund wouldn't meet future expenses. With Julia's surgeries practically unavoidable, the need was real. Yet he also saw that the corn alliance was a gamble, and that couldn't easily be rationalized. Glancing around the room, reading the faces and postures of men he'd known his whole life, Seth realized few men saw both sides. And that didn't bode well for restoring peace and harmony in the district.

The bishop raised his hand for silence. Soon the grumbling ceased and the men waited for his decision. "What's done is done," he said, in a clear voice. "The land has been leased. The crops have been planted. We shall pray for a bountiful harvest." He looked at his fellow elders to emphasize the appeal for unity. "We shall pitch in if someone needs help with harvest or comes up short with livestock feed or other necessities. If the profits are what you say they will be," he nodded at the younger spokesman, "then the community fund will be restored and whole district will benefit."

A noise from overhead drew everyone's attention. The bishop's gaze drifted upward where swallows flitted between the rafters. "But this will be the last of it...this speculation." He refocused on the men before him. "As I understand it, the leases were for one year. Next spring they'll be no alliance of corn growers with their get-rich-quick schemes." As the bishop spoke, some men nodded sagely, while the hotheads stood like statues in the town square. "Each farmer of this district will plant a variety of crops to carry us through good times and bad, like the *Ordnung* instructs."

For a moment silence filled the barn as dust motes danced in the last rays of the setting sun. Then murmuring resumed as the men either agreed with the decision or expressed some final grouse on the subject.

Simon was busy talking to the other deacon, so Seth slipped

outside to the cooler evening air. At least the topic had been laid to rest. God held their future in His hands, and Seth would patiently wait for the outcome.

Warm apple pie, crowned with a scoop of vanilla ice cream, and a tall glass of iced tea beckoned. He couldn't wait to get back to his wife...and his long overdue dessert. He concentrated on those two things on the way home, putting all thoughts of corn aside.

The kerosene lamp burned low on the kitchen table when he arrived, casting dancing shadows on the walls. The counters had been cleared and wiped down with lemon water, the faint scent still lingering in the air. A jelly jar of larkspur, picked by Phoebe, graced the center of the table. "Hannah," he called in the empty room. "Phoebe?"

His wife, wrapped in a robe over her nightgown appeared in the doorway. "She's long asleep, Seth. Let's not wake her."

The realization that something was wrong hit him like a slap of cold water. Hannah's eyes were red and swollen, her face pale and wan. She appeared somehow diminished, as though she'd shrunk a full size during the meeting.

"What's wrong, Hannah?" he asked. Fear snaked up his spine as his gut tightened into a knot. "What has happened?"

"Oh, Seth," she cried and ran to him. Burying her face in his shirt, she fisted her hands against his chest.

All thoughts of pie vanished in an instant.

He waited several long moments while she sobbed in his arms. When he could no longer stand the suspense, he gently lifted her chin to peer into her dark green eyes. "Tell me, *fraa*." He took a hanky from his pocket and pressed it into her hand.

She sniffed and dabbed her nose. "I was so happy, so hopeful. I thought I...we were expecting a *boppli*. Then tonight I got my monthly. Oh, Seth," she wailed. "I'm not pregnant." She dissolved into a sea of misery. "It's not to be. It's never to be."

～

Simon was sitting at the table when Emma and Matthew returned home. A mug of warm milk sat before him, cooling. "About time," he said when they entered the kitchen.

"Sorry, Pa," Matthew said. "Long way home on the back roads."

"How's *mamm*?" asked Emma, simultaneously.

"I know where Mount Hope is, son. Go to bed. You need your rest." To Emma, he said, "You can ask her that yourself tomorrow. It's been a long day. I'm going to bed."

"*Gut nacht,*" she said. Her father looked as old as *Dawdi* Eli. Deep creases and dark shadows ringed his eyes. He shuffled his feet across the linoleum floor. The joy of seeing James tonight, the thrill of discovering he wanted to be her beau diminished with the reminder that her dear mother was sick.

A wave of guilt followed her up the stairs to her room. When she kneeled beside the bed, she prayed for her parents, not for a future with a blue-eyed man with strong hands. *Mamm* and *daed* seemed to have aged so much during the past year.

Emma lay awake tossing and turning for a long while. Twice she woke Leah with her thrashing. The girl pulled the top sheet over her head without hiding her annoyance. When Emma finally did sleep, the sound of James' laughter and memory of his gentle touch haunted her dreams until dawn.

At breakfast, Leah was in a better mood than the previous night. "How did you like the horse pull?" she asked. Her face glowed with good health as she heated the frying pan for an omelet. Chopped peppers and ham were ready to be added to the eggs.

"Good," Emma said, not admitting she'd paid little attention to the huge horses pulling weighted sleighs. Men got excited over the dullest things while her mind had been elsewhere. "How is *mamm*?" she asked, glancing toward the steps.

"*Ach*, don't worry," Leah said. "She'll be asleep for a while. They gave her shots in both knees with a long needle and stronger pain pills." Leah flipped the omelet with skill. "But the news isn't good.

The X-rays showed more deterioration of her knees and feet. If the steroid injections don't work and the pills don't bring relief, they'll have to operate."

"Oh, my," Emma murmured. "Poor *mamm*." She hung her head, focusing on making toast so her sister wouldn't see her shame. *What am I doing? Falling in love with an* Englischer? *Only heartbreak for my family will come from that.* Yet she seemed helpless to stop. Maybe it was a good thing he would leave soon for college. No point upsetting her parents over a silly summer infatuation.

When Simon and the boys trooped in for breakfast, a glaze of sweat already dampened their faces. "It'll be another hot one today," Simon announced. But other than his weather prediction, the meal was short and silent. Even Matthew didn't chatter endlessly about the horse pull or share news from his schoolmates. The boy kept glancing at her, as though waiting for some kind of announcement.

When Leah volunteered to do the dishes by herself, Emma gratefully headed to the henhouse. She much preferred cleaning roosts and sweeping floors than answering unexpected questions. Emma completed her chores that day as though sleepwalking. Her small flock was thriving—growing rapidly and gaining weight. She'd lost no lambs to illness or predators. Her weaving skills had vastly improved—no longer did she produce the loose, puckered cloth she had first created. She had plenty of wool to spin into yarn, a task that calmed her mind and filled her with a sense of purpose.

Except for today.

None of her domestic activities took her mind off James Davis and what their future might hold. Could she one day become his wife—watching television, riding to town in his big truck, maybe even buying a microwave oven? What could a person do with one of those they couldn't do in a regular oven?

When nothing brought peace of mind, Emma slung a burlap bag over her shoulder and headed for the woodland path. In the quiet forest she hoped to find more than fresh grapevines to cut. She sought to calm her troubled spirit. While blackbirds squawked and sparrows twittered, Emma pulled out her clippers and attacked low-hanging vines. When her bag was full, she turned her face skyward and closed her eyes. Rays of sunlight reached down to warm her skin, filling her with the serenity that had long eluded her. In the forest clearing, she felt God's presence and prayed for guidance and forgiveness.

Renewed, Emma picked up her bag brimming with vines and marched home, humming a favorite song along the way. But her serenade came to an abrupt stop once she reached the high pasture. A shiny green truck pulling a livestock trailer was parked in their driveway, and James was just getting out of the driver's side.

With a shiver of fear, Emma picked up her skirt and started to run.

Matthew arrived first to greet their guest. As she was hopping a log, the two young men were shaking hands. Then they walked to the back of the trailer and opened the door. Emma shimmied between the fence rails, knocking off her *kapp* along the way. When she stopped to fix her head covering, she watched the tableau unfold in the yard below. And her heart rose into her throat.

A sleek brown-and-white Appaloosa marched down the ramp—the same one she'd admired the night before. From where she stood, she saw the horse raise its head regally and toss its mane. "Oh, no, what have I done?" she muttered and ran the rest of the way without stopping.

"James!" she huffed upon reaching her brother's side.

"Hi, Emma," James said, tightening up on the horse's reins. "What do you think of her? Isn't she a beauty? Not too big, yet strong enough to pull a pony cart up the highest hill in the county." He smoothed a hand down the Appaloosa's well-groomed coat.

Emma stared wide eyed and out of breath, but her *bruder* was almost jumping up and down. "I've never seen a filly so spirited that doesn't balk on short lead," Matthew said. His face reflected his appreciation of superior horseflesh.

Emma cleared her throat. "What a nice purchase you've made. I hope you won a good price at auction. Thank you for stopping by to show her off." She sounded primmer than her former schoolteacher, Miss Stoddard.

James tucked his cap into a back pocket. "Stopping by?" he asked, laughing. "No, Emma. This filly is for your pony cart. So old Belle can live out her days munching clover instead of taking you to town. Do you like her? I know Matt can train her with the cart. She's smart as a whip; I can tell that already." He looked as joyous as a person possibly could.

Emma was struck speechless. She dropped her sack of grapevines to the ground. "You bought this Appaloosa pony for me? Why would you do such a thing?"

"*Jah*, why would you do such a thing?" Simon Miller asked over her shoulder. His voice sounded cold enough to freeze the pond on a warm summer day.

"Well, Miss Emma can use a new pony, and they had this fine one for sale in Mount Hope yesterday." James looked confident and determined.

Simon stepped around his daughter. "If my girl's pony needs replacing, her family will buy another. You've got no business buying such an expensive gift. What do you mean by this nonsense?"

James ran a hand through his hair and then handed the reins of the prancing filly to Matthew. "I mean to say, Mr. Miller, with all due respect, that I'm in love with your daughter. This gift is a token of my serious intention to marry Emma once I'm done with college."

Julia gasped as loudly as Emma did. She didn't know her *mamm* had come from the house.

Simon turned to face Emma. "Did you know anything about this, young lady?"

"No, I didn't. But I do like the horse, and I could certainly use her."

Simon held up his hand. "Enough," he boomed. "This is a most inappropriate gift, and you'll not accept it." His complexion was drained of all color.

"*Daed*, it's my *Rumschpringe*," Emma said boldly. "And I like James very much." She couldn't say the word "love" in front of her family. She didn't even possess the courage to say the word to James when they were alone.

"*Rumschpringe* or not, you will not take this expensive horse from an *Englischer*. Go in the house now, Emma." Simon wasn't discussing the subject anymore.

Emma stepped backward to stand by her *mamm*, but she didn't go inside. She couldn't leave James alone to deal with her father's wrath.

"Mr. Miller, if you'd just hear me out, sir," James said.

"No, there's nothing you could say to make me change my mind. I'll thank you to put that fancy horse back into your trailer and be on your way. Hopefully, you can get your money back from the seller, but that's not my concern. You had no business buying it without checking with me first." Simon's grip tightened on his suspenders.

James crossed his arms over his chest, but he didn't move. No one said a word for several painfully long moments. Then Matthew broke the tense silence. "Here you go, James." He handed the reins back and pulled on the horse's halter. "I'll help you load her into the trailer."

James looked like he might continue to argue, but he decided against it when he met Emma's gaze. "Thanks, Matt," he mumbled and started to push the horse's backside up the ramp.

A flush crept up Emma's neck and her lower lip began to tremble. "Thank you anyway," she managed to say as tears streamed down her cheeks.

Simon faced her with fury. "I told you to go in the house. Now go."

Julia tugged on the sleeve of her dress. Emma couldn't take another minute of her domineering father. She turned on her heel and ran for the house. Only from the kitchen window did she watch James and Matthew coax the Appaloosa into the trailer and secure the gate behind it.

While her *mamm* resembled a startled rabbit and her *daed* a stubborn bull, James paused to say something else to her parents. Leah crept up behind Emma and slipped an arm around her waist. The two sisters viewed the final scene play out in silent, abstract motion. James talked with his hands out and palms up. He appeared to be pleading to be given a chance to prove himself. Matthew stood somberly on the sidelines, looking back and forth between the three.

Emma and Leah didn't need to hear the conversation to understand what was going on. Simon shifted his weight from foot to foot and then straightened his spine. He shook his head back and forth the same way Belle liked to do. Julia dropped her chin almost to her chest as she rubbed the backs of her knuckles.

James looked at each Miller once more, and then he nodded his head and climbed into his truck. The vehicle, pulling the trailer with the best present Emma had ever been given, turned around in the gravel and drove down the lane. Soon the blinking taillights disappeared around the bend in the road.

Leah stared at her as Emma felt the heat of anger replace her sadness. She was mad at *daed* and *mamm*. This was her *Rumschpringe*. They had no right to deny her this. She loved James and he loved her. She needed some rightful space before making up her mind about the rest of her life.

She hugged her sister tightly and then fled up the steps to her room. She was too angry to face her parents right now and too afraid she would say something she could never take back.

TWELVE

Julia didn't sleep well that night, and for a change it had nothing to do with arthritis. She was between a rock and a hard place as a mother. She knew very well what happened if you pushed a teenager too far—whether Amish or English. Emma would only rebel all the more.

Yet as a wife, she couldn't go against Simon's decision. He wanted what every Amish father wanted for his daughter—a loving, stable home in which to raise a family. He saw James Davis of Charm as an evil force that could ruin everything for his little girl. Simon might be a church deacon, but he couldn't remember being sixteen years old.

Julia had her own fears about the situation. She knew Emma needed some freedom, but also suspected Emma wouldn't want to leave her faith or the lifestyle she'd been raised in. But what if she compromised her reputation with this *Englischer* and no Amish man would take her for his wife? Once gone, a girl's good name could never be restored. This was a nightmare, but tossing and turning wouldn't help. Julia rose, swallowed her pills with a sip of water and went downstairs.

Simon hadn't left for his morning chores yet. He'd brewed a pot of coffee and a mug sat steaming before him. "*Ach*, Julia, up already?

You should lie back down and give the medicine a chance to work." He looked as bad as she felt.

She wasn't the only one unable to sleep last night. "No, Simon, we need to talk before the *kinner* get up."

Surprisingly, he nodded in agreement. "I lost my temper...again," he said, pouring her a cup of coffee.

"Who could blame you?" she asked. "But we must figure something out before Emma gets up. How we deal with this is very important. We mustn't drive her away." Julia sipped her coffee for fortification.

Simon's eyes were bloodshot and heavy lidded. "What do you suggest?"

"Give me a minute to think," she said, grasping his hand and closing her eyes. Suddenly, a thought, an insight, popped into her head—God speaking to her through intuition. When she opened her eyes, she smiled brightly. "I've got an idea. Hear me out and tell me what you think."

Later, when Emma came downstairs wearing a faded dress and a determined frown, her parents greeted her with renewed assurance.

"Guder mariye," Julia said.

"Good morning," Emma answered in English. "Oatmeal today for breakfast?"

"Sit for a minute. We need to talk." Julia nodded toward the other chair.

Emma sat, but she lifted her chin defiantly. "I heard everything you said yesterday. You made yourself quite clear."

Julia wouldn't let her face reveal her shock over Emma's tone of voice. "Calm yourself, young lady. Your father and I have discussed the matter, and you may court James if that's what you want. But you mustn't allow any undue familiarity between you two. Once lost, a girl's virtue cannot be restored. You might change your mind about young Davis and wish to court Amish fellows, but they'll have nothing to do with you if they feel you have disgraced yourself."

Julia allowed time for this to sink in. The battery wall clock ticked steadily while Emma pondered their decision. Squirrels noisily raided the bird feeder outside the window.

Emma blushed profusely. "And the gift? What about my new horse?" she asked.

Julia glanced at Simon. With his nod, she said, "If James still chooses, he may bring the horse back and you may accept it. But..." she placed unmistakable emphasis on the word, "...for now it's not a gift. If you want it so badly, you must pay him every month from your wool sales until it's paid in full. If you part company down the road, the animal will not become an embarrassment. The horse will be yours once the debt is paid off. And should this courtship eventually lead to marriage?"

Simon's face sagged with sorrow as Julia drew in a breath. "In that case, the money you've paid to James simply has gone to your future husband." Julia released a sigh and waited.

Emma focused on the wall. Then her demeanor brightened by measurable degrees until a smile blossomed on her young face. "*Danki, mamm* and *dead.*" She jumped up from her chair and hugged Julia tightly around the neck.

Julia didn't protest even when her back contracted sorely. Seeing a bridge reconnect them to their girl was worth the pain.

"May I send James a letter to tell him about your change of heart?" Her question had been directed to Simon.

He appeared to steel himself, as though waiting for a tooth to be pulled. "*Jah*, you may write to him, but sit back down, daughter. Your *mamm* isn't finished yet."

Emma obeyed, glancing from one to the other.

"We've made this decision because it's your *Rumschpringe* and we shouldn't force your choices, but you must think long and hard about the repercussions if you court this boy for very long. If the English world loses its appeal, you might not find a good man and a happy home in the world you left behind. Be very careful, Emma. Do nothing you'll regret should you wish to marry within your community." Julia exhaled and then reached for Simon. He clasped her hand wearing a sour-lemon expression.

Emma didn't jump up and down with the new conditions. Some of her earlier enthusiasm faded. "All right," she whispered. "I will not dishonor myself...or you." She bravely looked them in the eye. "But I cannot imagine wanting to marry any other man than James."

"And leave the Amish faith?" Julia asked. "You might not be shunned since you haven't joined the church yet, but you couldn't remain part of the family like you are now."

"The English world—that is what you want?" Simon couldn't hold his tongue any longer. "We have raised you to seek a simple lifestyle as the surest path to the kingdom of heaven. And you're anxious to toss away salvation just to wear fancy clothes and paint your face?"

Emma's eyes welled with tears. "I'll never turn from God. James would never want me to do that."

"*Ach!*" was Simon's final comment on the topic. He struggled to his feet and stomped out to his chores.

A large teardrop fell to the oak surface of the table. "Jesus loves more than just Plain people," Emma whispered.

Julia couldn't argue with that even if she wanted to; the fight had gone out of her. "*Jah*, that is true. Go write your letter. Do it now and get it out of the way. I'll manage breakfast with Leah whenever she gets up. Where is that girl, anyway?"

"I'll send her down." Emma rose and walked to the steps, trying to hold her head high.

Emma found the girl hiding, eavesdropping in the stairwell. Leah looked like a twister had just picked up their house and carried it across the street. Emma had never seen that expression on her sister before.

~

Seth walked between the rows of corn a happy man. Shiny green stalks held plenty of firm well-tasseled ears. The early harvest would be a good one. Enough rain showers and abundant sunshine had produced a bumper crop in the first acres planted.

And the late-planted field would mature in the waning days of summer. Turnip stayed close to his heels as they wandered through the long rows of corn. Overhead, fluffy puffs of clouds danced across a perfect azure sky. Grasshoppers jumped before each fall of his work boots, tormenting the dog with their quick movements. Days like today made Seth grateful to be a farmer—working the land allowed him to be close to nature and near the family he loved so much.

When he finally reached the end of the row, he looked out over the second cornfield where he usually grew alfalfa hay. This larger crop still had a ways to go, but he felt confident it would produce a record harvest too.

During his trek back to the barn, he contemplated what he might buy with his portion of the profits—shoes for Hannah and Phoebe, boots for himself, maybe a new cook skillet since he'd overheard Hannah complaining that food stuck and scorched in hers. Maybe they would even take a trip to Lancaster County to visit *Mammi* and *Dawdi* Kline. There would be plenty of cash to build the community medical fund and still allow a few expenditures.

Seth hummed a tune while he cleaned out horse stalls and refilled hay stanchions and water troughs. Even unloading the wagon of barn waste onto the compost pile failed to dampen his high spirits. He rode his mare bareback to the pond for a quick dip and then went searching for his wife.

"Hannah, where are you, *fraa*?" he called once inside the house.

"I'm here, Seth." Hannah emerged from the cellar doorway, carrying a jar of pickles. Her apron was filled with root vegetables. "What's going on? Dinner is hours away. I've barely started my beef barley soup." She set the jar on the counter and dumped the vegetables into the sink.

She looked so beautiful today, standing with her arms akimbo.

Had she gained some weight? A little extra meat on her bones would be a welcome addition, softening her angles with roundness.

"Get your cape and find Phoebe," he announced on impulse. "We're going to Mount Eaton for the afternoon." He lifted Hannah off her feet and spun her around.

"Whatever for? Put me down, Seth Miller, before someone gets hurt." She sounded only half peeved.

"Now me, *daed*," Phoebe cried from across the kitchen. She ran to him for her turn.

Seth set Hannah down and picked up his daughter, swinging her in a wide circle.

"Why are we going to Mount Eaton?" Hannah asked.

"To get an ice-cream cone," he said. "I heard they have the best!" He put the child down and then instructed, "Go wash your hands and face." Phoebe scampered off without being told twice.

"Their ice-cream is no better than ours in Winesburg," said Hannah with one hand perched on her a hip. "What are you up to?"

"I thought we'd ride up to the grain elevator and check the current prices. The first of our corn is ready to pick. And I've never seen so many plump ears. It looks like it'll be a good harvest." Seth couldn't control his excitement. "Forget about your pot of beef soup for today. We'll treat Phoebe to pizza in town."

Hannah grinned, deepening her dimples. "Oh, my. You are in a good mood." She put the pickles in the cupboard and loaded the vegetables into a bowl. "Give me a chance to change my dress." She hurried toward the stairs, calling, "Don't leave without me, you two. I'll be ready in two shakes of a lamb's tail." The excitement appeared to be catching.

Soon the Miller family was headed north on Route 186. They waved at neighbors, both familiar and not, and at every passing buggy. Tourist cars graciously gave them a wide arc while Phoebe and Hannah sang songs along the way. Seth admired acres upon acres of ripening corn everywhere.

Once in Mount Eaton, Phoebe hopped down from the buggy with Hannah in close pursuit. "We're heading to the ice-cream parlor," she called. "We'll meet you there."

Grain elevators seldom held interest for females, so Seth nodded in agreement. "I won't be long." He parked the buggy beside two others, tying the horse's reins to the rail.

Crossing the parking lot, he saw that two of his friends in the corn alliance had also come to the grain elevator. Both agreed with Seth's assessment of a wonderful harvest with big profits. They talked and joked and slapped each other on the back for thirty minutes. The price of corn listed on the chalkboard only heightened their exhilaration.

When Seth finally rejoined his girls, their ice-cream cones were long gone. Hannah and Phoebe browsed hand in hand among the bulk foods and handmade gifts. "How were the cones?" Seth asked.

"*Wunderbaar*," Phoebe answered, "*Mamm* had chocolate, and I had strawberry." Traces of pink still ringed her lips.

"Sniff this," Hannah instructed, holding a candle beneath his nostrils. "It's peach-mango. Isn't that the prettiest thing you've ever smelled?" She shifted the jar back to her own nose and inhaled deeply.

The fragrance wasn't much to Seth's tastes, but he nodded politely. "Let's buy that for you. Just think how sweet it'll smell up the kitchen once you're done boiling cabbage."

She giggled but placed it back on the shelf. "Don't be silly. They want twenty-five dollars for that candle." She clucked her tongue in disapproval.

"One indulgence per year won't hurt you or our wallet." He grabbed the candle and headed for the checkout counter. Hannah and Phoebe trailed after him exchanging shocked looks along the way.

It was an expensive extravagance, but he could afford twenty-five dollars to please his hardworking wife. They bought the candle and some bulk items and then started for home, stopping for a pizza supper in Winesburg. Even that bread-and-tomato pie tasted better than usual.

When he went out to chores that evening, Seth Miller was a content man. He had much to be thankful for, and that night, he didn't wait until bedtime to send up his prayers of thanksgiving.

~

Late September

A huge flock of birds settled in the harvested cornfield, scavenging the kernels left behind. Emma watched them in the thin light of dawn from her bedroom window. They squabbled and fussed while feeding and then rose into the air like a dark cloud. This was just the beginning of the fall migration from Canada as flocks paused briefly in the fertile farmland of central Ohio.

But Emma had better things to do than watch birds.

Today was her first real date with James since her parents had agreed to let them court. He usually stopped on his way to or from someplace to sip iced tea on the front porch or push her in the swing that hung from the tree.

But *mamm* always hovered nearby, either darning socks with her bad hands or reading a book. The one time they walked down to the creek and back, Leah had been forced to tag along. Her parents had meant every word of "you shall not compromise your reputation with this *Englischer*." But at least they were able to see each other.

James was taking her to the Swiss Cheese Festival with Sarah Hostetler and Sam Yoder—just the four of them, no hawkeyed parents watching their every move. It was all Emma could think about as she bathed, dressed, and helped Leah cook breakfast. She decided to eat later because anticipation had turned her stomach upside down.

"Remember, there will be plenty of Plain people in Sugar Creek to observe any improper behavior," Julia had warned at least three times.

Simon grunted and huffed while he ate his fried eggs. He said, "Make sure you're back by ten o'clock. No excuses." That particular phrase had been repeated more than once too.

Emma selected her favorite dress, a beautiful shade of deep rose, and applied her lip gloss and cheek blusher using a hand mirror. Leah watched her curiously while sitting on their bed. "I can't believe you're courting an *Englischer*," Leah said. "Nothing good can come from that." She flicked a piece of lint off her skirt.

Emma turned to meet her gaze. "That sounds like something *daed* would say."

"*Jah*, that's where I heard it," Leah admitted, blushing.

"James is a wonderful man. You would like him, I'm sure."

"But if you turn English, we'll never get to see each other," Leah wailed. "You're the only sister I've got! I would miss you so much."

Emma sat down on the bed and slipped an arm around her sister's shoulders. "Who says I'm turning English? I haven't decided anything like that."

"You will if you marry him. English boys never turn Amish. It's always the other way around." Leah pulled from Emma's embrace and ran from the room, her face pinched and teary.

With a sigh Emma finished getting ready and hurried downstairs. She ate a bowl of oatmeal to prevent getting carsick and was waiting on the porch when James pulled up the driveway and jumped out. "Hi, Emma," he called.

He was wearing dark blue jeans, a navy-and-white plaid shirt, and cowboy boots. His damp hair had been combed straight back from his face, accentuating his strong jawline and high, suntanned cheekbones. Emma thought him the handsomest man alive.

"Should I speak to your parents before we go?" he asked upon meeting her halfway down the pebble walkway.

"No, I've already said goodbye for both of us. Let's get going. I have to be home by ten." Emma hurried down the path, not mentioning how unhappy her folks were over the trip to Sugar Creek.

James pulled open her door. "Your carriage awaits, Cinderella."

"I beg your pardon?" she asked, climbing into the truck. She had heard of the book character but couldn't remember much of the story.

"Never mind. It's good to see you, and you look extra pretty today." James leaned over to tug a *kapp* string.

"Hello," she said to Sam, who was sitting in the backseat. "And you, keep your distance," she directed at James. "I'm sure *mamm* is watching from the window. I'm surprised she didn't want to ride to the Hostetlers with us and then walk back home." As soon as she uttered the spiteful words, Emma regretted them. She hung her head. "I have no idea why I said such a mean thing. My mother's only worried 'bout me, that's all." She glanced into the side view mirror as her farm faded from view.

"I know you love your family, Emma. What you said is already forgotten. You're just a little nervous. I am too."

She breathed deeply to regain her composure. How did James manage to stay so calm? He surely didn't seem nervous. But soon Sarah had climbed into the truck and they were on their way to the most enjoyable day of Emma's life.

They reached the quaint town nicknamed "Little Switzerland" in less than thirty minutes. The main streets had been closed to traffic. Everywhere, people were standing around and talking. They appeared to be waiting for something. Emma couldn't wait to join the throng. Booths had been set up that showcased more varieties of cheese than she thought existed. Girls dressed in Swiss costumes passed out free samples, while children in pigtails and old-fashioned outfits sang in street corner choirs.

An elderly gentleman, looking very distinguished, welcomed them and handed Emma a brochure of the day's events. James found a great spot to watch the grand parade, and soon people of all ages marched past singing and dancing and nodding like old friends. Emma imagined this is what a European village must look like, perhaps in Bavaria. Pretty young women, who were competing for the Festival Queen title, strolled by smiling and waving to the crowd.

"Do you want to listen to yodelers in the pavilion?" James asked when the parade concluded. "Later, there'll be square dancing and polka bands."

"What is a polka band?" she asked quietly, so Sam and Sarah wouldn't overhear.

"It's a type of music with an accordion player that people dance the polka to."

Emma thought better than to question this further. "You do know that Plain people don't dance," she said instead.

"Yeah, I know," he said close to her ear. The gesture tickled her already heightened senses. "If you'd rather, we could watch the Swiss cheese judging or find the midway where they have amusement rides."

Emma smelled the fried donuts, heard the music beginning to play, and felt the joy of a thousand people surrounding her. It swelled in her bloodstream like a tonic to an anemic man. She turned toward him, their noses only inches apart. "Let's see everything, James. I want to taste every kind of food and hear every type of music. And I want to see this *Steintossen*." She pointed to a picture in the brochure of a man hurling a boulder. "Plus, I want to see which girl is crowned the Festival Queen."

James peered over her shoulder at the brochure and laughed. "That looks bizarre."

Emma clapped her hands and impetuously grabbed his arm. "Maybe so, but I don't want to miss anything!" She knew she was behaving like a child, but she couldn't help herself. For the first time, Emma knew how a horse felt when finally released from its stall to an open pasture.

James clamped his hand over hers. The warm touch of his fingers raised her heart rate into the danger zone. "All right. Let's hope Sarah and Sam can keep up with us!"

The foursome walked from booth to booth and from one exhibition hall to the next. Sam tried his hand at yodeling. James won a stuffed giraffe by knocking down milk bottles. Sarah accurately predicted which beauty would win the Miss Swiss crown. Emma bought a huge round of cheese that James carried on his shoulder for half the day. And all of them became queasy from the quantity and combination of food consumed.

When they couldn't walk another step and collapsed at a picnic table to rest, James pulled four tickets from his shirt pocket. "I've got a surprise for us. I bought these the day after Emma said she would come with me today."

"What are they?" Three voices chimed in unison.

"Train tickets. We're going to sit back and watch the world go by." He hooked his thumb at the passenger cars waiting on the tracks at the edge of downtown.

Sam and Sarah jumped eagerly to their feet, but Emma felt frightened. It was one thing to come to Sugar Creek for the festival. She'd been here with her aunt many times before. But it was quite another to get on a train and ride to parts unknown without telling her parents.

"I don't know, James. I didn't tell my folks I'd be traveling somewhere other than here," she said.

James patted her shoulder. "Not to worry. This is just a scenic tourist train. We'll go down to Baltic, turn around, and come right back. Will that be okay? If not, I'll give our tickets away and we can watch more of the fair."

Emma thought for a moment. She'd never been on a train. Since they really weren't going anywhere, she didn't see any harm. "Okay, but don't forget that I must be home by ten."

The two couples walked toward the train station and then stood in line to board. "I wouldn't forget," James said softly. "I plan on doing everything possible to get on your father's good side."

A pig has a better chance of learning to ride a bicycle.

Once the train pulled out of Sugar Creek, a strange sense of wonder settled over Emma just as it had when she had been in the canoe. Towns, houses, and farms—all quite ordinary when observed from the road—were much more interesting when viewed from the train car. She loved peeking into strangers' backyards and gardens. Even laundry hanging from clotheslines became curious discoveries. One untidy yard was a veritable junkyard of broken farm implements and tractors. Another home had an enchanted garden of gazebos, topiaries, and flower beds. Farm fields stretching to the hills rippled with a bounty of oats, corn, and hay. Soon the train rounded a bend and crossed a river on a wooden trestle bridge. When Emma peered into the deep valley below, she slid back from the window and bumped into James.

"Sorry," she murmured. "I just realized I'm not fond of heights."

"Other than heights, what do you think? How do you like traveling?" he asked, snaking an arm around the back of her seat.

Most likely, her face expressed her opinion better than words. "Oh, James, I love seeing the world like this. I'd like to ride all the way to California and see the ocean! I've never been anywhere other than Ohio and Pennsylvania."

James took her hand. She didn't pull it back. "I love you, Emma, and I want to marry you when I finish college. I hope you'll wait for me, and that you'll have me for a husband someday." His face shone with delight.

Emma glanced over her shoulder. Sarah and Sam were absorbed in their own discovery of the backcountry of Tuscarawas County. "I love you too, James. And *jah*, I'll be your wife." Her mouth went dry after speaking the words. "I've got no problem with waiting. I've still got plenty to learn," she added, remembering her younger sister was already a better cook and baker than she.

James leaned over to kiss her lightly and sweetly on the lips.

Emma slid back against the window glass. "You are so bold," she said, hoping the other two were still distracted.

"I don't mean to embarrass you, Emma. I just wish we were older, that's all."

Emma felt she might float up to the ceiling of the train car. "Me too," she whispered hoarsely. She grinned so much her face muscles started to hurt.

"You'll love living on Hollyhock Farm. You can move your flock in with mine."

She shook her head. "It isn't much of a flock."

"It will be once we join the two together and babies start to come. We won't sell off any spring lambs until we have a respectable number." His fingers interlaced through hers. "And I'll build us our own house on the property, any style you wish—low and rambling or tall and stately—four, no five bedrooms. Would you like that, Emma?"

She felt nervous energy run up her spine. "I don't rightly know. Sounds like a lot of rooms to keep clean." Maybe it was the motion of the train, along with the strange assortment of food she'd eaten, but something was churning her stomach.

James squeezed her hand. "Sorry. I'm throwing too much at you at once. We'll have plenty of time to figure things out. For right now, you just think about where to go for our honeymoon trip—maybe California to see the Pacific Ocean, or we could hop on a jet to Paris or Rome. Wherever you like."

"I'll give it some thought," she said, smiling. But truthfully, Emma was grateful when the train stopped to switch over in Baltic. They had reached their destination, and the engine at the other end would bring them back to Sugar Creek.

Emma tried concentrating on the scenery during the return trip. Thankfully, James talked about smaller topics than the rest of their lives. It was a lot to digest—too much for one afternoon. But her younger sister had been right about one thing: James automatically assumed she would turn English when they wed.

And that was another frightening thing to consider.

Yet in the back of her mind, a picture of herself in blue jeans and a sleeveless top riding in a train car to California started to grow.

THIRTEEN

"W*ho-wee*, Sarah," Sam Yoder said. "That was some kiss. I believe we've just witnessed something momentous."

James and Emma immediately pulled back to a respectable distance. "It *is* a momentous occasion," James declared. "Miss Emma Miller has agreed to be my wife." James turned around just in time to catch a startled expression on Sarah's face, but she managed to recover quickly.

"Best wishes," Sarah said, placing a hand on Emma's shoulder. "I take it we're the first to hear the good news."

"*Jah*, you are," Emma said. "And for now, I'll thank you not to tell anyone. We won't be formally announcing our engagement yet."

She sounded more frightened than James would have thought, but he reminded himself that she was only sixteen.

"Congratulations, Jamie!" Sam cried enthusiastically. "But why does this not surprise me? You've been acting strange ever since you met Emma, or at least stranger than usual. And you've been off the farm more times this summer than in the past two years put together."

Everyone laughed, but Emma's laughter sounded forced.

"Will your *daed* announce your engagement by Christmas?" Sarah asked. "Once the harvest is in and things settle down?"

Emma glanced back at her friend and then focused her attention out the window. "No, we'll wait a little longer than that."

"I've got college to finish before we get hitched," James said, starting to doubt the wisdom of telling anybody their good news. He should have allowed Emma time to adjust to the idea.

Sarah stared at James in disbelief as the train clattered into Sugar Creek. "You expect an Amish gal to wait four years for you, James Davis?" She lifted an eyebrow with a mischievous grin.

"She'll only be twenty years old, Miss Hostetler, not exactly a senior citizen." James tried his best at indignation.

"Hmm," Sarah taunted. "You better be nice to my girlfriend. I'm not sure if any fellow is worth that long a wait!"

"Hey, what about me?" Sam asked, pretending to be offended.

Sarah punched him in the arm. "Not by a long shot." General tomfoolery ensued as the train braked to a screeching stop in the station. The foursome exited the train in high spirits—all but Emma, that is.

"Why are you talking about me like I'm not here?" Emma asked, sounding peeved. "I'm standing right in front of you."

"Of course you are, sweet girl," James said, slipping his arm around her waist. "We didn't mean anything by it. We're just having fun."

Surprisingly, Emma didn't shrug off his protective arm as they walked through the station and back to where the Swiss Cheese Festival continued in full swing. People strolled on the street carrying things they had either purchased or won from one of the midway booths. Music could still be heard coming from the pavilion. The sun, about to drop behind the western hills, bathed the streets of Sugar Creek in a magical, golden glow.

"I'm hungry again," Sam announced to the utter amazement of the others. "Let's get some bratwurst sandwiches." He rubbed his stomach with a circular motion.

"Oh, my, not for me," moaned Emma, looking stricken.

"We'll wait for you over there," James said as he pointed to an out-of-the-way grove of trees. A park bench sat temporarily unoccupied.

"I'll stand in line with you," Sarah said to Sam, "but I'm not eating another thing until tomorrow." The two strolled toward the vendors.

James and Emma walked hand in hand away from the hubbub. They didn't talk, but her head on his shoulder felt better than he could have imagined. "I'm glad you promised to wait for me, Emma, because Monday I move into the dorm on campus."

"Your classes have already started?" she asked, her blue eyes flashing with alarm.

"Yeah. I've been commuting back and forth, but I'm getting behind on my homework. I promised my folks to take school seriously and study hard. So it'll probably be a few weeks before I can come home for the weekend."

Emma nodded while her smile vanished into an unreadable expression. She appeared to be giving his news serious thought. "You probably shouldn't have told Sarah and Sam our plans...considering it'll be a while before we marry."

"Sorry. I'll remind them again not to spill the beans when I drop them off. I just couldn't stop myself. You made me the happiest man on earth when you said you loved me."

She pivoted on the bench to face him. "I do love you, James, but I don't see why we have to wait so long. Four years might as well be forever."

He chuckled and then patted her hand. "You're only sixteen. You would need your parents' consent. Anyway, you're too young to get married. Heck, I'm too young and I'm already eighteen. English people wait longer to get hitched."

"But I'm not English; I'm Amish. And I don't see why you need so much schooling to be a farmer. I would think your pa would've taught you plenty by now." She stood up, straightened her *kapp*, and smoothed the wrinkles from her skirt.

"He has taught me plenty, but there's always more to learn. You've got to compete with the big agri-corporations out there, or you'll be put out of business."

She arched one delicate blond eyebrow. "Oh? I don't see many families in our district forced off their farms by foreclosure."

James bit down on the inside of his mouth. Perhaps he should sign up for a class in diplomacy at OSU instead of crop rotation, because he sure could use it right now. "Sorry, Emma, but it's different on English farms. Lots more stuff to worry about. That's why I'm going to college." He braced his boot against the tree trunk, and for a minute, became distracted by a monster truck leaving the parking lot. It made a ruckus spinning gravel as it changed gears. When he looked at Emma, she had covered her ears with both palms.

"My goodness. Hasn't that man heard of a muffler?"

James grinned as he pulled her hands from her ears and kissed the back of her fingers.

She met his gaze. Her eyes looked cool and dark, like a deep pool far beneath a waterfall. "You're going away for four years so you won't have to worry so much about things?" she asked. "Seems to me you could save yourself time and your folks a lot of money by just turning to the Good Book. And maybe asking God for a little help."

James marveled at the wisdom of someone so young without benefit of higher education. "You're right. I can't argue with that. The truth is I'm going to college to please my parents. It's something they want me to do, and I want to respect that. Anyway, I doubt I'll stay four years. Most likely I'll cram the necessary courses into two."

Emma leaned back against the bench. "All right, James. I can understand your wish to honor your parents. It's the right thing to do. So you'll understand when I need to honor mine at some point in the future." One corner of her mouth turned down sadly.

James wanted to ask what she meant by that. He yearned to reassure her that two or even four years would pass quickly. Then they could announce their engagement and start planning a wedding, but Sam and Sarah had returned from the bratwurst booth.

Sarah was picking at a cone of purple cotton candy, while Sam chomped on a sausage sandwich covered with grilled onions and peppers. "You two don't know what you're missing," he said, taking a huge bite.

James' stomach lurched from the greasy smell.

"We'd better head for home," Emma said. "We don't know how the traffic will be leaving the festival, and I don't want to be late."

The two couples walked uptown to where they had parked the truck, seemingly a long time ago. Despite the fact that everyone was tired, Sam managed to keep the conversation lively all the way to Winesburg.

Emma, quiet and subdued, stared out the window, offering only occasional *jah*'s and noes to questions. James regretted making a promise to his mom and dad, and he felt even sorrier he wasn't able to convince Emma of the wisdom in waiting until they were older.

Some cultural differences were harder to bridge than others, but he knew with absolute certainty that he loved Emma. He would overcome any obstacle in his path, and he would marry her someday.

~

Moonlight reflected off the polished truck hood while stars sparkled high above the open sunroof. James drove slowly, as he was in no great hurry to get home. The longer it took, the longer he could remember and savor each special detail about Emma. She had kissed him goodnight while Sam had been walking Sarah to her door. James had smelled the fresh scent of peaches and tasted peppermint, like candy canes at Christmas. Her soft lips returned his kiss with innocence. Every time she pronounced his name, the sound of her accent made him believe all things were possible when two people fell in love.

James drove up their road and parked in front of an almost dark house. Only one light burned in the kitchen, like at the Miller house when he'd taken Emma home. Except this light was electric, not kerosene. James toed off his boots in the mudroom and then headed for the back stairs.

"Jamie?" A soft voice called from the kitchen. "Is that you?"

Apparently, Emma wasn't the only one with a worrying mother. "Yeah, Mom, it's me." He stepped into the kitchen where Barbara sat with her Bible, Sunday school manual, and a cup of tea. She looked both tired and somehow anxious.

"You're home early; that's good. It's not even ten thirty." She peered at him over her half-moon glasses.

"I took Emma Miller to the Sugar Creek Swiss Cheese Festival. She had to be home by ten."

His mom's face dropped. "Emma the Amish girl? Oh, Jamie. She's still a child! This is not a good idea. You're eighteen now." Creases across the bridge of her nose deepened, while her eyes narrowed into a pronounced squint. With her sudden change of mood, his mom looked very old.

James felt a surge of anger but tamped it down. "We shared only one little kiss goodnight. And that's all it will be until I'm finished with school. I thought you trusted me better than that." His righteous anger echoed off the oak-paneled walls.

But his mom offered no apology. "It's not a question of trust, son. You're both young and mistakes can be made—lapses of judgment. Remember, I was young once too." Her brown eyes pleaded for understanding.

"Yeah, well, I intend to behave myself so she'll still want to marry me when we're older." He crossed his arms over his chest and leaned on the door frame.

Barbara settled back in her chair. "You have no idea what you're asking her to give up. If you care about this girl, you shouldn't ask her to leave the only life she's ever known. Encourage her to date her own kind, and you do the same."

Her own kind? He felt his face flush as his blood started to boil. "You make me sound like a chicken wanting to date a Canada goose. I assure you, Mom, she is my kind. We're both human beings!"

"I realize that, son, but for Emma to seriously court you she would have to leave her faith and everything she loves behind."

He wanted to say more. He wanted to accuse her of being controlling—first demanding college, now telling him whom to date—but he couldn't. His mom had sacrificed so much for her children and never asked for anything in return...until now.

He would go away to college. He planned to buckle down and finish his education. Tomorrow after church services, he would start packing.

But he would never give up Emma.

～

Julia rose from her bed and walked to the window, hugging her shawl together with a shiver. The wind had picked up and it had started to rain. Leaves and large drops pelted the glass as she looked out over her backyard. With difficulty, she pulled the window sash down. Earlier, when she had gone to bed, a full moon had bathed the bare fields with shadowy light. Now she peered into nothing but inky blackness.

"What are you gawking at?" Simon asked, concerned for his wife.

"Absolutely nothing, *ehemann*. A front has come in and brought the rain."

"Come back to bed then. Emma is home safe and long asleep. She kept to her curfew. Despite the fact she's courting an *Englischer*, at least we can rejoice in that."

Julia turned from the window and smiled at her husband. How unlike him to make light of something she knew troubled him greatly. "*Jah*, she's home safe and on time. Her young man is leaving for college. Perhaps their interest will wither on the vine like grapes after an early frost. But Emma is not the reason I can't sleep." Julia hated troubling him in the middle of the night, but she saw no alternative. She'd waited too long already.

"What is it, Julia?" Simon asked. He threw off the quilt and sprang up faster than she'd seen him move in years. In a moment, he was at her side by the window.

Julia began to weep, unable to keep her secret any longer. "*Ach*, Simon, the pain has become more than I can bear." With the words came a deluge of emotion. She had remained quiet about her misery for weeks, but the time had come for honesty.

Simon enfolded her, drawing her close. "My dear Julia, I had such hope for those steroid injections," he said, careful not to hug too hard.

"As did I," she whispered, laying her head on his shoulder. "They helped at first, but now the pain is worse than before." She cried harder, dampening his nightshirt with her tears.

"What about those pain relievers the doctor prescribed? Aren't they doing anything for you?" He stroked the back of her head, his fingers tangling in her hair.

"They worked at first, but not anymore," she answered in a strangled voice. "I dare not increase the dosage, since the doctor said too many or for too long could damage my kidneys or liver."

Simon released a weary sigh. "Oh, my. We must do something. We can't let you suffer like this."

She pushed against his chest. "Let's go sit down. I'm tired of pacing the floor or staring out the window at nothing. I'm glad you finally know."

Simon helped her into bed, settling her against the headboard. He cushioned her back with their pillows and then gently tucked the quilt around her legs. "You should have said something before," he chided softly.

Even his admonishment soothed her spirit. She regretted not being forthright sooner. "You've had so much on your mind with the harvest and with Emma starting to court, I didn't want to burden you."

"You are my life, besides my wife. You could never be a burden."

Julia let her tears fall freely, starting to feel better already. And she was charmed by Simon's tenderness. His years of devotion had never included such romantic declarations, but hearing them warmed her heart. She reached for the top sheet. "And I love you, husband."

"Should I talk to the Lees about another trip to the Canton specialist?"

"No, there's no reason for another office visit." Julia breathed easier as the reality of what she must do became apparent. "The doctor explained six weeks ago that if the effects of the injections wear off quickly, or the medications can't control the pain, I will need replacement surgery on both knees. There are no other options. Perhaps he'll repair the joints in my feet at the same time, or maybe he'll wait till the knees recover. But at this point, the only thing to do is schedule the operation. If you take me to Mrs. Lee's tomorrow, I'll call his office."

Simon patted her leg gently atop the covers. "I won't have you suffering. You should have told me sooner. We'll call from the Lees' as soon as the doctor's office opens."

Julia pulled up the quilt. "Get under the covers. The first chill of fall is in the air."

Simon snuggled next to his wife of many years. "*Jah*, I can feel it in my back tonight. My, aren't we becoming a pair of old crows?"

"This operation will be expensive, husband. The surgeon understands we have no insurance. He'll minimize the length of time I'm in the hospital and send me to the rehab unit as quickly as possible, but I'll have to stay there at least a week before I continue my recovery at home." She inhaled a breath that caught in her throat. "The hospital requires a thousand dollars up front and then will set up a payment plan. The surgeon will accept whatever we can afford for down payment, and he too will wait for the balance."

Simon drew her head to his chest. "This will be a long, painful road, *fraa*. Don't worry about the bill. I heard that the early corn received a good price. By the time everyone has harvested and delivered to the grain elevator, the medical fund should be bulging at the seams. We'll use it for the hospital bill and pay the doctor off on our own. That's what a rainy day account is for." He cocked his head to one side. "Listen to that downpour on the roof. Even the weather coincides with our plan."

They both laughed. What else could they do? Julia felt a weight lift from her shoulders. "I hate depleting our savings when it took so long to set that sum aside."

"It's only money. It's not as important as you are to this family...or to me." His words trailed soft and low, but Julia heard him clearly.

"Simon Miller, you are becoming passionate in middle age."

"Don't be ridiculous, Julia. Let's go to sleep. I have plenty to do in the morning before I take you to the Lees.' And you need your rest."

His tone had changed back to the familiar, but Julia smiled as she struggled to find a comfortable sleeping position.

Her Simon really was romantic after all.

～

If Emma thought things would get easier now that her folks had agreed to let her court James, she was mistaken. She felt more confused than ever. All his talk about building a fancy house on his parents' farm with five bedrooms and taking her to Paris or Rome had only distressed her. Why would they need a mansion for the two of them? And going to Europe sounded unappealing and a little scary. She had heard that people who lived there ate fish eggs, pigs' feet, and a strange cheese made from cow brains.

Oh, good grief. Just thinking about such things turned her stomach queasy. It was still rebelling after yesterday's conglomeration of greasy sausage, funnel cakes, and candied apples. The drive home in James' truck hadn't helped matters. *Did all* Englischers *drive so fast?*

She didn't need a big fancy house and didn't want to get on an airplane to fly halfway across the world. But she did want to marry James. His proposal had left her stunned, with a heart pounding so loud all Sugar Creek could have heard it.

She loved him, plain and simple. English or not, he was a gentle man who shared her goals and dreams of raising crops and animals and, if God was willing, children someday. She would be content with a cottage in the woods and a honeymoon trip to Cleveland, or maybe to one of those Lake Erie islands. *If only we didn't have to wait so long...*

"What in the world are you doing, Emma?" Leah's sharp tone startled Emma from her reverie.

"Nothing," Emma said, moving to fill the coffeepot at the sink.

"I can see that. Breakfast isn't even started?" Leah sounded a bit cross. "Couldn't you have at least put the coffee on? What was the point of getting up so early?"

Emma shot her sister a warning look. "I had things to sort out, and I couldn't think straight with you snoring so loudly in bed."

Leah laughed good-naturedly. "Was I? Sorry. My sinuses are stuffy from allergies."

Emma lit the stove burner and then dumped bacon into a frying pan. "I'm sorry that I didn't get things going down here. You're always stuck with the lion's share of the cooking."

Leah set the griddle across two burners to make pancakes. "I don't mind. The kitchen is my favorite place to be. But what was all the sorting-out about? Was it because you're seeing an *Englischer*?" She whispered the word as though afraid to speak it aloud.

Because Leah was still a child, Emma chose not to take issue with the comment. "*Jah*, there's plenty of thinking to be done once a girl starts courting."

Leah clucked her tongue the way their mother often did. "I do want you to be happy, sister, but I hope you end up with an Amish fellow so things won't change around here."

"Life keeps changing, Leah, no matter what, but you'll be happy to hear I won't be seeing much of James for a while. He's gone to the university and will stay on campus until his assignments are caught up. I'll be lucky to see him before Thanksgiving. By then, a pretty college girl will probably have caught his eye."

Leah wiped her hands on her apron and then hugged Emma. "I'm sorry to hear that. Truly I am, but I'm afraid we'll both be so busy around here, Thanksgiving will be here before you know it."

Emma stepped back from the embrace and flipped the sizzling bacon. "Why? What's going on?" she asked, expecting news of sick livestock or a wallpapering project about to begin.

Leah glanced at the doorway to make sure they were alone. "It's our *mamm*. Don't get yourself worked up, but her legs and feet are worse—much worse."

"Oh, no," Emma breathed, feeling ashamed. She had spent so much time thinking about nonsense like Paris and California that she hadn't bothered to ask how her mother was feeling. "The pain has become unbearable?" She held her breath while waiting for the answer.

"*Jah*. She can barely walk. *Daed* and Matthew will carry her downstairs when she wakes up, and she won't be going back upstairs anymore." Leah poured perfect circles of batter onto the heated griddle so that each pancake would be uniform. "Pa tried to talk her out of using those steps long ago, but you know how stubborn our mother can be." Leah again glanced across the room, but the house remained eerily silent. "She would grip those banisters and drag herself up to their bedroom. She said she couldn't bear the thought of sleeping apart from *daed*."

Emma felt the sting of tears in her eyes, but she willed herself not to cry. "What's to be?" she asked. With a shaking hand, she lifted the slices of bacon out to drain on paper towels.

"They are turning the front room into a bedroom for them. *Daed* says he'll sleep downstairs with her. She is going ahead with the operation on both knees, and maybe her feet too."

The two sisters exchanged anxious looks. These operations came with no guarantees. Their *mamm* might end up never walking again.

Emma took hold of Leah's forearm. "You won't get much help with *mamm* so bad off, so I promise to help more with the housework. Maybe Henry can tend my flock and see to my outside chores. I won't run off and leave you alone inside again."

Leah patted Emma's hand as though comforting a younger sibling and then walked off to set the breakfast table. "*Danki*, sister, but what we really need is for you to earn money—as much as possible. Make as many grapevine wreaths as that gift shop will take, plus wool scarves and shawls and throws. Winter is coming—time for stores to stock up on woolens. How many skeins of yarn do you have ready to sell?"

Emma scratched her head. "I don't rightly know, maybe a dozen or so." She didn't think Leah knew what went on in the barn loft because the dust and animal dander made her allergies worse.

"I think you should double your production. I'm going to bake pies to sell in town in my spare time. We'll need extra money for *mamm's* prescriptions. If I know her, she'll insist on paying the other bills first and not take the proper dosage of medicine."

"But Leah, you're only thirteen years old. You can't possibly do all the housework for this family."

Leah gazed at her patiently. "Who do you think has been handling it lately? *Mamm* hasn't been able to help for some time now. I will need you on laundry day, that's for sure, but the canning and herb-drying is done for the season." Leah slid the rest of the pancakes onto a platter. "When I need you, I will know where to find you, won't I? Please, Emma, just make all the money you can. I'll be fine in here." She hurried to the refrigerator for milk and juice.

"I did notice a carpet and rug manufacturer when I was riding with James. They buy bulk wool. I've got plenty of wool that's too stiff and scratchy to spin on my wheel. Nobody wants a sweater made from that next to their skin. I should never have let *daed* buy those Dorsets and Suffolks to build my flock. Merinos would've been a better choice."

Leah set the plate of bacon on the table. "A rug sounds like the perfect use for that stiff wool. It'll never wear out." She cocked her head to the side. "I think I hear them on the steps bringing her down. Why don't you go see if you can help. I've got things handled here."

Emma took a long look at her sister before heading toward the stairwell. When had the child turned into a capable and generous-hearted young woman? It must have been while Emma had been busy daydreaming about a big, fancy English wedding.

FOURTEEN

October

G et up there," Seth called to his team of draft horses. Two of the four Percherons lifted their gray heads and shook their manes side to side. Although a human would interpret the action as a negative response, they nevertheless picked up their feet and started down the long row of corn. With a final wipe of his brow, Seth settled his hat back in place and tightened the reins. Breaktime was over. The team was pulling a motorized corn harvester that picked the corn and fed it into the wagon following alongside. His nephew Matthew drove the horses pulling the wagon.

When the bishop allowed the district to switch from ground-driven harvesters to motorized, speed and efficiency greatly improved. And it was a good thing too, because he needed to get the last of the corn picked. He had waited, hoping the ears would grow larger and fill out. But the rain he'd prayed for never came. A particularly dry September with near-drought conditions yielded a crop far less than his expectations. Since October so far had been equally dry, there was no sense in waiting longer.

Sitting on the corn harvester for hours at a time gave a man opportunity to think. And the thoughts Seth dwelled on this autumn afternoon were filled with recrimination. He'd been farming long enough that he didn't need a scale to know this crop was light. A meager harvest with poorly formed ears meant a lower price. This delivery wouldn't compare with the earlier one, but he had no choice but to keep going. He still had to bundle stalks and shred into silage before a heavy frost. If cold weather hit before he filled his silos, the feed would mold and become unusable.

With great joy Seth spotted Simon and his nephew Henry along with their wagon and team of Belgians. They entered the field from the opposite end with Simon's corn harvester. Despite his *bruder*'s position against the corn alliance, he'd come over with his son and team to help. Seth sent up a prayer of thanks for his family. And he also asked for forgiveness for his stubbornness and pride. Why hadn't he listened to Simon's wise counsel? If he'd stuck to the tried-and-true Amish ways, he would be cutting hay for the last time and facing the long winter with full silos. Instead, he was playing a game of beat-the-clock—a game he was fairly certain he would lose.

When his horses needed rest, he provided feed and water and headed to the house for lunch. Hannah greeted him at the door with a warm smile and cool drink. "How goes it, Seth? How much longer?"

He entered the kitchen, fragrant with the rich smell of simmering soup. "The picking goes well, but the quality of the harvest leaves much to be desired."

Hannah murmured words of consolation as she ladled soup into three bowls. Phoebe was already at the table with spoon in hand. Her faceless doll had been propped up in the opposite chair with a toy bowl before it. "Don't forget my dolly, *mamm*," Phoebe said.

Hannah pretended to fill the small bowl with her ladle. "I saw from the window that Simon came with Henry and their team. That should speed things up."

"*Jah*, it will. I invited him for lunch but Simon won't stop yet. He brought sandwiches in a sack for when they get hungry. Matthew will be in soon." Seth tried not to convey his downheartedness. It wasn't his family's fault he had made a bad decision.

They bowed their heads in silent prayer and then Seth stared into his bowl. "There's more corn in my soup than on the ears I've been picking," he said wryly.

No one laughed at his joke. Luckily, Matthew walked in with his hair wet and plastered to his head. "Sorry I'm late, Aunt Hannah. I took a quick dip in the pond to wash off. It might be October, but that sun is still hot."

Hannah handed him a towel. "Not to worry. We're grateful for your help. How is Julia today?" She filled her nephew's bowl to the brim.

"The same, I guess." He slurped his first spoonful noisily. "She's not happy we turned our front room into a sick room. That's what she called it. She says it's disgraceful to have grown adults sleeping in a room with eight windows." The boy ate his soup faster than Hannah had ever seen done before.

Hannah and Seth exchanged amused glances. "After she gets her new knees she might be able to move back upstairs, maybe in the spring," Hannah said, refilling his bowl again.

"*Jah*, maybe, but she's making Pa close in the back porch and turn it into a bedroom. That will be his wintertime project. Leah's excited about getting her own room upstairs."

Seth took another helping too, not to be outdone by a fourteen-year-old boy. "Tell your *daed* I'll help him with the room addition. And thank him for sending you over. You're a big help, Matty."

The boy grinned with delight. "I like helping, Uncle Seth. Are you taking a wagonload to the elevator this afternoon?"

Seth nodded. "I'll be back as soon as possible. If it's all right with Simon, you can deliver the corn tomorrow."

Matthew looked ecstatic. "*Danki*, Uncle Seth. I'll check with Pa tonight. Now I'd best get back out there." He stood, carried his bowl to the sink, and headed for the door. "*Danki* for lunch, Aunt Hannah."

"You're welcome," she called. He had wolfed down two bowls while she was still eating her first.

Seth poured a cup of coffee and spent a full minute studying the dark liquid.

His preoccupation didn't escape Hannah's notice. "Something wrong, Seth? Or is something curious swimming around in your cup?" She leaned over to look.

"I'm only delaying the inevitable, *fraa*. And I won't allow anymore self-indulgence. I'm heading for Mount Eaton." Seth rose, patted his daughter's head, and kissed his wife. No peck on the cheek or buzz across the forehead—this kiss expressed his love and respect for a patient woman. Hopefully, her patience would still remain after he returned from the corn buyer. Although he certainly deserved it, he prayed he wouldn't hear "I told you so" from his cherished bride.

By the time he reached Mount Eaton with his fully loaded wagon, a flock of crows was trailing behind, ready to devour any ears that fell out. The crisp fall air heightened every sensory nerve in his body. With long sunny days and without the humidity of summer, October was his favorite month. Turkey vultures wheeled high in the wind currents, apparently not ready for southern migration. Seth settled back and enjoyed the ride with little traffic and beautiful scenery.

But his peace of mind was short lived. The grain elevator in town buzzed with activity; long rows of horse-drawn wagons waited their turn to deliver corn. Men congregated on the loading dock, talking animatedly in tight knots. No one was smiling. Seth parked around the corner and entered the building from the front. He recognized a few familiar faces from his district and walked over to join them. They were speaking in German so fast he could barely keep up. One friend pointed at the grain buyer standing in the office doorway. Another wildly gestured at the chalkboard hanging on the wall. Seth squinted his eyes to read the scribbled numbers.

His jaw dropped open when he saw the current price being paid per bushel of corn. It was bad enough his crop had been inferior to expectations, but this price was a fraction of what the alliance had counted on.

"What...how?" he croaked in a raspy voice.

Everyone began talking at once—what they had heard from other farmers, what the grain dealer had explained, and what they had read in English newspapers. A large surplus of Ohio corn, coupled with a recent drop in oil prices, had reduced interest in ethanol production and triggered a price free fall.

Seth listened to one man after another and then moved to a different group, where he only heard more of the same. His mouth went dry as he felt the burn of stomach acid working on Hannah's chicken soup. He glanced at the chalkboard once more before walking onto the loading dock, feeling lightheaded and disoriented.

He had no choice but to join the queue of wagons and deliver his low-weight corn. The price he would get made it hardly worth his investment in extra seed corn and fertilizer. And he realized his crop not only didn't produce the windfall that the community fund needed, but he had to go home and face his brother and wife with his well-deserved shame.

~

"*Mamm*, are you awake?" Emma asked. She crept into the front room, looking around as though seeing it for the first time. The sofa had been moved out to the porch and covered with plastic. The chairs remained, but they had been grouped around the bed for visitors. Julia's sewing projects had long ago been turned over to Leah, who had arranged a table under the window with her notions.

Julia's eyes fluttered open, focusing on her daughter. "*Jah*, I was just dozing. Your pa insists I take extra pills, but they only make me sleep too much."

"I can come back later if you prefer," Emma said softly from the doorway.

"Nonsense. I'd like to visit with my girl." Julia patted the side of the bed. "Sit by me. Tell me about your trip to Sugar Creek. We were happy you kept your curfew, early by twelve minutes, I believe." She smiled, looking briefly as though pain didn't cloud every day of her life.

Emma hurried in and perched on the edge of the mattress. She began talking about the yodelers, the Grand Parade, the assortment of food, and the costumed dancers. She mentioned riding the Ferris wheel, Sarah's accurate selection of the pageant winner, savoring a taste of the championship Swiss cheese, and the scenic train ride to Baltic.

Julia smiled during the narration but asked no questions and offered few comments.

Emma did not mention James' kisses or holding hands as they left the station, or how happy she felt when they were together. She also kept quiet about his grandiose plans for a big house and wedding trip. No sense causing a fuss over things unlikely to happen.

"Say little to your *daed* about this date unless he asks you, especially not the train ride," Julia cautioned. "Even though he won't stop you, he isn't happy about this courting."

Emma nodded. "They'll be no more dates for a while. James has left for college and must stay on campus to catch up with homework."

Julia patted her hand. If the news pleased her, she hid it well. "You have a long life ahead of you, Emma. Don't rush things. Since he will be busy, I'd like you to start going to Sunday singings. Don't miss the activities other Amish girls will be enjoying."

Emma had always looked forward to Sunday singings before she met James. Now, however, wouldn't the young men there think she was interested in courting? And wouldn't that make her fickle or a phony? Each passing day brought no clarity, only more confusion.

"Do this for me, Emma. I've not asked many things of you before."

When Emma looked into her *mamm's* moist brown eyes, the answer was clear. *Isn't James going off to school to please his parents? Don't I love my mother just as much?*

"*Jah*, I'll go to singings. Sarah mentioned there's one this week."

"*Danki.* Go meet new people—boys and girls. You only get one

Rumschpringe. Enjoy it. Don't look back on this period of youth with regret. Even if you choose not to follow our path, you'll at least understand exactly what you gave up."

There it was. Not in so many words, but her *mamm* acknowledged that she might someday turn English. How difficult that must be for the woman who had changed her diapers as a baby.

By the time the three-hour preaching service was over on Sunday, Emma was looking forward to the singing. Sarah's family was hosting the evening get-together, so Emma had planned to walk until Matthew insisted on taking her, even though he wouldn't be able to attend for another two years. Emma baked a batch of Apple Betty bars for the snack table—the kind James had so loved at the bonfire. She felt a bit disloyal, but unlike Leah, Emma had few special recipes up her sleeve. She knew how to bake pie, cornbread, cookies, and muffins, but a variety of treats to impress new friends was beyond her experience.

Matthew drove the pony cart pulled by Emma's new horse. She hoped her *bruder* wouldn't pester her with endless questions about James on the way, but she needn't have worried. The boy prattled on endlessly about the Appaloosa he'd been training with excellent results.

James had brought the filly back the very day he received Emma's letter explaining her parents' decision. He'd accepted her down payment, produced a bill of sale, and agreed to the payment terms all under Simon's watchful eye. Emma named the new pony Maybelle to honor her predecessor. Belle now contentedly grazed in the high pasture, preferring to sleep outdoors in mild weather rather than in her stall.

"Here you are, sister," Matthew said, bringing the pony cart to a smooth stop with only a light tug on the reins.

"*Danki.* I'll be able to get a ride home," Emma said. "Several in the district pass right by our farm."

"I could wait for you," he suggested while helping her step down.

"I could hang out with Sarah's *bruders* in the barn." He tipped his hat back and grinned.

"No, *daed* gave you no such permission. Help yourself to something from the snack table and then go on home. You're time will come soon enough."

He tied the reins to the rail and ran off, leaving Emma alone to walk to the Hostetler outbuilding. Suddenly, she felt like an outsider, as though everyone would know she might someday leave the Plain community. But soon Sarah spotted her and enveloped her with warm friendship. She introduced Emma to the people she didn't know and then sat down beside her.

At a singing, boys sat on one side of a long table and girls on the other. The young people visited and caught up with news while the songbooks were passed out.

"*Guder nachmittag*, Miss Miller."

Emma's head snapped up. She'd been studying notches carved into the walnut surface of the table.

"Hello. Joseph Kauffman, right?" she asked politely. "You live over near Berlin."

"*Jah*, that's right. Nice that you remembered me." His clean-shaven cheeks flushed to a shade of bright pink. "That is my sister, Elizabeth," he nodded to the girl sitting next to Emma. The girl smiled shyly.

Emma remembered the very bashful boy from a few weddings. Tall and thin, his jacket cuff revealed quite a bit of wrist, an indication that his poor *mamm*'s sewing probably couldn't keep pace with his growing. "Your father is the harness maker, right? My *daed* bought new harnesses from him a few weeks back."

Joseph's blush deepened to cherry red as he leaned forward and whispered, "I didn't think it right what my pa told yours, but I know he didn't mean to cause trouble." He settled back on the bench.

Emma had no idea what Joseph was talking about, but the singing was about to start, so any explanation would have to wait. Within a few minutes Emma forgot Joseph's odd apology and relaxed into the evening. They sang all her favorites in German and a couple new songs that were fun to learn. They even sang one gospel-type song in English. Many girls and boys exchanged secret looks, because singings often led to courting for many young people, but Emma refused to think about courting or entertain any romantic notions of her beau, James Davis. Whatever he was doing on the campus extension of Ohio State was sure to be far different than this.

Sarah clutched her hand tightly several times, smiling. In between songs, Emma asked her why Sam wasn't there.

"Only our district and the next one to the west were invited," she whispered. "No New Order districts." Yet that fact didn't appear to trouble her. She seemed to glow with an inner joy and contentment. It was impossible not to be uplifted in her company.

During the last few songs, Emma noticed Joseph stealing glances at her. Each time she met his eye, he blushed and glanced away. Perhaps he was fascinated by her choppy bangs, which had grown out long enough to hang in her eyes. She constantly kept tucking them under her *kapp*.

When the singing concluded, everyone milled around the snack table, helping themselves to desserts and cups of cold cider. With a jolt of horror, Emma noticed not one of her Apple Betty bars had been taken from the plate. A woman's worst nightmare—to go home with your food contribution untouched! Taking one for her plate would only draw attention to her embarrassment.

Then Joseph and his sister walked up to the table. He selected one chocolate chip cookie and two Apple Betty bars, while Elizabeth did the same. Emma felt her back muscles relax while she fixed a small plate of cut-up vegetables and Rice Krispies squares. She glanced around for Sarah but saw no familiar faces in the crowd.

"Miss Miller, would you like to sit with us?" Joseph asked from over her shoulder. "We saved some hay bales outside with our coats. It's nice out tonight."

Emma craned her neck to scan the crowd, but she still saw no

Sarah. "*Jah* sure, *danki*." She followed them out of the barn and shared a hay bale with his sister.

Elizabeth Kauffman was also tall and thin with a lovely smile and dark brown eyes. Both siblings had silky, shiny black hair. Most of Elizabeth's was hidden beneath her *kapp*, but it definitely was Joseph's best feature.

For several minutes the three sat quietly eating their snacks and enjoying the nighttime serenade of owls, crickets, and tree frogs.

"I love those sounds," Emma said when she had finished the snack on her plate.

"Very soon the world will become silent again. The first frost is coming," said Elizabeth with sadness edging her words.

"Good. I'll be able to get a good night's sleep without all that racket," said Joseph, not sharing their sentiments. "Say, did you make these, Miss Miller?" He bit into his second dessert bar.

"Why do you ask?" Emma returned the query. "Did you break a tooth?"

He laughed and then shook his head. "No, I think they're the best I've ever tasted."

Emma snickered. "They're okay if you have plenty of cider to wash them down. I think they're a little dry." She tipped up her cup and drained the contents.

"I'll get us both refills." Elizabeth sprang to her feet and grabbed Emma's cup without hesitation.

Once the girl disappeared into the barn, Emma asked the question that had been bothering her. "What were you saying about your pa not meaning to cause trouble?"

Joseph studied her and seemed to choose his words carefully. "He told your father that you had an English friend—one who wasn't female."

The night chorus crept in around them as though even the creatures waited for her reaction. "I see. That's how my *daed* found out about James. He's another sheep farmer from Charm." She tried to remember the conversation with her father that night to no avail.

"This is your *Rumschpringe*, Miss Miller, same as it's mine. You've got a right to make new friends, even if they're English." He set his empty plate on the ground. "How will you ever know what you want if you don't know what's out there?"

Emma nodded in agreement, but she doubted her folks saw things the same way.

Elizabeth was headed back from the barn with two brimming cups of cider. Joseph spoke in a low voice only Emma could hear. "I hope we can be friends, Miss Miller. It would be nice to talk to a gal that ain't my sister." His earnest brown eyes met her gaze.

Emma noticed that his olive skin was sallow and his long limbs seemed out of proportion. But there was something endearing about his bashfulness, as though he would be incapable of deception. "All right, Joseph. I don't have many friends either. And a person can always use one more."

His grin made his thin face seem a bit fuller. She offered a tiny smile too and then said, "So I guess you should start calling me Emma."

～

That night Emma knelt by her bed for prayers, but then she decided to read some Scripture before sleep. Lighting a candle, she flipped through her *mamm*'s worn Bible. Her eyes settled on Proverbs 10:23-24: "Doing wrong is fun for a fool, but living wisely brings pleasure to the sensible. The fears of the wicked will be fulfilled; the hopes of the godly will be granted."

She wondered which category God would put her in.

～

Leah certainly had been right about one thing. The weeks before *mamm*'s surgery were so busy, Emma had no time to pine over James or wonder what he was doing on campus.

Julia was no longer able to get out of bed on her own. She had to be helped to the bathroom or to the kitchen table at mealtimes.

She hated being an invalid, by her description, and would only allow someone to carry her to the kitchen for supper. Breakfast and lunch she ate from a tray while propped up in bed.

Leah did all the cooking, baking, ironing, and sewing—the latter two tasks could be accomplished in the sunny front room with Julia for company.

Emma oversaw her flock, fed the chickens and gathered eggs, helped Leah with cleaning and laundry, and spent every other available minute spinning, weaving, grinding dried flowers for dye packets, and assembling grapevine wreaths. Mrs. Dunn had given her a large order for the coming holiday season. Emma would have to rise earlier and sleep less if she had any hope of filling it, but that was fine with her because more work meant less time dreaming of a blue-eyed *Englischer* who had proposed and then not written to her in two weeks.

Despite her pain, Julia always mustered a patient smile for either daughter, who often came for domestic advice. Emma usually carried in the lunch tray, bringing her own along to eat with *mamm* because her chores often kept her outdoors. During their shared lunchtime, Julia never asked questions about courting, and Emma mentioned only that she had enjoyed the singing and making new friends. Both seemed grateful for the peaceful truce.

Today, though, the Miller world would once again be turned upside down—the day of Julia's surgery. Mr. and Mrs. Lee, their English neighbors, arrived before dawn to drive Julia and Simon to the Canton hospital. Julia wouldn't permit any of her *kinner* to "waste the day sitting around a waiting room," as she put it. She ordered Leah, Matthew, and Henry to school as usual, and left Emma in charge at home.

But when Mr. Lee and *daed* carried Julia to the Lees' van, Emma begged to come along without any success. *What if something happens to* mamm? *What if I don't get a chance to tell her how much I love her?* Memories of sharp words and glowering expressions plagued Emma all morning. After they had left for the hospital and her siblings had gone to school, Emma was alone in the quiet house with recrimination and regret as her sole companions. Only a sharp rapping interrupted her ceaseless worries.

Aunt Hannah seldom waited for someone to open the door, so she marched in with determination, carrying a bag of dried flowers. She spotted Emma's red-rimmed eyes before even shrugging off her cape. "Are you worried about your *mamm*? Me too. That's why I came over as soon as Phoebe left for school. Fretting never solved a thing. It only shows God how little faith we have. And that's the last thing we need."

Emma dabbed her nose and then looked at her aunt carefully. Dark smudges hollowed out the skin beneath her eyes. "You don't look like you slept very well, either."

Hannah hugged Emma's shoulders tightly. "True enough, but I know she will be all right. In fact, she'll be better than ever with her brand-new knees."

Emma returned the embrace and felt better having someone near. "This won't be the last of it," she said. "Once physical therapy restores her legs, *mamm* will have to endure operations on both feet, one at a time." A few tears slipped from beneath her lashes.

Hannah reached over and brushed them away. "If I know my sister, she didn't plan to run in one of those marathons anyway. Everything she loves is right here, and all she still wishes to accomplish she will be able to do, given a little time. Don't worry about your *mamm*, Emma. She's stronger than you think."

"I hope so. And I hope she knows how much I love her." Emma spoke the words, but she couldn't look her aunt in the eye.

Hannah lifted Emma's chin until she met her gaze. "She knows, *liewi*, she knows. Now let's stop moping and get to work. I hear you've been busy in the loft, filling a big order. I've got wool from my last shearing in the buggy. We'll work together today and every day while Julia's in the hospital. I'll spin the wool into yarn while you weave on the loom or make wreaths. By the time she gets home from the rehab center, we'll have plenty to deliver to Mrs. Dunn." Hannah already was settling her shawl back over her shoulders. "Whatever I would've earned I was planning to put toward the hospital bill anyway, so if we work together we might be able to pay the thing off in one fell swoop."

Both women laughed. "You overestimate my abilities on the loom, Aunt Hannah."

"And you underestimate what two Miller women can do when they put their heads together. Grab that sweet wool poncho you made and let's get busy."

They walked into the crisp October day arm in arm. The breeze was cool, but the sun still felt warm on their backs. Yellow, red, and orange leaves swirled in eddies around their feet, while the crystalline blue sky overhead made a person forget that the season would soon change once more. A sharp wind would bring cold, pelting rain with chilly nights that seeped into the bones and thinned the blood. Then finally the snow would come, covering the fields and meadows with a blanket of soft, peaceful white. But today was perfect, and niece and aunt enjoyed the bright sunshine.

Each day for the next week, Emma and Hannah worked the entire time the *kinner* were at school. They made packets of dye and festive Christmas wreaths, spun raw wool into skeins of yarn, and wove shawls and scatter rugs on the loom. They might not have earned enough to pay off all the medical bills, but they forged a bond between them that nothing in this world could ever break.

FIFTEEN

Late October

At dawn Hannah lowered the purple martin house with the pulley Seth had rigged for her. With her bushel basket, stiff brush, sponge, and bucket of bleach water ready, she decided to clean out their summer quarters. The birds had flown south a while ago, abandoning Holmes County for a sunnier climate. They had done their job of eating the insects that would have devoured her garden. Hannah brushed the decayed nesting material into the basket, trying not to inhale spores of mold and mildew. She would miss the purple martins playfully gliding into their home, but at least the majestic red-tailed hawks and turkey vultures had stayed behind for the past few winters, filling the winter sky with something to watch.

Hannah's thoughts turned to her sister and her dear niece during the mindless chore. Julia's operation had gone well. She'd struggled through a week at the rehab facility in so much agony the therapists doubted she would be able to continue. But stubborn, determined Julia agreed to higher doses of pain medication and had prevailed. She was walking again—slowly and clumsily with a walker, but walking nonetheless. She would continue her rehabilitation at home, surrounded by her family. A physical therapist had stopped by to teach

Simon and Emma what needed to be done, and Julia was following the regimen to the letter.

"*Danki*, Lord," Hannah murmured for perhaps the one hundredth time since Julia came home. With her sister on the road to recovery, Hannah's thoughts returned to the one sorrow she couldn't seem to forget. Her nightly prayers for a *boppli* of her own had gone unanswered. She and Seth had been married for a year with normal newlywed enthusiasm, yet no pregnancy had resulted. How she longed to experience the thrill of new life growing inside her. Would she never know the joy of holding their child in her arms? Each time she looked at the oak cradle, hand-carved by Seth's *dawdi* and used by generations of Millers, her heart sank. Finally, she'd asked Seth to store it in the attic to remove the constant reminder that she was barren. Someday she would pass it on to Emma, upon her marriage.

Seth had reminded her about Zechariah and Elizabeth, a couple long past childbearing years, and yet God granted them a son to bring them joy in their old age. Hannah had often turned to Luke 1 to read about the story of John the Baptist. The Scripture used to console her, because it reminded her that in God all things were possible.

But lately Hannah had come to the realization that her nightly prayers hadn't gone unanswered. God *did* answer her—He had said no. He, who with infinite wisdom saw all things at once, had chosen a different path for her. And it was about time she accepted His will and appreciated the grace she'd already been shown. Phoebe was thriving. The child had come to accept her during the past year as her own mother. Gentle, affectionate, and obedient, Phoebe was everything a mother could ask for in a daughter. And Hannah loved her so. She also loved Seth more than she thought possible. God had given her a second opportunity to love. She should stop wallowing in self-pity, dwelling on things not meant to be, and start looking for ways to serve others.

Hannah finished cleaning the birdhouse, but she left it down for the winter to discourage undesirable birds from moving in. She hurried inside to wash and change clothes before going to Julia's. With Phoebe gone for the day at school, she and Emma had planned a long-overdue trip to Sugar Creek. Both needed to deliver orders to A Stitch in Time. Emma had created so many lovely Christmas wreaths Mrs. Dunn might have to expand her store. They both had skeins of yarn, bags of wool, and handmade woolens to sell on consignment. Hannah was amazed how much Emma had accomplished since Julia came home from the hospital. The girl must never sleep—which was why her sister had insisted that Emma take a day off from the farm. On Saturday, Simon planned to drive Leah to town to eat in a restaurant—a popular tourist spot—for her much-deserved break. But today was for Emma, and Hannah planned to make it special.

Half an hour later, Hannah pulled into the Miller driveway and parked her buggy under the tree. *"Guder mariye,"* she called to Simon and Emma.

"Hi, Aunt," Emma said. "What do you think?" The girl flourished her hand toward the well-packed wagon. *"Daed* hitched up the Belgians instead of the standardbreds since I had so much to deliver to Sugar Creek."

"I think you've been busier than any bee I've ever seen," Hannah said, looking at the amazing assortment.

Simon pulled a tarp over the contents and secured it tightly. "You let your aunt drive the team," he instructed. "She has more experience. This is different than driving your little pony cart." He finished with the ropes and then settled his gaze on Hannah. *"Guder mariye,* Hannah. You're looking well." He offered a small smile.

"Ach, my cooking might be improving. I've put on a bit of weight."

"My *bruder* never complains about your meals, nor does he fill a sack with leftovers when he's here. You must be getting the hang of it."

Emma stood with the reins, looking rather impatient. "Please get in, Aunt Hannah, and let's be off."

Hannah stepped into the wagon, chuckling over Simon's uncharacteristic teasing.

"Remember what I said at breakfast," he warned his daughter.

"*Jah, daed*. Please don't worry. No one will steal my purse. I'll watch it very carefully after Mrs. Dunn pays me." Emma gave Simon a peck on the cheek and climbed up onto the seat.

Simon stood blushing, embarrassed by the display of affection. "Enjoy yourselves today and don't scrimp on lunch. Eat at some place nice. We will be fine here." He demanded this with the same tone of voice as though ordering Curley out of the garden.

Hannah glanced over her shoulder at Simon, trying to suppress a grin as the wagon reached the end of the drive and turned onto the road.

Emma noticed Hannah's reaction however. "*Jah, daed*'s been in a better mood now that *mamm* is walking again. She has been sitting at the kitchen table every afternoon, teaching Leah plenty of new recipes. You can't believe what a fine cook Leah is turning into."

"I'm sure he's very proud of you too," Hannah said. "I've never seen such beautiful work as those wreaths." She glanced back at the covered wagon.

Emma folded her hands in her lap. "*Danki*. I hope Mrs. Dunn feels the same."

Once they reached Sugar Creek and Hannah pulled back the tarp, they discovered Mrs. Dunn more than felt the same. The shopkeeper walked around the wagon twice, gushing with praise for Emma's handiwork. She lifted one wreath after another, insisting she'd never seen any finer. After her inspection, the three women went to her office while her two helpers unloaded the wagon. The contents would be sorted, counted, and then weighed in the back storeroom.

Once cups of tea had been passed around, Mrs. Dunn stated her business proposition. "I'd like to pay you thirty-five dollars outright for each wreath. I know I can sell every one of them and make a profit. I'll take the woolens on consignment as usual, and I'll also buy all the dye packets and skeins of yarn. Your work is exceptional, Emma."

"Thank you, ma'am."

Then Mrs. Dunn remembered there were two women in her office. "Excuse me, Hannah. I didn't mean to slight you."

"No offense taken, Audrey," Hannah murmured with a smile.

"The quality of your wool is excellent, as usual," the shopkeeper continued. "I'll take yours at our agreed price and the woolens on consignment as well. Your handmade items have the smoothest, tightest weave." Mrs. Dunn smiled warmly at her two favorite suppliers.

"Aunt Hannah's weaving is much better than mine," said Emma, focusing on her hands in her lap.

"But yours improves with every piece you complete," Hannah said. She reached for Emma's hand to give it a squeeze.

"By the way, Emma," Mrs. Dunn said, taking a sip of tea. "What do you hear from the Davis boy? His dad delivered their load of wool instead of him. Last time I saw Jamie, he was going on and on about a horse he'd planned to buy for you."

Emma blushed to the roots of her hair. "I haven't seen him lately. He's moved to Wooster to attend college."

Hannah set her teacup on its saucer with a clatter. "He purchased the horse on Emma's behalf, not as a gift," she clarified. "Emma makes regular payments to him and will continue to do so until the horse is paid in full." Hannah knew Simon wouldn't appreciate false rumors floating around, not even in the English world. Sugar Creek was a small town.

Audrey bobbed her head. "Ah, yes. Every one of the Davises has a good eye for horseflesh. I'm sure you did well having Jamie pick out your purchase." A horn blared from the direction of the loading dock. Mrs. Dunn rose to her feet. "Looks like I'm about to receive another delivery. Do you have other stops to make? The men will finish weighing your bulk wool, and then I can have a check ready in about an hour."

"*Jah*, we're going to lunch," Hannah said, also standing. The three women shook hands and a still-glowing Emma hurried for the door. "We'll stop back later."

Hannah glanced at her niece as they walked to the restaurant. The teenager's mood had taken a tumble. "I'm hungry. Are you ready to eat? I daresay the profits today were better than expected. Your father insisted we treat ourselves to something special. They'll be plenty left to put toward your *mamm*'s medical bills."

Emma seemed to barely pay attention as they passed shop windows loaded with lovely things for sale. "You pick where, Aunt Hannah. I'm not particular."

"All right. Then let's go to Beachy's," Hannah said enthusiastically to Emma's modest nod.

Inside the restaurant, the younger woman picked at her food, despite a buffet of delicious choices. Hannah ate more than usual and then walked over to peruse the dessert area. "Oh, my," she said, returning to the table. "They have an ice-cream sundae bar with chocolate syrup, candy sprinkles, and real whipped cream."

The confectionary bounty failed to pique Emma's interest. "Not for me, *danki*. No room for it."

Hannah couldn't see herself indulging alone, so with disappointment she too skipped dessert. With growing uneasiness, she picked up the bill and headed toward the cashier. "What's wrong, child? Don't you feel well?"

Emma didn't answer until they left the restaurant. "I feel fine physically, Aunt, but inside it feels like my heart has been torn in half." Two large tears slipped from beneath her lashes. "When Mrs. Dunn asked about James, I remembered just how much I miss him." She shuffled her feet like an elderly woman as they walked back uptown.

This was more than Hannah had bargained for, preferring not to get between Simon and Emma during her *Rumschpringe*. But considering her niece's misery, she decided to break her rule this once.

"Haven't you received any letters from him since he left?" she asked. "I know your parents said that you two could write."

After Emma climbed into the wagon, a torrent of tears let loose. "I didn't for the longest time, but I got a letter yesterday." She dabbed at her nose with a tissue. "It was ever so nice a letter. He told me all about his dorm and classes and the town of Wooster." Emma tried to take in a breath, but it caught in her throat. "And he said he missed me more than he thought possible!" Her voice sounded strangled.

Hannah patted her knee. "It is hard to be young. I do remember that." With the sympathetic gesture, Emma's sobs increased.

"James invited me to come visit him. Truly, he *begged* me to come. He said he had so much to show me. They have a special farm for the students where they test new seed hybrids and fertilizers and whatnot. I guess they practice farming." She shook her head in confusion, setting her *kapp* strings swinging. "I don't really understand it, but I do want to visit him. *Mamm* and *daed* would never allow it. They'll say it's not proper for me to go to Wooster alone." She hung her head inconsolably.

Hannah spoke without thinking. "What if I accompanied you for the day? What if you were never out of my sight? Then they might agree to the visit."

Emma turned her watery blue eyes to meet Hannah's. "You would do that for me, Aunt Hannah?"

"I would if they say it's okay. And they just might. Your parents know how hard you've worked during Julia's recuperation."

"Oh, *danki* so much." Emma threw her arms around her aunt's neck and hugged so hard, Hannah couldn't breathe.

"Goodness, Emma. If you choke me I won't be able to chaperone." She wiggled from the embrace.

"Sorry." Emma scooted back on the bench and straightened her skirt. "I can't wait to get home to ask them. And pick out which dress I'll wear in case they agree to the trip. I'll write to James the minute they say yes. Do you suppose my bangs will be grown out enough that they won't keep falling into my face?" The waterworks had mysteriously stopped.

"Perhaps a tighter *kapp* will help. I'm going in to get the check from Mrs. Dunn. You wait here in the wagon." Hannah handed her niece the reins and went inside the shop. When she returned, Emma was still staring at the horses' backsides with the same wistful expression on her face.

"Did you miss me, child?" Hannah asked, clucking to the horses.

"Pardon?" Emma asked, waking from her daydream of a joyous Wooster reunion.

"Nothing. Just hang on to the seat so you don't bounce out of the wagon on the way back." To the team she called, "Get up there," and slapped the reins lightly on their backs. The team picked up the pace and they soon left Sugar Creek behind.

Hannah was eager to get home to fix dinner for her husband and daughter...but not quite so anxious to face the music with her brother-in-law.

~

Emma could hardly believe her good fortune. When she'd received the invitation from James, her pleasure had been short lived. She was sure her father would never permit a visit to a college campus. Rumors abounded even in the Plain world as to the poor behavior of young women and about far too much alcohol consumption. She had tucked the letter into her drawer, preferring not to ruffle any family feathers. But Aunt Hannah's willingness to come along changed everything. Emma tried to concentrate on the scenery during the trip home so she wouldn't float right up into the clouds.

Matthew came running from the barn the moment the wagon rumbled up the driveway. He was smiling and waving as though they had been gone for weeks.

Emma and Hannah exchanged surprised looks. "I've never seen

a boy so eager to rub down horses before," Hannah said, chuckling. "Either that, or he certainly missed his big sister this afternoon."

"Probably the first possibility. My *bruder* has never met a horse he didn't like."

Hannah brought the wagon to a stop close to the pasture gate and set the brake.

"Emma, Emma! I've got some great news," Matthew shouted as he joined them. He grabbed onto the lead Belgian's bridle as Aunt Hannah climbed down.

Emma held up an index finger, like a schoolmarm. "One moment," she said to him, and to Hannah, "*Danki* for taking me to Sugar Creek and for the delicious lunch." Emma spoke very primly. "I shall keep you informed regarding the other matter we discussed outside Mrs. Dunn's." Then she faced her brother. "Where are your manners, young man?" She scolded him as though far more than two years his senior.

Matthew swept his hat from his head. "*Guder nachmittag*, Aunt Hannah. 'Cuse me. I hitched up your mare a little while ago so your buggy would be ready. Want me to drive you home and then walk back?"

"No, Matthew, I'm perfectly able to get myself home. Good day, you two. Tell your *mamm* I'll be over in the morning for a visit. I need to start dinner now." Hannah climbed into her buggy and set off without another word.

"Thank you for a lovely day!" Emma hollered, waving her hand frantically. Then she wheeled around to Matthew, who seemed incapable of standing still. "Now tell me your news. What is so important that I couldn't properly see off my aunt?"

Matthew tipped his hat back and scratched his forehead. "What else did you plan to say other than goodbye?" He looked thoroughly perplexed.

Emma lifted her tote bag from the wagon and crossed her arms. "Never mind. You wouldn't understand."

Matthew needed no further prodding. "I got a job, Em. A real job with a paycheck!" His freckled face lit up like a dozen burning candles.

"Doing what? You're still in school till May. Does *daed* know? What about your chores?" Emma rattled off one question after another.

"Training horses. After school and Saturdays until I'm done with school." He paused to recollect. "*Jah, daed* knows; he slapped me on the back. I'll still get all my chores done. Pa made me promise. Besides, Henry is no *boppli* anymore. He should take on a bigger share."

Emma walked beside her brother as he unhitched the team and led them to their stalls. "That is good news," she said. "Where is this job?"

"Over at Macintosh Farms on the county road. They're English folks. Mr. Macintosh breeds quarter horses and thoroughbreds, and he hired me to work them in the ring. Mainly, I'll just be an exercise boy, but I'll apprentice to a real trainer and work my way up." He started brushing the first draft horse with so much zeal it could end up a show horse...or bald.

"I'm real proud of you, Matty," Emma said. "Mr. Macintosh must have recognized your talent with four-legged beasts." She patted the Belgian's rump and then jumped back when he suddenly reared his head.

"Stay back, sister. You're making him nervous." He calmed the horse with a long, smooth pat down his flank. "Mr. Mac—that's what he told me to call him—said I was a natural. I understand animals and can figure out what they're thinking." He wielded the brush with finesse on the neck and mane.

"Thinking?" Emma giggled. "Horses don't think. *Daed* said they must have brains the size of a pea."

Matthew shook his head. "You had better get on the other side of the stall if you're going to talk like that! Horses are not only smart, but they know when someone doesn't like them. And they'll treat you accordingly."

Emma clucked her tongue with skepticism but stepped back just the same.

"A horseman learns to read an animal's body language and uses that information in training." Matthew scratched the Belgian's large wet nose.

"Body language?" Emma asked. "What do you mean—they talk by scraping their hooves in the dirt or shaking their tails?"

"Oh, forget it, Emma." Matthew was rapidly losing patience.

"Well, I am happy for you, and I wish you luck with the new job." She reached in between the slats to pat his arm. The horse turned his head and focused one dark brown eye on her. She yanked her hand back. "I should go in and help Leah. I'll see you at supper."

Emma fled the barn before the beast decided that her "pea-sized brain" comment had been in poor taste. Anyway, she had more important things to think about than horses communicating with their tails.

All of them had to do with a tall, blond-haired fellow from Charm.

～

November

A stiff wind, cold enough to cut a person almost to the bone, blew the last of the leaves from the trees the day Emma was to visit Wooster. Standing on her aunt's porch, she tightened her wool cape around her shoulders. Hannah was feeding the chickens and had suggested that Emma wait inside the kitchen for James' arrival. But Emma was so excited she couldn't stand another moment in the overheated kitchen.

James had selected a Friday for their trip to campus for two reasons: First, he had no Friday morning classes, and second, the labs would be fully staffed for an accurate picture of the agricultural college. He was due at eight o'clock. If he thought it strange to pick her up here, and not around the corner, he hid it well. Although her father had agreed to the visit after much prodding by Julia, he wasn't in favor of his daughter mingling with "heathens of loose morals."

Emma had become indignant, knowing how much James loved the Lord. In his last letter, he'd told her that he joined a church and a Bible study group in Wooster. But Simon Miller had not been mollified.

Do not leave your aunt's sight.

Do not dawdle in public restaurants or shops.

Do not drink anything that didn't come from your tote bag. Someone could add a drug to your beverage.

Simon left these instructions before storming off to his milking parlor.

With shame, Emma remembered stamping her foot in response. A show of defiance would never win her *daed* over, but she'd lost her temper. Thus, she decided it would be best if the shiny green truck didn't pull up their driveway this morning.

The rooster marched down the henhouse ramp to deliver his message well after dawn, just as James turned into the Miller lane. "At long last," Emma murmured.

"It's only five minutes after eight," said Hannah, coming up the steps with a full basket of eggs. "I'll set these inside and we can be off."

She didn't sound very excited, but Emma didn't care. The man of her heart had just jumped out of his truck and was headed her way. He carried the largest armload of roses Emma had ever seen.

"Hi, Emma!" he called while still twenty paces away.

He was wearing a wool sport coat, a navy blue sweater, and dark jeans. His boots had been polished, and his hair freshly washed.

"Hello, James." She hoped she didn't appear as eager as she felt.

"These are for you." He held out the enormous multicolored bouquet.

"I'm not sure if she can accept those, James, knowing how her father feels about expensive gifts," Hannah said. She had put the eggs away and returned to the porch in record time.

"Oh, no, ma'am," James said. "These weren't expensive at all. They were grown in a greenhouse on campus. The students can buy them for their moms or…friends…for next to nothing."

"All right," Hannah said to Emma. "Put them in water in the kitchen and let's be off."

Emma felt a tingle of static electricity snake up her spine as she accepted the bouquet. "Thank you, James. I love how they're different colors. I didn't even know green roses existed."

James blushed the traditional shade of long-stem roses as he slipped his hands into his back pockets. "The horticulture students experiment with different hybrids to see what colors they can come up with."

"Seems to me they should leave God's handiwork alone," Hannah muttered, already walking toward his truck.

Emma went inside to put the roses in water and decided not to let anything dampen her spirits on her day with James. When she got to his truck, Aunt Hannah was seated in back, so she took the front seat. It wouldn't be polite to make him feel like a professional chauffer. The drive to his campus took less than thirty minutes, and their route took them through the village of Apple Creek, where Emma saw Amish folk milling on the street and spotted several tied-up buggies. "Are we still in Holmes County?" she asked.

"No, we're in Wayne County," James said. "Plenty of Amish live here as well. In fact, three Amish farms surround the land owned by my school."

"There are lots more people in general, I expect," Hannah said petulantly from the backseat. "The traffic up here is worse than where we live."

Emma had counted only a few cars on the road but decided not to argue. Her aunt had allowed her to sit in the front seat. She and James were mere inches apart.

"Perhaps you could slow down, young man? I'm feeling sick to my stomach." Hannah crossed her arms over her belly.

"Yes, ma'am. I'm sorry." James immediately braked to reduce his speed. "We're almost there."

Emma reached over the seat to take her aunt's hand. Hannah did indeed look pale as she peered out the window.

"We're almost there," James said, glancing into his rearview mirror.

Emma had expected tall college buildings, but instead she saw rolling fields, fenced pastures, well-tended paddocks, and several large buildings.

"This is the farm laboratory," James explained, driving slowly up the lane. "Or at least, part of it. It spreads out in all directions. We have dairy, beef, swine, and agricultural facilities, besides the land lab, farm office, and the equine center."

"Equine center as in big horse barn?" Emma asked.

James smiled. "It's much more than that, Em. It's a state-of-the-art facility for horse breeding and genetic engineering, veterinary trials, and clinical studies of diet, supplements, and pharmaceuticals."

"Looks like a bunch of horse barns to me," Hannah mumbled.

"Should we get out and walk around? You can watch some of the work being done." James parked outside a large set of double doors.

Emma wanted to investigate, but her aunt answered first. "No, thank you. We'll tour the campus from inside the vehicle. It looks muddy and like it might rain at any minute."

Emma rolled her eyes while James chanced a sly wink at her. "Where exactly do you take your classes? Inside these barns?"

"Oh, no. We work on projects here, but the classroom complex is down the road. We'll go there next."

As he explained the research projects going on, Emma heard a tone of condescension in his voice she'd never noticed before. None of it made much sense, nor was it very interesting.

James pulled the truck into a parking lot. "Here are the classroom buildings and dorms. The student activities center and the apartment village for married students are over there." He stole another glance in Emma's direction—one that made her stomach tumble. "Want to see the residence hall?"

"Absolutely not!" Aunt Hannah screeched, reminding Emma of a barn owl.

"I only meant the dining hall, not the rooms, Mrs. Miller. I thought maybe a bite to eat might settle your stomach."

"Oh…thank you," Hannah said, dabbing at her forehead with a hanky. "I'd prefer to eat in a restaurant when we get to Wooster."

"Okay," he agreed. "But first let's take a stroll through the campus conservatory. I think both of you will enjoy that."

Emma had no idea what to expect, having never heard of a conservatory before. It turned out to be nothing more than a big fancy greenhouse—overly warm, very humid, and smelling of chemicals and fertilizers.

James walked by her side, pointing out plants, shrubs, and trees she had never seen before, nor even heard of. Hannah lagged behind them, looking greener than some of the foliage in the giant pots.

"What are all these strange plants?" Emma asked.

"Tropical varieties from exotic locations from around the world," he explained. "Look, there's a banana tree." He pointed as though she were a child.

"But why are they *here*? And why are you studying about them? I thought you came to learn how to be a better farmer." She sounded peevish, because the strange smells were making her a little queasy too.

"I did, Emma. I only thought you would like to tour the conservatory. I couldn't believe how many pretty flowers the horticulture students grow here."

"Horticulture—that's just a fancy word for plants!" She bumped her head on a low-hanging branch.

"I know that, but I thought gals liked flowers." James tried to take her hand, but she pulled it back as though touching a hot stove. Aunt Hannah was close behind.

"What's wrong with you, Emma?" James asked. "Aren't you happy to see me? I planned our day together down to the smallest detail when you said you could come." He sounded wounded. "I was so excited I couldn't sleep."

Emma looked into his face. His summer suntan had faded to a few freckles across his nose, while his blond hair had dried into soft waves. He looked the same, yet somehow different in his sport coat. "*Jah*, I'm happy to see you. I just thought you'd be learning about crops and critters and useful stuff, not about banana trees. They won't grow in Holmes County no matter how many expensive textbooks you read."

James looked as though she had slapped him.

Aunt Hannah stepped forward. "You two may finish looking through the greenhouse by yourselves. I'll wait for you outside the door. I can use some fresh air."

Since Aunt Hannah overheard our exchange of words, she probably no longer fears a quick kiss or a stolen embrace, Emma thought.

"I know that, Emma," James said. "I'm not studying this stuff. I'm taking general sciences, biology, English, history, and mathematics. Plus, I go to a writing lab a couple afternoons a week."

"Whatever for? Are you planning to write books on farming now?" she asked. A headache was building behind her eyes.

James looked miffed. "No, Emma. It's to help me with term papers and other assignments. I'm afraid I didn't study hard enough in high school, and I'm behind the other students."

"We mustn't keep my aunt waiting." Her schoolteacher voice had returned. They finished the tour as though trying to catch a bus rather than enjoying a leisurely stroll through a garden. Once they were reunited with Aunt Hannah, no one talked much during the drive into Wooster. Everywhere Emma looked she saw pretty girls in pretty clothes doing normal English things. Workers on ladders were decorating the charming town with strings of tiny white lights for Christmas, but she couldn't muster any gaiety.

In the restaurant James had chosen, everyone seemed to be staring at Emma and Aunt Hannah as though they had never seen Amish people before. The white tablecloths, long-stemmed goblets, and three different forks at each place setting was much too elegant for Emma's tastes. Why would anybody need three different forks?

James tried his best to make the meal special by suggesting this menu selection and that herbal tea, but Emma couldn't relax. Part of the problem was that Aunt Hannah's queasiness hadn't diminished. Even bland chicken soup with saltines failed to settle her stomach. And both Emma and James had to guard every word they said, lest something be deemed improper. All in all, Emma felt relieved when they finished lunch and Aunt Hannah announced she wished to start for home.

James looked disappointed. He had more to show them back at the agricultural college and in the town of Wooster, but Emma's headache had become tortuous, so she insisted they head back to Winesburg. She also felt disoriented and confused with the traffic, shoppers scurrying in all directions, drivers honking horns, and general commotion.

What happened to the gentle sheep farmer I fell in love with while floating down a lazy river in a canoe? This man, who was trying to explain his courses on entomology and environmental resources, was a stranger, despite his familiar piercingly blue eyes.

SIXTEEN

When the trip back from Wooster was finally over and James had dropped them off in Aunt Hannah's yard, Emma felt a little ashamed. If James never wished to speak to her again, she couldn't blame him. During the ride home, her aunt had moaned piteously with every pothole or sharp curve in the road. And Emma had sat there without talking like a bump on a log.

James had tried several times to engage her in conversation. He'd told her about his biology teacher who had moved here from Texas, wore a ten-gallon hat, and had once tried his hand as a rodeo rider. James had tried to explain his progression of courses—the fundamentals he must take before delving into true agriculture courses. He even mentioned a few Mennonite classmates who were having equal difficulty with grammar in their English class.

Emma hadn't felt like talking. She was feeling inferior, as though shortcomings in her own education would be all too apparent now that James was attending college. And she'd felt left behind.

Now, standing in her aunt's driveway, she only felt rude.

Aunt Hannah had thanked James, called goodbye to her, and fled inside her house, clutching her stomach. James walked her as far as the porch and then left without trying to sneak a kiss. Emma hugged her arms across her chest in the fading daylight. She didn't want to go inside Uncle Seth's house, yet she wasn't ready to go home either. So she stood in the November chill and tried to sort out her life.

She discovered today that she didn't like Caesar salad dressing or gazpacho soup. Twice-baked potatoes seemed like too much work for the small amount of improvement. She also knew she didn't want to go to college. And the idea of turning English—of learning to drive a car someday, or buying fancy clothes in shops with white lights around the windows, had lost much of its appeal.

Emma wondered how those people could keep their faith. How could they manage to stay close to God while fighting over parking spaces or waiting in long lines for the ATMs at the bank? Maybe that's why young college girls often ran into trouble with drinking and misbehaving at parties. There seemed to be so much chaos. And Wooster was only a small town compared to the cities in California or Italy where James wished to take her. It was much easier to talk to God in her sheep pasture, along her woodland path, or sitting by the creek than in a high-rise apartment or while riding in one of those underground trains.

Emma heard a tapping sound and turned toward the house. Phoebe had spotted her dawdling in the yard and started knocking on the glass. Emma smiled, waved at the child, and then walked toward the barn. Time to go home and stop fretting before Aunt Hannah came back outdoors to see why she hadn't left.

On the path that connected the two farms Emma gave over her dilemma to Someone better qualified. Picking her way through scrub vegetation and boggy low ground, she paused by the beaver pond. Brooding about her current state of confusion wasn't working. God knew her heart and the hearts of everyone involved. He would set into motion the perfect solution within His time frame.

But she didn't think the answer would be so quick in coming.

When Emma entered the surprisingly quiet kitchen, her *daed* was sitting alone at the table, his head propped up with one weathered hand. A Bible lay open before him; his concentration was absolute.

Since Simon hadn't heard her come in, Emma had a few moments to study the man who had once bounced her on his knee. When had his hair turned so gray? His long silky beard was nearly pure white. His dark eyes squinted behind his spectacles, while his shoulders were hunched over the book. The skin beneath his chin sagged, and Emma noticed a slight tremor in the hand holding the coffee mug. He looked frail for a man who had labored hard his entire life.

She fought to swallow the lump in her throat.

"Emma! Why are you sneaking up on people? I didn't hear you come in."

Emma kicked off her shoes in the hallway and hung her cape on a peg. "I wasn't trying to be especially quiet. You must have been distracted."

Only then did he study his daughter carefully, perhaps making sure she hadn't dyed her hair red or painted her fingernails purple. "You're back earlier than I expected you to be."

"*Jah*, Aunt Hannah wasn't feeling well. The drive along twisty roads made her carsick. And I think some of the food she sampled at the restaurant wasn't to her liking."

His brows knitted together over the bridge of his nose. "What did she eat?"

"She tried some of my cold soup and Caesar salad and didn't like either one of them."

"Cold soup? Did someone forget to turn on the stove burner?" Simon sounded shocked.

"No, it was supposed to be served that way," she answered, stifling a smile.

Simon waited to see if she was kidding, and then he uttered a dismissive *ach* and drained the rest of his coffee.

She slipped into the opposite chair. "*Daed*, where is everyone? Why are you sitting here alone? Why isn't Leah fixing dinner? It's not late."

Simon looked up, but not at her. He focused his gaze on the darkened window, outside of which a hard rain had begun to fall. "Dinner was cooked, eaten, and cleaned up afterward early tonight. Leah is helping Mrs. Lee bake cakes and cookies for a bridal shower for her daughter this weekend. Matthew is over at Macintosh Farms. Henry is out in the barn trying to build birdhouses. Your *mamm* felt tired after the therapy session and went to bed. That leaves me… and you." The last word hung in the air like the smell of sulfur after lighting a match, but still he didn't look at her. He returned to his Bible and tried to find his place with an index finger.

He asked nary a word about her trip to Wooster.

She so much wanted to talk about things weighing on her, but she didn't know where to begin. Finally she said, "Did you know that plenty of Plain people live around Apple Creek in Wayne County?"

He raised his head to stare at her. "I'm well aware of that fact. There's also plenty who live in Lodi and Dalton too. Is there something you wish to discuss with me, Emma? If so, spit it out, but if not, I'd like to get back to what I was doing."

Emma's throat tightened. His harsh tone didn't encourage a father-daughter chat. He sounded as though he didn't like her anymore, or at least that he was very angry that she went to see James.

She contemplated running up the stairs, burying her head beneath a pillow, and not coming down until January, but her legs wouldn't cooperate.

"I was wondering what you were studying." She sounded like a spring peeper, freshly broken through its shell.

Simon exhaled through his dry, chapped lips and rolled his eyes. He made a great show of inserting his bookmark—one that she had crocheted as a little girl—and shutting the Good Book. "I am reading the book of Ecclesiastes, searching for guidance since my eldest *kinner* is determined to destroy everything good and run to a life we had tried to protect her from. I need to find out where I failed."

Such stark honesty had not been expected. Emma started to cry silently, not wishing to wake her mother upstairs. "I don't want to destroy my life."

"I know that," said Simon. "But you cannot dally with this boy, no matter how nice he is, and then return to Amish ways like nothing ever happened." The sorrow in his eyes made him look very aged.

Emma's shame rose a notch upon realizing she had caused untold grief to both parents. That hadn't been her intention. She just wanted some fun during *Rumschpringe*, never intending to fall in love with an *Englischer*. "You have not failed, *daed*," Emma whispered, reaching out to place her small hand over his.

He didn't pull back or flinch with the show of affection. Instead, Simon wrapped both his hands around hers. "But I did. I have failed you both as your father and your deacon." He squeezed her hand for a long moment before returning to his Bible. "There's still hot water in the kettle if you wish to take a cup of tea to your room. You must be tired after your trip." He spoke in the gentlest voice she'd ever heard. And Simon Miller never condoned such self-indulgence as sipping tea bedside. His motto had always been: "Drink your beverage at the kitchen table and be done with it."

This dear man loved her enough to take on the burden of her waywardness and still show her compassion. If he had hollered or blustered it would have somehow been easier.

What she must do came to her in a flash of insight. As much as she loved James—and she did love him—she loved her parents more. She wouldn't cause them another minute of pain, not when she had the power to stop their anxiety. Emma straightened her spine, willed herself to stop crying, and spoke before she lost her courage. "You haven't failed me because I have no intention of leaving the Amish faith. You and *mamm* raised me to love the Lord and be obedient to His will. I found out today that I don't much like the fancy world. Although I like James, I don't wish to become English as he expects me to if we ever became engaged." She forced herself to breathe. "So tonight I will write to him and say I won't court him any longer. He needs to concentrate on his schooling, and I…have my own life." Her stream of words ran out. Her resolve faltered, but she had done it. For the first time, she had put others before her own selfish desires. Emma folded her hands together and waited for his reaction.

Simon stared at her and then said, "I'm glad to hear you've come to your senses, Emma. Why don't you go upstairs now and look in on your *mamm*. I'm certain she's still awake." He gestured with his head toward the doorway and then lowered his focus to his Bible.

If Emma had expected jubilation or a sudden outpouring of emotion, it was not forthcoming. Her *daed* returned to his reading calmly. But when she glanced back at his hunched form, she saw a teardrop fall to the well-worn page.

That memory she would hold in her heart for a very long time. It would fortify her as she climbed the stairs to her room. It had to carry her through the ordeal of taking paper and pen from her drawer and pulling a chair up to the windowsill. The memory of her father's tears of relief sustained her as she wrote to the young man she loved.

Plenty of her own tears were to fall that evening before Emma was able to sleep.

~

When James returned to his dorm a week later, he was almost too tired to listen to his answering machine. He'd eaten his bland dinner without paying much attention to what meat had been part of the casserole. His writing and math labs after his regular classes were starting to wear him down with extra assignments. If he had known all this studying lay ahead of him, he would have paid better attention to his classes in high school.

As he stretched out on his bed, the blinking light would not let him relax. James pressed the button and listened to his mom's cheery voice. His favorite mare had foaled without complications, the last of the fields had been prepared for winter, one of the pond pumps broke and had to be replaced, and he'd gotten a letter from Miss Emma Miller of Winesburg.

James sat up so fast he saw stars.

Emma. It had been a week since her visit to OSU—a week of wondering what had happened between them. She had seemed more than distant; she'd seemed downright hostile toward his school and the curriculum. He had no control over the required courses or the advanced technology of the facilities. If she had bothered to listen to him, she would have found out he didn't plan to pursue horticulture. He'd just thought she might like to see some pretty flowers and exotic plants.

He sure had been wrong about that.

Nothing had changed for him regarding his future plans. Yet much seemed to have changed for Emma during the past few weeks.

Were her parents pressuring her not to court him?

Was the stress of a sick mom making her cranky?

Or had she simply lost interest in him? He still had homework assignments before bed, and his favorite show was on TV tonight, but he couldn't consider either right now. Emma had written him a letter. Maybe she offered an explanation for her short temper last Friday. He didn't care about an apology—everyone was entitled to an occasional bad mood. What he needed was confirmation that she was still his girl.

James punched in his home phone number and listened with anticipation. His mom picked up on the sixth ring.

"Jamie! How are you? How are you doing in the labs? I trust you heard my update on our farm news."

He answered her cursory questions and commented appropriately regarding the new thoroughbred foal. When he couldn't be patient another moment, he blurted out, "What about Emma's letter? Have you any idea what's in it?"

For a few moments of total silence ensued. Then his mom said softly, "It's a sealed envelope, Jamie. Do you think I would steam it open and read your personal mail?" She chuckled.

"Sorry, Mom. I know you wouldn't. I'm just curious about what Emma had to say."

To that, she had no response.

"We didn't exactly get along well when she visited with her aunt last week."

"I'm sorry to hear that, son. The letter will be waiting for you on your dresser."

"I'm coming home tomorrow after my last class," he said impetuously.

"Is that wise? Aren't you loaded down with assignments?"

"Yeah, but I gotta know what's in that letter. I'll bring my work home and do it there. I could use a little home cooking anyway. The food here can't compare with yours."

"Jamie—"

He didn't let her finish. "Ma, I gotta go. I have things to do, but I'll see you tomorrow after my last class." He hung up before she tried to change his mind.

After the call he was able to study and sleep like a baby. Tomorrow afternoon he would hold in his hand words from Emma—whose sweet face and gentle ways were never off his mind.

～

James had only the one-hour drive to Charm to believe things were still good with his young girlfriend. Only one hour to imagine what interesting tales Emma would share with him. He still tried to come up with possible reasons for her frosty behavior but came up empty. With the last of autumn leaves swirling in the breeze, he arrived at the entrance to Hollyhock Farms. Driving slowly up their road, he saw no people bustling about as they often did during the summertime, only horses, cows, and sheep—the sheep that had become dearer since he'd met Emma.

Mom and Dad were sitting at the kitchen table when he pushed open the door. Mom sipped her afternoon tea while his father savored a cup of coffee.

"Jamie, welcome home," his mother said, greeting him with a smile.

"I've only been gone a few weeks. You couldn't have missed me yet."

"That's more than enough time. How goes it, son?" Dad asked. "How are your classes?"

"Not too bad." James shrugged off his coat and hung it on a peg.

"Pull up a chair and tell us all about it." His father looked intrigued.

"Dinner will be ready in twenty minutes," Barbara added. "We're having your favorites—fried chicken, creamed corn, and coleslaw."

James looked from one parent to the other. They both wanted him to succeed so badly. "Give me just a few minutes, and then I'll divulge the exciting news from Wooster land lab," he teased, "but first I want to read Emma's letter."

"We're not going anywhere, son." His dad picked up the newspaper.

James ran up the steps two at a time. He found the letter where his mom said it would be, read his name and address—twice—and then ripped open the envelope.

Dear James,

I must apologize for my rude behavior on your school campus. You went to a lot of trouble, and it probably seemed unappreciated. I must confess the fancy world made me uncomfortable. Although I have enjoyed our outings together and have treasured our friendship, I do not wish to turn English. Your world isn't for me. I don't want to dishonor my parents, and I am afraid to leave my faith. So I think it would be best if we no longer see each other and I start courting Amish fellows. I wish you much success with college, and I

*hope nothing I said last Friday will discourage you from getting your
degree.*

Your friend,
Emma Miller

Your friend, Emma Miller? This was the girl he had proposed to—
the one he wished to pledge himself to for the rest of his life. And
she referred to herself as a friend...a companion for horseback riding,
canoeing, and Swiss Cheese Festivals? But it seemed that now that
she wanted a serious beau, she would look only among the Amish.

He felt as though he had been punched in the stomach. He wanted to cry but wouldn't allow himself. He was a grown man, not a
spoiled little boy. Instead, he reread the flowery sheet of stationery
three times to make sure he didn't miss a detail that would clear up
his confusion.

Five or ten minutes passed, yet no rational explanation arrived.
Vacillating between anger and sorrow, James tucked the letter into
his sock drawer and trudged downstairs. Apparently, his disappointment was written across his face.

"Oh, dear, Jamie. Bad news from Miss Miller?"

"You could say that," he said, slumping into a chair.

"What happened, son?" Dad asked. His forehead furrowed with
concern.

"Emma broke up with me—just like that, without a reason other
than the English world wasn't for her." He couldn't look at either
parent—not his dad, for fear his weakness would be all too apparent,
and not his mom, for fear he'd see some sign of relief. So James stared
at the rooster wall clock, whose silly face failed to cheer him up.

"She's very young, Jamie. I'm sure she's simply not ready for serious commitment." His mother spoke without a trace of satisfaction
in her voice.

"I love her, Mom. I love Emma. I thought she felt the same. And
Amish girls get serious around this age or at least start courting.

That's all I wanted for right now. We have a lot in common, despite the fact I'm English."

The rooster on the wall marked the passage of time as three people tried to find the right words to say.

"Don't get too upset, Jamie. Your ma and I had plenty of rocky patches before we took that stroll down the aisle," Dad said, trying to lift his spirits.

"I'm willing to work out rough patches. I don't like the part where she won't see me anymore and wants to court Amish guys." Unfortunately, James' voice rose in intensity while anger welled from deep within.

James Davis Sr. looked to his wife.

His mom stared at her hands for a minute before meeting his eye. "You say that you love this girl. And I believe that you do. But when you love someone, sometimes you have to put their best interests ahead of your own. Emma may have fallen in love with you too, but she might not be ready to disappoint her family and face shunning from her community. Everything that Emma knows in this world would be lost to her."

James slicked a hand through his hair. "You're saying her family would disown her if she married me? That doesn't sound very Christian."

"They wouldn't disown her exactly. Their actions would be more along the lines of ostracizing her. They believe they must maintain separation from the modern world in order to obtain salvation. They see the tremendous amount of sin, temptation, and evil in our English world and want no part of it. The main difference between their Christian faith and ours is they believe we can never feel *assured* of salvation, but must walk the narrow path until the moment of our death. They would ostracize Emma to protect the family from falling away from Amish ways. Do not judge them, son. We are all struggling to maintain a lifestyle acceptable in God's eyes."

"So there's nothing I can do?" he asked, recognizing hopelessness when he saw it. "If I convince her that I love her and wish to make her happy, and if she marries me...she might grow to resent me if she can't find contentment being English. Everything will be lost to her." He slumped in the chair and hung his head.

"There are two things you can do," Barbara said, walking to the oven. She pulled out the pan of fried chicken. "You can give her time to sort things out while you finish your studies. Keep your mind busy while she has a chance to grow up. She may see things differently in a year or two." Barbara emptied a jar of corn into a saucepot and turned on the stove.

James folded his arms and tried to calm down. "What's the second thing?" he asked. "You said two."

His mom looked at him with eyes full of compassion. "You can pray. If it's God's will for you to be together, nothing can stand in the way. But if God has other plans for you or for her, then trying to win her will only result in heartache. For the time being, give it up to the Lord and pray that He watches over your little Emma."

James felt his face grow hot and his scalp start to tingle as emotions rose to the surface. His mom's empathy clutched at his heart. This wasn't the resolution he'd sought, but he knew she was right. He inhaled a deep breath and said, "I'm going out to the horse barn for a while so I can think. I'll eat later, if that's okay."

With a nod from both parents, he rose and headed for the door. "Thanks, Mom," he mumbled.

If he had stayed longer or had tried to speak louder, they would have found out that a small Amish girl from Winesburg had brought him to his knees.

SEVENTEEN

Hannah awoke the day after Thanksgiving at dawn. She washed and dressed as quickly as she could and hurried downstairs. Her dear Seth had already started breakfast. The smell of frying bacon failed to whet her appetite as it usually did, but after seeing that he had fixed a pot of cinnamon oatmeal, she relaxed. No way would she get into a moving vehicle with an empty stomach again, not after her experience on the way to Wooster.

"*Guder mariye,*" she said upon reaching the kitchen. "Am I later than usual? Or are you an especially early bird today?"

"The latter, *fraa.* I wanted to make sure you ate a hearty meal before your trip to Canton. You arrived home green around the gills from your last outing with Emma."

She peeked into the pot. "You sliced up bananas into the oatmeal? Just how I like it! *Danki,* Seth." She wrapped an arm around his waist.

He buzzed a kiss across the top of her head. "You're welcome, but tell no one what you have seen this morning. I don't want to ruin my reputation among Amish men."

Hannah laughed as she poured a cup of coffee, but she also knew there was truth to his jest. Amish men seldom attempted domestic chores.

Seth took the remaining bacon from the pan with tongs. "Sit down and start eating, Hannah. I'm going out to see what's taking Phoebe so long in the henhouse."

He disappeared before she could volunteer to go, so Hannah settled into a chair with her bowl of cereal and contemplated the second trip in a month with her niece.

Julia was worried about her daughter. Ever since Emma wrote to young Davis to terminate their friendship, the girl had done nothing but work. If she wasn't in the herb shed or loft, she was baking or sewing or cleaning house. And if she ran out of tasks, she would read the Bible curled in a chair close to her *mamm*. She never left the farm except for preaching services. And Simon had noticed that his eldest was losing weight.

Emma was brokenhearted, even if she didn't admit it.

Mrs. Dunn's invitation to attend a giant craft fair in downtown Canton couldn't have come at a better time. The two-day exposition would give them a chance to sell handmade woolens and wreaths at good retail prices. And sleeping in a hotel and eating in restaurants might provide enough change of scenery to boost Emma's spirits.

Hannah had broached the subject yesterday during the family turkey dinner. Simon readily agreed to the *Rumschpringe* trip. Julia and Leah both gushed with excitement about staying overnight. However Emma's reply had been, "Okay, Aunt Hannah, if you think we can sell some crafts."

Not exactly bubbling with enthusiasm, Hannah thought while packing her overnight bag. She didn't like leaving her family even for one night, but they would be fine. It was Emma who needed her. And Hannah wanted to help.

Because Seth had packed her saleable woolens the night before, they were able to leave for Simon's right after breakfast. Phoebe came along for the ride and to visit her cousins. Within half an hour of Mrs. Dunn's arrival, Hannah and Emma had loaded their goods inside the large paneled van, and they were on their way.

Emma seemed happy enough. Although Mrs. Dunn did most of the talking, Emma explained her ideas on how to set up the booth. After they reached the convention center, they were so busy hauling, unpacking, and arranging stock that no one had time to mope. The craft fair proved hectic but rewarding. Emma was paid plenty of compliments on her workmanship, and all three ladies earned more than they had hoped by day's end.

Emma said little during dinner, and once back to their hotel room she seemed only interested in slipping on her nightgown and going to bed.

"Come look, Emma," Hannah called. "I made us hot chocolate in the micro-oven. Audrey explained how to do it. Let's sit at the little table and talk for a minute." Hannah heated the beverage to near scalding to prevent quick consumption.

Emma reluctantly complied, eyeing the cocoa suspiciously. "How come the Styrofoam cup didn't melt in the oven?"

"I have no idea," Hannah answered, studying her cup also. "How did you like the Mexican food for supper? I thought the steak fajitas were quite tasty once you added all those toppings."

Emma wrinkled her nose. "They tasted good, but they were awfully messy to eat. I took a bite and half of it shot out the other end onto my dress. The Mexicans must have to do lots of laundry." Her attention returned to the steaming cocoa.

Hannah tried again. "Isn't this craft fair amazing? There are so many different kinds of things for sale. It's much bigger than I ever imagined."

Emma turned stormy. "Some people brought mass-produced wreaths from foreign countries that they were able to sell cheaper than mine. I thought this was supposed to be for handmade crafts." She sipped her drink, burned her tongue, and emitted a yowl similar to the cat's when someone stepped on her tail.

Hannah pushed their two drinks aside for a moment and opted for the direct approach. "Emma, your *mamm* wanted you to come to the fair primarily for a change of scenery—to get your mind off your broken courtship. It doesn't seem to be working. Are you still pining over James Davis?"

Emma met her eye and then glanced away. "I'm trying not to, believe me, but I can't seem to forget him. He was the nicest *person* I've ever met, let alone the nicest boy!" She burst into tears.

The direct approach had been a disaster. Hannah patted Emma's hand until her sobs subsided.

"I still love him, Aunt Hannah," she whispered, "but please don't tell my parents. I don't want them to worry about me since I don't plan to see James again. I must be content with spinsterhood and being a good aunt to Matt, Leah, and Henry's future *kinner*, like you've been to me."

Her young face was so filled with despair, Hannah willed herself not to laugh at a sixteen-year-old's grim summation of her future. "There might still be a chance for happiness, dear, but not if you're always hiding in your loft. You told your mother you'd go to Sunday singings. Julia said you've only gone to one so far."

Emma slid her drink back and cupped her hands around the warmth. "*Jah*, that's true. My heart hasn't been in it." One teardrop fell into her cocoa. "But I suppose I had better go again before *mamm* finds out how miserable I am and starts worrying."

Hannah smiled inwardly, knowing a parent never stopped agonizing over their offspring. Before she slept tonight, Hannah would toss and turn, fretting over what Phoebe ate for supper and if Seth remembered to feed Turnip and the barn cats. She reached for her own drink. "Good idea. Try to go out as much as possible. These are the years to do so, and it will take your mind off your lonesomeness. You don't know what God has in mind for you, Emma. Give your problems over to Him and be brave." She took a sip of the hot chocolate. "Now tell me how you plan to prevail over the cheaply priced wreaths at tomorrow's fair."

Emma took a cautious sip from her cup. "Mmm, this is delicious once it cools down." A corner of her mouth turned up. "Tomorrow, I plan to hang a poster board sign that reads: 'Handmade Christmas Wreaths.' I'll make the first word huge with red letters. And since the other booth had a bunch of sourpusses, I intend to smile at every shopper who walks by." She grinned to practice her technique.

Hannah relaxed against the chair back. "Sounds like the perfect solution. Your competition doesn't stand a chance."

~

Hannah would be pleased to know Emma didn't have to wait until the next singing to enter back into Amish society. *Daed* announced the following Saturday that today was a cider-making frolic at a district member's farm and they would all attend. Julia was hobbling around much better with her aluminum walker. Leah, Emma, and Henry would accompany their parents immediately after lunch. All chores were to be completed beforehand. Matthew would ride over in the buggy after finishing his shift at Macintosh Farms. He couldn't wait to get to the cider-making party since hearing that a hayride for young people had been planned for the evening. Simon would let Matthew attend as long as he sat with the driver and not with the courting couples.

Emma tried not to think about courting couples while they loaded the last of their apples into the back of the wagon. They had already canned enough applesauce and sliced apples for pies to last the winter. Today the remainder would be pressed down to make cider. She loved a glass of cold cider with a meal or a mug of warm cider in the winter.

"This is my favorite kind of frolic," announced Henry during the ride. He was wedged in between his two sisters in the small second row of the wagon.

"Why is that?" Emma asked. "Because apples are your favorite fruit?" She gave his suspenders a playful snap.

"No, because it's a lot less work than a barn raising or house painting. Most of us get to stand around and just watch."

"And drink the cider and eat plenty of goodies," Leah added. "I've baked chocolate chip and peanut butter cookies. Did you make your famous Apple Betty bars when I wasn't looking?" she asked Emma.

"No, and they are not famous. I figured we'd get our fill of apples today. I made a pan of Rice Krispies squares."

"Joseph from Berlin will be mighty disappointed. His sister Elizabeth told me he's fond of your Apple Betty bars," Leah said, and then she pretended to be fascinated by the stark, empty field on her left.

"Joseph Kauffman?" Simon asked, glancing back at Emma. "He comes from a fine, hardworking family."

When their *daed* turned his attention back to the road, Emma muttered under her breath. "You're a tad young to be carrying gossip like that, Leah." She pulled the lap robe up to her waist.

"It's not gossip, sister, if the man truly enjoys your baking. And there's nothing wrong with him paying you a compliment." Leah tugged the robe back over her own knees.

Henry began squirming on the bench. "Could you two settle this when I'm not stuck in the middle?" He pulled the flaps of his hat down over his ears.

Leah smiled sweetly, Emma clucked her tongue, and Henry rolled his eyes. And so it went on the drive to the frolic. Luckily for Henry, the hosting family lived only forty minutes away. When the Millers turned up the lane, the yard and barn were already buzzing with activity.

"Looks like everybody in the county is here," Julia murmured.

"Oh, good," came from Leah.

"Oh, dear," was Emma's reply. But by the time they helped unload the baskets of apples, she had caught some of the infectious conviviality.

Since it took a bushel of apples to yield three gallons of cider, much work went into preparations. Apples needed to be fully ripe; windfalls made an excellent choice as long as they weren't wormy. They discarded any heavily bruised or damaged apples and then washed, cut up, and ground the rest into applesauce consistency. Finally, they fed the mash through a large apple press to separate out the juice. The resulting sweet cider was usually dark brown in color and contained plenty of pulp. It had to be kept cold and would remain sweet and unfermented for about two weeks. If a facility filtered and pasteurized the cider, it became apple juice, which had a longer shelf life.

Their host tasted the first glass from the press, declared it too tart and stirred in castor sugar. At long last, the batch was pronounced acceptable and folks lined up for a sample. Emma accepted a glass of cider and moved away from the crowd. She found a quiet spot near the door to sip and watch without becoming part of the hubbub. She especially wanted to avoid Sarah Hostetler and Sam Yoder. Seeing those two together, laughing and talking, reminded Emma of the fourth member of their group.

But she refused to be drawn back into despair. Despite herself, Emma was having a good time at the frolic. Sometimes if you acted as though you were having fun, life started moving in that direction.

"Whew, there you are, sister." A panting Leah joined her in the doorway with her *kapp* askew and the bottom of her hem muddy.

"*Jah*, here I am. Where have you been? Stomping around in the bog?" Emma was glad to see her sister acting like a child instead of a mini-version of *mamm*.

"A friend and I challenged two boys to a race to the pasture fence and we won." Joy radiated from her face while her breath came in great gulps.

"Was one boy limping and did the other have a cast on his foot?" Emma asked.

"No, neither one." Leah looked mystified. "Why would you ask that?"

"Just curious." Emma smiled as she turned to see the other runner.

It was Elizabeth Kauffman, Joseph's sister. Her thin face was streaked with perspiration. "Hullo, Elizabeth," Emma said.

"Hi, Emma. I'm glad you remember me from the singing. You haven't been back since." When Elizabeth smiled, her plain face took on unusual prettiness.

"I've been busy around the house, but I'll come to another singing very soon."

"Your sister and I are getting in line for supper. Will you sit with us? They're having ham, hot potato salad, and plenty of cold salads."

"All right," Emma said. "That way I can make sure Leah takes one of my desserts to get the ball rolling."

Leah snaked an arm around Emma's waist, but not before she pinched her sister's arm. "I'll be the first guinea pig since I know they're delicious."

With plates of food, the three girls found space at a table far away from the buffet line. Emma had just popped a baby beet into her mouth when Leah sprang to her feet. "We forgot drinks. I'll get us some cider."

"I'll help you carry them," Elizabeth declared. Off they scurried as though every movement should be deemed a race to the pasture fence.

"Good evening, Miss Miller...eh, Emma. Mind if I join you girls for supper?"

Emma swallowed hard and gazed into the near black eyes of Joseph Kauffman. His silky hair hung almost in his eyes. He desperately needed a haircut.

"Sure, sit there," she said, pointing to the other side of the table.

"Mind if I sit here?" he asked, gesturing to the spot beside her. "Then I won't have to carry this all the way around. He set down his plate as a corn muffin toppled off the pile. "I'm afraid I made a pig of myself." He stepped over the bench and squeezed in beside her.

"It's the cool weather that makes a person hungrier." She glanced again at his meal, amazed that someone could eat like that and remain thin.

He noticed her focus. "Anything you care to sample, Emma? You can help herself."

She felt herself blush. "No, *danki*. I've taken more than enough on my plate." She turned her attention to cutting her ham into very small pieces until the girls returned. While they ate, Leah and Elizabeth chattered about everything under the sun, from who brought the wormiest apples to who would host the next singing. Emma had begun to relax when she realized Leah was purposefully trying to draw her and Joseph into conversation.

"I don't see a Rice Krispies square on your plate, Joseph," Leah stated, pointing accusingly with her index finger.

"Perhaps he wishes to go home with all his teeth intact," Emma said, as she tried to kick Leah under the table. She connected with the table leg instead.

"Oh, no," Leah argued. "Your Rice Krispies squares aren't too sticky. They're always soft and crunchy. Emma makes the best desserts, but she's too modest to admit it." Leah directed this assertion at both of the Kauffmans.

Emma rolled her eyes and concentrated on eating. "I'll tell you what's really good—this ham! The glaze has plenty of brown sugar and molasses."

"Joseph, some day you'll have to try Emma's Apple Betty bars. They're loaded with brown sugar too."

"I have had that pleasure, Leah. And I must agree they're *wunderbaar*."

Emma drained her cup and held it out to Leah. "Could you please get more cider? I'm blocked in and I'm still parched dry. *Danki*." She smiled graciously.

Leah looked puzzled. "Sure, Emma," she replied and dashed off with the empty cup. For some reason, Elizabeth jumped up to follow.

Emma released an audible sigh of relief. "I hope my younger sister isn't making you uncomfortable. She seems bound and determined to make me look good in your eyes and has the subtlety of a rooster at dawn." Emma stared down at her plate.

Joseph laughed without embarrassment. "I'm not the least bit uncomfortable, Emma. We're friends, remember? We agreed to that at the singing. And Leah needn't worry about my opinion of you. I thought highly of you the first time we met. Never let little sisters get under your skin. I seldom pay much attention to mine." He pushed away his plate and wiped his hands on a napkin. "I'm going to take the rest. It's too much to waste and I'm full."

"*Danki* for not running for the door." Emma finished her potato salad and pickled cucumbers. Her appetite was finally returning.

"Will you do me a favor?" he asked. "I want to ask this now before Miss-Buttinsky-one-and-two come back with the drinks."

Emma wiped her mouth and hands. "What kind of favor? Send Elizabeth and Leah on a wild goose chase for the rest of the night?"

One corner of his mouth lifted and a smile filled his angular face. "I'd like you to sit with me on the hayride tonight." He looked away. "Truth is I love hayrides, but I can't bear to go on another one alone or with my sister." Suddenly, Joseph Kauffman looked earnest and melancholy.

With his change in demeanor, Emma realized she'd only been thinking about herself. She had agreed to be his friend, and then she made little effort to be friendly. "Of course I will. I was hoping you would save me from sitting with Leah. She keeps pinching my arm. I've got purple marks to prove it."

"She can ride with Elizabeth. That one is always pulling my hair or doing something ornery. They can sit together and annoy each other."

Emma rose from the bench. Joseph held her elbow as she extricated herself from the picnic table with as much dignity as possible. Just as they were about to throw away their trash, the sisters returned with brimming cups of cider.

"Where are you going? We brought you more to drink." Elizabeth looked suspicious.

"*Danki*, we'll take these with us," Joseph said, taking both cups. "I need Emma's advice on a matter. And I wish to see her new pony. We'll catch up with you two later. Much later."

Emma hurried toward the barn door, trying not to laugh. Leah rather deserved this—she'd been making a nuisance of herself.

"Should I wrap up your leftovers in foil, *bruder*?" Elizabeth called.

"Emma didn't bring her pony cart today. We came in the wagon." Leah hollered. Neither received any response.

When Emma and Joseph reached outdoors, they sped toward the largest oak to hide behind until certain they weren't being followed. "I think we've lost them," Emma whispered, peering around the trunk. When she glanced back at Joseph, he was watching her oddly.

"My sister said you and that English fellow weren't courtin' anymore and that he went off to college."

This was the last topic she wanted to discuss, but she couldn't be rude. "*Jah*, that's true. He's in Wooster." She stared past him at horses silhouetted in the pasture.

"I know you would never do anything to dishonor yourself. And the fact that you rode around in his pickup truck doesn't matter a hill of beans to me. You are the finest woman I've ever met, and I'm glad you're my friend." He crossed his arms over his jacket and waited for her response.

Problem was, Emma didn't know what to say. She thought maybe she should thank Joseph for his faith in her, but that sounded rather stiff. She picked up a cup of cider from where he had set them in the grass and drank it down. "I'm glad to hear that, Joseph. Shall we see if they're loading the hay wagon for the first ride? I'm really getting excited, because I haven't gone on one in a long time."

He tipped his hat and offered his arm as they crossed the lawn toward the farm road. Emma didn't know what to make of Joseph.

The older she got, the more confused she became. Didn't people say, with age comes wisdom? She hoped some would hurry up and get here already.

~

December

"Git up there," Seth shouted to his team of Percherons. He threw his full weight against the wagon wheel that was stuck in a deep furrow. His lead horse picked up his ears and pulled hard against the traces, dragging the wheel from the rut. A spray of cold muddy water, smelling faintly of decay, splashed Seth from head to toe. This was his just reward for not paying attention as he drove his team.

"*Ach,*" he muttered, pulling a handkerchief from his pocket. With the wagon headed in the right direction, he dared not worry about his appearance right now. He needed to deliver hay to several round stanchions for his cows and horses, and to Hannah's sheep in another pasture.

A cold wind cut through his damp jacket and trousers, adding to his discomfort. He would be glad when it turned cold enough to freeze the mud into solid footing for his wagon. This had been the third time he'd become mired this week. But he couldn't blame the horses for his lack of concentration. Each time he fed the livestock, he remembered the hay had been purchased from a neighboring English farmer—hay he should have grown himself.

Simon had cautioned against veering from traditional self-sufficiency; even his wife had advised against focusing on one cash crop. But Seth thought he could solve district financial woes with one big harvest. Proverbs 3:5-6 said, "Trust in the Lord with all your heart; do not depend on your own understanding. Seek his will in all that you do, and he will show you which path to take." But Seth hadn't done that. He had been a foolish, stubborn man, and now he must pay the price for his pride.

He would consider himself blessed if he didn't lose his farm. And his sweet wife and child would face winter with a lean purse because of his misjudgment. For the hundredth time, Seth clenched down on his back molars, wishing he could do things over. Feeling cold, wet, and frustrated, he delivered the rest of the hay to his hungry animals and headed to the pump house to wash up. It was time to face his wife, and he wouldn't compound her woes by tracking up the kitchen.

"My goodness, Seth," Hannah exclaimed, spotting him in the back hall. She stood with her hands on her hips and her green eyes flashing. "Did you wash in the freezing cold pump house? Why didn't you clean up inside?" She reached for a towel to hand him. "Quick, dry your hair before you catch your death."

"I'll leave my coat on the throw rug since it needs washing." Seth shucked off his wet garments and then toweled his hair, face, and arms. "I got splashed by the wheels and didn't want to bring any mud inside."

Hannah shook her head. "*Danki* for that. Come eat some hot stew and get warmed up. Isn't that the third time you got stuck in the mud? What's wrong with those horses? Should we buy them glasses next time we're in town? Sit here by the oven. It's still warm from this morning. I baked banana bread with the last of those ripe bananas I bought on sale." She quickly finished preparing lunch.

Seth let Hannah rattle on the way she usually did when he came in from the fields. While Phoebe was at school, Hannah would save up things to say during the quiet morning and release them in a barrage at lunchtime. Pouring a cup a coffee, he sat down to watch his fireball of a wife unwind.

Finally, she halted mid-sentence, halfway through a list of the recently announced December weddings. "What's wrong, Seth? Why are you staring at me like that?" She scooped up two bowls of stew and set them on the table.

"Hannah," he said. "Stop flitting around like a bumblebee and sit down."

She complied with a forehead creased with worry. "What has happened?"

Seth tried to smile. "Nothing's happened, but we need to talk. I've been acting like a turtle—pulling my head into my shell, hoping the threat will go away, but I must confess that I was wrong to follow the corn alliance." He took several slow breaths. "When the price of petroleum fell, so did the price paid for a bushel of corn. Not much demand for ethanol if it costs more to produce than a barrel of fossil oil. We thought...I thought we would reap huge profits to fatten the medical account and replace worn-out equipment, but once I delivered the last of my corn to the elevator, the profits barely covered the cost of extra seed and fertilizer." He forced himself to pause and not dump the news on her like an avalanche.

Hannah was sitting in the opposite chair, clutching her mug of lemon tea. "You meant well, Seth. Your heart was in the right place." She reached for his hand. "We make mistakes. God doesn't expect us to be perfect, only to keep trying. We all fall short. I expect you'll return to the old ways come spring." She winked at him in an attempt to lighten his mood.

Seth patted her hand. "*Jah*, that is true, but I'm worried about the months between now and then." He gazed into her emerald green eyes. "I'll need to buy more hay and livestock feed. I've got no hay left from my first cutting and not enough ground corn in the silo to last the winter. And the price of feed sure hasn't fallen any. I drew up a budget for our expenses including land taxes for the next six months. We're going to have enough. Right now, I accepted a delivery of hay on credit, but I must pay for it soon. I'll not have another family suffer because of my pigheadedness." He focused on the oak table. "I'm sorry, Hannah. I should've listened to you and my *bruder*. Then we wouldn't be facing winter with empty silos. Now my family is going to suffer."

Hannah pulled his clenched fists toward her. "We are *not* going to suffer, Seth Miller. We may have tribulation, *jah*, because the Lord wants us to learn our lessons—either the easy way or the hard way. But we won't be walking that road alone. He'll be right there next to us." The slanted light from the window made her eyes sparkle. "If times are lean, we'll economize and be more frugal, but I won't have you punishing yourself because of an error made with good intentions. We'll get through this. It will strengthen us as Christians and as a family." She exhaled and relaxed against the chair back. "And we can use the last of my farm sale proceeds to pay for hay."

She pulled the bowl of stew over and began to eat. "Whew, Seth. You had me worried at first that something was seriously wrong. Money is just…money. It ebbs and flows like the tides. We're better off when we don't worry too much about it."

Seth stared at her and then picked up his spoon and also started to eat. The stew smelled wonderful. He was a fortunate man. He'd been blessed with the sweetest woman on earth for a wife.

EIGHTEEN

Emma sat alone in her loft, spending more time staring out the window than spinning wool into yarn. Snow was falling, blanketing the fields in a cloak of pristine white. Winter was a time of rest and rejuvenation. After the whirlwind of harvest, a farm took a deep breath and restored itself. Farmers also used this time to relax, plan for spring, and contemplate whether the path they were on was the right one.

Emma wasn't so sure. She'd gone on the hayride with Joseph and made every effort to be friendly. She laughed at his jokes, listened to his plans for expansion of the harness shop, and drank hot cider around the bonfire under the stars.

He had asked to take her home.

She had declined and ridden home with Matthew. At her *mamm*'s prodding she'd attended the next singing, but she found it far less enjoyable than the first. Elizabeth had kept watching her like a bug under a magnifying glass. And Joseph nearly tripped over himself trying to be helpful.

Would you care for more cider, Emma?

Could I bring you some more cookies?

Are you warm enough? Would you like me to get you a lap robe?

What she wanted was peace and quiet and found that only here in her cluttered workroom. *Daed* had installed a small potbellied stove to keep her from freezing to death while contemplating the rest of her life. She wasn't hiding from her family as much as she was trying to find herself. She still missed James so much. It was his handsome face she saw every night when she closed her eyes and tried to sleep. She would hear his voice on every walk through the forest or while passing near the beaver pond on her way to Aunt Hannah's. She had prayed for guidance and for the strength to forget him, yet her love hadn't diminished one bit.

She pictured herself rocking on the porch as a very old woman, replaying in her mind their canoe trip and train ride. Fate could be so cruel. She wouldn't leave her faith or shame her family, but she couldn't seem to forget him, either.

"Emma? Are you up there?" A voice from below jolted her from the daydream. It was her *mamm*.

"*Jah*, I'm working," she called, which wasn't exactly the truth.

"You have a visitor," Julia called. "I'm sending her up. Come into the house if you two get cold."

"Okay," she hollered and expected to see Aunt Hannah poke her head at the top of the steps.

Instead, Sarah Hostetler appeared on the landing. "There you are, Emma Miller, at long last. You can't hide from me any longer."

Emma hung her head, mortified. "I'm so sorry. Please forgive me." She wasn't about to compound her sin by lying.

"You are forgiven," said Sarah and ran to embrace her.

Emma stumbled to her feet as pieces of wool fell to the floor. She allowed herself to be enfolded in a hug.

"I know why you've avoided me. I'm not a *dummkopf*. Every time you see Sam and me you're reminded of James."

Emma nodded. "True. I'm a selfish woman and a poor friend."

"No, you're a normal woman." Sarah glanced around the room. "*Ach*, what a mess up here. How do you stand all this lint and dust?" She sneezed as though on cue.

Emma laughed and brushed a pile of raw wool off the other chair. "It doesn't bother me, but Leah won't set foot up here with her allergies."

"Hmm, I have little sisters too. This lint can be a blessing in disguise."

Both girls laughed as Emma realized how much she'd missed her friend. "I have missed you, Sarah," she blurted out.

"And I, you," Sarah said. "I saw you sitting with Joseph at the cider-making frolic. And I also saw you climbing into the wagon for the first hayride with him. Sam and I went on the last ride. Has Joseph asked to court you?" Her pretty brown eyes grew round as her voice dropped to a whisper.

Emma rose from her stool and began pacing the floor. "Not in so many words, but I think he wants to. I'm dreading the question."

"Why?" Sarah dabbed at her nose with a hanky. "He's a nice boy from what I hear…and as an only son he'll eventually take over his pa's harness shop."

Emma tried not to reveal her feelings. "*Jah*, he's very nice and quite attentive. He'll make some woman a good husband some day."

"But not you?" Sarah pulled the hanky from her face.

"I really don't know how I feel. I just know things are impossible with James. Joseph asked me to an ice-skating party next Saturday if the cold snap holds. I will wait and see what happens."

Sarah nodded sagely. "When in doubt, do nothing." She gazed toward the skylight, where dust motes floated and swirled in the winter sunlight. "Have you heard any news from James since your visit?"

The question hung in the air unanswered for a few minutes. "No. I told him not to stop by or write any more letters."

Sarah crossed her arms and tilted her head. "A clean break…always the best way. If you *were* to hear news of him, it might just get your hopes up, and we couldn't have that, could we?"

This question took half a minute to sink in. Then Emma stared at her friend. "Have you heard something, Sarah Hostetler? If so, I sure wish you'd spit it out instead of dangling it like catnip."

Sarah's grin filled her face. "I only know that James Davis Jr. has been coming home every Thursday after his last class. He doesn't spend a single minute on campus more than necessary. He's home working on the farm until dawn on Monday, and then he drives back to Wooster." She stood and moved closer to the potbellied stove to warm her hands.

Emma added more kindling, stirred the embers, and shut the little brass door. "That's hardly news, dear girl. He loves farming and would spend as much time home as possible." She held her palms above the radiant heat too.

"*Jah*, but I also know he's been attending church services with Sam and his family. You can guess who told me that little tidbit." She winked at Emma.

Emma's head snapped up. "James has been attending New Order preaching services?" Her voice revealed her disbelief. "Whatever for? He's not Amish."

"That I do not know. Why don't you write him a letter and ask him?" She smiled with satisfaction.

"Oh, no, I could never do that."

"Suit yourself, Emma, but you'll spend the entire winter up here wondering." Sarah glanced around the untidy but serviceable workroom again, sniffed, and then sneezed.

Emma was about to list the reasons she couldn't contact James when the barn door opened and a shout came from down below. A gust of cold air accompanied Leah's words up the stairs. "Emma, Sarah? Are you two still up there? *Mamm* says to come in now and get warmed up. She made a pot of blackberry tea and I baked lemon-poppy seed muffins."

Emma shook her head as she walked to the landing. "*Danki*, Leah. We'll be right down. I just want to bank the stove."

Sarah waited until Emma finished with the fire before she grabbed her sleeve. "Before we go in, I want to tell you something in private." She lowered her voice in case the little-mouse-with-big-ears was still in the barn. "Sam has proposed, but we're going to wait to announce our engagement for a while."

"Congratulations!" exclaimed Emma, hugging her friend tightly. "But why the wait and why keep it a secret? You and Sam are perfect together."

"My parents don't quite agree, at least not yet, so we're waiting to marry until I turn eighteen."

Emma knew that Sarah was Old Order, but Sam Yoder wasn't. "What will you do? Have you decided?" She also kept her tone a whisper.

"*Jah*, I've decided to become New Order when we marry. I won't be shunned since I haven't taken the kneeling vow yet, but *mamm* and *daed* still won't be too happy. We're giving them time to get used to the idea." Sarah smiled with her face flushed with the promise of new love. "So for now, this is our secret, okay?"

"Of course," said Emma, "but we'd better go in before Leah returns. She'll drag us out by our capes. She thinks even five minutes spent in a barn is five minutes too long."

Both girls started down the stairs. At the bottom Emma looked at Sarah earnestly. "*Danki* for coming over today. And for not being angry with me and for the news about James." She glanced at the doorway and then back toward the loft. "You're right, I'll probably mull over that information all the way till spring."

～

Early January

The skating party had to be postponed several times. Temperatures had warmed into the forties just before Christmas and melted all the snow, including the ice on ponds. Emma breathed a sign of relief. She wasn't eager for the date with Joseph. Reminding herself that they were friends, she feared he wished for something more permanent. She tried to picture herself courting him, but every time it was a blond-haired, blue-eyed man who escorted her to singings or for rides in his courting buggy. It was all very silly—the imaginings of a foolish young woman. James Davis wasn't even Amish.

Emma's loneliness abated somewhat at Christmastime. Visits from *Mammi* and *Dawdi* Kline and from Uncle Thomas and his bride, Catherine, filled the house with love and laughter. She, Leah, and *mamm* were so busy cooking or baking up goodies during the two-week visit that she had no time to feel sorry for herself.

Aunt Hannah was usually there, along with Phoebe and Uncle Seth, to lend a hand but mainly to visit with her parents. The menfolk stayed out in the barn until frozen fingers and toes drew them back to the woodstove in the front room. *Daed* said they were busy planning for spring, but Emma knew they mostly visited and swapped stories during the quietest time of the year. Everyone attended Simon's evening Scripture readings as they sought inspiration from the Gospel accounts of the Savior's birth.

Hannah, usually far more talkative than an average Plain woman, had grown quiet during the waning days of Catherine and Thomas' visit, ever since the night Catherine announced she was expecting a *boppli* in the late spring. Everyone had been joyous, slapping Thomas on the back and hugging Catherine, including Hannah. But Emma had seen Hannah's eyes full of tears when she carried dessert plates to the kitchen, probably because she wasn't in a family way yet. Emma pitied her aunt, knowing how it felt not to get your heart's desire.

New nightgowns from *mamm*, chocolate candy kisses from *daed*, a birdhouse from Henry, and Matthew's gift of new leather harnesses for her pony cart had brightened the season's festivities. Leah had surpassed herself with a gift of cookbooks and jars of colored icing. Emma loved and treasured each gift, yet just one inexpensive greeting card from Charm could have made her holiday perfect.

Yet no card had come, and Emma knew James would respect her

request to stay away. Today, very cold and sunless, she would drive over to the Hershberger farm with Leah for the rescheduled ice skating party. Dressing in many layers, she waddled downstairs feeling as though she faced a trip to the dentist rather than a social outing.

"Ah, Emma," said Simon, "ready to go? I hope you don't fall down on the ice. Bundled up like that, you'll never get back up." He laughed heartily as he finished his coffee.

Emma also laughed. Picturing herself helplessly flat on the ice was funny, and she laughed because her father seldom cracked a joke. "I'll just have to wait for a thaw and float to shore." She grabbed some carrot sticks for her pony, Maybelle.

"I'm sure Joseph will be close by to pull you upright." Simon chuckled again, but Emma lost her good humor.

The fact that her parents were pushing her toward the harness maker's son only made her more resistant. Luckily, at that moment her sister lumbered into the room, equally overdressed. "Ready to go, Leah? Let's be off." Emma brushed a kiss on her father's cheek and headed outdoors.

Her dear *bruder* had the pony hitched up and ready to go. Leah chattered about one topic after another along the way, giving Emma time to think. Unfortunately, even a forty-five minute ride wasn't sufficient for the solutions she required.

Joseph practically ran to their pony cart when they parked near the barn. "Hullo, Emma. Leah." He swept off his hat and then settled it back in place. "I'll put your Appaloosa inside a barn stall. There's room. They've started the bonfire if you're cold from the ride over. Food tables are set up in the north outbuilding in case you're hungry." He pointed with one long finger in the general direction. "I'll eat whenever you want, Emma. Should I carry your skates to the pond?"

The two sisters exchanged glances; neither had ever heard him talk so much or so fast. "I'll see you later, Em. I'm going to look for Elizabeth." Leah grabbed her skates and ran—not walked—away from the pony cart.

She smiled weakly at Joseph and tried to remember his questions. "I'm not hungry yet, nor am I too cold. Why don't you put away Maybelle and then we can skate for a spell?"

He looked confused and then realized Maybelle was her pony. "Sure. I'll be back in a few minutes."

Emma grabbed the hamper of baked goods and her skates and walked toward the pond. She didn't wait while Joseph put the horse away. Young people and courting couples were already skating. Slab wood benches sat close to the ice for donning skates, while the bonfire's flames leaped in the air, promising to warm chilly fingers and toes.

It didn't take Emma long to spot Sarah and Sam out on the ice. They skated very close together with crossed arms, while exchanging moon-cow glances. Emma bit the inside of her cheek to stem the tide of envy. Sarah was her friend and deserved happiness even if she spent the rest of her life in a dusty workroom.

"Ready, Emma?" Joseph asked over her shoulder. He was smiling sweetly at her.

She wasn't worthy of the attention from such a kind and gentle soul. Mean-spirited, jealous people like her deserved to be shut away in a barn loft. "*Jah*, let's skate," she said, sitting on the bench. They laced on their skates and glided onto the sparkling ice. It was smooth and free of snow after the quick freeze. Emma soon found her stride. With one hand locked on Joseph's elbow and the other hand aloft for balance, she circled the pond many times, weaving in and out of slower skaters. The sun peeked from behind the clouds, turning the gray January day into a sharp contrast of light and shadow. Emma relaxed while skating and allowed the physical activity to occupy her mind and body completely.

Finally, it was Joseph who demanded a break. "Whew, let's rest for a spell. My ankles are getting sore. Today's the first time I've had these things on in quite some time." He hobbled clumsily up the bank to where they had left their boots.

Emma noticed that all other benches were empty. Everyone was either skating, inside the barn having a snack, or by the bonfire. She stretched out her legs with her feet balanced on the skate blades. The crisp air filled her lungs, giving her a boost of energy. "My, I've been cooped up too long indoors. It's so good to breathe fresh air."

Joseph nodded vigorously. "*Jah*, true. Are you getting thirsty? Or maybe I can get you a few cookies to tide you over till supper?"

Either he was very nervous or he thought that she never went longer than ten minutes without eating or drinking something. "Neither, *danki*. I'm fine just to sit a moment and watch the skaters." She reached over and patted his forearm with her gloved hand. It was a meaningless gesture, one she used with her siblings all the time.

But Joseph Kauffman did not find it so meaningless. Without warning, he leaned over and kissed her—not on the forehead or cheek, but squarely on the mouth.

She was so shocked the kiss was over before she could respond. Then Emma's reaction was sheer terror. She had played her friend falsely, somehow giving him the impression that she wished to be courted. "Nooooo," she moaned. Her hands flew to undo her skates' laces, and then she pulled off her skates, tugged on her boots, and ran pell-mell away from the pond.

"Wait, Emma. Stop, please," called Joseph.

Emma ran wildly, stumbling and almost falling in her untied boots. She didn't stop until she reached a stand of pine trees, far from the skating party. Panting and with her nose running, she threw herself against a tree trunk and sobbed.

One or two minutes passed before she heard his tender voice. "Forgive me, Emma. I had no right to behave so boldly. Please, slap my face or kick my shins, but I beg you not to cry. I'm so sorry."

Emma pulled her wet face from the pine bark and turned to face him. He stood with his hat in hand, looking like a condemned man.

"No, Joseph. It's me who's sorry. I should have told you the truth right away and we wouldn't be in this predicament. I'm in love with the *Englischer*. I honestly tried not to be, but I still am!" The tears resumed like a waterfall in spring. "I haven't been kind to you, and you're…a…very…nice…man." Her declaration sounded like a string of hiccups.

"*Ach*, Emma, I'm not that nice a guy or I wouldn't have stolen that kiss. Cry your eyes out on my shoulder if you like, and then we can go back to being what we were—friends. I can still use a few more of those." He drew her to his chest while she buried her face in his soft wool coat. When the crying stopped, she stepped back and wiped her face with his hanky. "*Danki*, Joseph."

"Okay, what do you want to do now? Get something to eat?"

Despite her misery, a smile she couldn't resist began in the corner of her mouth. *We're back to the topic of food again.* "No, not yet. I want to skate and skate and skate…all the way until dark."

And so they did, but eventually they ate sloppy joes and sat around the bonfire sipping hot chocolate for him and warm cider for her. It felt good to have a friend, and Emma felt an enormous weight lift from her shoulders. Despite the stolen kiss and emotional upheaval, she had enjoyed herself at the skating party.

But Joseph didn't ask to take her home. And Emma knew he never would. He was looking for a wife and it would not be her. One day he would find the perfect one, while she faced a lonely lifetime of spinning wool into yarn, hidden away in her barn loft like some fabled storybook character.

~

Late February

"I'll take that egg if you don't mind," Hannah said to the chicken. After a ruffle of feathers and a loud cluck, the hen rose from her roost and strutted toward the ramp. She marched from the henhouse without a backward glance.

"*Danki* very much." Hannah placed the egg with the others in the basket and then grabbed for the support post. A wave of dizziness overtook her as her stomach churned and somersaulted. The taste of bile inched up her throat as Hannah tried steadying herself with deep breaths.

Inhaling deeply in a henhouse was always a bad idea. Hannah set down the basket and ran for the door. Something she ate at breakfast had upset her stomach, so she hurried toward the house. Maybe it was the scrambled eggs or the fried bacon playing havoc, but Hannah didn't make it to the bathroom. She doubled over, gripped her knees, and vomited into the bushes on the side of the henhouse. When the wave of nausea finally passed, Hannah sucked clean cold February air into her lungs and waited for her head to clear. From the branches overhead, she heard the distinctive chirping of songbirds heralding the return of spring to Holmes County. The early birds were back. She spotted thickening buds on the rhododendron bushes and turkey vultures soaring high in the wind currents.

Spring couldn't arrive soon enough for her.

When she felt better, she fetched paper towels and a bucket of water from the pump house to clean up and then went indoors. Seth would have to retrieve the basket of eggs later. This was the third time she'd been sick this week. She prayed over and over in her head: *If it be Your will, Lord, please let it be.*

She dared not name her heart's desire. God knew she yearned for a *boppli* of her own to love in the *wunderbaar* home Seth had made for her. She had all but given up hope, remembering with shame her initial reaction of envy upon hearing that Catherine was pregnant. Now Hannah couldn't wait for her *bruder's* blessed event, only a couple months away. Seth promised they would travel back to Lancaster once the baby arrived and spring planting was finished. Would she have news of her own to share with Thomas and Catherine?

Walking through her warm kitchen, smelling faintly of cinnamon and spice, Hannah headed for the bathroom to wash her face and hands and then brush her teeth. Feeling refreshed, she went back to the kitchen and knelt by her chair and bowed her head. Her prayer was simple and earnest. She prayed for a safe delivery of Catherine's child, a lifting of Seth's worries over family finances, a salving of Emma's wounded heart…and that she might, indeed, be pregnant.

Seth found Hannah still kneeling, with her head bent in silent prayer, when he returned from town twenty minutes later. He walked quietly to her side and laid a large hand upon her shoulder. "What troubles you, *fraa,* that you would seek counsel in the middle of the day? Has something happened? Are you ill?"

His tender words soothed her nerves like nothing in the herb book ever could. "Not now I'm not. It has passed. But I have much to pray for and to be thankful for. Didn't want to save it all up for evening." She struggled to her feet, feeling clumsy and stiff.

Seth lifted her up effortlessly. When they both settled themselves at the table, he asked, "Tell me, Hannah, what is bothering you. I'm worried."

She remained mute for several moments, while insecurity and fear over voicing her hopeful speculation surfaced. "I'm afraid to speak, *ehemann.* I don't want to seem prideful or overly confident and ruin my chances of it being true."

Seth laughed. That wasn't exactly the response she'd expected. "God doesn't punish us for boldly speaking that which is true and just. If you have good news, be brave. Speak up and share it with me. I think I have an idea what this is about. I haven't been living in China for the past few weeks." His grin crinkled the skin around his eyes.

"Seth Miller! You're impossible." She playfully slapped his arm and then rose to her feet. "I'm getting our sandwiches for lunch. If you don't mind, I'd like to wait a couple more months just to be sure, so please don't tell your *bruder* or my sister about your…suppositions."

"Hannah—"

She raised a palm to stem his protests. "Only two months, Seth, and then I promise—you'll be the first person I tell the good news. After that, I don't care if you take out an ad in the *Daily Journal.*"

He sneaked up from behind as she searched the refrigerator and hugged her waist. "It's a deal. Then I tell the world."

While they ate lunch, Hannah thought it best to change the subject. "How did it go in town? Were you able to order the feed that we'll need?"

"*Jah*, they will deliver it tomorrow." Seth set his sandwich on the plate and pushed it away.

"Something wrong?" she asked. "Too much mustard?"

"The sandwich is fine, but I heard some talk at the elevator today that got me worried."

"Go on," she prompted, not liking his change of mood.

"Many that had been in the corn alliance are still talking big. Some want to go to the bishop to demand that certain machinery be permitted to speed up planting and harvesting. They are upset about our financial straits. Apparently, we're not the only ones with money difficulties." He met her gaze. His dark cool eyes did not look happy.

"And what did you say to these hotheads?"

"I said it was bold talk like this that got us into this predicament. We need to let the bishop guide us through the crisis instead of causing more dissension."

"You have no desire for additional machinery?" she asked.

"None. I intend to bow my head in prayer after lunch and ask for guidance. This time I plan to listen to what He tells me."

Hannah saw some of the uneasiness in Seth drain away. She reached for his plate and pushed it in front of him. "Then I suggest you finish eating your lunch. It'll help keep up your strength."

NINETEEN

Late April

Emma decided that even a hermit must come out of her cave on a day like this. By eleven o'clock, the sun had burned off the morning dew and had risen high enough for temperatures to reach sixty degrees. With no wind and not a cloud in the sky, the little hermit decided it was a good day to go to town.

Mamm was hobbling around well enough to not need her help fixing lunch. Leah, Matthew, and Henry were at school—soon to be a distant memory for Matthew, who would graduate in a couple weeks. *Daed* was busy with spring planting and would stay in the fields until supper. Considering she had caught up with her spinning and carding and had just completed a piece on the loom, Emma felt she deserved a day off.

Her *mamm* had even encouraged her to go, supplying a list of items she wanted from the bulk food store with additional money for a rare family treat—take-out pizza. When Emma reached the barn, she unexpectedly found Simon hitching up the pony cart.

"*Danki* for getting Maybelle ready to go, but you shouldn't have taken time away from planting. I know how to hitch a horse into the traces."

"*Ach*, I needed a break from plowing. Too much dust. Anyway,

I rarely get to see you, daughter. You're always working so hard in the shed or barn, or you're up in your room." Simon smiled at her, looking rather sad.

Emma didn't mention the fact she sat at the dinner table each evening, because she knew what he meant. She had spent little time with her family, seldom rocking on the porch or sitting in the front room, never lingering over coffee after supper. She'd been wallowing in loneliness, and her father's expression almost broke her heart. "Sorry, *daed.* This morning I came to the same conclusion that I spend too much time alone."

She grabbed the seat back and stepped into the cart. "That's why I decided to drive to town—to look at something other than the walls of my loft. And I promise to stop being such a stranger." She took the reins from him and then clucked to Maybelle.

But Simon held tight to the bridle. "Do you want your *mamm* to ride along for company? Or maybe your old gray-haired *daed?*"

Emma was taken aback. *Taking a day from chores during the busiest time of year? Unheard of!*

"No, *danki.* I won't be gone long. Just a quick trip."

"Oh, I saw Amos Kauffman from Berlin yesterday. He seems to think his boy, Joseph, is courting Martha Hostetler." Simon clung to Maybelle's halter.

Emma lifted an eyebrow. A deacon never discussed who was courting whom, at least not until today anyway, "*Jah,* I heard the same from Sarah."

Father and daughter locked gazes—Simon's watery gray eyes with Emma's cornflower blue. "Did you two have a fight?" he asked. "I thought you liked him. Your *mamm* said you stopped going to singings again."

Emma felt no anger with the question, only an odd sense of pity. She answered softy, "I still like him. He's a nice young man and we're friends. Martha Hostetler is a nice person too, so they sound perfect for each other, *jah?*"

Simon swept off his hat and turned his face skyward. "I suppose so." He didn't sound very convincing. "But what about you, Emma?"

"What about me? I'm soon to be seventeen, not thirty. Am I that loathsome a daughter that you and *mamm* are anxious to get rid of me?" Her voice rose a notch.

Simon looked just as surprised as when Curly delivered an unexpected head-butting. "No, Emma. Why would you ask such a thing?" He cocked his head to the side.

She felt her face flush. "Because you sure sound eager to marry me off to Joseph Kauffman."

"No, no, no, not if you don't have feelings for each other. Your *mamm* and I...we just hate seeing you so lonely and unhappy. Do you think we haven't noticed?" He touched the sleeve of her dress. "We would be content if you never wed and lived here forever with us, as long as you laugh and smile again. You haven't taken me to see your new lambs yet, like you did last year." He lifted her chin with two fingers to meet her gaze. "I love you, daughter. I only wish to see you at peace."

Emma swallowed hard. "I am happy. I just have a hard time showing it." She felt the salty sting of tears in the back of her throat. "And I love you too." Abruptly, she shook the reins on the pony's back. "Git up there, Maybelle." As the pony cart started rolling, she called over her shoulder, "We'll take a walk to see the lambs as soon as I get back."

Simon waved while Emma headed for Winesburg. There would be no crying today. The weather was too nice for tears.

In town Emma chatted with the shopkeepers as she found everything on her list and *mamm*'s, and then she treated herself to an ice-cream cone while they baked the pizza. She sat outside at an umbrella table, waving at passing buggies and enjoying the perfect spring weather. Across the street, sparrows were busily building a nest in the crook of a tree while bees went from flower to flower among the lilacs.

Now that she was out and about, Emma didn't want to go home. But her afternoon chores awaited besides a promise made to *daed*. Tucking the fragrant pizza into the wooden storage box, Emma clucked her tongue to the small horse and left the charming town.

She wasn't the only one who appreciated the warm, sunny day. Everywhere Emma looked she saw children on swing sets, women hanging clothes on the line, men tilling small gardens or large fields, even one English teenager stretched out on a lounge chair, working on an early suntan. Emma waved at them all as the last of her winter melancholy faded in the bright sunshine. Her thoughts turned to the Sunday singing this week—maybe she would go after all. She needn't worry about Joseph. He was busy courting Martha with her blessing. She also mulled over Aunt Hannah, who'd been keeping closer to home lately. Something was going on at the other Miller brother farm, and she had a good idea what it involved.

Thoughts of her *bruder*, happy to be done with school, and of Leah, quite the accomplished baker these days, ran through her mind. But as usual, thoughts of James came creeping back too. But no heartache was attached to these reminiscences, only the fuzzy memory of a different springtime in her young life.

The face of James Davis, with his ruddy, suntanned complexion and bright blue eyes, was the last thing she saw in her mind's eye. Then the horrible sound of screeching tires, the crunch of gravel, the discordant blare of a car horn, and finally the mournful wail of an animal in pain filled her ears. Emma's world turned black. For a moment, she experienced the weightless sensation of flying through the air…and then she felt nothing at all.

~

James jammed his English and math textbooks into his backpack and swung the heavy bag over his shoulder. Emma had hit one nail right on the head: What did a farmer need with all this book learning?

At least in the fall when he returned to school, most of his courses would be agriculture oriented. And then he wouldn't feel like such a box of rocks, not that he didn't appreciate the help from his tutors. His grades wouldn't be as high as they were without their coaching.

But it was Thursday afternoon. The weekend stretched before him like a sweet field of four-leaf clover. Maybe he would drive to Sam's tonight and shoot hoops after chores. If this fine weather held out, maybe he'd go for a trail ride into the hills and get lost among the pine trees. Or maybe he and Dad would take the rowboat out on the pond and do some fishing. This time of year, he might even get lucky and catch a fish.

Or maybe not.

Trail rides reminded him of sweet Emma, while anything near water brought back their canoe trip on the Mohican River. How he wished they'd paddled down to the Ohio River when they had the chance. And how he still missed that girl! So, other than maybe basketball tonight at Sam's, he would probably work the entire weekend on the farm. There was always something needing to be done, plus the busier he stayed the less he thought about the prettiest girl in Holmes County.

James usually took the roundabout way home on Thursdays to forget about school and soak in the countryside he loved so much. Especially on gorgeous spring days like today. He didn't even bother to tune in to his favorite country music station, preferring peace and quiet, except for the occasional buzz of truckers talking on the CB radio. The CB caught snippets of conversation from people on Highway 30, hurrying either in one direction or the other. He had thought about seeing the world, or at least visiting different parts of the country, but without someone special to travel with, he'd just as soon stay home.

The town of Apple Creek was busier today than usual for a weekday as he drove through. The sight of the Amish ladies coming from the grocery store made his mouth dry and his palms clammy. He hoped that one day he could gaze on those gentle Plain people and not be reminded of Emma.

But today wouldn't be the day.

Suddenly, the CB radio crackled to life, and James heard a rescue worker on his way from home to the fire station. He was talking about a wreck on a Holmes County road—an accident involving an Amish buggy and a full-sized pickup. James' spine stiffened while his blood turned to ice. His truck quickly built up speed until he eased off the accelerator. As horrible as any accident was, he had no reason to believe he knew the victims.

Thousands of Amish families lived in Holmes and the surrounding counties.

Nevertheless, he grabbed the CB transmitter and began asking rapid-fire questions. He heard fear in his voice and felt his stomach turn over. When the emergency worker came back on line with information, his worst nightmare was realized. The Amish buggy driver was a young woman, riding alone, and the Amish conveyance was described as a small two-seat trap.

A pony cart. James swallowed several times to keep the stomach acid from rising up his throat. The CB responder had no information regarding the condition of either driver.

But the scene of the accident was along the same route Emma Miller took to town.

James fought back tears as horrific images flooded his brain. He tried to tell himself that plenty of Amish ladies owned pony carts for short trips to neighbors or to run errands. There was no logical reason to assume the victim was Emma, yet in his heart he knew. With mindless concentration, he drove toward the location as fast as safety would allow.

While still half a mile from the accident site, traffic crawled to a dead stop. For a moment, James considered driving on the wrong side of the road to reach the scene. From where he sat at the bottom of a hill he couldn't see anything. A visualization of crashing head-on with the ambulance carrying injured people to the hospital flashed through his brain. He slapped his palm on the steering wheel several times in utter frustration. Without a logical alternative, James threw the truck into reverse and backed up the shoulder into the first driveway he came to. Feeling fingers of panic closing around his heart, he turned off the ignition and abandoned his truck in the front yard of a ranch house with morning glories climbing up the mailbox post.

Then he started to run—toward his past and, God willing, toward his future. He couldn't think about what he might find at his destination, but something inside told him Emma would be there. He ran past cars and trucks, semis and Amish buggies. A few people hollered questions to him, but he paid them no mind. He passed up people impatiently glancing at watches, mothers scolding restless children, even an older man who had leaned his seat back and closed his eyes for a nap. On James ran, heedless of the blistering sun or the fact he'd lost his favorite Indians ball cap on the side of the road.

He was oblivious to the countryside he passed—the things he and Emma cherished about their rural county: tidy farmhouses, rolling fields abundant with golden grain, the cows and sheep and horses that occupied so much of their lives, and the people who had left their chores to see if they could help. Someday he would again appreciate the world, but right now he had to see what had stopped traffic in both directions.

He needed to know.

James saw flashing lights around the next bend in the road. Police cars, ambulances, and a fire truck had parked at odd angles, forming a cluster around something he still couldn't see. But at least nothing was burning. He slowed down to a fast walk and struggled to catch his breath. Beads of sweat formed on his upper lip while perspiration soaked through his shirt.

Close to the accident, people had left their vehicles and stood in groups; talking, wondering, maybe some were praying. James hurried on, trying not to listen to their conjectures. In the next moment he heard a sound that stopped his heart—the piercingly cold report of a single gunshot. All chatter around him ceased; even the birds and insects turned eerily silent.

Fighting back a gag reflex, he pushed through the crowd of onlookers, including one heartless fool who was taking photos with a digital camera. James resisted the impulse to punch out the ghoulish photographer. His goal was to reach Emma, if it was Emma, and nothing else.

"Hold up there, young man." A highway patrolman reached out and grabbed onto James' arm.

"Please, let go of me," he said, trying to shrug off the officer. "I'm family of the female victim in the buggy." It was a bold, outright lie. James had no idea who had been injured in the accident. It might be a total stranger, but he couldn't stay back with the crowd, immobile and impotent.

Surprisingly, the highway patrolman released his hold on him. "All right, go on up, but don't get in the rescue workers' way."

"I won't," James promised and hurried on. In another twenty feet, he caught sight of an animal on the side of the road, lying very still. A sheriff's deputy stood beside it along with Dr. Longo, the county veterinarian. *Emma's family uses Dr. Longo, same as us,* he thought abstractly. He turned away from the heartbreaking scene, preferring not to lock the visual into his mind.

But within fifty paces lay something he couldn't turn from—the mangled remains of a wooden pony cart. It had been knocked clear off the pavement into a soybean field. James crept closer to examine the wreckage. Splintered slats of wood jutted in all directions. The metal wheels had broken off the axle while the steel frame had crumpled from the impact. The twisted heap was barely recognizable as to its former function.

Then James spotted something among the soybeans he could identify—a multicolored patchwork quilt. It had been made by Leah and given to Emma to keep her legs warm. Although torn and wadded up, James was certain it was the one he'd seen when Emma arrived at the volleyball party. Bending closer to inspect, he realized it was sodden with blood—Emma's blood. A searing pain began in the pit of his stomach, paralyzing him as it inched its way up his spine. He felt dizzy and light-headed, while his throat started to close as though he had been stung by a bee.

James Davis did what he hadn't done in years—alone in a soybean field on what had been a perfect spring day—he began to cry.

The highway patrolman tentatively placed a hand James' shoulder. James quickly swiped at his face with his shirtsleeve.

"It's okay, son," the officer said. "Your relative is alive. She's in that ambulance over there." He gestured with his gloved finger. "You can go see her, but remember what I told you before—don't get in anybody's way. They're getting ready to head for the hospital right about now."

James' head turned until he focused on the rescue vehicle. People were swarming around the back door. "Thank you," he called to the patrolman. And he whispered a second thank-you to God, who held the life of even the humblest creature in His hand. On wobbly legs, James started moving toward the flashing lights.

~

Simon watched the young man approach and felt nothing but pity. James' face was pale and his eyes were red and puffy. Thank goodness his dear, sweet daughter was already inside the ambulance. Her clothing, stained with her life's blood, had been covered by a sterile white blanket. The EMTs had strapped her to a board to prevent further injury to her spine and immobilized both her broken legs and arm.

But she was alive. And Simon Miller was a grateful man.

"Mr. Miller, can I have a word with you, sir?" James Davis asked. "Please."

Simon walked from the open ambulance door to meet Emma's English friend. He did not want their conversation to be overheard.

"I know you don't much care for me, but I want to know how Emma is. I must know." He stood resolute less than a foot away, out of breath and sweaty.

Simon crossed his arms over his jacket and answered as accurately as he could. "She has multiple injuries to both legs, arms, back, and…" His voice faltered as his fortitude waned. He gasped for air and then continued, "…some head injuries. No way of telling how severe until they get her to the hospital."

Simon would have made it through the description—one he knew he would have to repeat many times—if he hadn't looked up and seen tears streaming down the young man's face. *Men his age never cry.* Simon felt his own eyes sting with moisture. "But she's conscious, James. She talked to me and knew that I was her *daed*. The medics say she has a good chance for recovery."

James swiped at his face with a handkerchief as his expression turned joyous. "Oh, thank God," he said huskily.

"*Jah*, indeed, we have much to be thankful for. I was riding back from the chiropractor with my neighbor and came upon…this, or else I wouldn't have known or been able to see her."

James shoved the hanky into a back pocket and straightened to his full height. "Thank you, Mr. Miller, for letting me know." He took a step backward.

Simon observed the change in the young *Englischer*'s demeanor. His relief that Emma was alive was almost palpable. On impulse he asked, "Would you like to see her, James, before they take her to the hospital?" He felt a tear fall but brushed it away quickly.

James couldn't have looked more surprised if the skies had opened and a team of chariots arrived to transport Emma to the emergency room. "Yes, sir, I sure would." He shifted his weight from one leg to the other. "I know she doesn't care about me anymore, but I just want to see for myself that she's okay. Then I'll be on my way.

Simon walked back to where EMTs were hooking Emma to monitors and IVs, stabilizing her for transport. He gestured for James to enter and then spoke as the boy stepped past him, "I wouldn't be so sure about that."

Inside the ambulance, James asked softly, "Emma, are you awake?"

To his astonishment, her eyes fluttered open. "*Jah*, I'm awake. Oh, Jamie, I thought I'd never see you again." Two tears ran down her bloodied cheeks.

"Don't talk like that, Em. Even if you don't love me, I'll always care about you…and pray that you are safe and well." He touched the blanket gingerly.

Emma lifted up her unfettered arm in protest. "But I do care about you. I never stopped caring." She sounded weak but very sure of herself.

"Time to go, Miss Miller," a female medical tech said, eyeing James impatiently. "There'll be plenty of time for romantic reunions after we get you patched up." She pointed toward the door for James.

"I'll see you soon, Em." He patted her hand and stepped out quickly.

"Hop in, Mr. Miller. We're ready to go," she hollered. "We're heading to Mercy Hospital in Canton."

"Wait," called Emma in a raspy voice. "I want…both of them to ride with me."

"No, Miss Miller, there's no room. *I'm* riding with you. Pick one or the other," said the EMT.

Simon, standing in the doorway, looked at his daughter's swollen face and felt nothing but gratefulness that she was not only alive, but speaking up for what she wanted.

So very like my Emma.

"Go ahead, son. Ride with Emma. I'll follow behind with Mr. Lee in his van."

James lifted his chin and suddenly looked older than eighteen.

"No, sir. You ride with your daughter. I'll send Mr. Lee back to pick up your wife and children to take them to the hospital. Then I'll drive to Emma's aunt's farm and tell them. They can ride to Canton with me if they like."

Simon shook his hand and climbed into the ambulance before it left without either of them.

With sirens blaring and lights flashing, the ambulance sped off, carrying the love of his life. James watched it disappear before running back to his vehicle. He didn't look at the destroyed pony cart or the pitiful Appaloosa he had so optimistically bought Emma as a gift. He ran as though competing in the one-mile sprint in the state finals. When he found Mr. Lee beyond the police barrier, the man was beside himself with anxiety. Upon hearing that Emma would recover, he galvanized into James' plan of action.

A worried-looking elderly woman was standing next to his truck when he reached her yard. "Sorry, ma'am, that I left my truck there. I had to reach the crash site in a hurry."

She smiled indulgently. "No harm done. Is there anything I can do to help?"

James jumped into the driver's side and turned the ignition key before an idea struck him. "Yes, ma'am. Could you please call my parents so they don't worry? Tell them Emma's been in an accident and that I'm going to Canton. Tell them she'll be all right." He jotted his phone number down on a fast-food receipt, thanked her, and left before she could ask him any more questions.

He didn't have any answers.

He only knew one thing. Emma still cared for him, and that was the only thing he needed to know.

～

From the window in the doctor's office, Hannah could see two Amish buggies, three cars, and the forest-covered hills to the east.

She also spotted her husband with his metal-toothed brush, working the tangles from the standardbred's coat. That man did not know how to be still, so sitting patiently in a doctor's waiting room was out of the question.

Hannah watched him grooming the mare while she tried to calm her overexcitement. It was what she'd suspected for weeks. It was the midwife's logical explanation for her weight gain, heightened appetite, and frequent morning sickness. The woman had laughed at Hannah's naïveté. Usually women raised on farms could recognize the signs of pregnancy. *It might be a bladder infection, a slow-growing stomach tumor, or perhaps a mysterious allergic reaction.*

But today's visit to a Mount Eaton English doctor confirmed her fondest hope—she was expecting a child. Hannah couldn't stop grinning the entire time she redressed, and then she thanked every staff member she encountered on her way out.

Seth stopped brushing the horse when he saw her crossing the parking lot. "Well, Mrs. Miller?" he asked, holding back a smile.

"Well, what, *ehemann*? Must a wife discuss every *little* thing with her husband?" She tried to sound impatient. "Let's go. I want to pick up a pizza on the way home."

Without warning, he lifted her off her feet and swung her away from the buggy. "Not every little thing…only this particular one."

"Put me down this instant! Let's not jar the *boppli* with all your foolishness!"

He immediately complied, but he lifted her chin to meet her gaze. "*Jah*, Hannah? You're really having a child?"

"*Jah*," she said. "I'm expecting. Let's hope it's a child and not a lamb or calf." Despite her attempt at humor, she began to cry. "Oh, Seth, I am so happy."

"Me too, *fraa*, me too. But there is one thing I gotta say." He offered a hand as she stepped into the buggy.

"What's that?" she asked, expecting to hear "I love you" or perhaps "I wonder if it's a girl or boy."

"I told you so!" He winked and shook the reins.

Business as usual in the Miller family.

Hannah and Seth teased each other all the way home. Seth suggested baby girl names that were unusual, to put it mildly, while Hannah promised to name the baby Zephaniah—Seth's middle and his least favorite name—if the child was male. They didn't reach agreement until almost home, the pizza already half eaten.

Hannah was filled with contentment as they turned down their township road. At long last, a *boppli*...a sister or brother for Phoebe. Now maybe that child would stop asking so many questions about where babies came from. Hannah mused on whom she would tell first—Julia or Emma, or perhaps crusty Simon, who had softened toward her considerably since the marriage to his *bruder*. She pondered what color to paint the baby's room—traditional white, or if Seth permitted, maybe a soft yellow.

The sight of a shiny, green pickup parked at odd angle in their driveway curtailed her thoughts of paint colors. Hannah knew immediately who had come to call, but she couldn't fathom why. The young English sheep farmer from Charm knew where Emma lived these days. Hannah felt an ominous sense of dread.

"I wonder who this might be?" Seth asked, parking the buggy close to the barn.

Hannah remained silent as they walked toward the house. They could see a tall, blond head at the back door. He'd been knocking to no avail—Phoebe was at Julia's for the day.

Suddenly, the man spotted their approach and hurried down the steps.

The look on his face chilled Hannah's blood.

"Mr. and Mrs. Miller?" he asked. "I'm afraid I have some bad news for you."

TWENTY

Late August

A bead of sweat ran down Emma's temple as she painstakingly moved one leg and then the other through the long grass. She lifted her hand from the aluminum walker long enough to swipe the perspiration away and then braced her weight evenly on both palms. With difficulty, she took another step and shifted her weight forward. It hurt worse than sticking your head in a beehive. *Thirty more paces,* she told herself. *Twenty-nine, twenty-eight.* Slowly the bench *daed* had placed under the willow tree drew closer. Sitting in the shade would be her reward after the mandatory afternoon walk.

Three times a day, she endured agony as her muscles, tendons, and joints regained their usefulness. She had thought that once the casts came off her two broken legs, life would improve. It had felt *wunderbaar* to get rid of those itchy monstrosities. But with the casts gone, the daily physical therapy started. And with it came more suffering than a seventeen-year-old could ever imagine. *I guess I'll be more understanding of* mamm, she thought, remembering Julia's arthritis.

After twenty minutes Emma reached her cool oasis and lowered herself to the bench. When her breathing returned to normal, she turned her face skyward and offered up a heartfelt prayer. She knew she had much to be thankful for. Many people did not survive truck-buggy collisions. Given time, her legs would mend, and she would walk normally again one day. Her arm had sustained a simple break and was healing nicely. Already it was able to bear a certain amount of weight. The cuts, scratches, and purple bruises had faded. A competent plastic surgeon had stitched the deep gash by her eyebrow. It too would diminish into little more than a white line, according to her mother, and in the meantime it was usually hidden by her *kapp*. The broken cheekbone, nose, and eye socket bone had also mended without any permanent impairment to her vision. After prompt medical attention to her fractured skull, no residual effects remained other than occasional headaches in bright sunshine.

All in all, Emma was one lucky girl. More accurately, God had shown great mercy that day last April when an impatient young driver decided he couldn't wait behind a slow-moving vehicle and swerved over the double yellow line...on a hill and going around a curve. He hadn't thought anybody would be in that lane on the seldom-used back road.

He would think twice before driving recklessly again. The twenty-five-year-old mechanic from Millersburg had visited her several times in the hospital until she had asked him not to come anymore. She harbored no ill will toward him, but after a while his downtrodden expression, hand-wringing, and endless apologies only made her feel worse. He kept looking at her as though she were horribly crippled or disfigured. She wasn't. She would be fine, and she didn't wish to think about the accident any more. She also didn't like to consider the enormous medical bills from her surgeries and subsequent rehabilitation. Several attorneys had approached her father regarding a lawsuit against the young man's insurance policy for pain and suffering.

That was not the Amish way.

The mechanic's insurance had covered the medical bills. For the emotional trauma, Emma would trust in God and the comfort of her family to see her completely healed.

But poor, poor Maybelle. The sweet pony that she had recently finished paying for was gone. That was the most heartbreaking part of the whole mess. It would be a long time before Emma would drive a buggy again or have further need for a pony.

Oddly enough, there was a bright spot. Her father had allowed James Davis to come calling again. Because he was home from college for the summer break, *daed* permitted James to visit each Wednesday evening and Saturday afternoon. Wednesdays they would sit on the porch swing under *mamm's* watchful eye and read aloud to each other. Sometimes James would read Old Testament Scripture, stories of people who triumphed over adversity through their faith. Emma was heartened by these biblical heroes, and she knew a few broken bones were minor hardships by comparison. Sometimes he would read inspirational novels of modern people overcoming great challenges. Once in a while, they would sit quietly and listen to the night sounds—crickets, cicadas, nightjars, and tree frogs putting on a serenade.

If Julia excused herself for a few minutes, James would hold her hand and speak softly from his heart. He loved her. He always would. And with that knowledge, Emma would continue to endure walks to the park bench even if *daed* moved it all the way to Aunt Hannah's beaver pond.

Her father made no mention of the inappropriateness of courting an *Englischer*. He no longer dropped hints about Joseph Kauffman or other Amish fellows that he favored. And he smiled often when he looked at her. Her *mamm* released her from any chores after the accident and had divided her work between Matthew, Leah, and Henry. Leah had waited on her hand and foot until Emma put a stop to it.

Emma, do you want some cookies?

Shall I get your shawl?

Would you like me to bring some lambs out of the pasture for you to see?

Leah, the girl who would start sneezing whenever she was within ten feet of a wooly critter.

Yes, Emma had much to be grateful for.

On Saturday afternoons, James arrived after chores with damp hair from the shower and unlimited enthusiasm. At first he pushed her in the wheelchair on warm sunny days to see her sheep, or into the barn where her spinning wheel and baskets of wool had been relocated to the first floor. Any work with the wool was comically impractical until her arm cast was removed, but Emma still loved to sit near her various projects. James even tried his hand at spinning under her tutelage and proved adequate for someone with large, calloused fingers. When weather permitted, James pushed her wheelchair down the path to the beaver pond or into the cool woods. Leah accompanied them on these sojourns, entertaining them with funny stories and feeding them from her hamper of snacks and cool drinks. The three watched the not-so-graceful landing of mallard ducks, the industrious hummingbirds among the shrubbery, and lazy box turtles sunning themselves on fallen logs. The damp swamp air smelled sweet to Emma after weeks of confinement in hospital beds and in *mamm*'s enclosed back porch.

Leah and Emma grew inseparable as sisters, and Leah bonded in friendship with James as they both fussed over the invalid. Despite her condition, Emma couldn't remember summer days as lovely as those of June and July.

When the legs casts came off and the physical therapy began, her days turned from idyll to tortuous. James helped her to exercise lead-heavy limbs and cajoled her to continue when she wanted only to retreat back to her chair. He was present when she gingerly took her first two steps as *daed* and the therapist supported her on both sides. Now that she could ambulate on her own with the walker, James had become her slave driver, pushing her to overcome each difficult threshold to recovery. Despite the added pain, Emma's heart swelled each time his green truck drove into the yard. Saturdays had become her favorite day of the week.

And as Emma finished her silent prayers of thanks, she smiled brightly. Today was Saturday.

~

James parked in the driveway under a shady tree and reached for the bouquet he had picked for Emma. He had no trouble finding her. She sat where she always waited for him on Saturdays, under the low-hanging willow tree. A book lay beside her, but her attention had been diverted toward the heavens. Perhaps she prayed for rain for the corn crop or maybe for relief from the pain in her legs and back. He had been praying too, that Emma would see his idea as the logical solution and not some crazy Yankee notion.

"Hi, Emma," he called at the midway point.

"Good afternoon, James. What are you hiding behind your back? Better not be a snake or a toad."

He presented the flowers with a flourish when he reached her bench. "Flowers, and not an exotic bloom to be found. Picked by me in my mom's garden just this morning. Every last one of them indigenous to Holmes County, Ohio."

"Indigenous, hmm. At least they're teaching you big, fancy words up in Wooster." She accepted the bouquet but arched one eyebrow. "Did you *ask* before you went wild with your clippers?"

"I did. Ma said I should take all I wanted, and she sends her get-well wishes." He sat down beside her under the sheltering willow.

"I'm not sick," she protested. "Tell her I am well, just my legs are still a little rusty. Shall we lumber on down to the pond? You can check if Leah's ready to take a break from the hot kitchen. She's been baking up a storm. I'm not sure if you come to visit me or eat my sister's creations."

James placed an arm on the back of the bench, careful not to touch her. The enormous bouquet sat between them. "Only you, sweet girl, but let's sit a spell and not walk quite yet. I've got something on my mind, and I might as well come out with it. School is starting back up next week." He could feel his palms start to sweat with nervous apprehension. Emma folded her hands primly in her lap, waiting.

He looked away from her innocent face. "Shucks, Emma. You know I love you, don't you?" He glanced back from the corner of his eye.

She cocked her head to the side. "I suspected as much, considering how many times you visited me in the hospital and in the rehab unit. After I came back home, you haven't missed a Wednesday evening or Saturday afternoon since my father said you could come calling."

He met her gaze. "Do you love me, Emma? I need to know before I go any further with my big ideas for the rest of our lives."

A sad expression flickered across her face. "I do love you, Jamie, but I know I wouldn't be happy being English. And that leaves us in the same tight spot we were in before."

He felt tremendously buoyed by her admission of love. *If she loves me, all things are possible, aren't they?*

"Well, not exactly." He couldn't stop grinning. "What if we met somewhere in the middle? I've been going to a New Order Amish church with Sam Yoder for the past nine months."

"*Jah*, I heard as much from Sarah Hostetler. I've been wondering why since Sarah said their services are in German, same as Old Order. Did you learn a second language while you were studying hard at your fancy college?" Mischief sparkled in her pretty blue eyes.

"Nope, I have enough trouble with English. And I'll admit, even though they throw in some English during the service, the language barrier still presents a challenge." He winked and then glanced around. "But when I talked to one of their ministers, I learned their Christian beliefs are pretty much the same as my evangelical church. And they use tractors to farm instead of teams of draft horses and mules. Most districts have electricity in both their houses and barns. If you changed to New Order, you would find their style of dress basically the same, and their church services are held in folks' homes like what you're used to. They study the Bible more than Old Order, but that's something we're both doing already." He couldn't tamp down his growing enthusiasm. "I wouldn't mind giving up blue jeans for Plain clothes and growing a beard after we get hitched. I'd planned to do that anyway. Shaving seems like a big waste of time for a farmer."

Emma shook her head, but she smiled. "Aren't you forgetting one little thing, James Davis?" She bobbed her head toward the drive.

"What's that, Miss Miller? I bought some 'Learn to Speak German' CDs already," he teased. "And I'll bet the bishop will allow me to keep my English-language Bible."

"I'm talking about something green and shiny and sitting right over there."

"Yeah, you're right. It won't be easy to give up my truck and start driving a horse and buggy. But since I'll still be managing my dad's farm, he can take me when I need to travel a great distance. I know it'll be a big adjustment for both of us. New Order is more vocal about their beliefs than what you're used to, and they get involved with community outreach, but why don't we at least give it some thought? Next year when I'm twenty and finished with college and you're eighteen, we can become baptized in the New Order church."

Emma looked happier and more relaxed than she had in a long time. "Why do you want to do this, Jamie? Why would you be willing to take up Amish ways and change your life so drastically?"

He didn't answer right away so she wouldn't think him impetuous or insincere. "I've had plenty of time to think while commuting back and forth to Wooster for the past year. And I've come to a few conclusions. I pretty much don't like school. I plan to cram the rest of my agricultural courses into next year to finish my education in two years instead of four. Sort of a compromise with my folks."

"No more research on growing bananas in Holmes County?" Emma teased, leaning back against the bench.

"Not for me, pretty girl. I'm willing to content myself with apples, peaches, and pears." James grinned and then gazed toward the western hills. They were bathed with the golden light of a setting sun. "I realized I've only ever wanted two things in life—one is to be a farmer. And the other is to marry Emma Miller of Winesburg. Everything else that comes my way I can adjust to if you'll be my wife. I plan to get baptized in New Order next summer, right after I finish my last semester. I'll give up my truck and pick out the plainest buggy I can find. Horses I've got plenty of, and I'm sure Matthew could train one to pull a buggy." He paused, giving her a chance to mull things over.

She appeared deep in thought and then she nodded her head as a smile turned her pretty face beautiful. "You really think you can give up zippers, buffalo plaid shirts, and your Cleveland Indians ball cap?"

"Yeah, I do."

"All right, next summer I'll be eighteen. If we both still feel the same, I'll take the kneeling vow in a New Order church too. But I won't marry you for another year after that." She set her jaw with determination. "You must live Amish for a full year before we wed. Marriage is a sacrament, besides a lifetime commitment. Plain folk don't believe in divorce, so you can't just shave off your beard and go out and buy some Levis. I want you to be very sure, Jamie."

James exhaled his pent-up breath. "Fair enough, Miss Miller, but I want one more thing before I go find your sister for that walk." He leaned close and smelled the clean scent of Ivory soap. "Tell me again you love me."

She arched her neck and met his eye. "I love you, James Davis, with my whole heart. And I have for a long time. I just didn't want to admit it...even to myself."

~

For Emma, pledging her love and fidelity to James, promising to marry him in two years, was the easy part. Telling her parents she planned to leave her Old Order district in a year before her baptism was another matter altogether.

Emma thought long and hard, and she prayed nightly for weeks before she was ready to broach the subject. Chicks flying too far from the nest were nothing but heartbreak to Amish parents. She also thought it best to tell her folks separately.

On a chilly but sunny October morning she found the opportunity. *Mamm* sat alone in the kitchen, sipping coffee and reading the *Daily Journal.* Leah, usually a fixture in the kitchen these days, was nowhere to be seen.

"Guder mariye," Emma greeted and limped to the coffee pot. The aroma drew her like a bee to nectar.

"Good morning to you, daughter," Julia said. "And where is the walker?"

"I left it in the hallway. My legs are getting stronger, so unless I'm going quite a distance, I don't plan to use it."

"That's good to hear. What a blessing." Julia sipped her coffee while studying her eldest child.

Emma slipped into a chair with her mug. *"Mamm,* are you going to the quilting bee this week to sort squares for the ladies?"

Julia laughed, a welcome sound since her recovery from knee surgery. "I do more gabbing and nibbling snacks than helping with the quilt, but I'm going. Why do you ask?"

"I'd like to come too. There's nothing wrong with my hands. I can help with the quilt. I hear it's for Sarah Hostetler."

Julia grinned with delight. "I'm glad you're getting out of the house. Does this mean you'll start back with Sunday singings?" Hope resonated in her question.

Emma patted her mother's hand. "No. No singings for me, but I'll attend any work bees or the like. If I go to singings...people might think I'm ready to start courting. And I have no wish to give that impression."

Julia's smile faded. "So you've decided on James Davis then? You want to become part of the English world?" She couldn't hide her disappointment.

"No, *mamm.* I do love James and hope to wed him in a couple of years, but I'm not leaving my Plain faith. James is becoming Amish."

Julia couldn't have looked more surprised if Emma had said they were relocating to Pluto after the wedding. "That is almost never done," she said.

"*Jah*, that's what I told him, but we will join a New Order district. That way he can continue to farm with tractors and electricity."

Julia nodded sagely. "I see, but it will still be a very big change— his clothing, giving up his truck, maintaining a lifestyle where God is the main focus. Giving up worldly pursuits."

"He is a devout Christian already. Living a Plain lifestyle will make it easier for him in some ways."

Julia furrowed her brow. "Does he realize that the preaching services will be in German, same as ours?"

Emma laughed. "*Jah*. He's been going to services already with Sam Yoder. And he's studying German along with his agriculture courses."

"*Ach*, Emma. You're not considering the cultural differences. It goes deeper than German preaching or a horse and buggy. *Englischers* have been raised to believe they should be unique, that they should stand out in some way. The Amish find comfort in conformity and blending into a community. Individuality has no purpose on the path to salvation. Are you sure you've both thought this through?"

Emma reached for her mother's hand. "I have. We will not marry until we've both lived as members of New Order for one full year. He must find a way to live Amish at his parents' farm. He must make the change long before the wedding."

Julia looked at her differently somehow, as though no longer seeing Emma as a little girl.

"I don't want him to have any regrets," said Emma softy. "He must be very sure about this."

"That is wise, daughter." Julia nodded and appeared to mull over the avalanche of news thrust upon her.

Emma knew her mother wouldn't give her blessing until Simon did. Amish wives never wished to be at odds with their husbands in matters involving *kinner*. "I think I'll go find *daed* and tell him," Emma said. "I might as well get this over with before I lose my courage. I'm afraid he won't be as willing to hear me out as you have been."

"Since your accident you have shown the courage of three women," Julia said. "Why don't you let me break the news to your father? I know how he can fly off the handle before listening to the particulars." Julia furrowed her forehead with wrinkles. "He will be more patient with me. You go sit on your bench under the willow. I'll send him over to talk once he's over the initial shock."

Emma hugged Julia tightly. "*Danki, mamm*. You are the best *mamm* in the world."

"Hush now, before you make me prideful with that kind of talk."

At that moment Leah breezed into the kitchen with a full bucket of late pears. "Who's in the mood for poached pears for dessert?" she asked. "Poaching will soften up these dried leftovers nicely." She placed the bucket in the sink and then turned toward the other women.

"I am," Julia and Emma answered together.

Emma struggled clumsily to her feet. "I'll be back later to help you, sister," she said. After a final glance at her mother, she limped from the warm kitchen to await her fate under the willow tree.

She concentrated on where she placed each foot along the path so she didn't stumble with her newly regained mobility. Emma hadn't noticed which way Julia had headed when they left the house. Once she lowered herself to the bench, the next five minutes were spent perspiring and trying to recover her breath. It would be a while before she got back the energy and stamina she'd had before her accident.

But she didn't have long to wait for her father. By the time her legs stopped aching and her heart rate returned to normal, Simon was heading her way. He crossed the lawn from the milking parlor with a posture stooped from back pain. But Emma noticed he walked faster than his usual slow shuffle...and he was smiling.

Emma also saw that his eyes were moist and glassy, as though on the verge of tears. How she yearned to run to him, but with her weak legs on uneven ground she didn't dare. Rising to her feet, she stretched both arms out to him. "Did she tell you?" Emma asked, with a voice sounding pitiably young for a recently engaged woman.

Simon took her hand and drew her into a hug. His chore coat smelled faintly of alfalfa hay. He settled one arm around her shoulders while he supported her back with the other. "She did, daughter. She also said you were afraid to tell me your decision."

Emma, though close to his height, laid her head on his shoulder the way she'd done years ago as a child. "I didn't want to upset you, not after what you've been through already."

He stroked the back of her head, knocking her *kapp* askew. "Emma, Emma, I'm so blessed to have my girl back safe and sound. It would take much more than you turning New Order to upset me these days. More than anything, I want you to live a long, healthy, God-fearing life. And if that means you must change to a different order, then so be it."

"You're not unhappy that I plan to marry James in two years?" She held her breath while waiting for his answer.

Simon glanced at the sheep grazing in the far pasture before replying. The animals happily chewed grass without a thought about their remaining days on earth. "God will guide your decision as to whom you marry when the time comes. Keep your heart always open to Him. If it be His will, then I'll not stand in your way, though the adjustments will be difficult for both of you." Simon turned Emma's face so he might peer into her eyes. "Right now, the only thing that could upset your *mamm* and me would be if you moved far away and we'd seldom get to see you."

Emma hugged her father tightly. Tears ran down her cheeks unchecked. "Don't worry, *daed*. I couldn't live apart from my family. No matter what happens during the next two years or whether or not I marry James, I'll never be far from home."

Autumn

Emma walked very slowly and began panting like a dog, but eventually she reached the fence of her sheep pasture. From there she could oversee Henry as he filled the water stanchions and delivered enriched grain to the troughs. She couldn't wait until she was able to resume her chores. Henry looked forward to that day too. Although he worked without grumbling, he cheered each one of her victories louder than anyone else. The road to recovery was difficult, but Emma pushed through the pain. She had a bright future ahead of her with James.

Gingerly, she stepped up onto the lowest fence rail and transferred her weight to the better of her two legs. Wincing with pain, she dragged her stiff leg up to the rail. From this vantage point, she could gaze over her late-season nursing lambs, her ewes in need of shearing, and the horned ram who strutted around as though he owned the place.

"What are you doing up there? Get down before you fall and break something!" a voice squawked from behind her. Leah-the-mother-hen grabbed her tightly around the waist and didn't let go until both Emma's feet were on the ground.

"Why do you coddle me worse than *mamm?*" Emma huffed, grasping the rail.

Leah ignored this and asked her own question. "Where have you been? I've been searching everywhere for you." A tiny hitch in her voice revealed her emotional state.

Then Emma noticed Leah's cheeks were streaked with tears. "I've been right here. What's wrong, sister? Have you been crying?" She braced a hand on Leah's shoulder.

"It's *daed,*" she moaned. "He said I'm too young to go to town alone and he's too busy to take me. And Henry's got chores, *mamm* has a headache, and Matthew is working at the horse farm." Another tear slipped from beneath her dark lashes. "I'll be fourteen next week; I'm finished with my schooling, and yet *mamm* still treats me like a *boppli!*" Indignation was rapidly replacing sorrow.

"You'll always be her baby," said Emma, tugging one of Leah's *kapp* strings.

"Henry is the baby. Besides, I have business in Winesburg." One hand perched on a bony hip.

"What kind of business do you have?" Emma laughed merrily until Leah's frown turned ominous.

"My pie-baking business. The cook who works at the auction barn cafeteria sampled one of my pies at a quilting bee. She said it was the best rhubarb she'd ever tasted." Pride glowed in Leah's young face. "She hired me to make the unusual pies, to see if any could become regular features on the menu. The cook will continue to bake apple, cherry, peach, and coconut cream."

Emma grinned with delight. "That's *wunderbaar!* What oddball pies does she want you to bake?"

Leah lifted one dark eyebrow. "*Danki*, Emma, but I prefer the word 'unusual' instead of oddball." She paused briefly to make sure her meaning was clear. "She wants rhubarb, sweet potato, and walnut pie."

"I've never heard of walnut pie."

"It's similar to pecan, but with a substitution of walnuts since no pecan trees grow here."

"Oh, that makes sense. How exciting this must be for you. What can I do to help?" she asked.

Emma regretted the hasty offer the moment the words left her mouth, knowing the answer already.

"Thank goodness. I was hoping you would offer. I need you to ride with me to Winesburg. *Daed* won't let me go unless somebody comes along."

Emma opened her mouth to argue, but Leah forestalled complaints with an upraised palm. "Don't worry, sister. I'll hold the reins, and I'm very good at keeping the buggy on the shoulder of the road."

Emma shuddered. She'd gone few places since the accident other than her doctor's office and a few preaching services. But considering how Leah had been doing all her chores plus waiting on her like a princess, how could she say no? "All right. I'll ask Henry to hitch up the buggy while you pack up your pies and tell *mamm*."

Leah hugged her so hard Emma's ribs hurt. "I'm so grateful. I know it's hard for you and I appreciate this." The girl ran toward the house like a schoolgirl instead of a businesswoman.

Emma watched her go, wondering if she would ever be able to run again. *No matter. At least I can walk.* "Get my purse from my room," she hollered. "I might as well pick up a few things while we're there."

Leah waved while Emma motioned over Henry to tell him about yet another chore and then started her painstaking meander toward the barn. She would get through a simple trip to town…but she uttered a silent prayer just the same.

As it turned out, Emma was glad she made the trip. Leah handled herself quite professionally when she delivered her pies to the cafeteria manager. If the pies tasted as good as they looked, Leah would have something to keep her busy this winter. The manager promised to send a note reporting on the popularity, or lack thereof, of each recipe.

Emma waited in the buggy while Leah shopped for the family. Her legs felt achy and tired, and she longed for one of her pain pills. But soon her sister returned toting several shopping bags, and their buggy headed for the back road out of town. They hadn't gone far when Leah pulled up on the reins and called to the horse, "Whoa, there." Leah turned the buggy off the pavement into an empty parking lot. Weeds, brush, and even a few tree saplings had sprouted in between cracks in the asphalt.

"What are we doing here?" Emma asked, glancing around but seeing no reason to stop.

"Oh, my. Just look at that!" Awe could be discerned in Leah's exclamation.

Emma stared where the girl focused but couldn't fathom any cause for exuberance. All she saw was an abandoned train car still attached to a woebegone faded red caboose. No glass remained in any of the windows. And the only explanation for the caboose remaining red was the extreme amount of rust. The train cars sat forgotten on an unused siding next to a vacant factory.

"Looks like the place went out of business and somebody dumped parts of a train there." Emma clucked her tongue with disapproval.

"It's a passenger car and a caboose," Leah murmured. "I wonder if it's for sale. It would be perfect."

Emma glanced around before replying. "What I see is two train cars barely this side of falling down."

"Oh, no, sister. Squint your eyes to soften the edges and use some imagination. What I see is a diner in the larger passenger car and a kitchen in the caboose. Wouldn't that make a sweet restaurant?" The words left her tongue as expressions of love.

"You'd better stay out of the sun without your full bonnet. You might have sunstroke. It's too small for a restaurant anyway. One busload of tourists and you'd be overflowing."

"It wouldn't be for tourists, in particular. I'm thinking a great breakfast and lunch spot for Amish folk when they come to town on business. I would close before the supper hour when folks need to go home anyway."

Even squinting her eyes and mustering every bit of imagination God had given her, Emma couldn't share her sister's enthusiasm. "I see no For Sale sign, so we had better head for home, although we probably have enough in our wallets even after shopping, considering its deplorable condition."

Leah obliged and started the horse back toward the road, but she couldn't resist one last glance over her shoulder. "I'd love to open my own diner someday. I'd call it Leah's Home Cooking, or Leah's Plain Cooking…no, Leah's Simple Delights." Her smile filled her entire face.

"What about Leah's Sure Path to Bankruptcy?" Emma asked, pinching her sister's arm.

Leah shook her head. "You have no vision. Just picture it all fixed up with curtains in the windows and potted petunias in flower boxes hanging beneath every window. English people would be welcome too, but I wouldn't advertise in the tourist magazines. It would remain a local hidden gem."

Emma smiled at the mental picture of Leah wielding her spatula at an eight-burner commercial stove. She allowed her little sister to wax poetic about the specials she would make each day of the week but Sundays. Everyone needed to have dreams, even if they were only fourteen years old and fresh out of school

If *mamm* and *daed* could handle her turning New Order Amish in one year and someday marrying James, having a chef in the family might not seem so extraordinary.

She would pray for her sister tonight. That busy little cooking bee deserved every happiness life could offer.

Everything is possible for the person who has faith.

ABOUT THE AUTHOR

~

Mary Ellis grew up close to the eastern Ohio Amish Community, Geauga County, where her parents often took her to farmers' markets and woodworking fairs. She and her husband now live in Medina County, close to the largest population of Amish families, and enjoy the simple way of life.

Never Far from Home is Mary's second novel with Harvest House, following up on her bestselling first book in The Miller Family series, *A Widow's Hope.*

www.maryellis.wordpress.com

A WIDOW'S HOPE
by Mary Ellis

CAN A YOUNG AMISH WIDOW FIND LOVE?

After the death of her husband, Hannah Brown is determined to make a new life with her sister's family. But when she sells her farm in Lancaster County, Pennsylvania, and moves her sheep to Ohio, the wool unexpectedly begins to fly. Simon, her deacon brother-in-law, finds just about everything about Hannah vexing. So no one is more surprised than the deacon when his own brother, Seth, shows interest in the beautiful young widow.

But perhaps he has nothing to worry about. The two seem to be at cross-purposes as often as not. Hannah is willful, and Seth has an independent streak a mile wide. But much is at stake, including the heart of Seth's silent young daughter, Phoebe. Can Seth and Hannah move past their own pain to find a lasting love?

An inspirational story of trust in the God who sees our needs before we do.